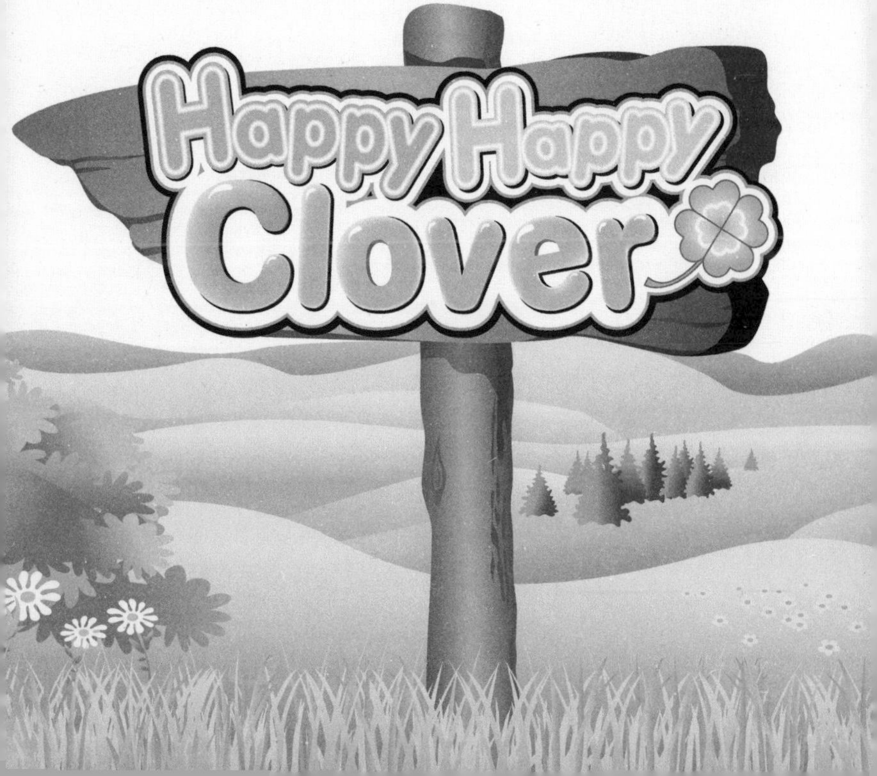
Happy Happy Clover

Vol. 2
VIZ Kids Edition

Story and Art by SAYURI TATSUYAMA

English Adaptation by Naoko Amemiya

Translation/Kaori Inoue
Touch-up Art & Lettering/James Gaubatz
Cover and Book Design/Carolina Ugalde
Editor/Annette Roman

HAPPY HAPPY CLOVER 2 by Sayuri TATSUYAMA
© 2007 Sayuri TATSUYAMA
All rights reserved.
Original Japanese edition published in 2007 by Shogakukan Inc., Tokyo.

Printed in the U.S.A.

Published by VIZ Media, LLC
P.O. Box 77010
San Francisco, CA 94107

10 9 8 7 6 5 4 3 2
First printing, June 2009
Second printing, April 2014

PARENTAL ADVISORY
HAPPY HAPPY CLOVER is
rated A and is suitable for
readers of all ages.
ratings.viz.com

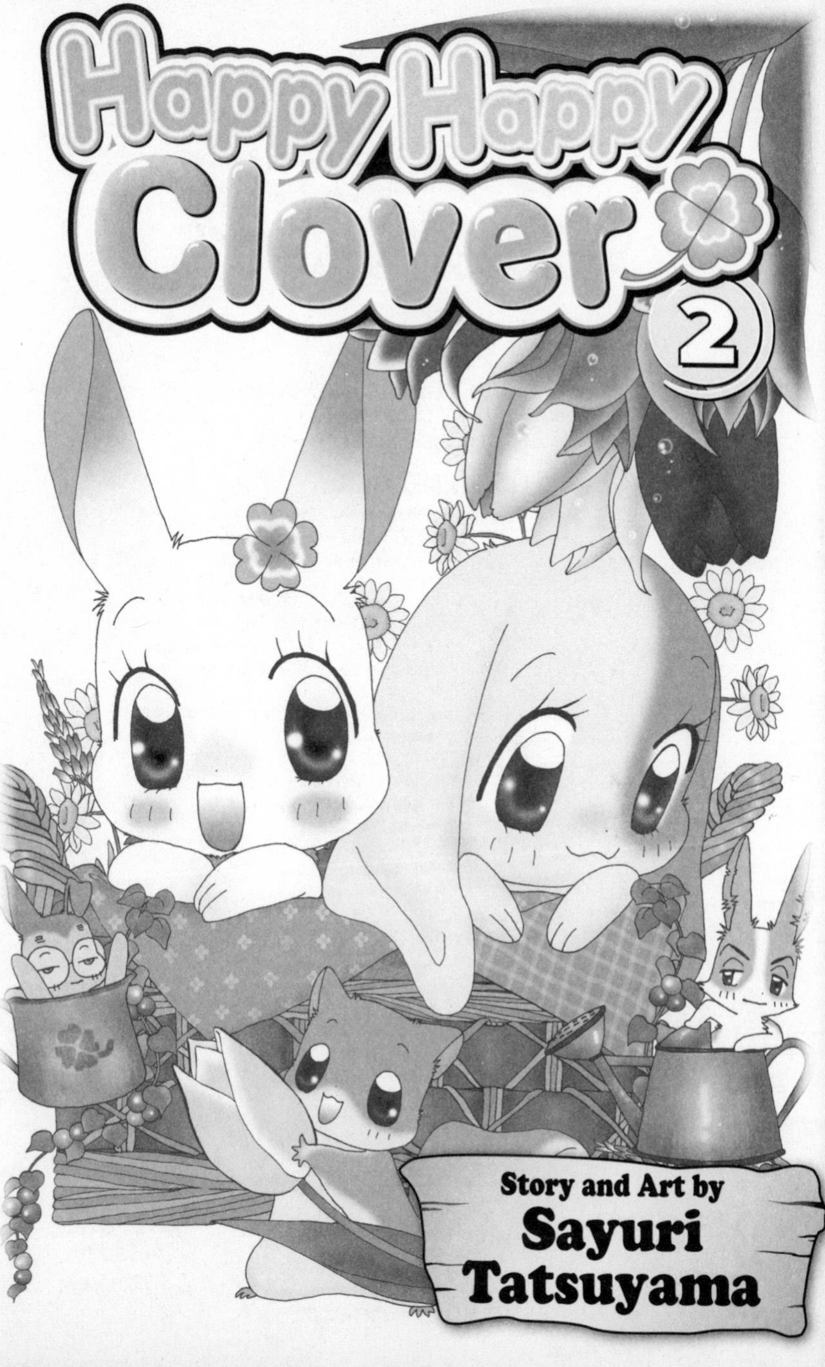
Happy Happy Clover
2
Story and Art by
Sayuri Tatsuyama

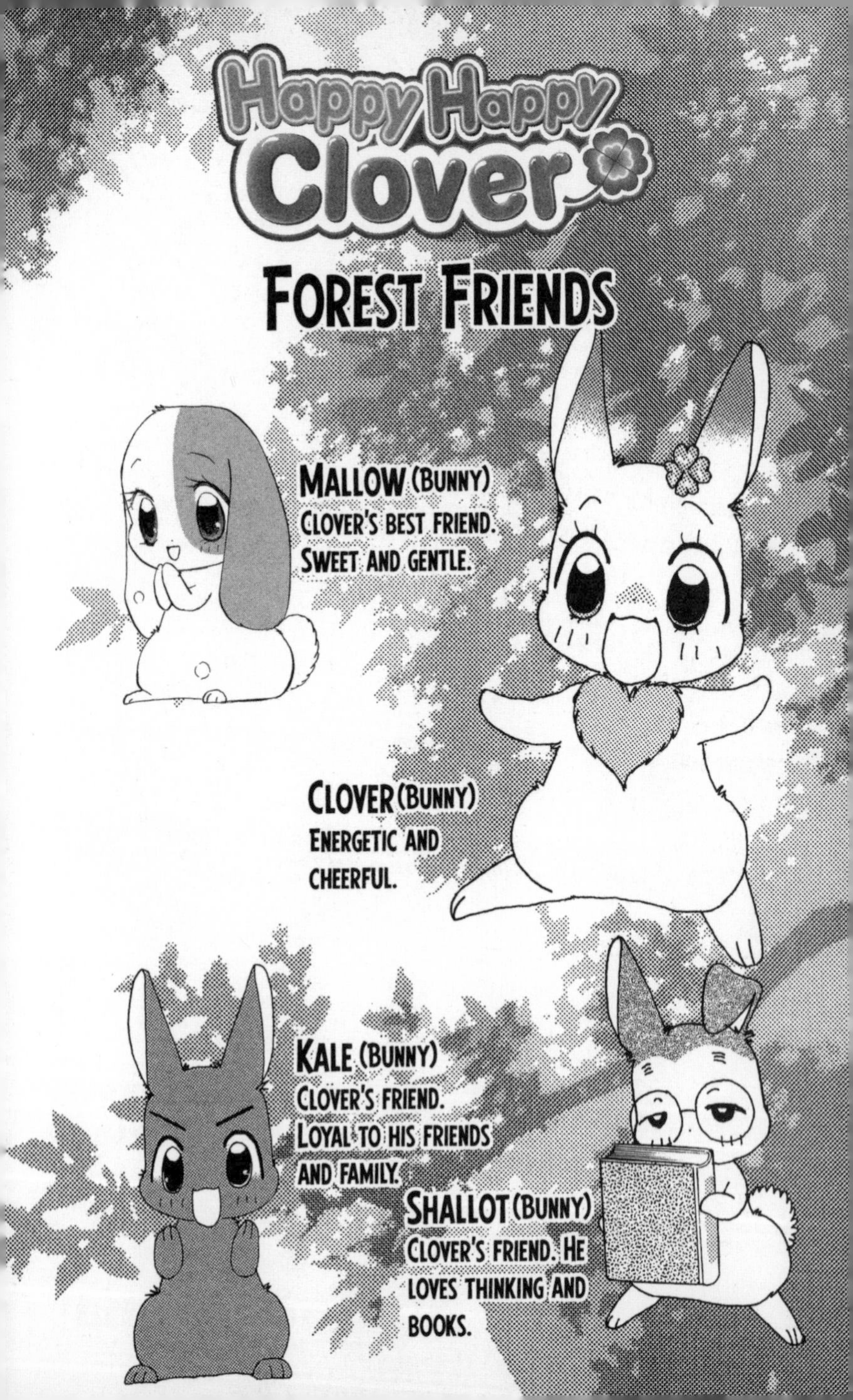
Happy Happy Clover
FOREST FRIENDS
MALLOW (BUNNY)
CLOVER'S BEST FRIEND. SWEET AND GENTLE.
CLOVER (BUNNY)
ENERGETIC AND CHEERFUL.
KALE (BUNNY)
CLOVER'S FRIEND. LOYAL TO HIS FRIENDS AND FAMILY.
SHALLOT (BUNNY)
CLOVER'S FRIEND. HE LOVES THINKING AND BOOKS.

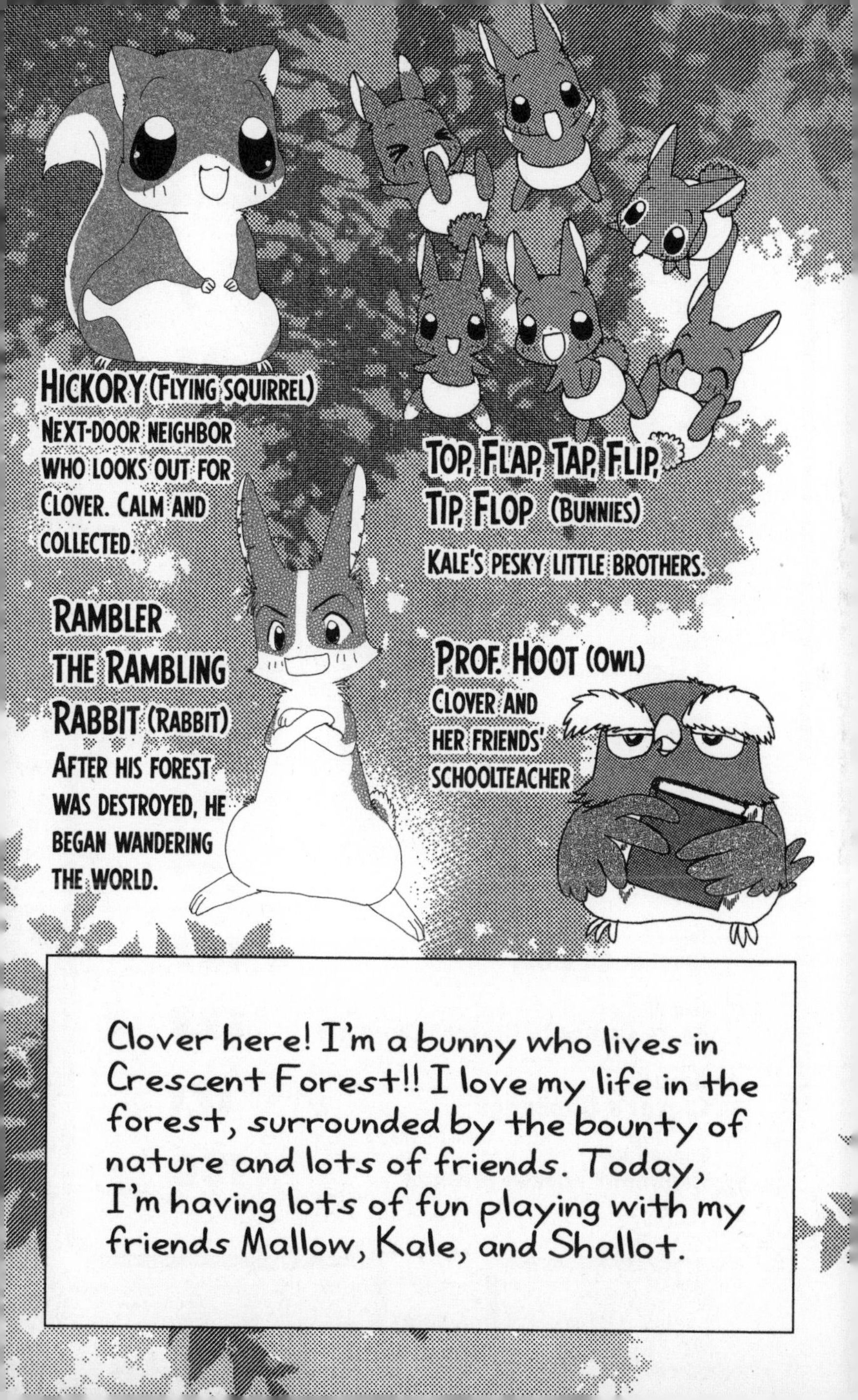
HICKORY (FLYING SQUIRREL)
NEXT-DOOR NEIGHBOR WHO LOOKS OUT FOR CLOVER. CALM AND COLLECTED.
TOP, FLAP, TAP, FLIP, TIP, FLOP (BUNNIES)
KALE'S PESKY LITTLE BROTHERS.
RAMBLER THE RAMBLING RABBIT (RABBIT)
AFTER HIS FOREST WAS DESTROYED, HE BEGAN WANDERING THE WORLD.
PROF. HOOT (OWL)
CLOVER AND HER FRIENDS' SCHOOLTEACHER

Clover here! I'm a bunny who lives in Crescent Forest!! I love my life in the forest, surrounded by the bounty of nature and lots of friends. Today, I'm having lots of fun playing with my friends Mallow, Kale, and Shallot.

Happy Happy Clover

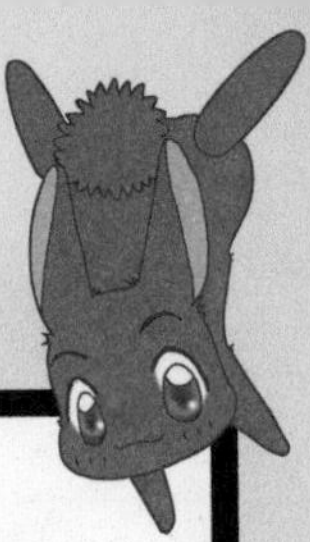

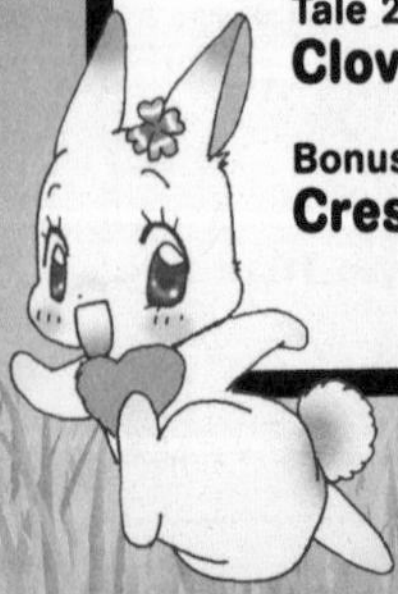

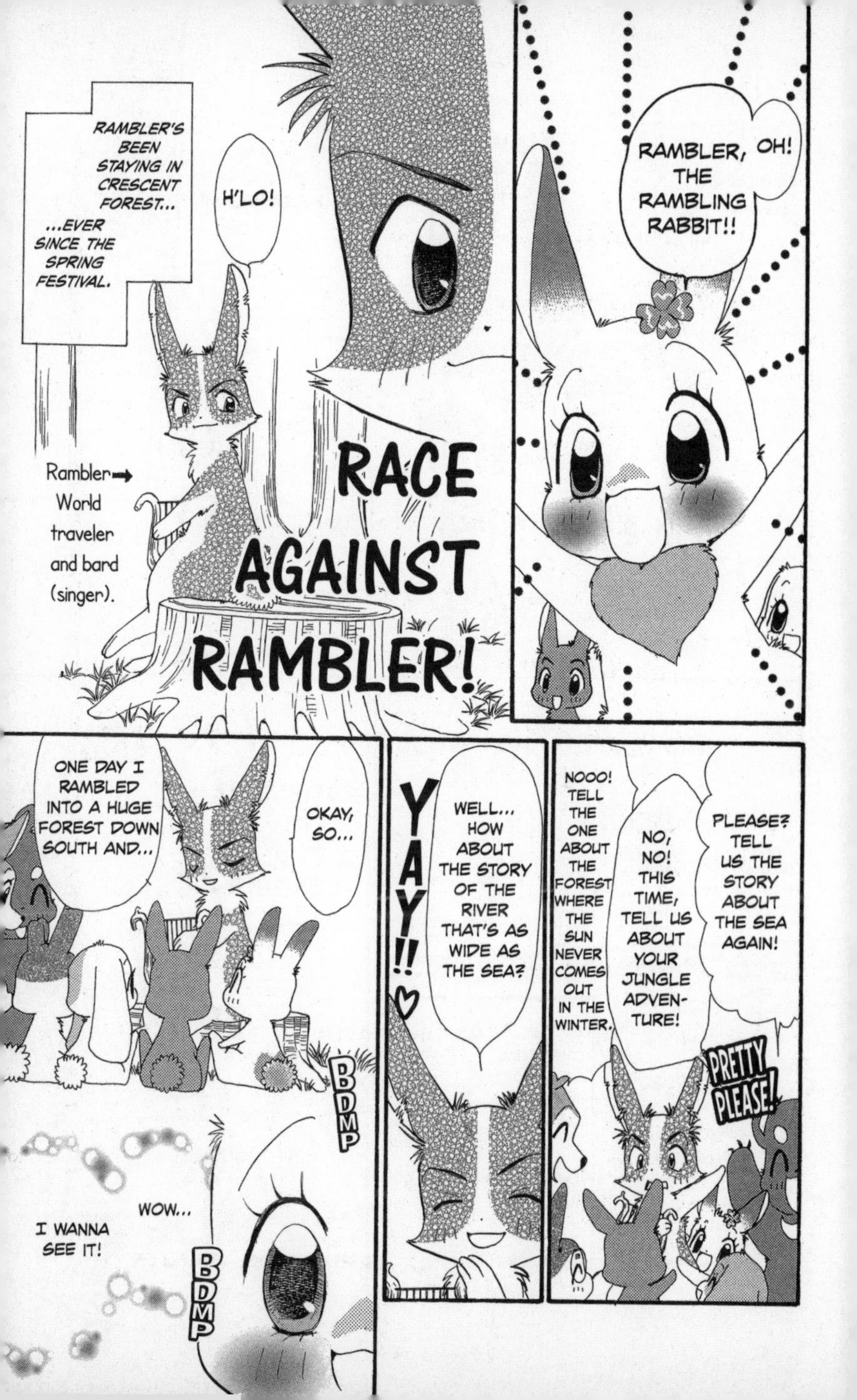
OH!
RAMBLER, THE RAMBLING RABBIT!!
H'LO!
RAMBLER'S BEEN STAYING IN CRESCENT FOREST... ...EVER SINCE THE SPRING FESTIVAL.
RACE AGAINST RAMBLER!
Rambler→ World traveler and bard (singer).
PLEASE? TELL US THE STORY ABOUT THE SEA AGAIN!
NO, NO! THIS TIME, TELL US ABOUT YOUR JUNGLE ADVENTURE!
NOOO! TELL THE ONE ABOUT THE FOREST WHERE THE SUN NEVER COMES OUT IN THE WINTER.
PRETTY PLEASE!
WELL... HOW ABOUT THE STORY OF THE RIVER THAT'S AS WIDE AS THE SEA?
YAY!! ♡
OKAY, SO...
ONE DAY I RAMBLED INTO A HUGE FOREST DOWN SOUTH AND...
BDMP
WOW...
I WANNA SEE IT!
BDMP

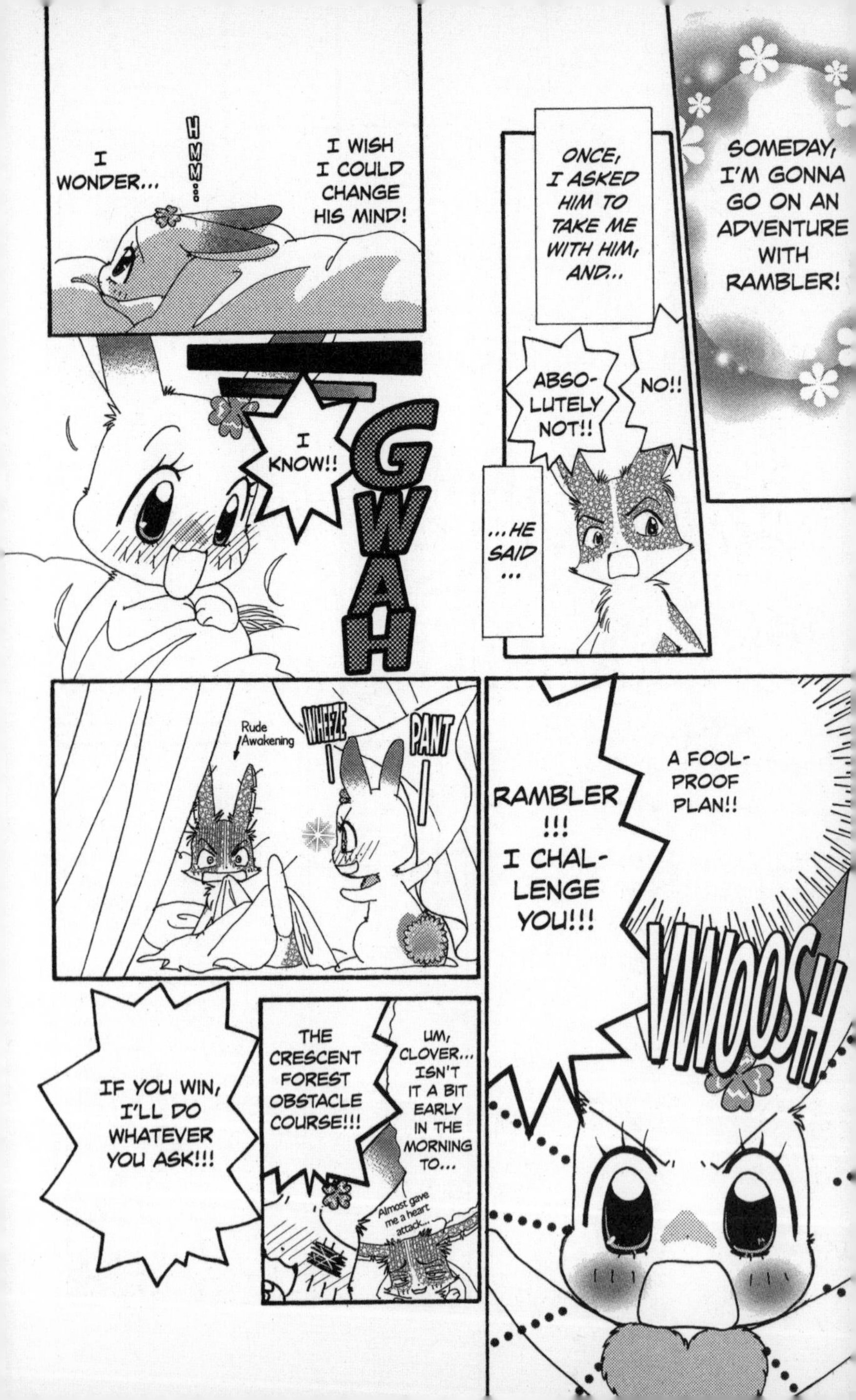
SOMEDAY, I'M GONNA GO ON AN ADVENTURE WITH RAMBLER!
ONCE, I ASKED HIM TO TAKE ME WITH HIM, AND...
NO!!
ABSO-LUTELY NOT!!
...HE SAID...
I WISH I COULD CHANGE HIS MIND!
HMM...
I WONDER...
I KNOW!!
GWAH
A FOOL-PROOF PLAN!!
RAMBLER!!! I CHAL-LENGE YOU!!!
VWOOSH
PANT
WHEEZE
Rude Awakening
UM, CLOVER... ISN'T IT A BIT EARLY IN THE MORNING TO...
Almost gave me a heart attack...
THE CRESCENT FOREST OBSTACLE COURSE!!!
IF YOU WIN, I'LL DO WHATEVER YOU ASK!!!

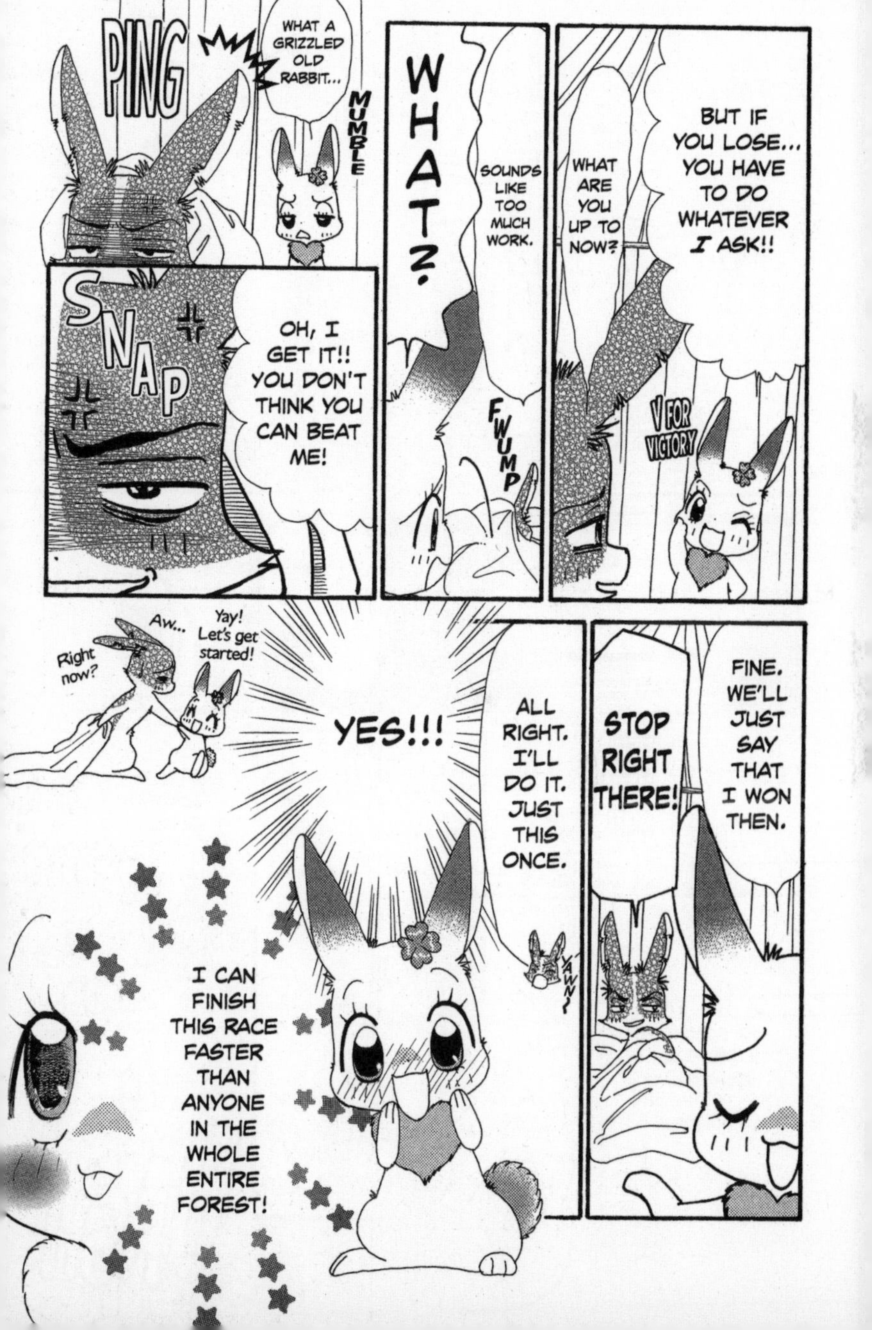
BUT IF YOU LOSE... YOU HAVE TO DO WHATEVER I ASK!!
WHAT ARE YOU UP TO NOW?
V FOR VICTORY
WHAT?
SOUNDS LIKE TOO MUCH WORK.
FWUMP
WHAT A GRIZZLED OLD RABBIT...
PING
MUMBLE
OH, I GET IT!! YOU DON'T THINK YOU CAN BEAT ME!
SNAP
FINE. WE'LL JUST SAY THAT I WON THEN.
STOP RIGHT THERE!
YAWN~
ALL RIGHT. I'LL DO IT. JUST THIS ONCE.
YES!!!
Yay! Let's get started!
Aw...
Right now?
I CAN FINISH THIS RACE FASTER THAN ANYONE IN THE WHOLE ENTIRE FOREST!

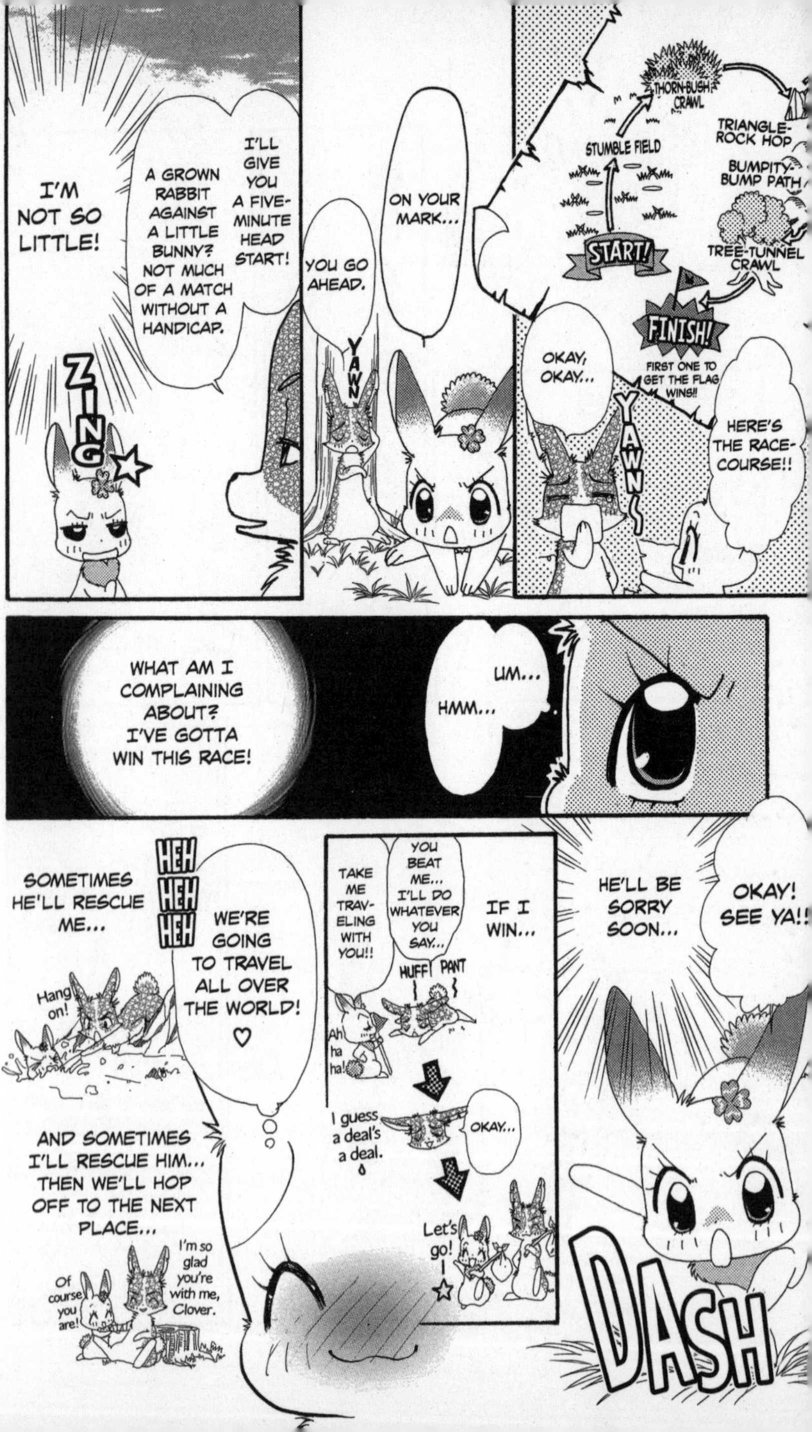
HERE'S THE RACE-COURSE!!
START!
STUMBLE FIELD
THORN-BUSH CRAWL
TRIANGLE-ROCK HOP
BUMPITY-BUMP PATH
TREE-TUNNEL CRAWL
FINISH!
FIRST ONE TO GET THE FLAG WINS!!
OKAY, OKAY...
YAWN~
ON YOUR MARK...
YOU GO AHEAD.
YAWN
I'LL GIVE YOU A FIVE-MINUTE HEAD START!
A GROWN RABBIT AGAINST A LITTLE BUNNY? NOT MUCH OF A MATCH WITHOUT A HANDICAP.
I'M NOT SO LITTLE!
ZING
UM...
HMM...
WHAT AM I COMPLAINING ABOUT? I'VE GOTTA WIN THIS RACE!
OKAY! SEE YA!!
HE'LL BE SORRY SOON...
DASH
IF I WIN...
YOU BEAT ME... I'LL DO WHATEVER YOU SAY...
HUFF PANT
TAKE ME TRAV-ELING WITH YOU!!
Ah ha ha!
OKAY...
I guess a deal's a deal.
Let's go!
WE'RE GOING TO TRAVEL ALL OVER THE WORLD! ♡
HEH HEH HEH
SOMETIMES HE'LL RESCUE ME...
Hang on!
AND SOMETIMES I'LL RESCUE HIM... THEN WE'LL HOP OFF TO THE NEXT PLACE...
I'm so glad you're with me, Clover.
Of course you are!

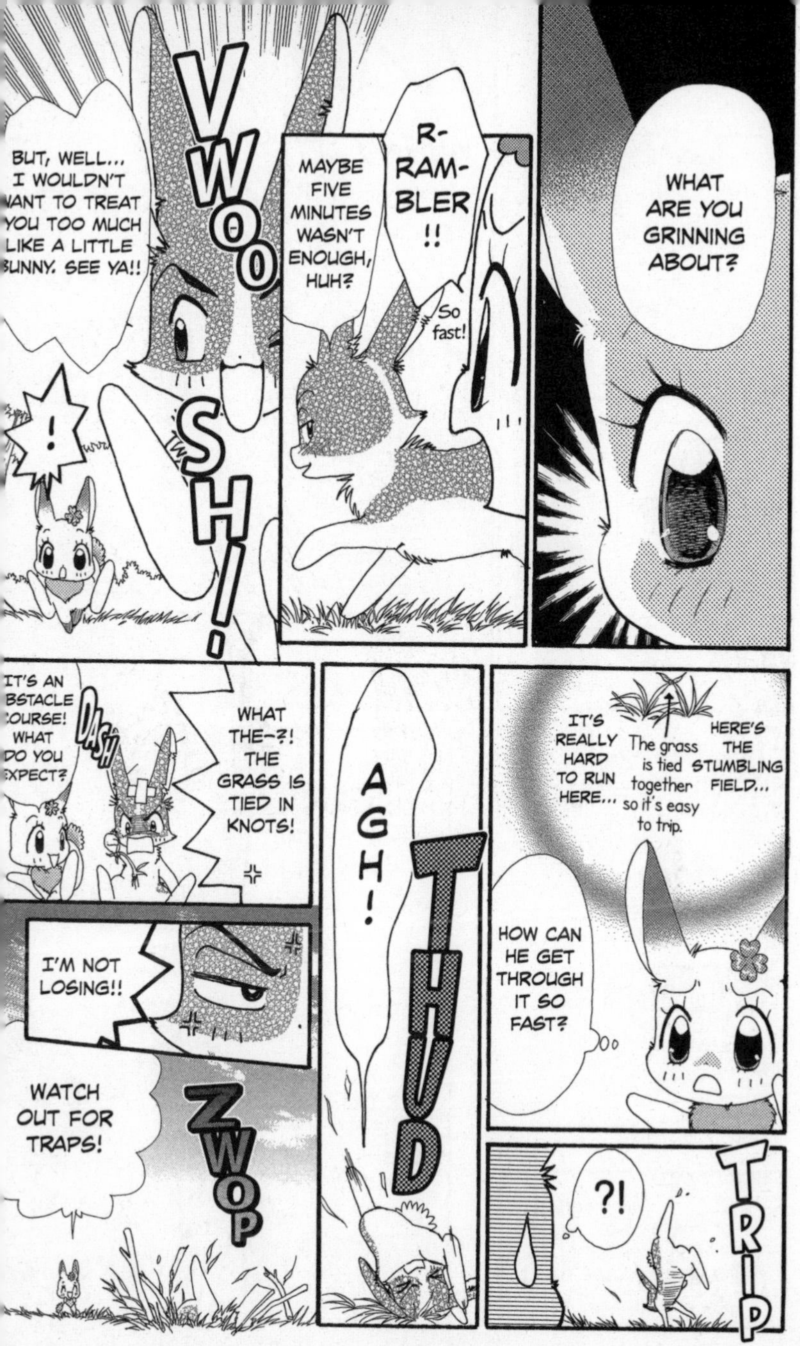
WHAT ARE YOU GRINNING ABOUT?
R-RAMBLER!!
MAYBE FIVE MINUTES WASN'T ENOUGH, HUH?
So fast!
BUT, WELL... I WOULDN'T WANT TO TREAT YOU TOO MUCH LIKE A LITTLE BUNNY. SEE YA!!
VWOOSH!!
!
HERE'S THE STUMBLING FIELD...
IT'S REALLY HARD TO RUN HERE...
The grass is tied together so it's easy to trip.
HOW CAN HE GET THROUGH IT SO FAST?
TRIP
?!
AGH!
THUD
WHAT THE—?! THE GRASS IS TIED IN KNOTS!
IT'S AN OBSTACLE COURSE! WHAT DO YOU EXPECT?
DASH
I'M NOT LOSING!!
WATCH OUT FOR TRAPS!
ZWOP

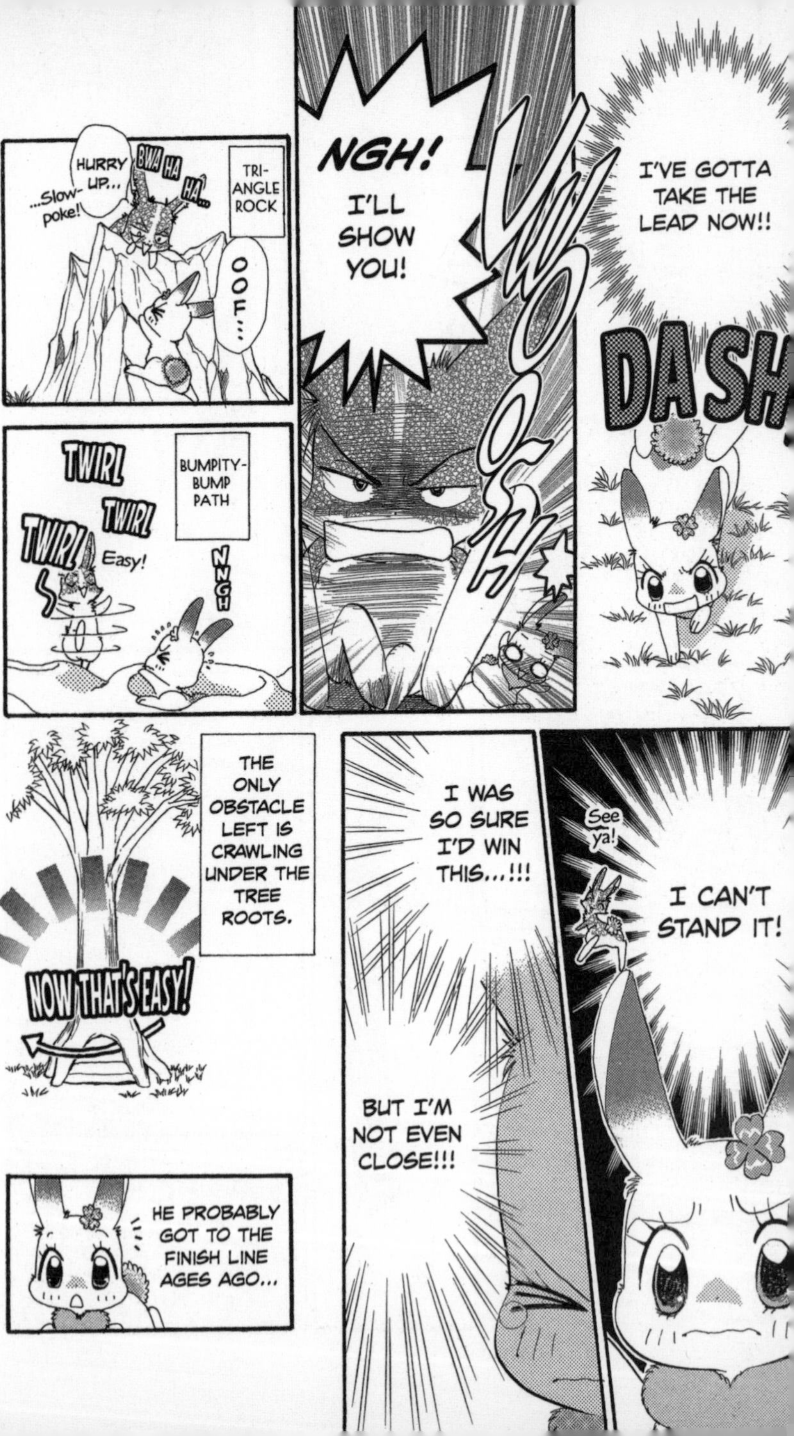
I'VE GOTTA TAKE THE LEAD NOW!!
DASH
NGH!
I'LL SHOW YOU!
WHOOOSH
TRI-ANGLE ROCK
BWA HA HA...
HURRY UP...
...Slow-poke!
OOF...
BUMPITY-BUMP PATH
TWIRL
TWIRL
TWIRL
Easy!
NNGH
See ya!
I CAN'T STAND IT!
I WAS SO SURE I'D WIN THIS...!!!
BUT I'M NOT EVEN CLOSE!!!
THE ONLY OBSTACLE LEFT IS CRAWLING UNDER THE TREE ROOTS.
NOW THAT'S EASY!
HE PROBABLY GOT TO THE FINISH LINE AGES AGO...

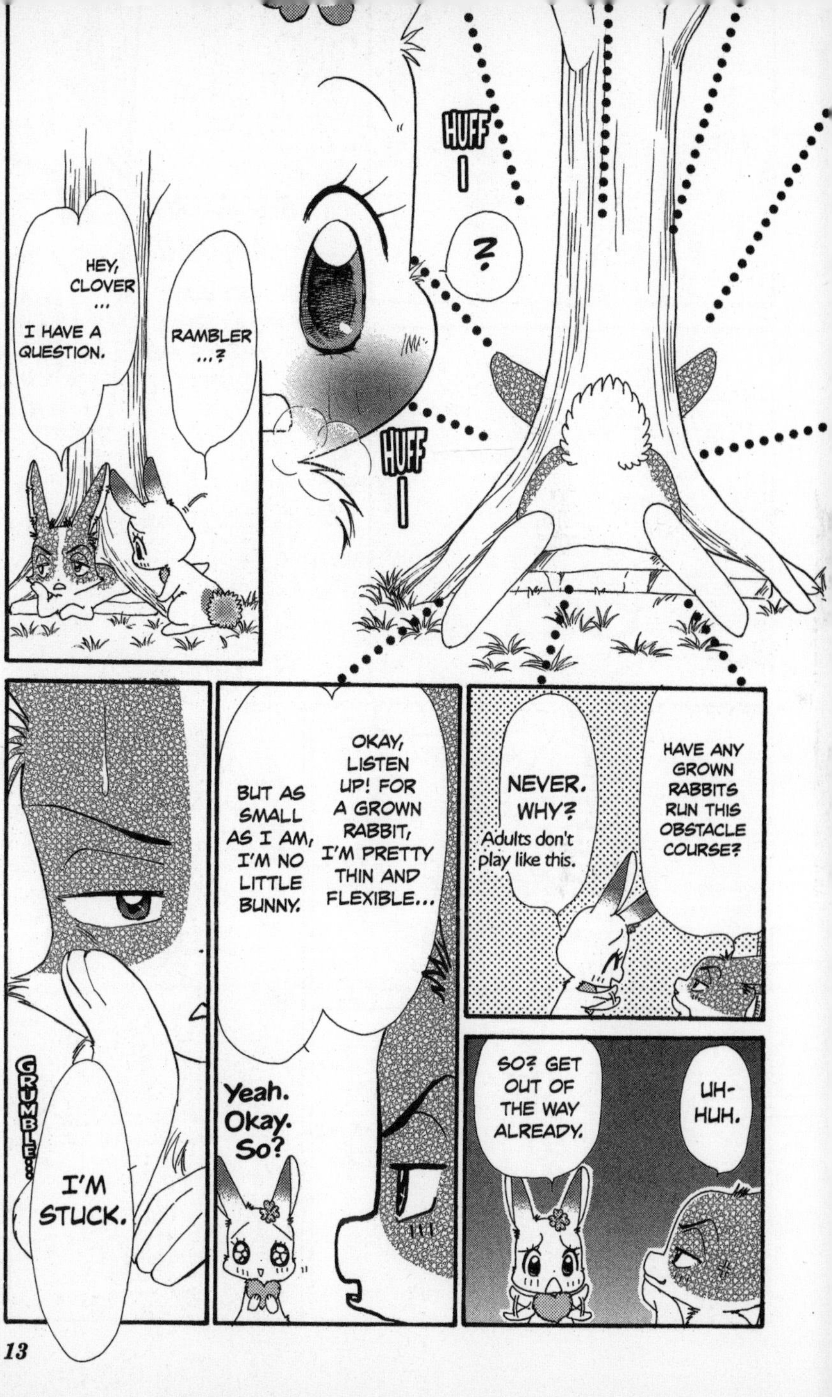
HUFF
HUFF
?
HEY, CLOVER ... I HAVE A QUESTION.
RAMBLER ...?
HAVE ANY GROWN RABBITS RUN THIS OBSTACLE COURSE?
NEVER. WHY? Adults don't play like this.
UH-HUH.
SO? GET OUT OF THE WAY ALREADY.
OKAY, LISTEN UP! FOR A GROWN RABBIT, I'M PRETTY THIN AND FLEXIBLE...
BUT AS SMALL AS I AM, I'M NO LITTLE BUNNY.
Yeah. Okay. So?
GRUMBLE...
I'M STUCK.

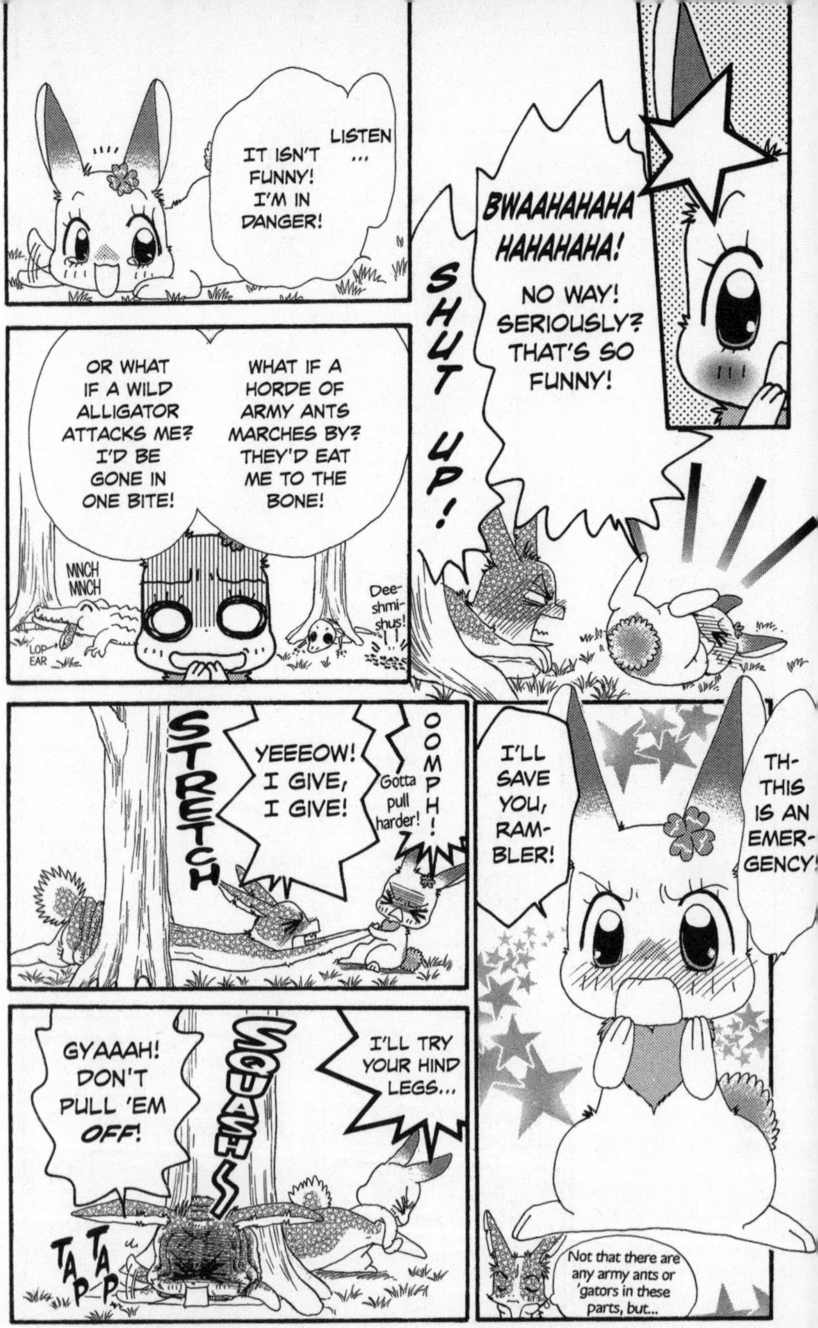
BWAAHAHAHA HAHAHAHA!
NO WAY! SERIOUSLY? THAT'S SO FUNNY!
SHUT UP!
LISTEN...
IT ISN'T FUNNY! I'M IN DANGER!
WHAT IF A HORDE OF ARMY ANTS MARCHES BY? THEY'D EAT ME TO THE BONE!
OR WHAT IF A WILD ALLIGATOR ATTACKS ME? I'D BE GONE IN ONE BITE!
Dee-shmi-shus!
MNCH MNCH
LOP EAR
TH- THIS IS AN EMER-GENCY!
I'LL SAVE YOU, RAM-BLER!
Not that there are any army ants or 'gators in these parts, but...
OOMPH!
Gotta pull harder!
YEEEOW! I GIVE, I GIVE!
STRETCH
I'LL TRY YOUR HIND LEGS...
SQUASH
GYAAAH! DON'T PULL 'EM OFF!
TAP TAP

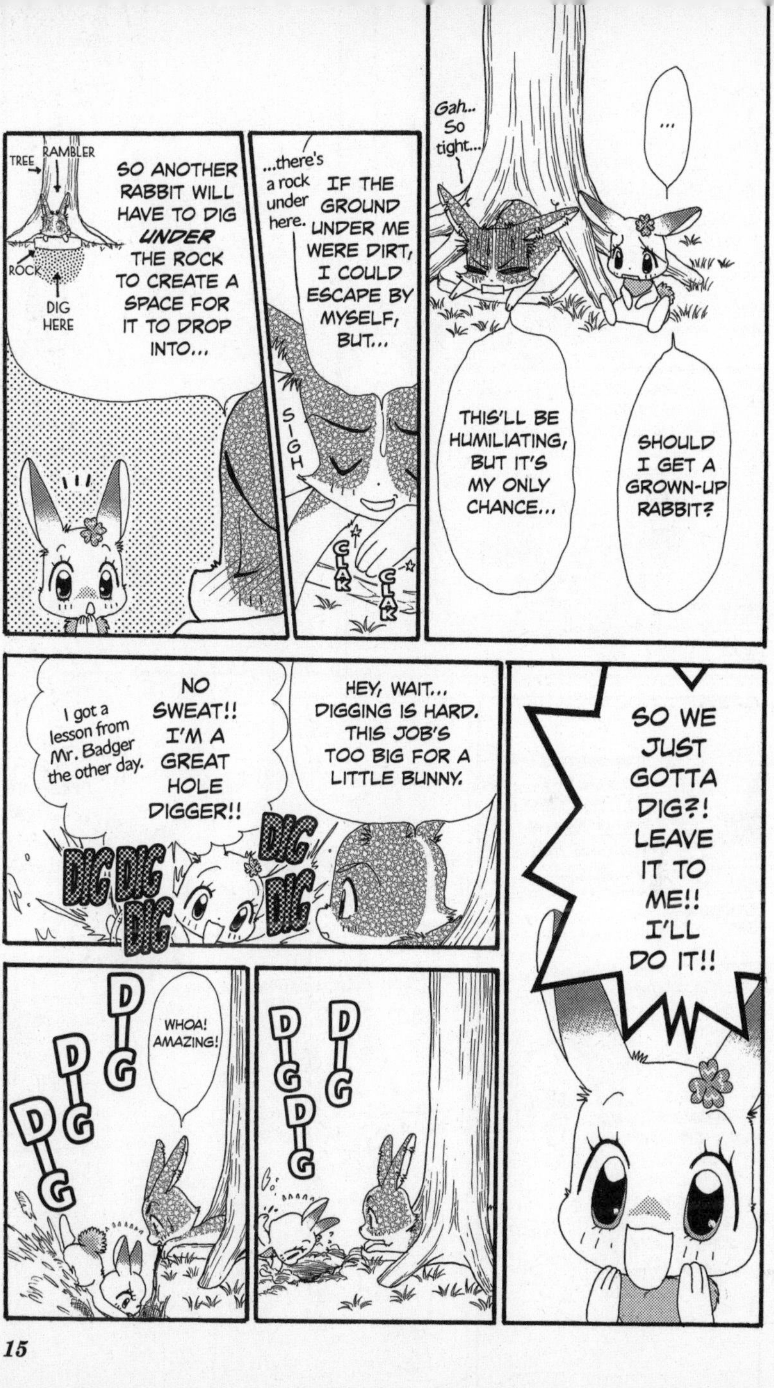
...
Gah.. So tight...
SHOULD I GET A GROWN-UP RABBIT?
THIS'LL BE HUMILIATING, BUT IT'S MY ONLY CHANCE...
...there's a rock under here.
IF THE GROUND UNDER ME WERE DIRT, I COULD ESCAPE BY MYSELF, BUT...
SIGH
CLAK
CLAK
TREE
RAMBLER
ROCK
DIG HERE
SO ANOTHER RABBIT WILL HAVE TO DIG *UNDER* THE ROCK TO CREATE A SPACE FOR IT TO DROP INTO...
SO WE JUST GOTTA DIG?! LEAVE IT TO ME!! I'LL DO IT!!
HEY, WAIT... DIGGING IS HARD. THIS JOB'S TOO BIG FOR A LITTLE BUNNY.
NO SWEAT!! I'M A GREAT HOLE DIGGER!!
I got a lesson from Mr. Badger the other day.
DIG
DIG
DIG DIG DIG
DIG
DIG
DIG
DIG
WHOA! AMAZING!
DIG
DIG
DIG

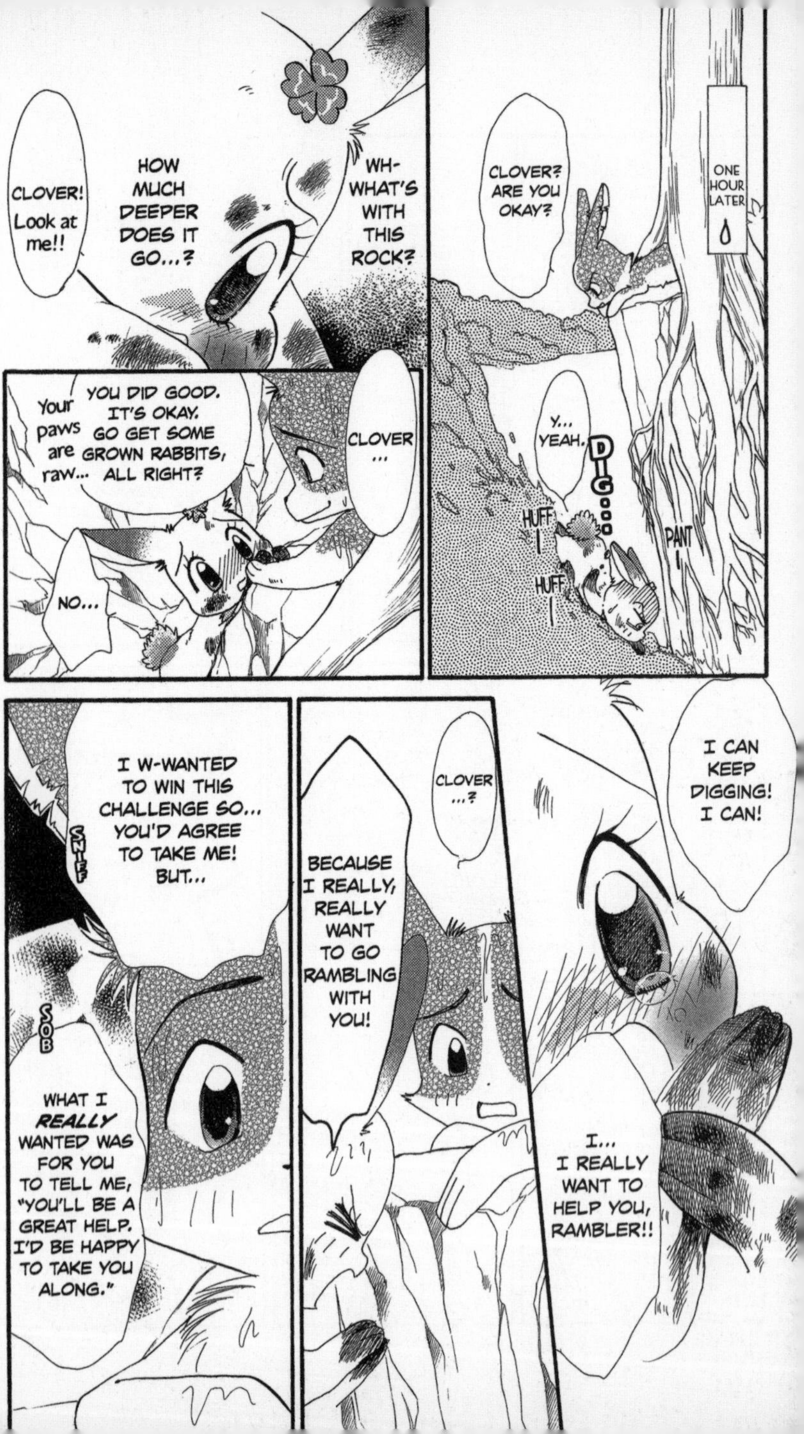
ONE HOUR LATER
CLOVER? ARE YOU OKAY?
Y... YEAH.
DIG...
HUFF
HUFF
PANT
WH- WHAT'S WITH THIS ROCK?
HOW MUCH DEEPER DOES IT GO...?
CLOVER! Look at me!!
CLOVER...
YOU DID GOOD. IT'S OKAY. GO GET SOME GROWN RABBITS, ALL RIGHT?
Your paws are raw...
NO...
I CAN KEEP DIGGING! I CAN!
I... I REALLY WANT TO HELP YOU, RAMBLER!!
CLOVER...?
BECAUSE I REALLY, REALLY WANT TO GO RAMBLING WITH YOU!
I W-WANTED TO WIN THIS CHALLENGE SO... YOU'D AGREE TO TAKE ME! BUT...
SNIFF
SOB
WHAT I REALLY WANTED WAS FOR YOU TO TELL ME, "YOU'LL BE A GREAT HELP. I'D BE HAPPY TO TAKE YOU ALONG."

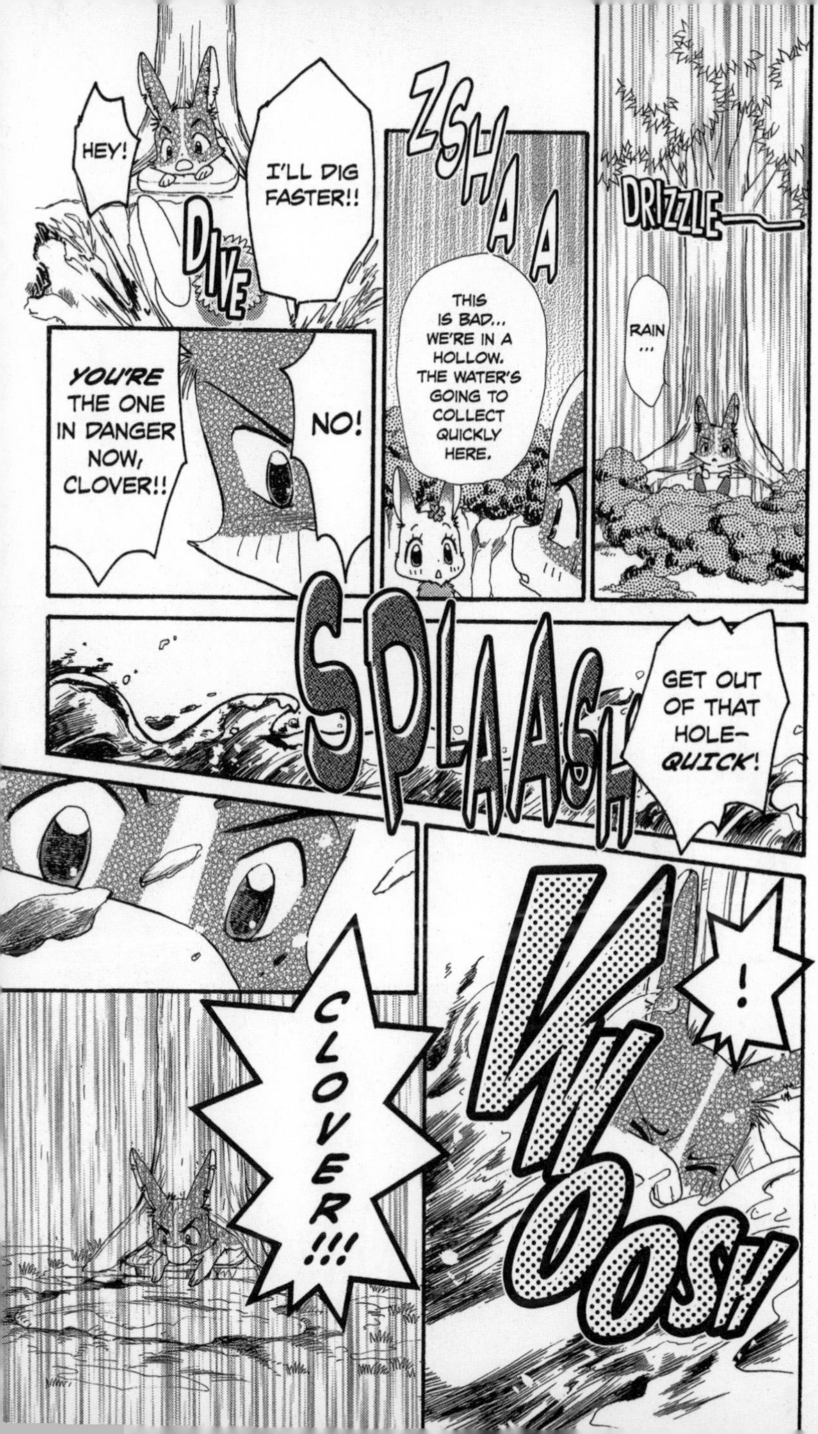
DRIZZLE
RAIN...
ZSHAAA
THIS IS BAD... WE'RE IN A HOLLOW. THE WATER'S GOING TO COLLECT QUICKLY HERE.
I'LL DIG FASTER!!
HEY!
DIVE
NO!
YOU'RE THE ONE IN DANGER NOW, CLOVER!!
GET OUT OF THAT HOLE- QUICK!
SPLAASH
!
WHOOSH
CLOVER!!!

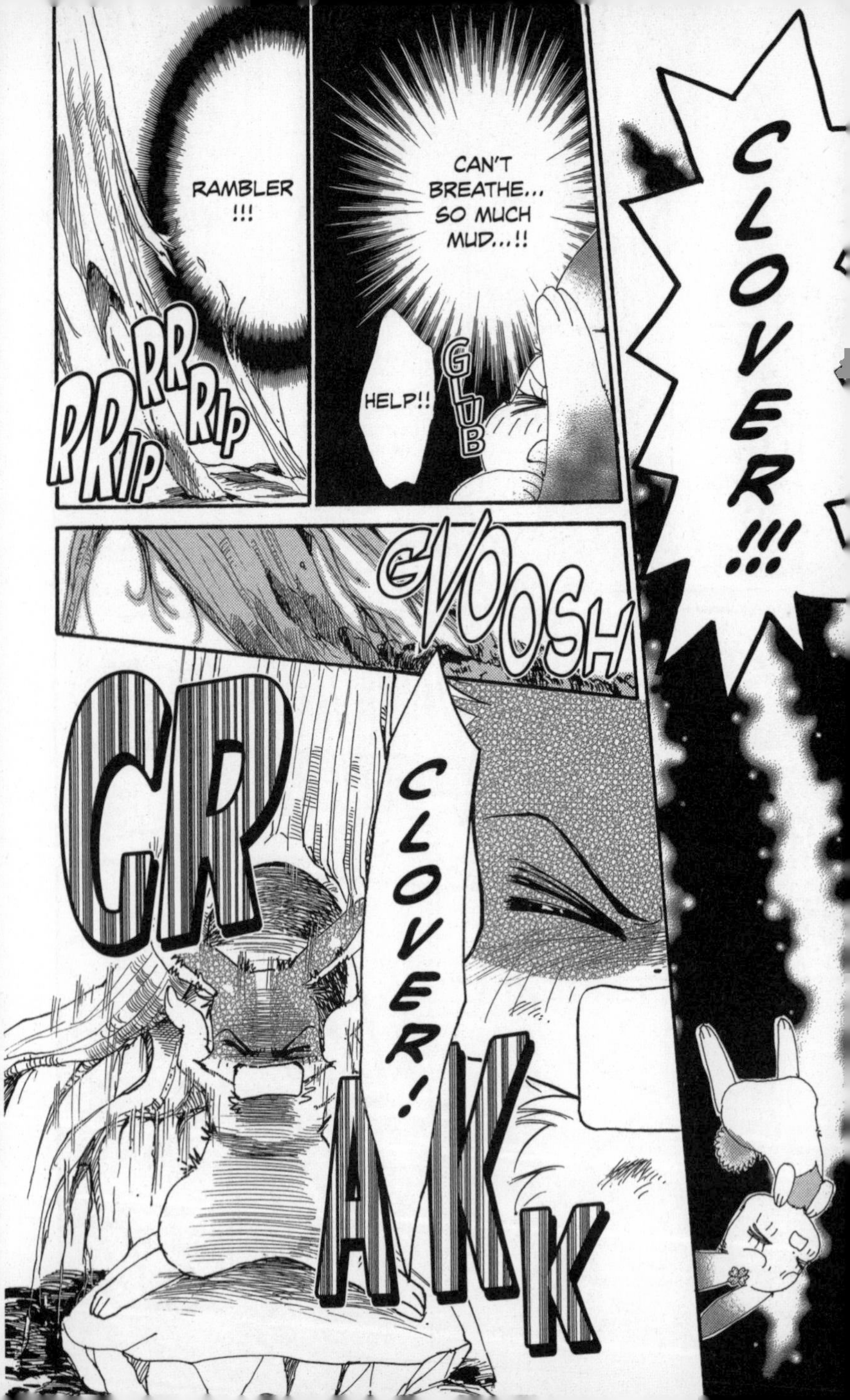
CLOVER!!!
CAN'T BREATHE... SO MUCH MUD...!!
GLUB
HELP!!
RAMBLER!!!
RRRRIP RRIP
GVOOSH
CLOVER!
CRAKK

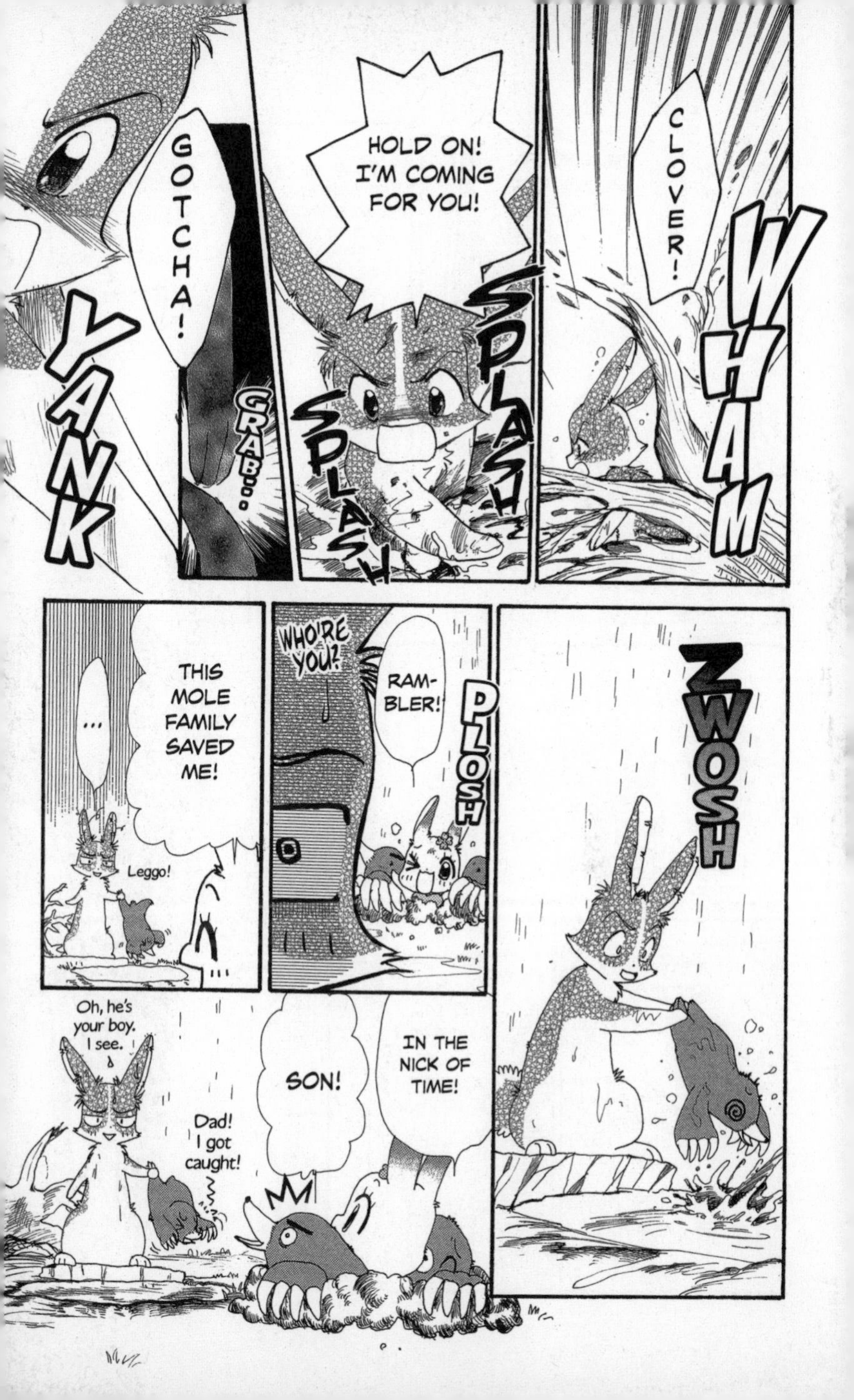
CLOVER!
WHAM
HOLD ON! I'M COMING FOR YOU!
SPLASH
SPLASH
GOTCHA!
GRAB...
YANK
ZWOSH
WHO'RE YOU?
RAMBLER!
PLOSH
THIS MOLE FAMILY SAVED ME!
...
Leggo!
IN THE NICK OF TIME!
SON!
Dad! I got caught!
Oh, he's your boy. I see.

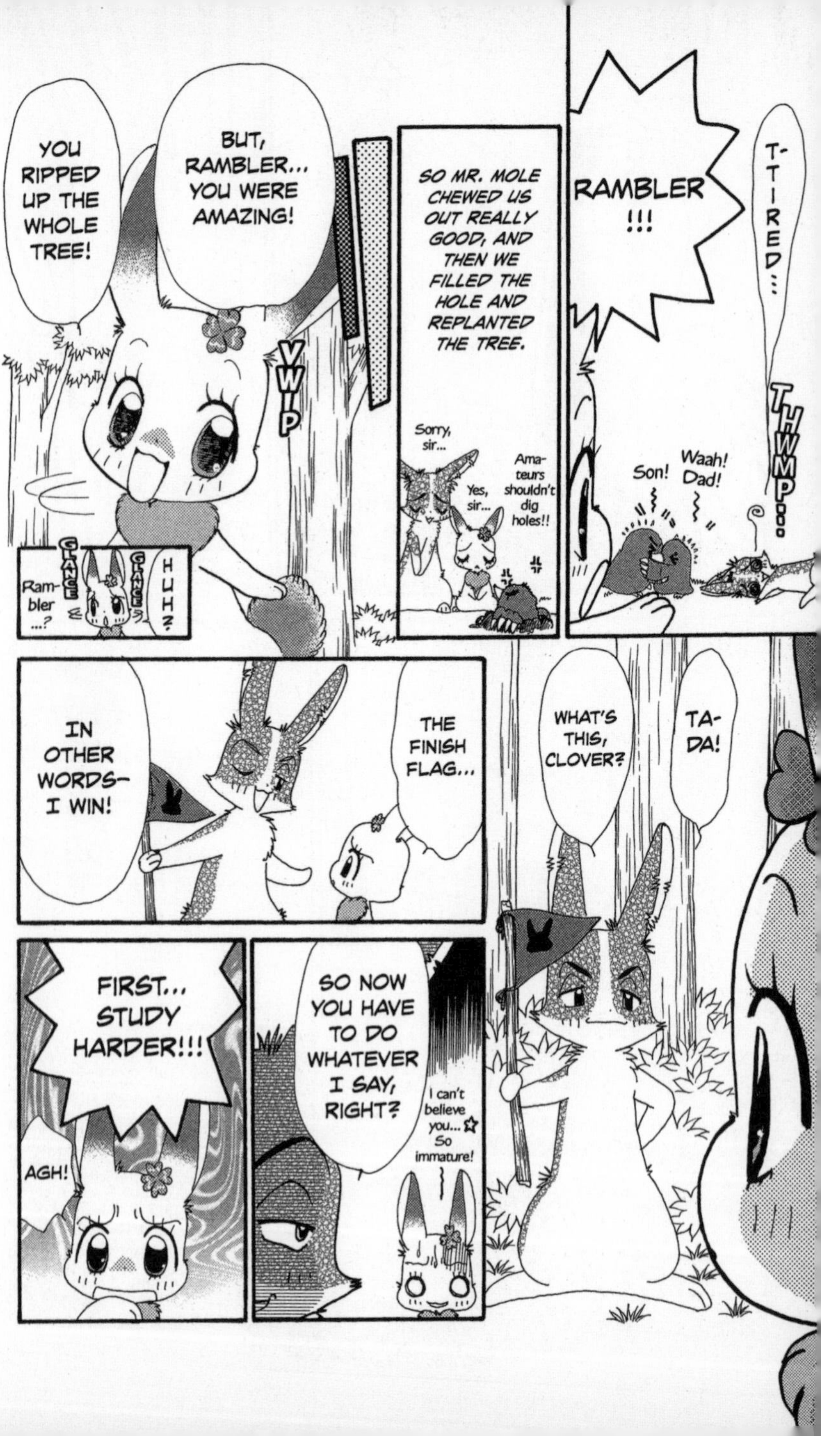

T-TIRED...
RAMBLER!!!
THWMP...
Waah! Dad!
Son!
SO MR. MOLE CHEWED US OUT REALLY GOOD, AND THEN WE FILLED THE HOLE AND REPLANTED THE TREE.
Sorry, sir...
Amateurs shouldn't dig holes!!
Yes, sir...
BUT, RAMBLER... YOU WERE AMAZING!
YOU RIPPED UP THE WHOLE TREE!
VWIP
HUH?
GLANCE
GLANCE
Rambler...?
TA-DA!
WHAT'S THIS, CLOVER?
THE FINISH FLAG...
IN OTHER WORDS— I WIN!
SO NOW YOU HAVE TO DO WHATEVER I SAY, RIGHT?
I can't believe you... ☆ So immature!
FIRST... STUDY HARDER!!!
AGH!

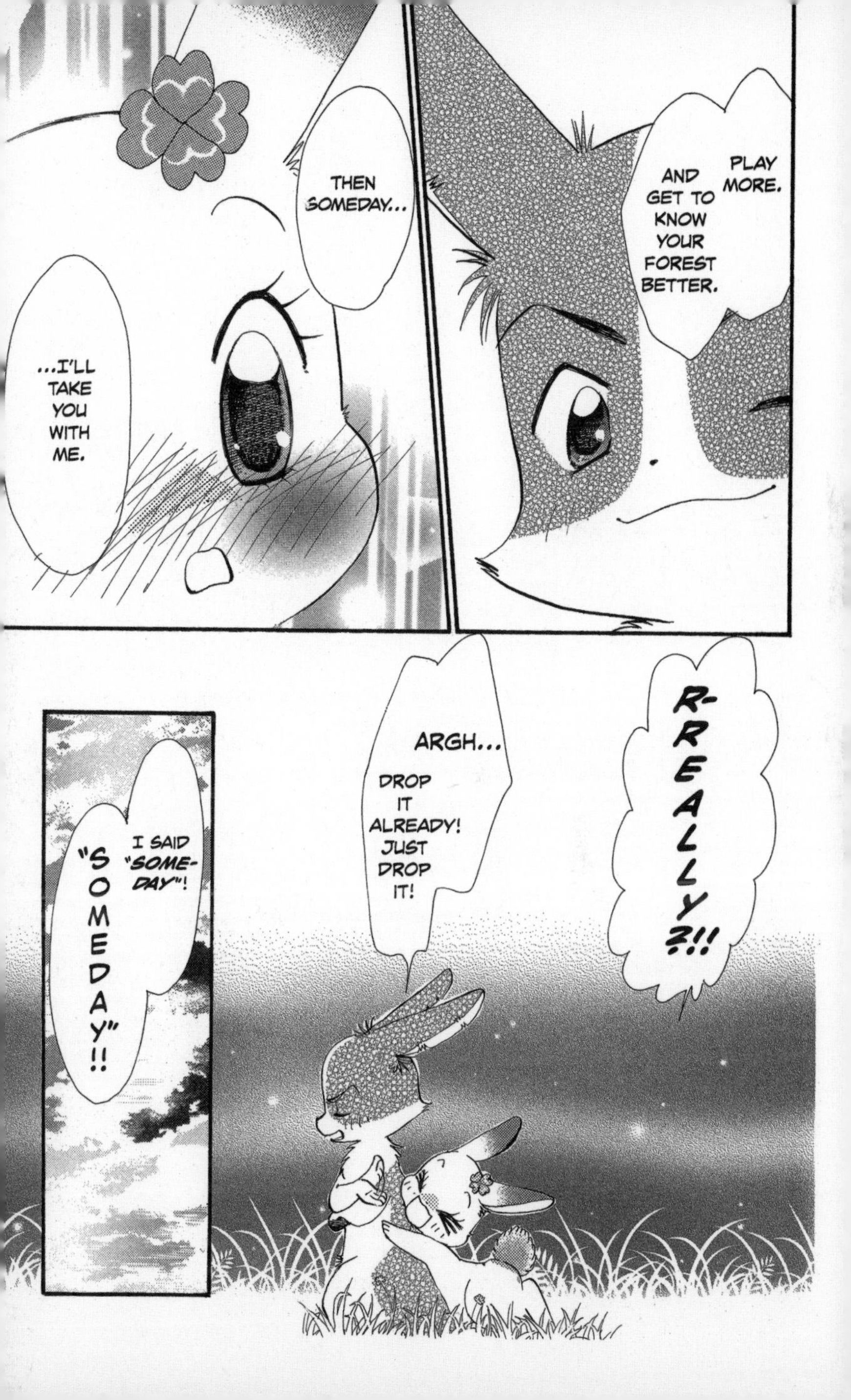
PLAY MORE. AND GET TO KNOW YOUR FOREST BETTER.
THEN SOMEDAY...
...I'LL TAKE YOU WITH ME.
R-REALLY?!!
ARGH...
DROP IT ALREADY! JUST DROP IT!
I SAID "SOME-DAY"!
"SOMEDAY"!!

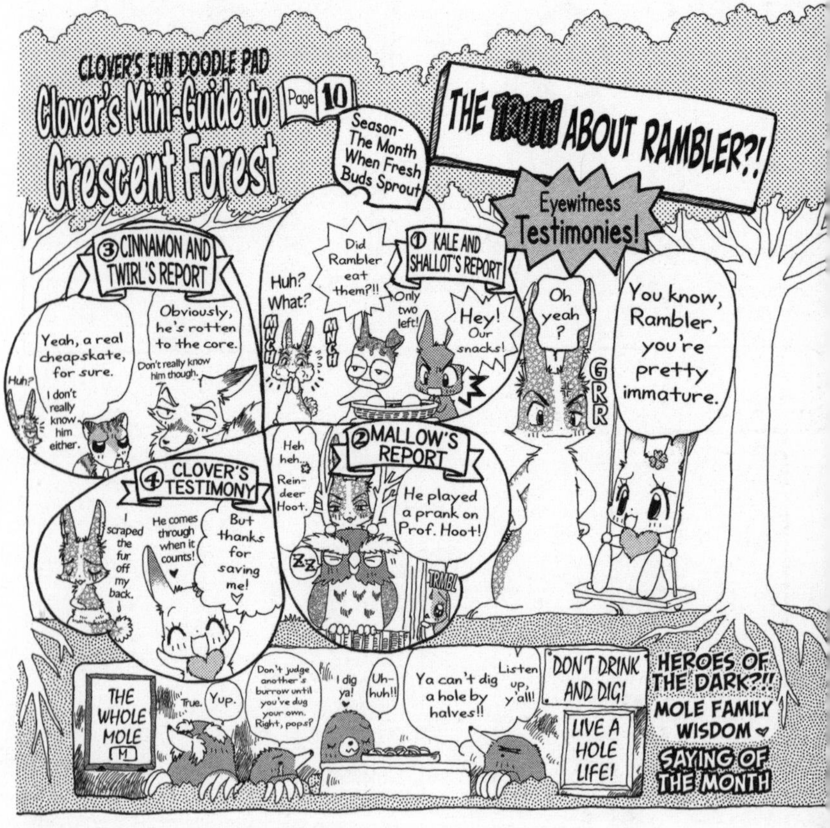
CLOVER'S FUN DOODLE PAD
Clover's Mini-Guide to Crescent Forest
Page 10
Season- The Month When Fresh Buds Sprout
THE TRUTH ABOUT RAMBLER?!
Eyewitness Testimonies!
You know, Rambler, you're pretty immature.
Oh yeah?
GRR
① KALE AND SHALLOT'S REPORT
Hey! Our snacks!
Only two left!
Did Rambler eat them?!!
Huh? What?
MNCH
MNCH
② MALLOW'S REPORT
He played a prank on Prof. Hoot!
Heh heh... Reindeer Hoot.
TRMBL
ZZ
③ CINNAMON AND TWIRL'S REPORT
Obviously, he's rotten to the core.
Don't really know him though.
Yeah, a real cheapskate, for sure.
I don't really know him either.
Huh?
④ CLOVER'S TESTIMONY
But thanks for saving me!
He comes through when it counts!
I scraped the fur off my back.
HEROES OF THE DARK?!! MOLE FAMILY WISDOM
SAYING OF THE MONTH
DON'T DRINK AND DIG!
LIVE A HOLE LIFE!
Listen up, y'all!
Ya can't dig a hole by halves!!
Uh-huh!!
I dig ya!
Don't judge another's burrow until you've dug your own. Right, pops?
Yup.
True.
THE WHOLE MOLE
M

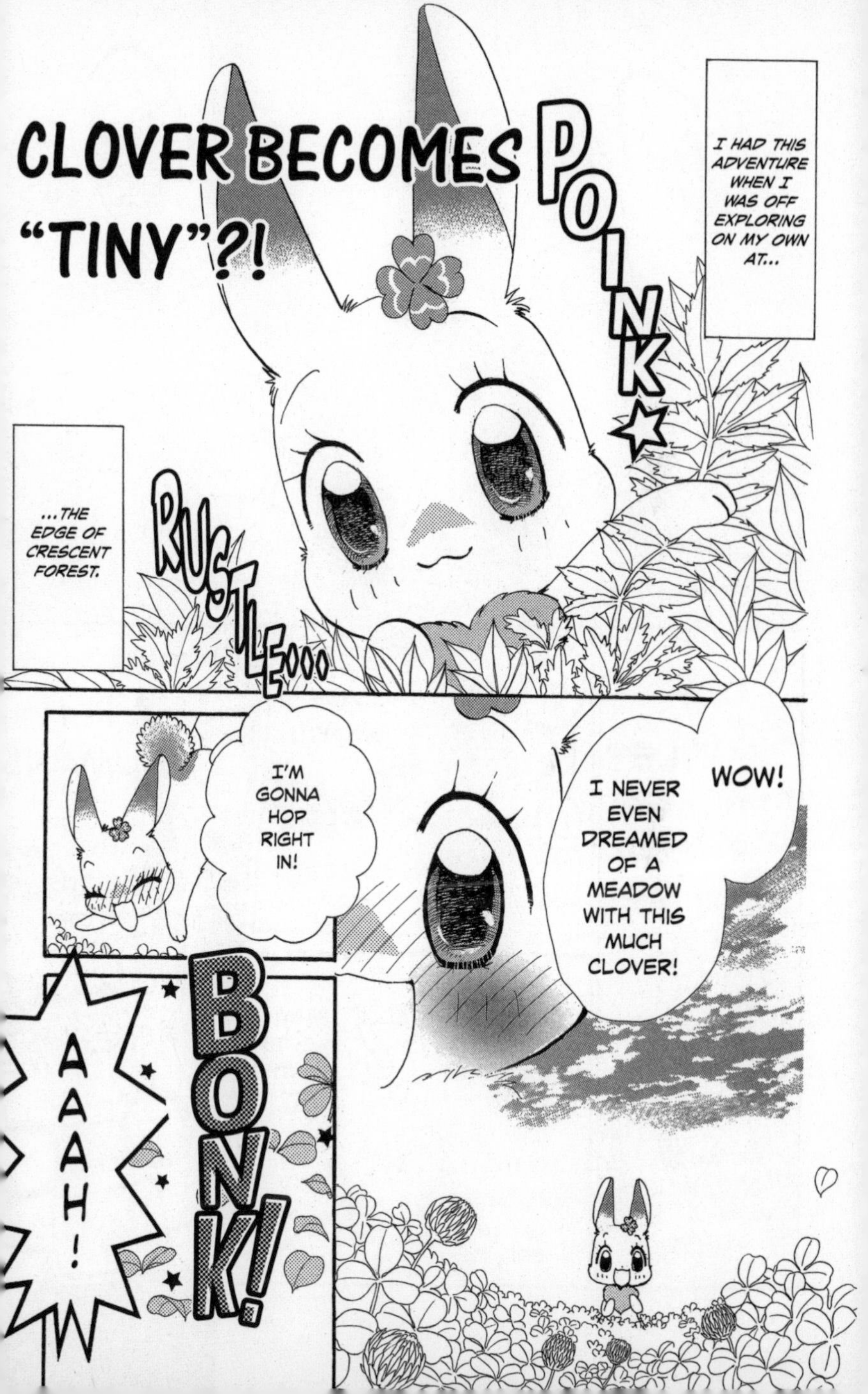
CLOVER BECOMES "TINY"?!
I HAD THIS ADVENTURE WHEN I WAS OFF EXPLORING ON MY OWN AT...
POINK☆
RUSTLE...
...THE EDGE OF CRESCENT FOREST.
WOW!
I NEVER EVEN DREAMED OF A MEADOW WITH THIS MUCH CLOVER!
I'M GONNA HOP RIGHT IN!
BONK!
AAAH!

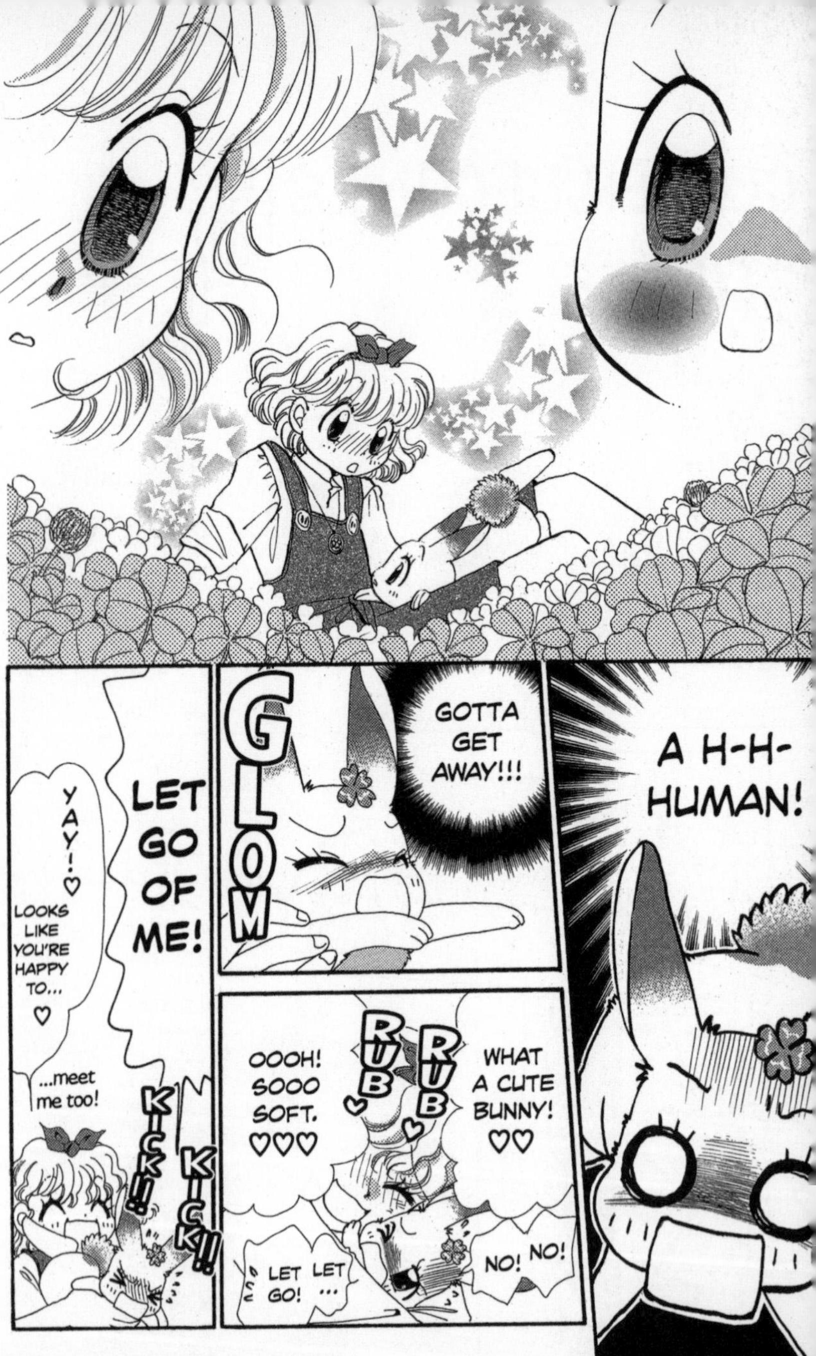
A H-H-HUMAN!
GOTTA GET AWAY!!!
GLOM
WHAT A CUTE BUNNY! ♡♡
RUB
RUB
♡
♡
OOOH! SOOO SOFT. ♡♡♡
NO! NO!
LET ...
LET GO!
LET GO OF ME!
YAY! ♡
LOOKS LIKE YOU'RE HAPPY TO... ♡
...meet me too!
KICK!!
KICK!!

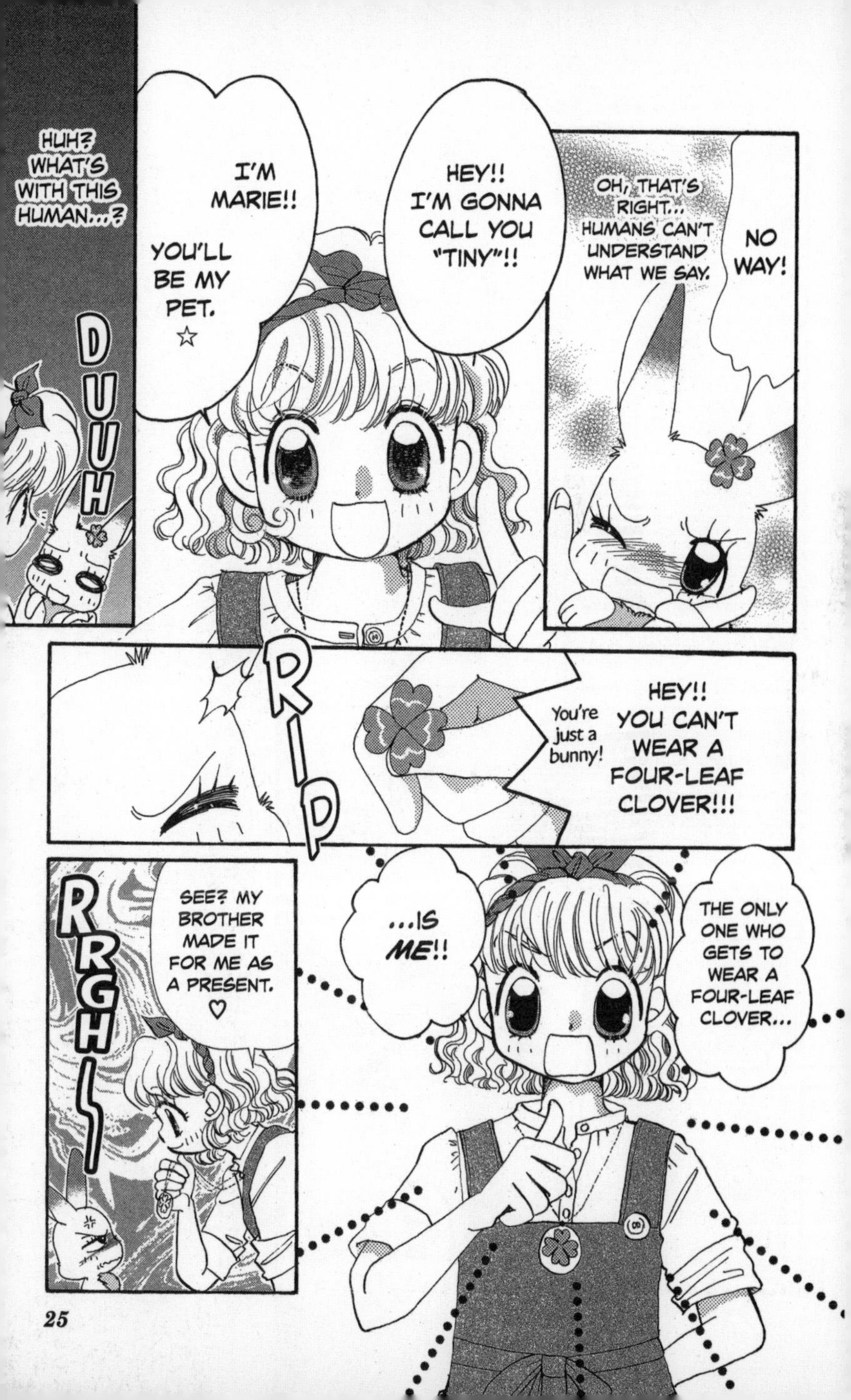
NO WAY!
OH, THAT'S RIGHT... HUMANS CAN'T UNDERSTAND WHAT WE SAY.
HEY!! I'M GONNA CALL YOU "TINY"!!
I'M MARIE!!
YOU'LL BE MY PET. ☆
HUH? WHAT'S WITH THIS HUMAN...?
DUUH
HEY!! YOU CAN'T WEAR A FOUR-LEAF CLOVER!!!
You're just a bunny!
RIP
THE ONLY ONE WHO GETS TO WEAR A FOUR-LEAF CLOVER...
...IS *ME*!!
SEE? MY BROTHER MADE IT FOR ME AS A PRESENT. ♡
RRGH~

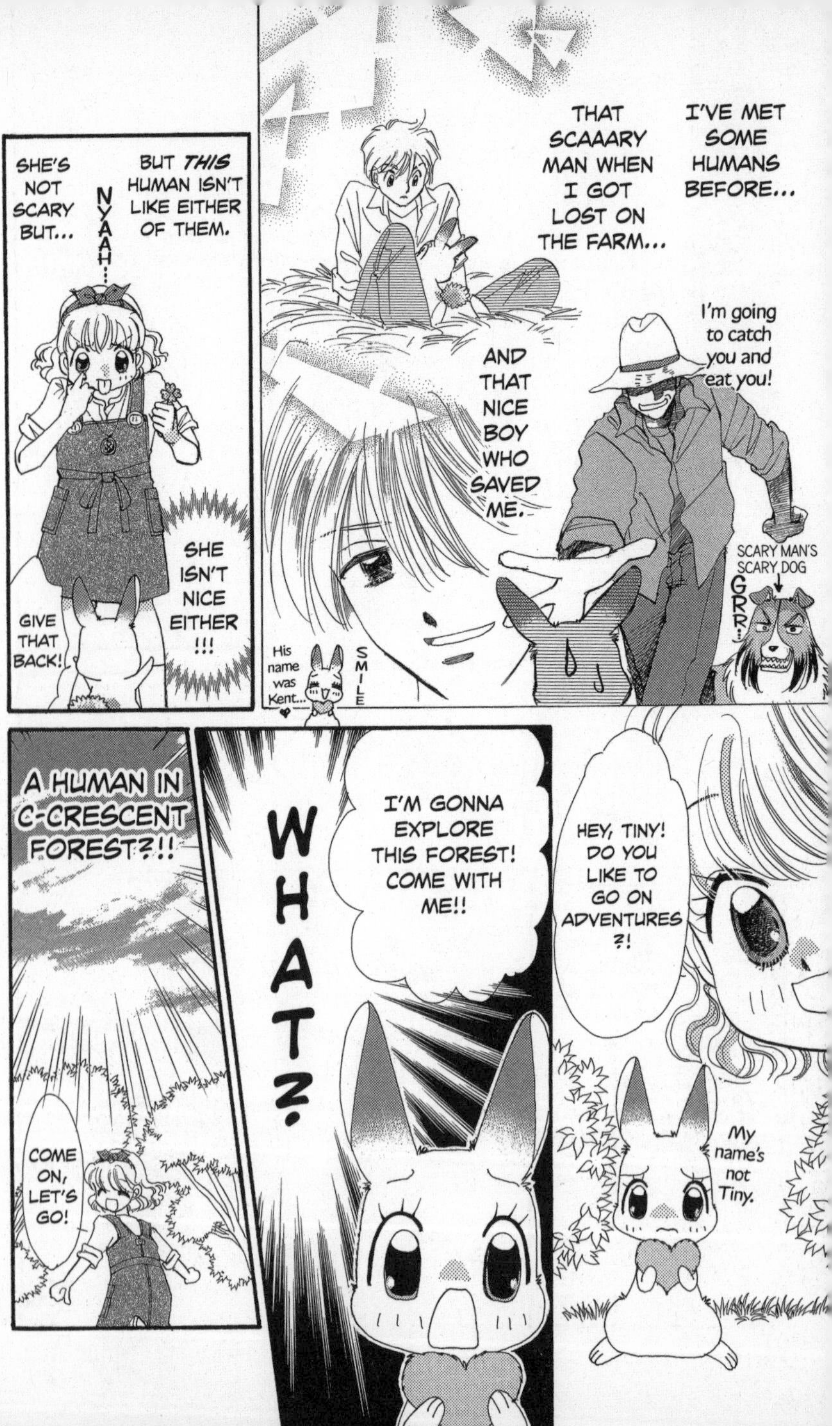
I'VE MET SOME HUMANS BEFORE...
THAT SCAAARY MAN WHEN I GOT LOST ON THE FARM...
I'm going to catch you and eat you!
SCARY MAN'S SCARY DOG
GRR...
AND THAT NICE BOY WHO SAVED ME.
SMILE
His name was Kent...
BUT *THIS* HUMAN ISN'T LIKE EITHER OF THEM.
NYAAH...
SHE'S NOT SCARY BUT...
SHE ISN'T NICE EITHER!!!
GIVE THAT BACK!
HEY, TINY! DO YOU LIKE TO GO ON ADVENTURES?!
My name's not Tiny.
I'M GONNA EXPLORE THIS FOREST! COME WITH ME!!
WHAT?
A HUMAN IN C-CRESCENT FOREST?!!
COME ON, LET'S GO!

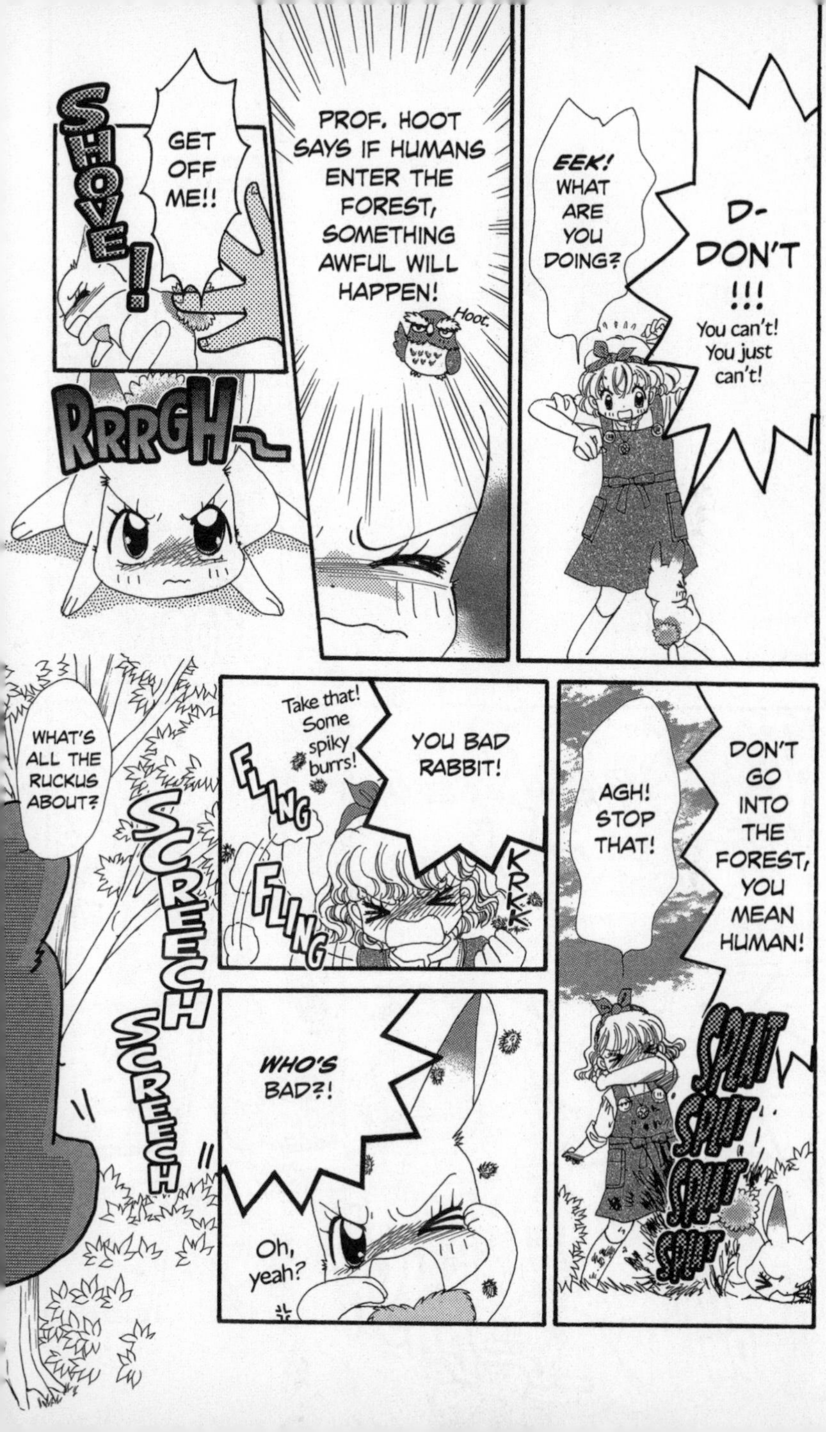
D-DON'T !!!
You can't! You just can't!
EEK! WHAT ARE YOU DOING?
PROF. HOOT SAYS IF HUMANS ENTER THE FOREST, SOMETHING AWFUL WILL HAPPEN!
Hoot.
SHOVE!
GET OFF ME!!
RRRGH~
DON'T GO INTO THE FOREST, YOU MEAN HUMAN!
AGH! STOP THAT!
SPLAT
SPLAT
SPLAT
SPLAT
YOU BAD RABBIT!
Take that! Some spiky burrs!
FLING
FLING
KRKK
WHO'S BAD?!
Oh, yeah?
WHAT'S ALL THE RUCKUS ABOUT?
SCREECH
SCREECH

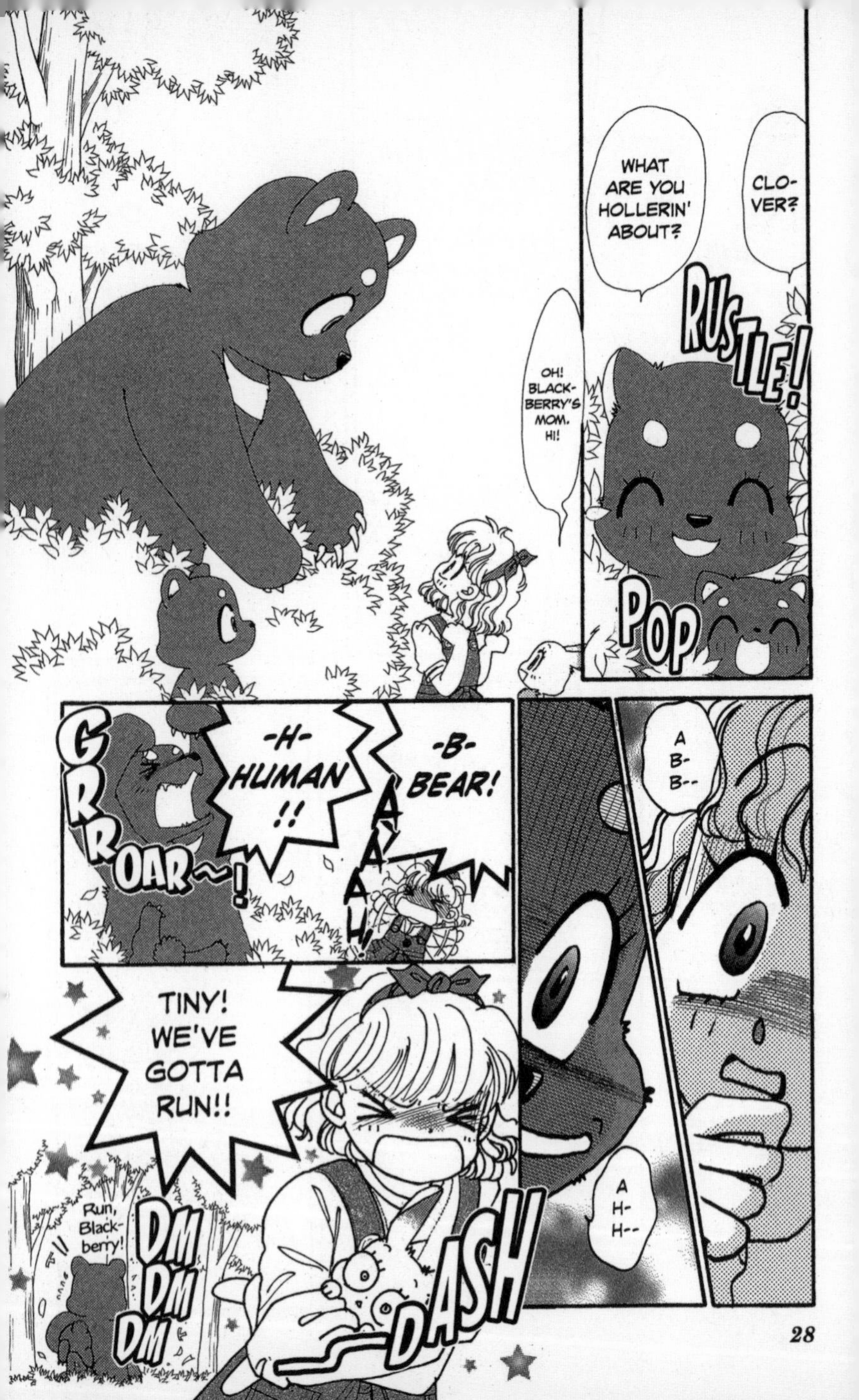
CLO-VER?
WHAT ARE YOU HOLLERIN' ABOUT?
RUSTLE!
OH! BLACK-BERRY'S MOM. HI!
POP
A B- B--
A H- H--
-B- BEAR!
-H- HUMAN!!
GRRROAR~!
AAAAH!!
TINY! WE'VE GOTTA RUN!!
Run, Black-berry!
DM DM DM
DASH

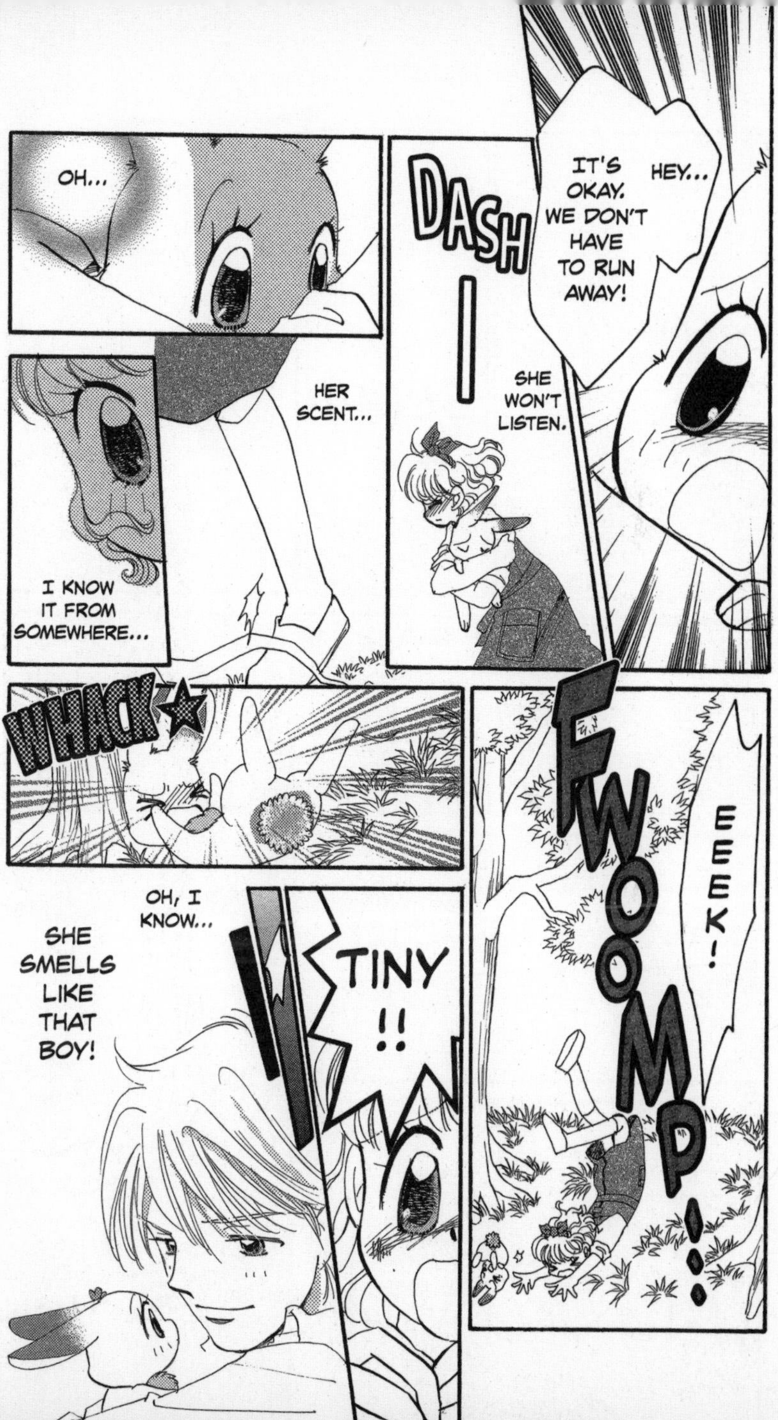
HEY...
IT'S OKAY. WE DON'T HAVE TO RUN AWAY!
DASH
SHE WON'T LISTEN.
OH...
HER SCENT...
I KNOW IT FROM SOMEWHERE...
EEEK!
FWOOMP!!
WHACK☆
TINY!!
OH, I KNOW...
SHE SMELLS LIKE THAT BOY!

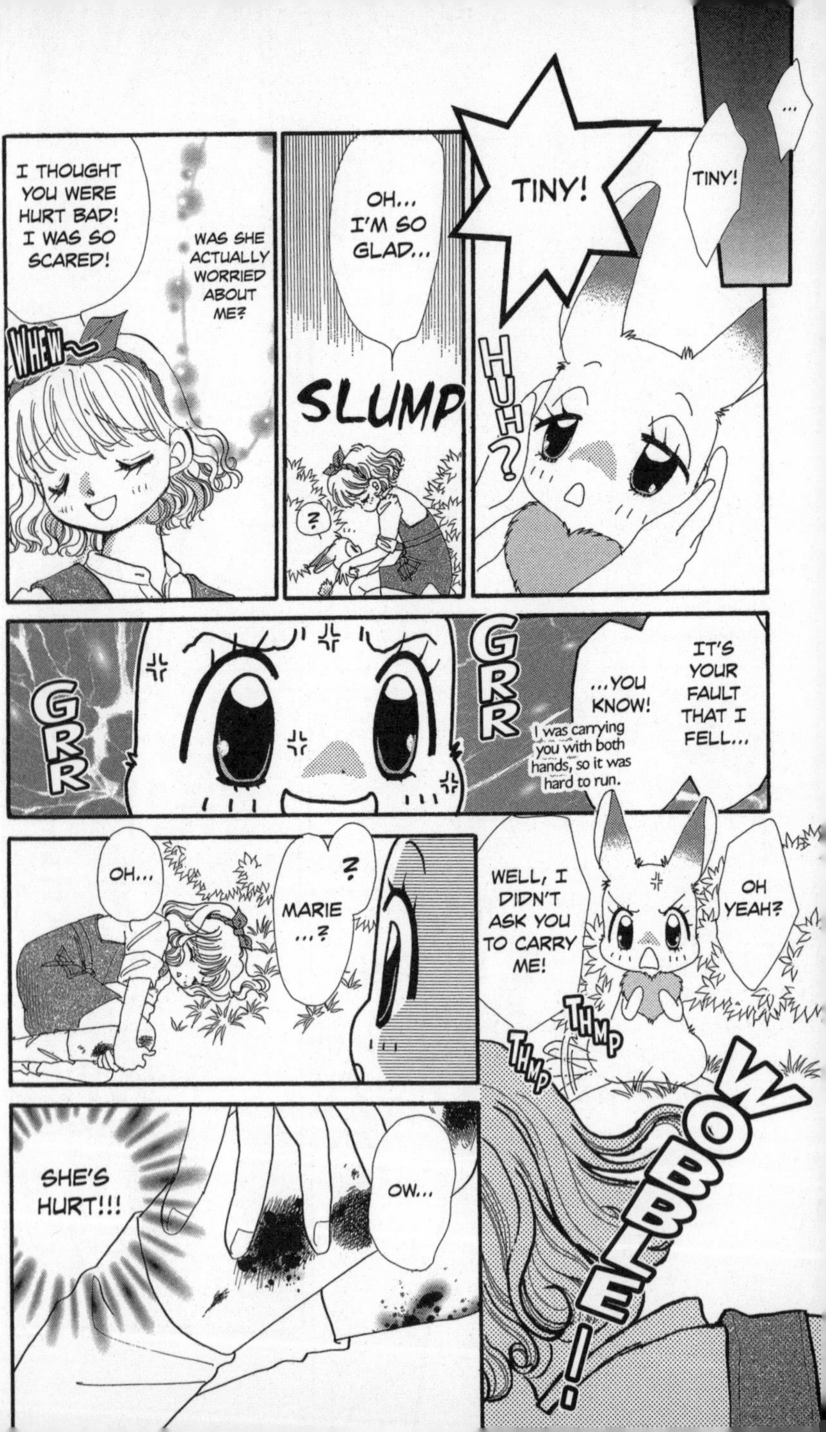
...
TINY!
TINY!
HUH?
OH... I'M SO GLAD...
SLUMP
?
I THOUGHT YOU WERE HURT BAD! I WAS SO SCARED!
WAS SHE ACTUALLY WORRIED ABOUT ME?
WHEW~
IT'S YOUR FAULT THAT I FELL...
...YOU KNOW!
I was carrying you with both hands, so it was hard to run.
GRR
GRR
OH YEAH?
WELL, I DIDN'T ASK YOU TO CARRY ME!
THMP
THMP
WOBBLE!!
?
MARIE ...?
OH...
OW...
SHE'S HURT!!!

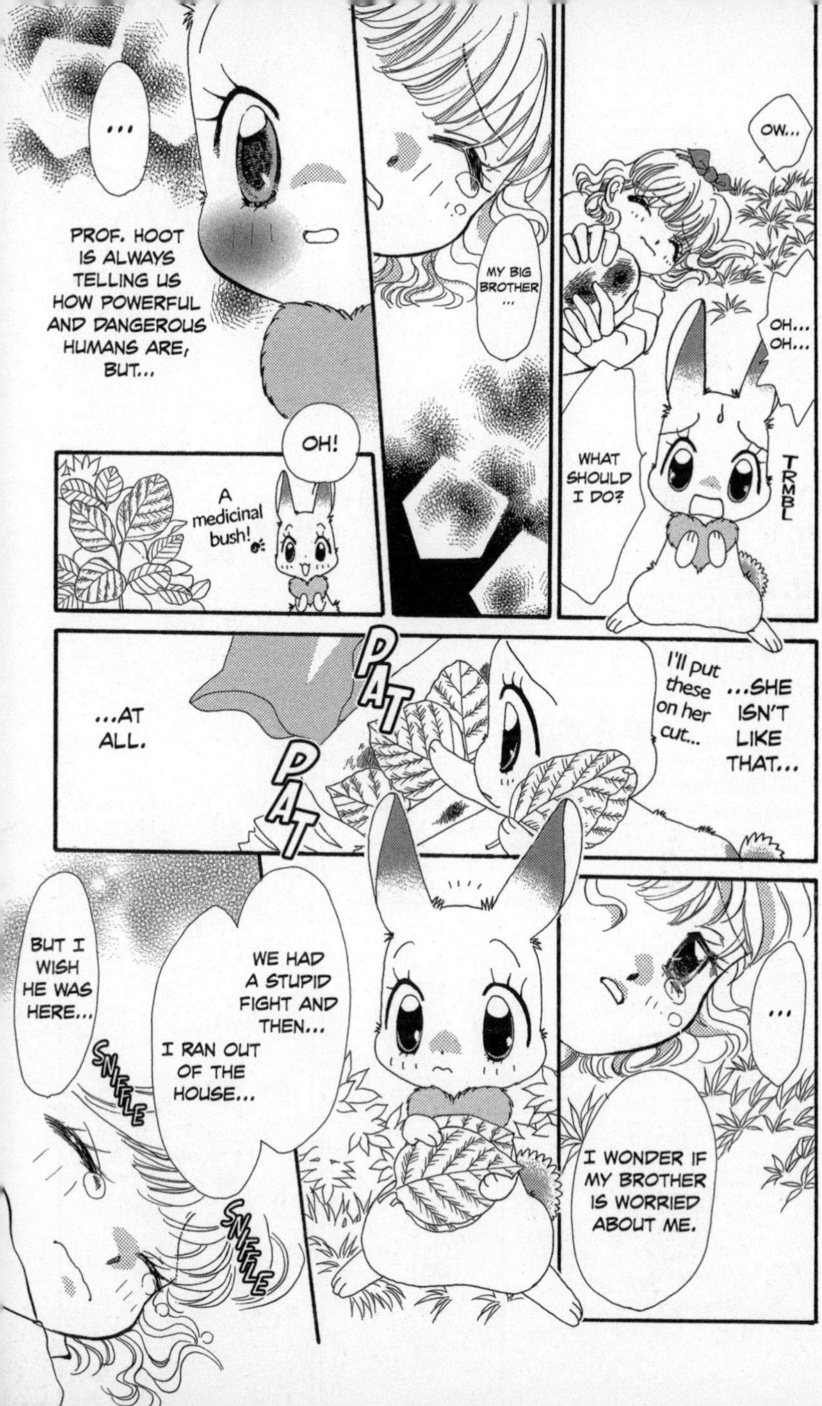

OW...
OH... OH...
WHAT SHOULD I DO?
TRMBL
MY BIG BROTHER ...
...
PROF. HOOT IS ALWAYS TELLING US HOW POWERFUL AND DANGEROUS HUMANS ARE, BUT...
OH!
A medicinal bush!
I'll put these on her cut...
...SHE ISN'T LIKE THAT...
PAT
PAT
...AT ALL.
...
I WONDER IF MY BROTHER IS WORRIED ABOUT ME.
WE HAD A STUPID FIGHT AND THEN...
I RAN OUT OF THE HOUSE...
BUT I WISH HE WAS HERE...
SNIFFLE
SNIFFLE

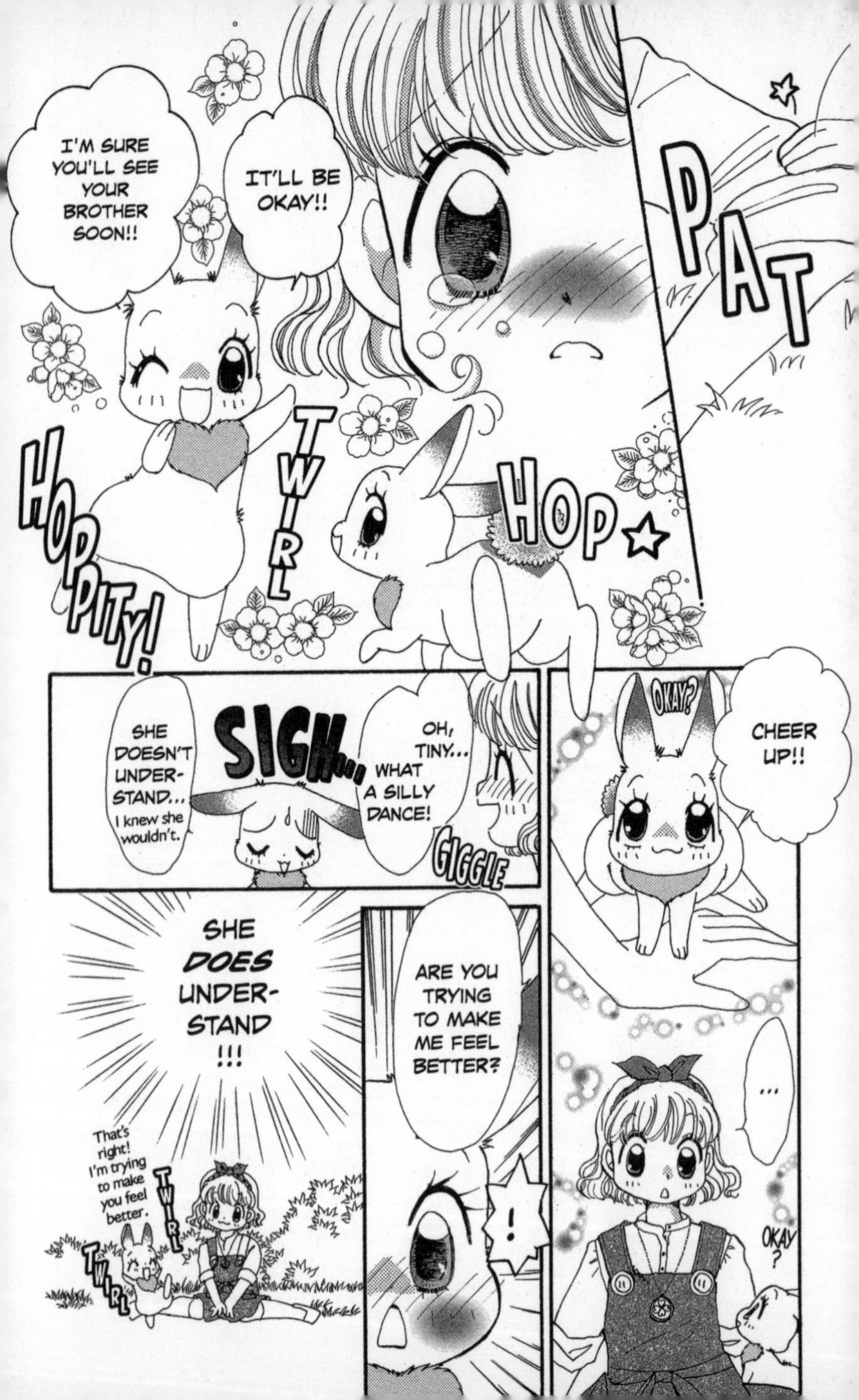
PAT
IT'LL BE OKAY!!
I'M SURE YOU'LL SEE YOUR BROTHER SOON!!
HOP☆
TWIRL
HOPPITY!
OKAY?
CHEER UP!!
...
OKAY?
OH, TINY... WHAT A SILLY DANCE!
GIGGLE
SIGH...
SHE DOESN'T UNDERSTAND... I knew she wouldn't.
ARE YOU TRYING TO MAKE ME FEEL BETTER?
!
SHE DOES UNDERSTAND!!!
That's right! I'm trying to make you feel better.
TWIRL
TWIRL

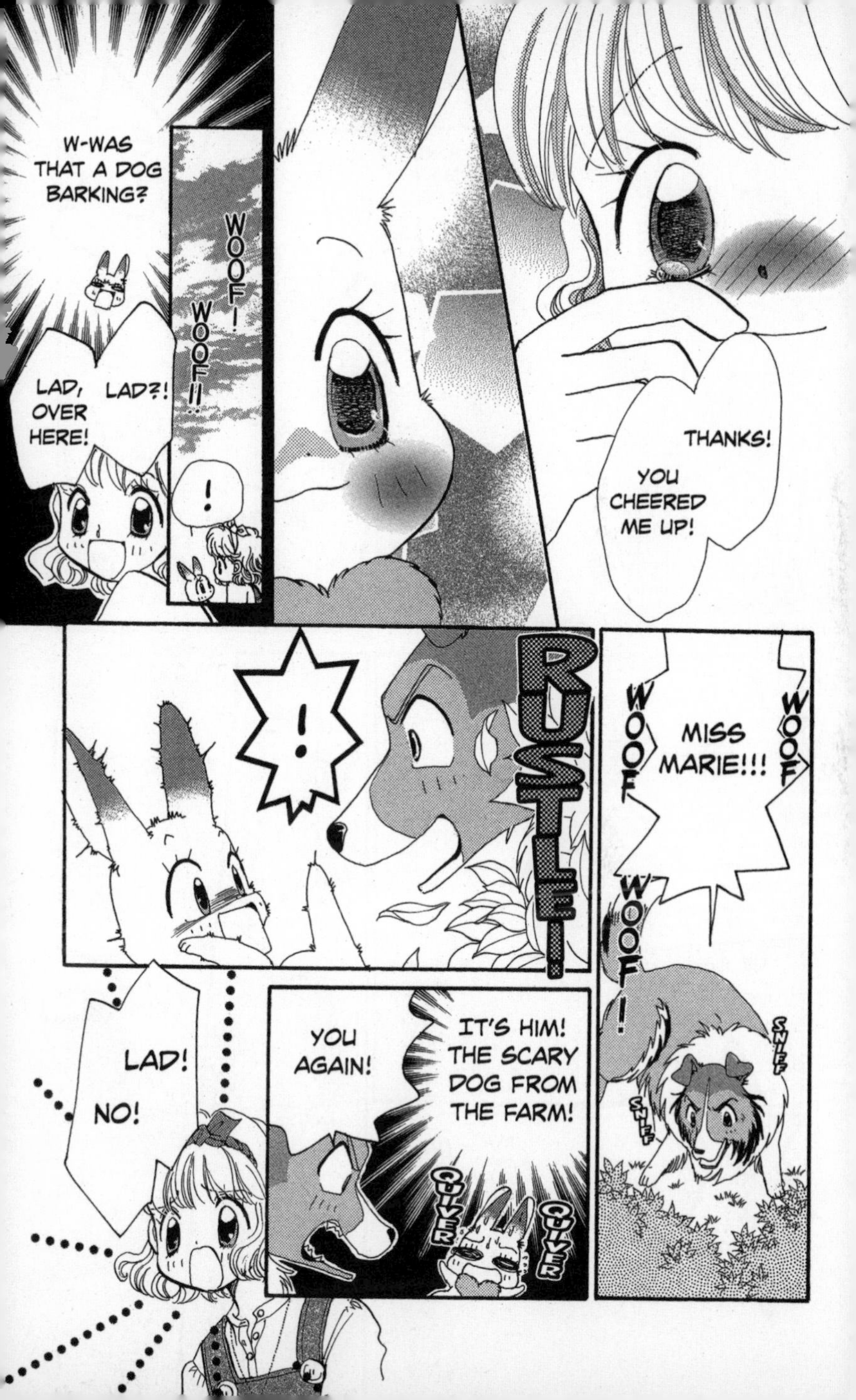
THANKS!
YOU CHEERED ME UP!
WOOF! WOOF!!
!
W-WAS THAT A DOG BARKING?
LAD?!
LAD, OVER HERE!
MISS MARIE!!!
WOOF WOOF
WOOF WOOF!
SNIFF SNIFF
RUSTLE!
!
IT'S HIM! THE SCARY DOG FROM THE FARM!
YOU AGAIN!
QUIVER QUIVER
LAD!
NO!

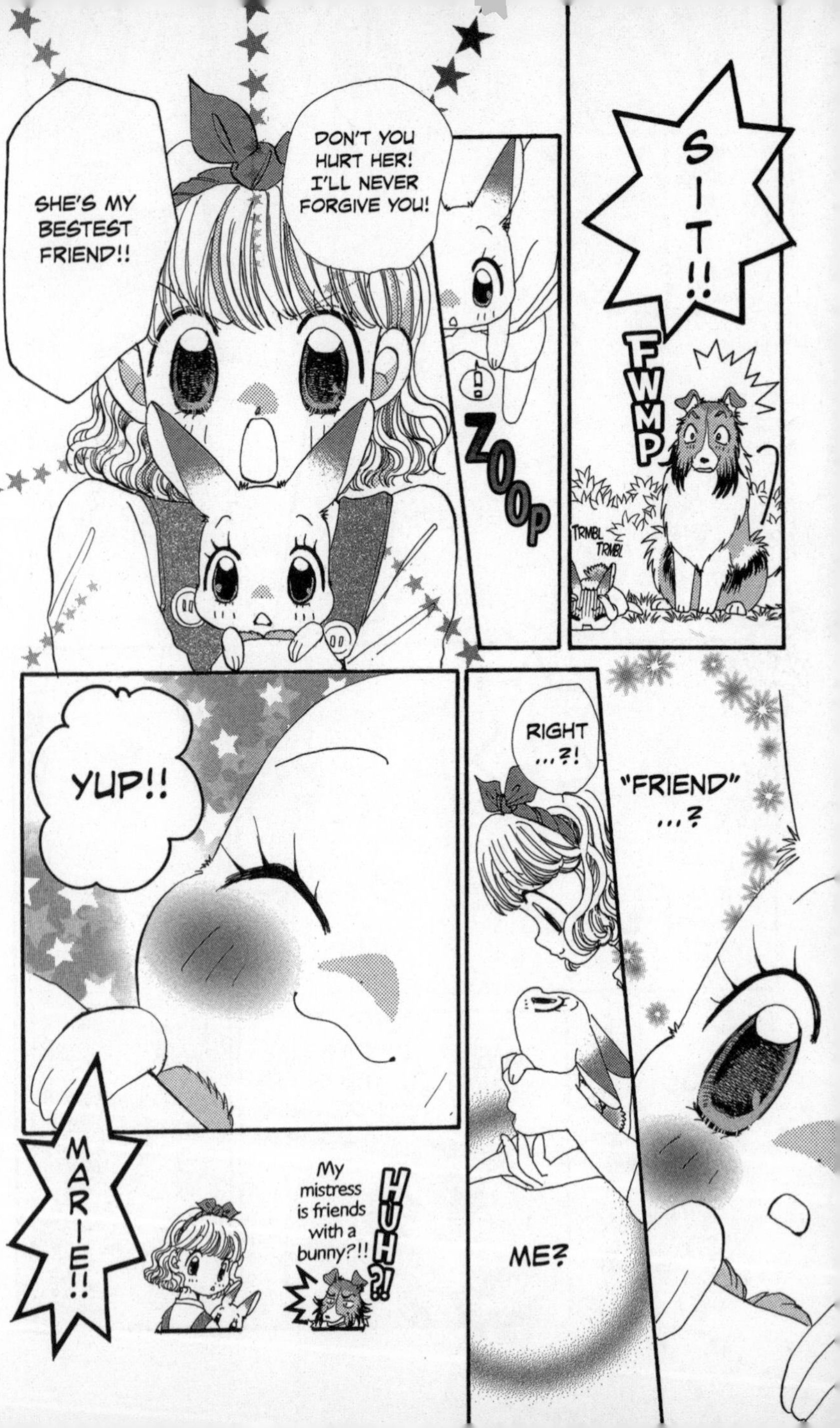
SIT!!
FWMP
TRMBL TRMBL
!
ZOOP
DON'T YOU HURT HER! I'LL NEVER FORGIVE YOU!
SHE'S MY BESTEST FRIEND!!
"FRIEND" ...?
RIGHT ...?!
ME?
YUP!!
HUH?!
My mistress is friends with a bunny?!!
MARIE!!

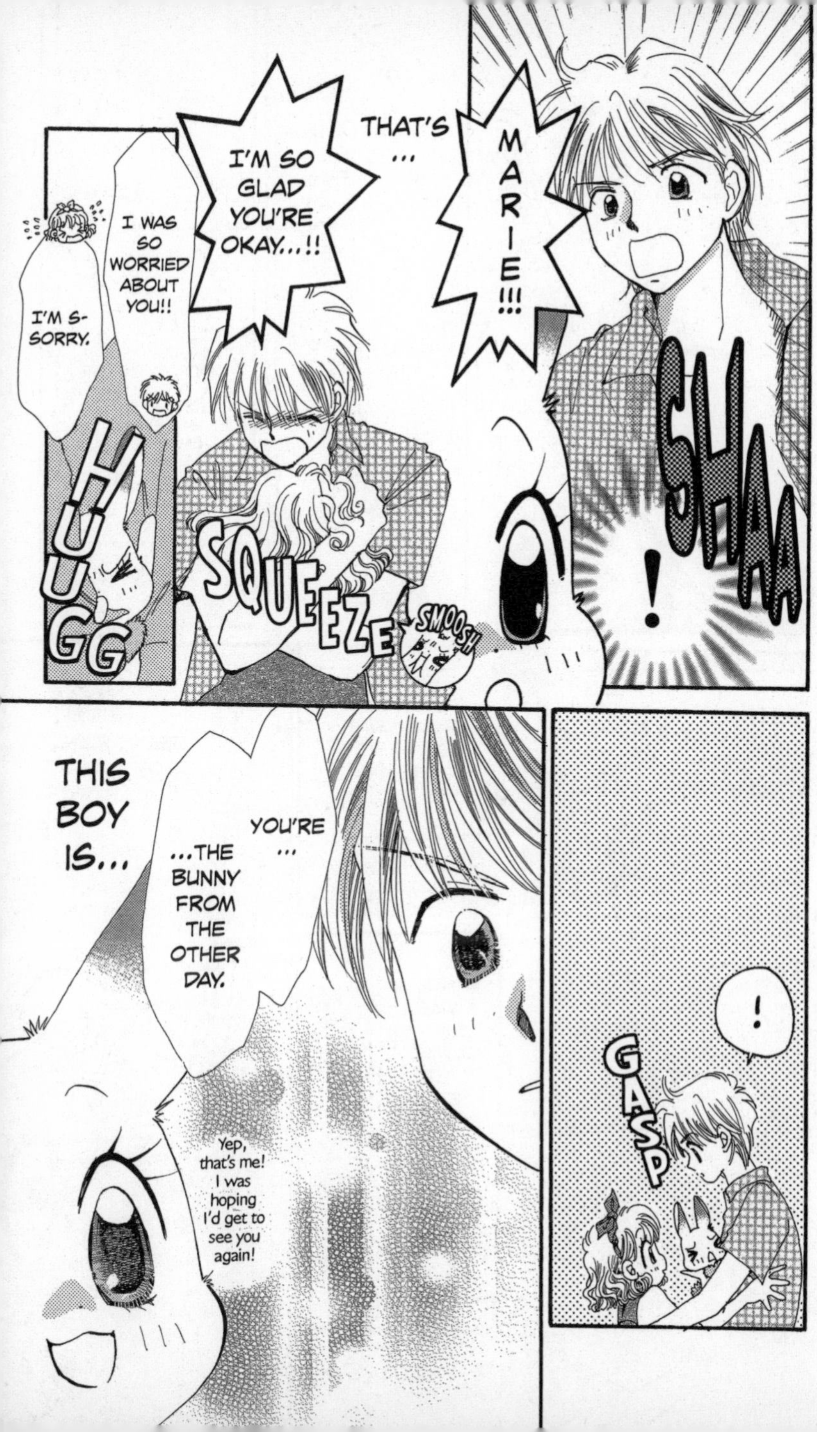
THAT'S...
MARIE!!!
SHAA
!
I'M SO GLAD YOU'RE OKAY...!!
SQUEEZE
SMOOSH
I WAS SO WORRIED ABOUT YOU!!
I'M S-SORRY.
HUUGG
!
GASP
YOU'RE...
...THE BUNNY FROM THE OTHER DAY.
THIS BOY IS...
Yep, that's me! I was hoping I'd get to see you again!

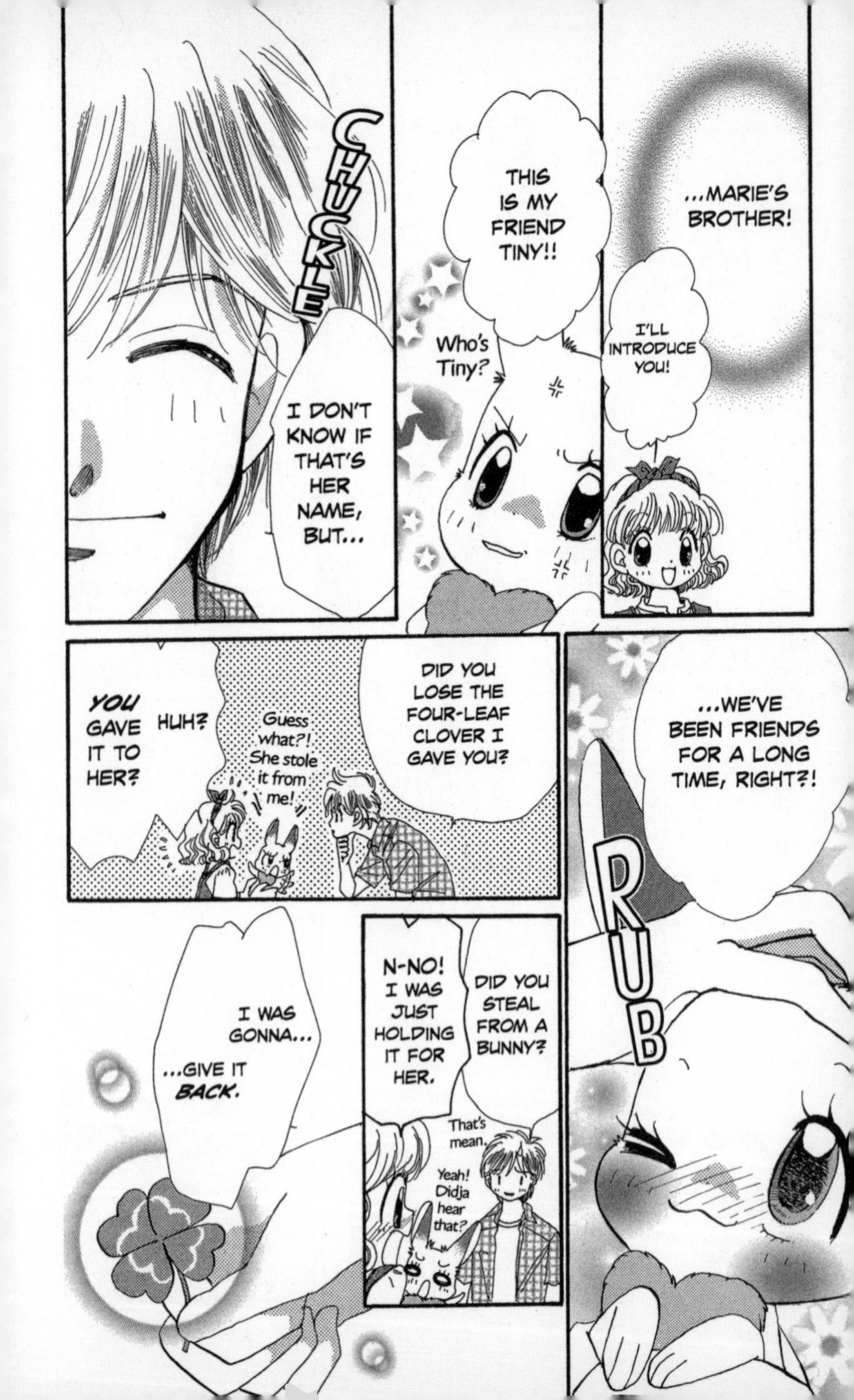
...MARIE'S BROTHER!
I'LL INTRODUCE YOU!
THIS IS MY FRIEND TINY!!
Who's Tiny?
CHUCKLE
I DON'T KNOW IF THAT'S HER NAME, BUT...
...WE'VE BEEN FRIENDS FOR A LONG TIME, RIGHT?!
RUB
DID YOU LOSE THE FOUR-LEAF CLOVER I GAVE YOU?
Guess what?! She stole it from me!
HUH?
YOU GAVE IT TO HER?
DID YOU STEAL FROM A BUNNY?
N-NO! I WAS JUST HOLDING IT FOR HER.
That's mean.
Yeah! Didja hear that?
I WAS GONNA...
...GIVE IT *BACK*.

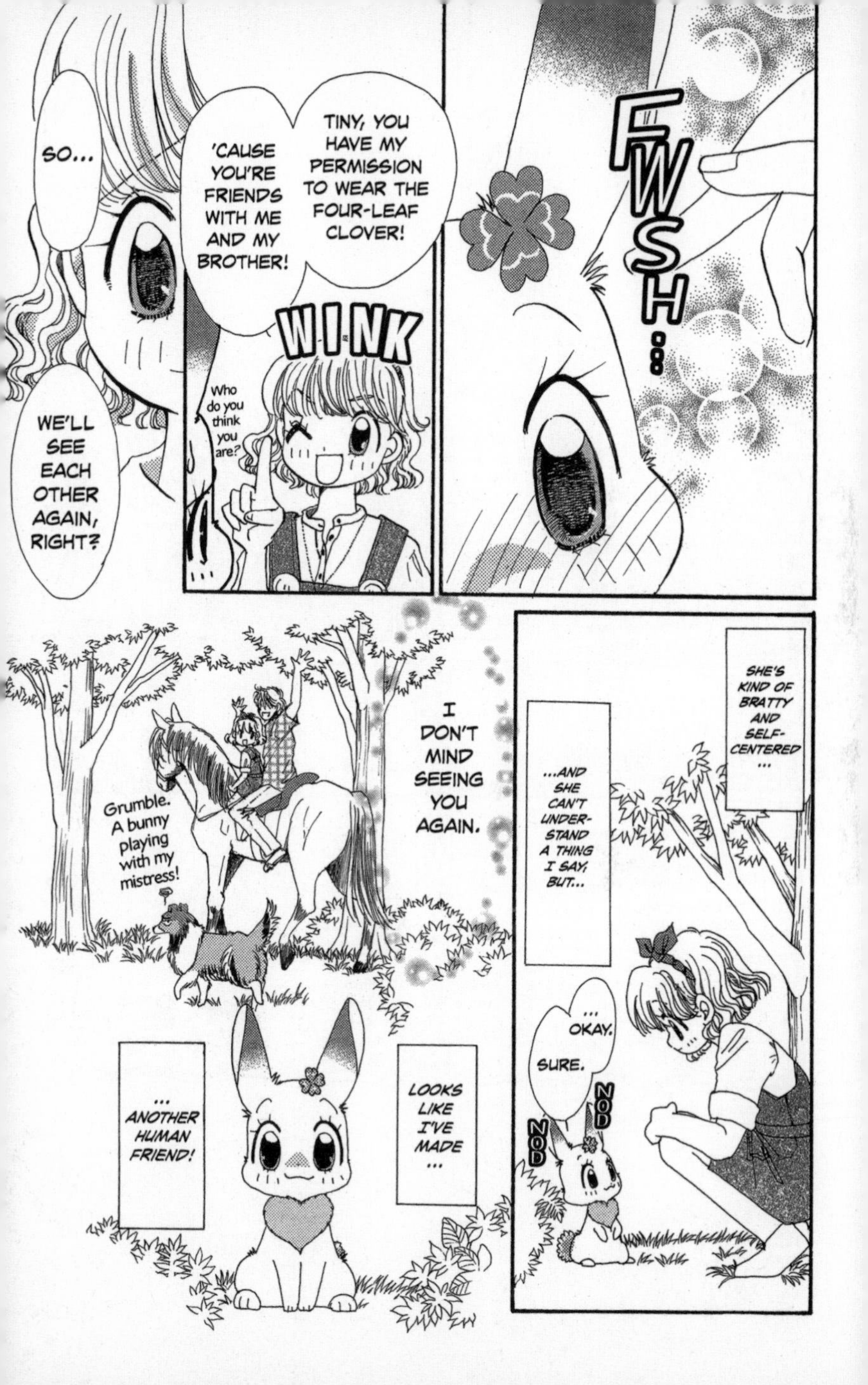
FWSH...
TINY, YOU HAVE MY PERMISSION TO WEAR THE FOUR-LEAF CLOVER!
'CAUSE YOU'RE FRIENDS WITH ME AND MY BROTHER!
WINK
Who do you think you are?
SO...
WE'LL SEE EACH OTHER AGAIN, RIGHT?
SHE'S KIND OF BRATTY AND SELF-CENTERED...
...AND SHE CAN'T UNDERSTAND A THING I SAY, BUT...
... OKAY.
SURE.
NOD
NOD
I DON'T MIND SEEING YOU AGAIN.
Grumble. A bunny playing with my mistress!
LOOKS LIKE I'VE MADE...
...ANOTHER HUMAN FRIEND!

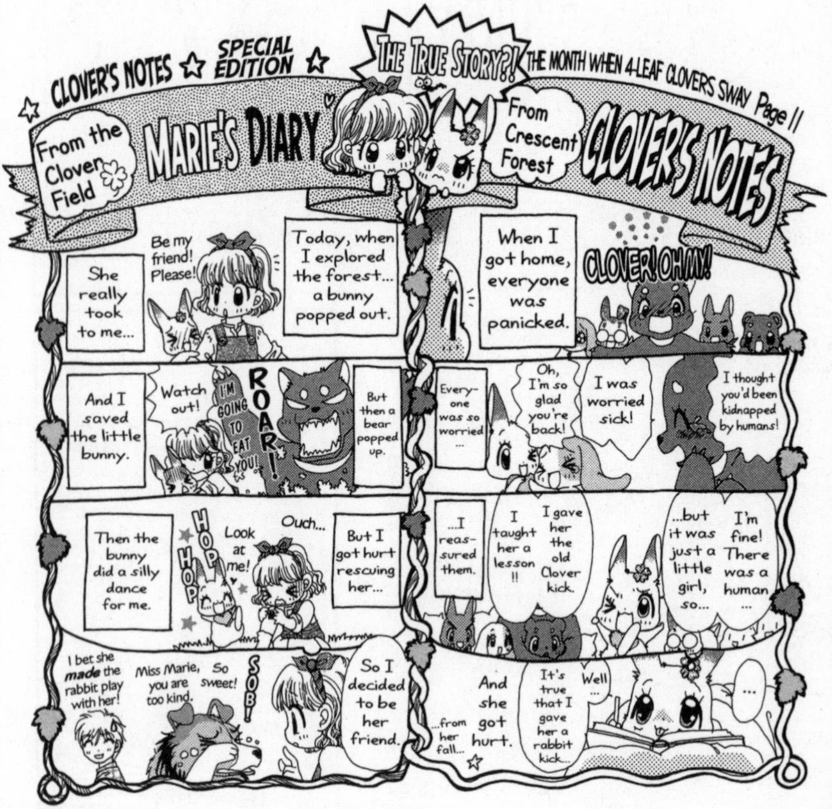
CLOVER'S NOTES SPECIAL EDITION
THE TRUE STORY?!
THE MONTH WHEN 4-LEAF CLOVERS SWAY Page 11
From Crescent Forest
CLOVER'S NOTES
CLOVER! OH MY!
When I got home, everyone was panicked.
I thought you'd been kidnapped by humans!
I was worried sick!
Oh, I'm so glad you're back!
Everyone was so worried...
I'm fine! There was a human...
...but it was just a little girl, so...
I gave her the old Clover kick.
I taught her a lesson!!
...I reassured them.
...
Well...
It's true that I gave her a rabbit kick...
And she got hurt.
...from her fall...
From the Clover Field
MARIE'S DIARY
Today, when I explored the forest... a bunny popped out.
Be my friend! Please!
She really took to me...
But then a bear popped up.
ROAR!
I'M GOING TO EAT YOU!
Watch out!
And I saved the little bunny.
But I got hurt rescuing her...
Ouch...
Look at me!
HOP HOP
Then the bunny did a silly dance for me.
So I decided to be her friend.
SOB!
So sweet!
Miss Marie, you are too kind.
I bet she *made* the rabbit play with her!

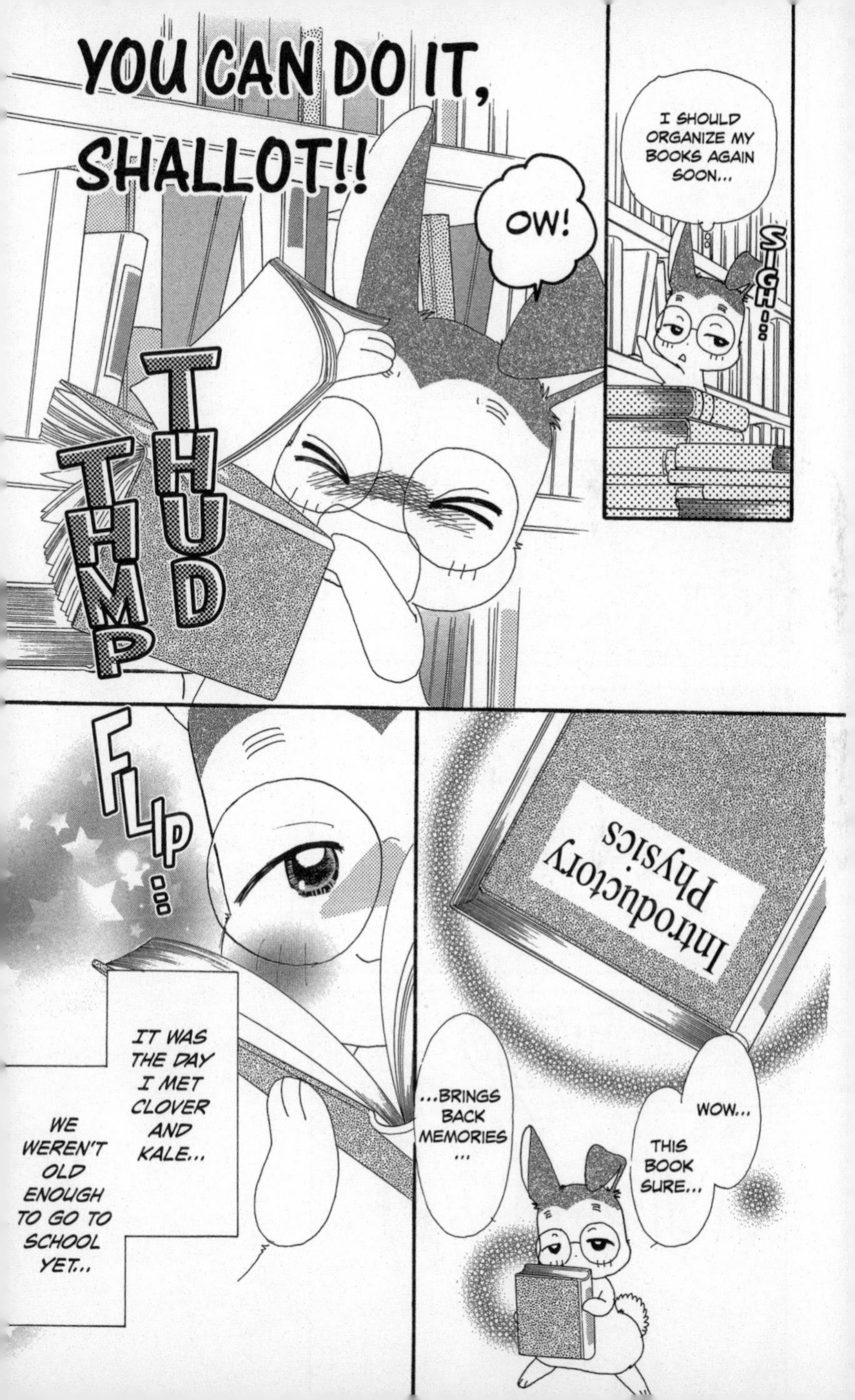
I SHOULD ORGANIZE MY BOOKS AGAIN SOON...
SIGH...
YOU CAN DO IT, SHALLOT!!
OW!
THUD
THUMP
Introductory Physics
WOW...
THIS BOOK SURE...
...BRINGS BACK MEMORIES...
FLIP...
IT WAS THE DAY I MET CLOVER AND KALE...
WE WEREN'T OLD ENOUGH TO GO TO SCHOOL YET...

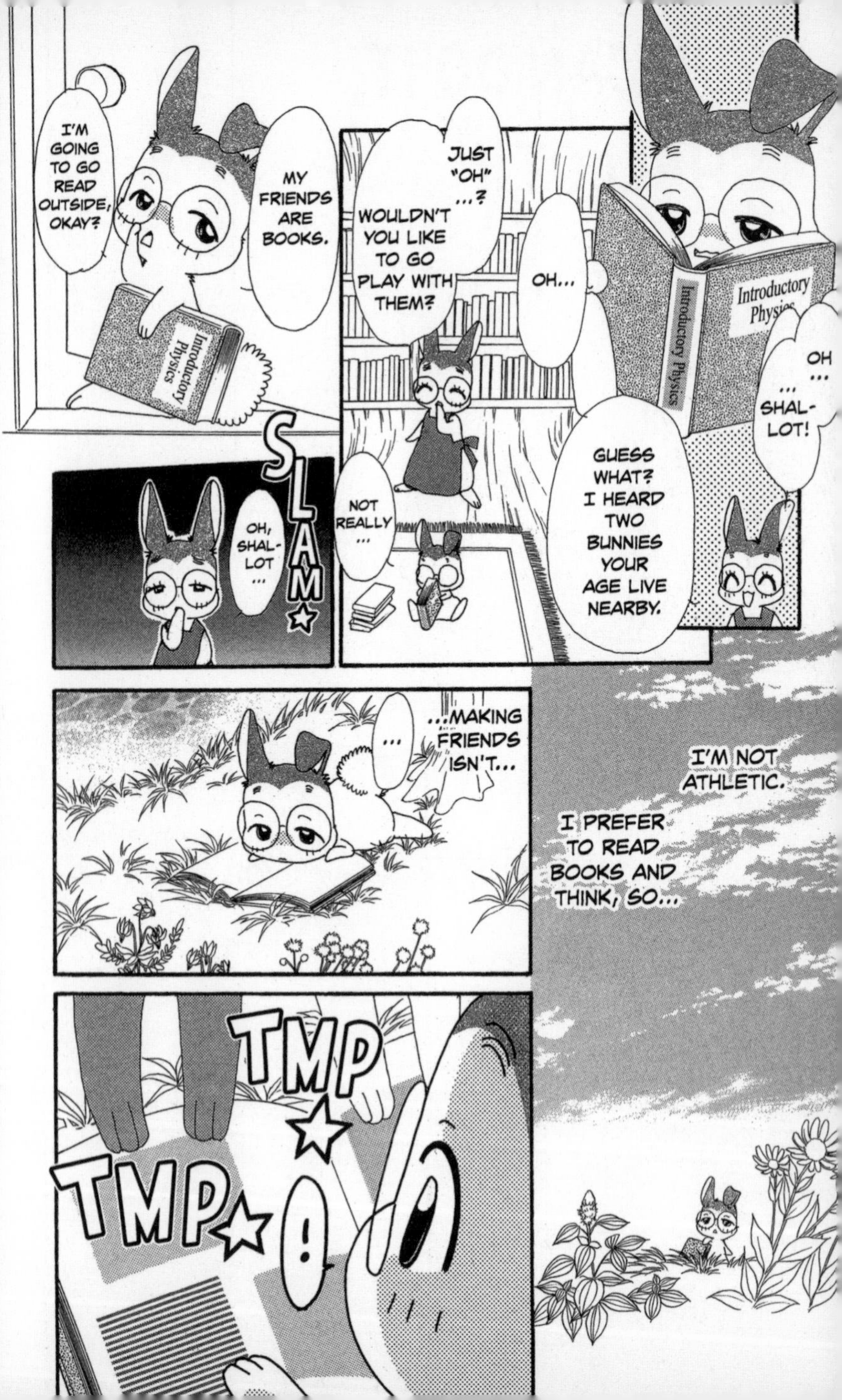
OH ... ... SHAL-LOT!
Introductory Physics
GUESS WHAT? I HEARD TWO BUNNIES YOUR AGE LIVE NEARBY.
OH...
JUST "OH" ...?
WOULDN'T YOU LIKE TO GO PLAY WITH THEM?
NOT REALLY ...
MY FRIENDS ARE BOOKS.
I'M GOING TO GO READ OUTSIDE, OKAY?
Introductory Physics
SLAM☆
OH, SHAL-LOT ...
I'M NOT ATHLETIC.
I PREFER TO READ BOOKS AND THINK, SO...
...MAKING FRIENDS ISN'T...
...
TMP☆
TMP☆
!

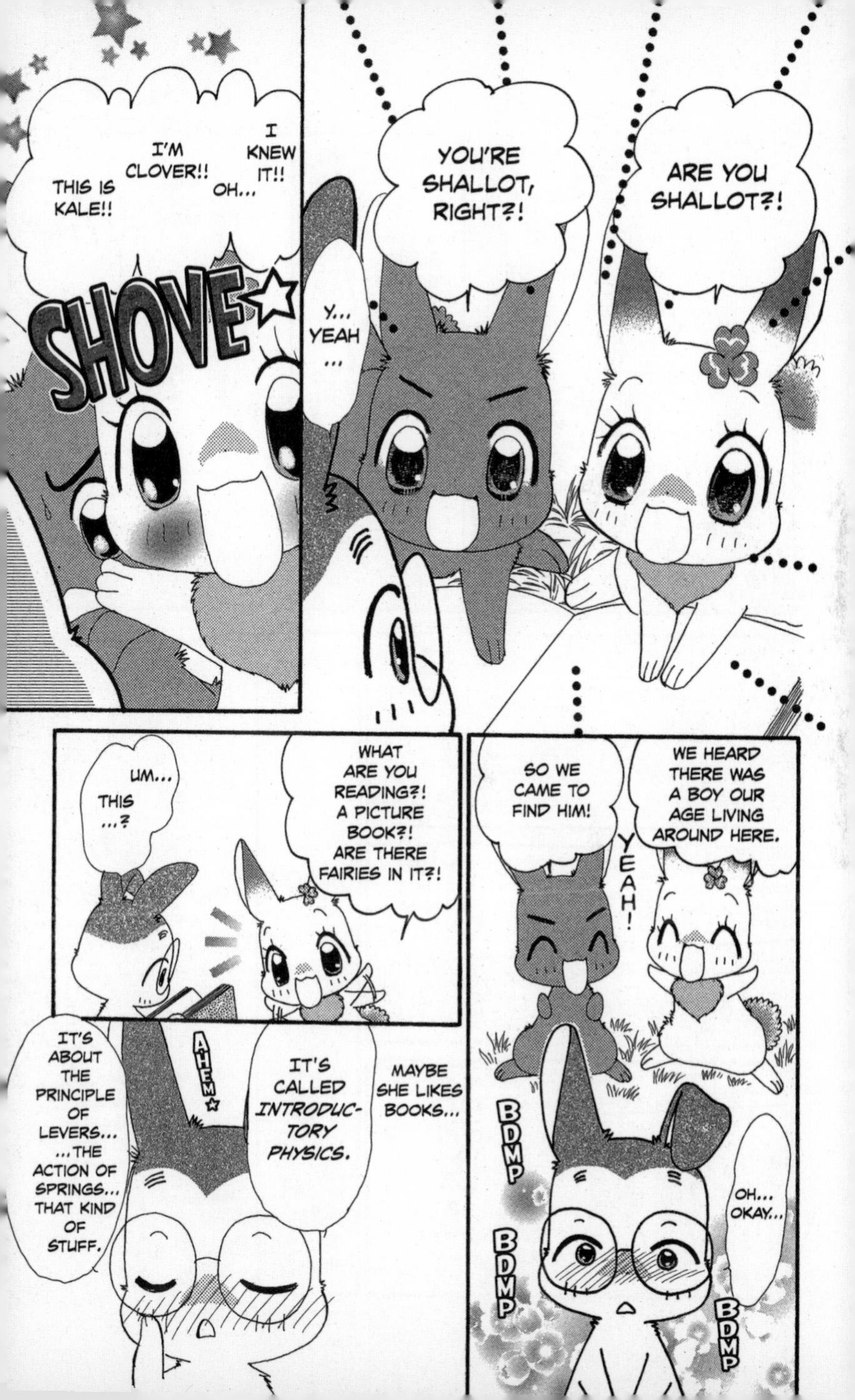
ARE YOU SHALLOT?!
YOU'RE SHALLOT, RIGHT?!
Y... YEAH ...
I KNEW IT!!
OH...
I'M CLOVER!!
THIS IS KALE!!
SHOVE☆
WE HEARD THERE WAS A BOY OUR AGE LIVING AROUND HERE.
SO WE CAME TO FIND HIM!
YEAH!
OH... OKAY...
BDMP
BDMP
BDMP
WHAT ARE YOU READING?! A PICTURE BOOK?! ARE THERE FAIRIES IN IT?!
UM... THIS ...?
MAYBE SHE LIKES BOOKS...
IT'S CALLED *INTRODUCTORY PHYSICS*.
AHEM☆
IT'S ABOUT THE PRINCIPLE OF LEVERS... ...THE ACTION OF SPRINGS... THAT KIND OF STUFF.

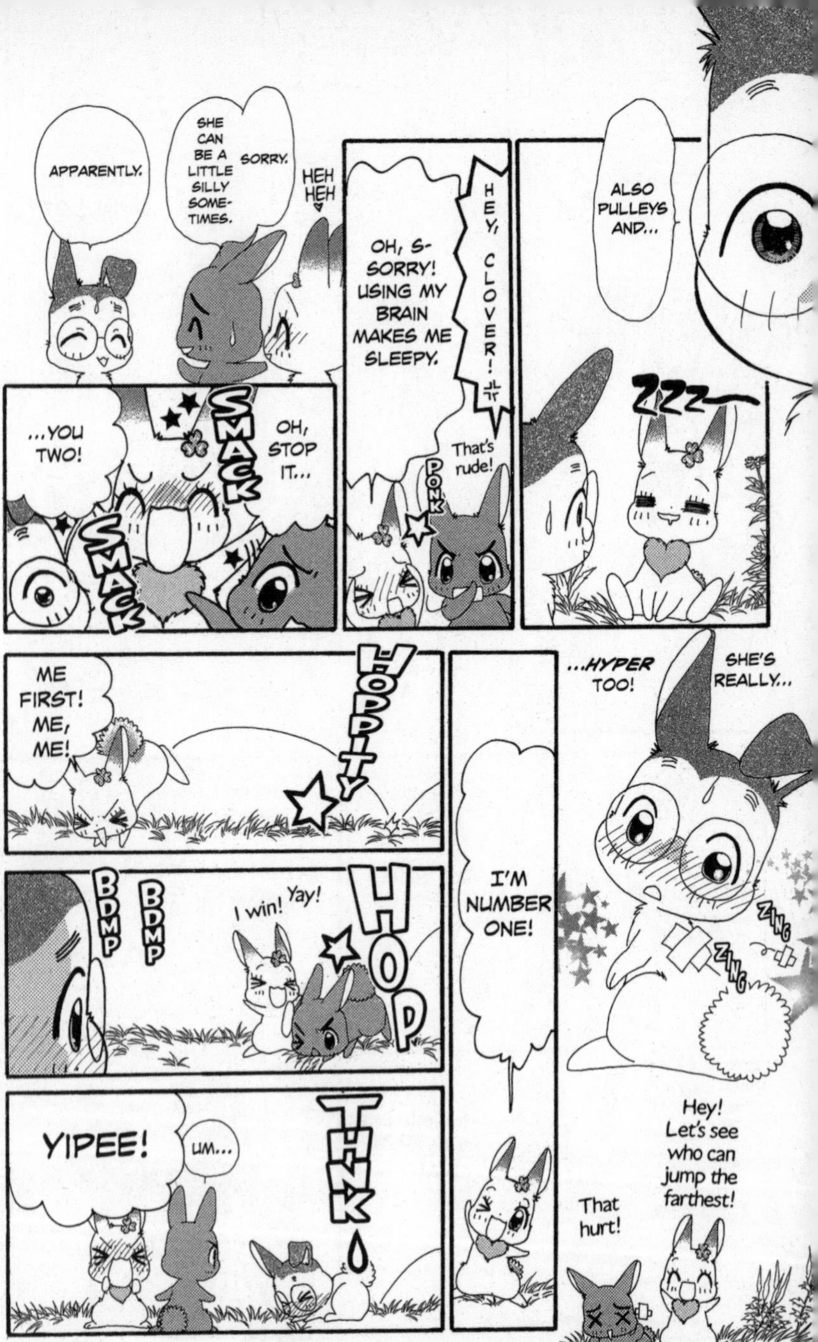

ALSO PULLEYS AND...
ZZZ
HEY, CLOVER!
OH, S-SORRY! USING MY BRAIN MAKES ME SLEEPY.
That's rude!
PONK
HEH HEH
SORRY.
SHE CAN BE A LITTLE SILLY SOME-TIMES.
APPARENTLY.
SMACK
OH, STOP IT...
SMACK
...YOU TWO!
SHE'S REALLY...
...HYPER TOO!
ZING
ZING
Hey! Let's see who can jump the farthest!
That hurt!
I'M NUMBER ONE!
HOPPITY
ME FIRST! ME, ME!
HOP
Yay!
I win!
BDMP
BDMP
THNK
UM...
YIPEE!

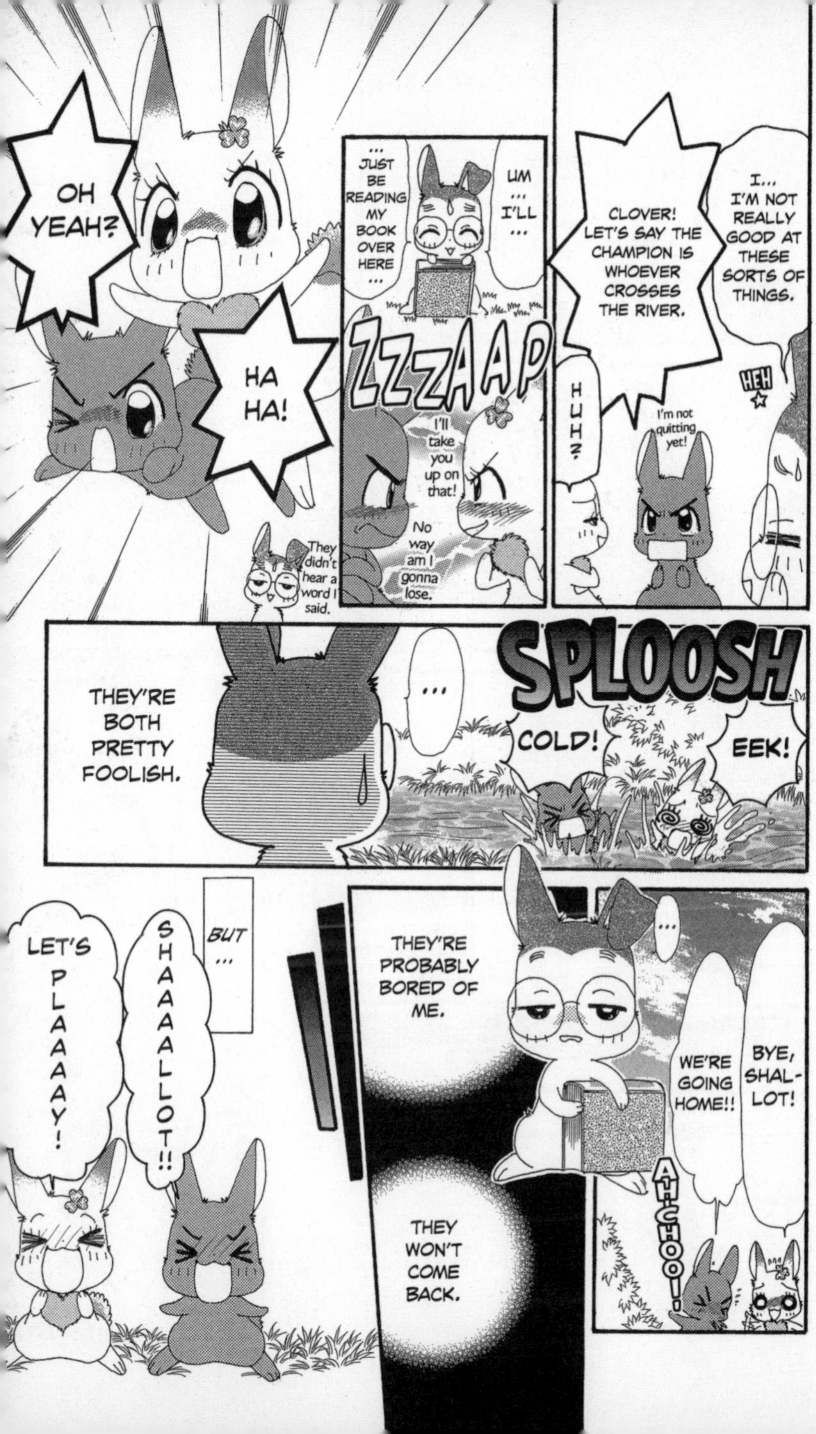
I... I'M NOT REALLY GOOD AT THESE SORTS OF THINGS.
CLOVER! LET'S SAY THE CHAMPION IS WHOEVER CROSSES THE RIVER.
HEH☆
I'm not quitting yet!
HUH?
UM... I'LL...
...JUST BE READING MY BOOK OVER HERE...
ZZZAAP
I'll take you up on that!
No way am I gonna lose.
OH YEAH?
HA HA!
They didn't hear a word I said.
SPLOOSH
EEK!
COLD!
...
THEY'RE BOTH PRETTY FOOLISH.
...
BYE, SHAL-LOT!
WE'RE GOING HOME!!
AH-CHOO!
THEY'RE PROBABLY BORED OF ME.
THEY WON'T COME BACK.
BUT...
SHAAAAALLOT!!
LET'S PLAAAAAY!

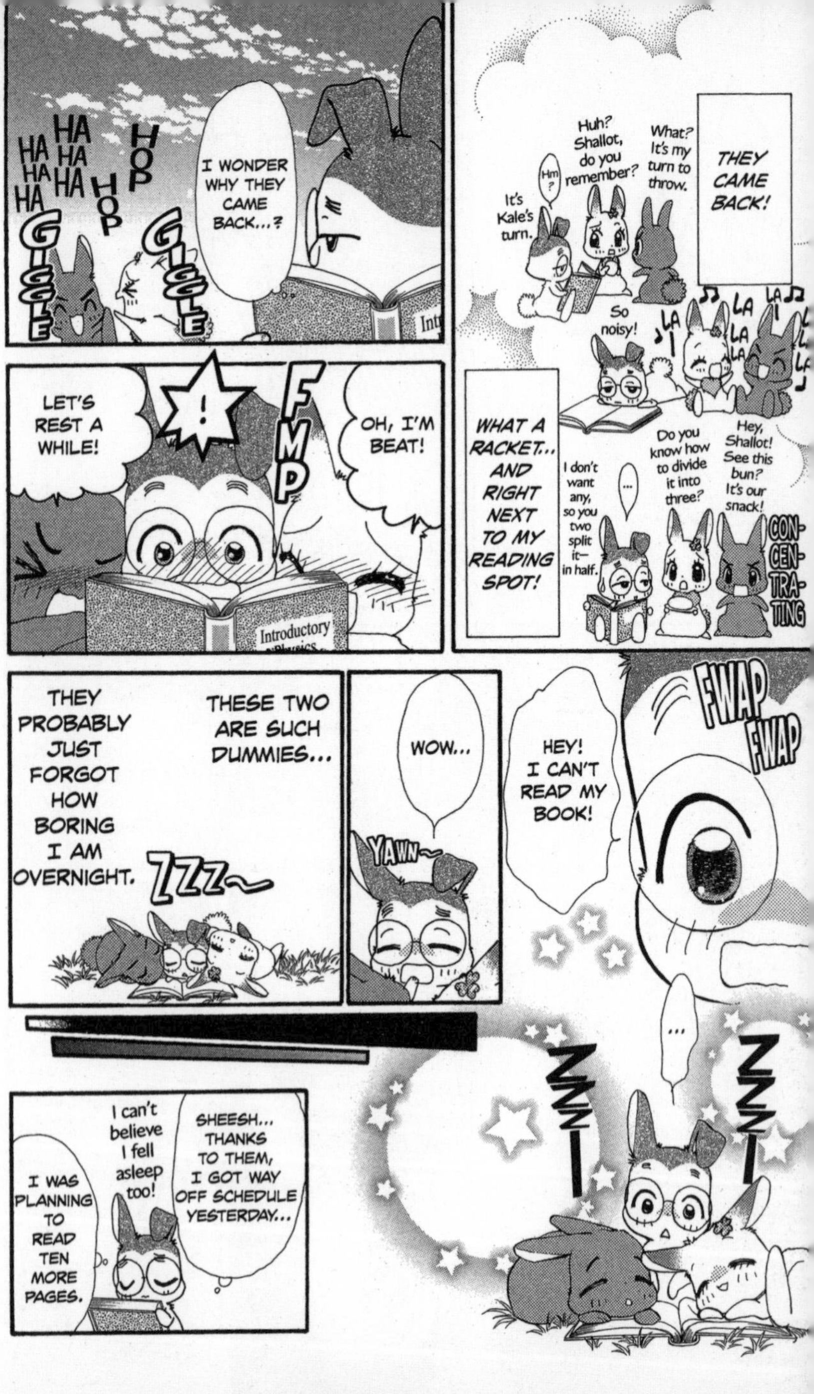
THEY CAME BACK!
What? It's my turn to throw.
Huh? Shallot, do you remember?
Hm?
It's Kale's turn.
LA LA LA LA LA
So noisy!
Hey, Shallot! See this bun? It's our snack!
Do you know how to divide it into three?
...
I don't want any, so you two split it—in half.
CON-CEN-TRA-TING
WHAT A RACKET... AND RIGHT NEXT TO MY READING SPOT!
HOP HOP
I WONDER WHY THEY CAME BACK...?
HA HA HA HA HA HA HA
GIGGLE GIGGLE
OH, I'M BEAT!
FMP
!
LET'S REST A WHILE!
Introductory
FWAP FWAP
HEY! I CAN'T READ MY BOOK!
WOW...
YAWN~
THESE TWO ARE SUCH DUMMIES...
THEY PROBABLY JUST FORGOT HOW BORING I AM OVERNIGHT.
ZZZ~
...
ZZZ
SHEESH... THANKS TO THEM, I GOT WAY OFF SCHEDULE YESTERDAY...
I can't believe I fell asleep too!
I WAS PLANNING TO READ TEN MORE PAGES.

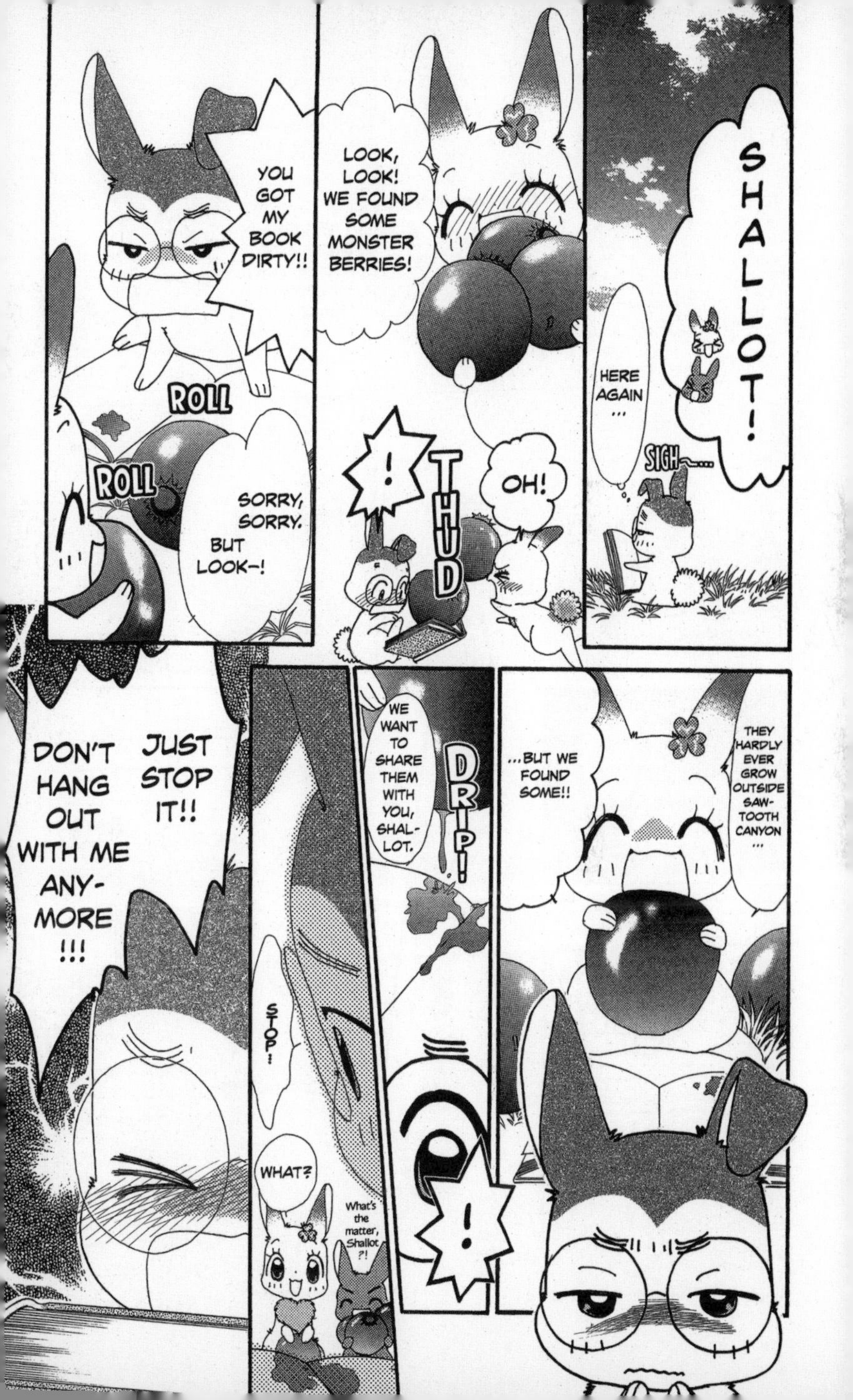
SHALLOT!
HERE AGAIN...
SIGH~...
LOOK, LOOK! WE FOUND SOME MONSTER BERRIES!
OH!
THUD
!
YOU GOT MY BOOK DIRTY!!
ROLL
ROLL
SORRY, SORRY.
BUT LOOK-!
THEY HARDLY EVER GROW OUTSIDE SAW-TOOTH CANYON...
...BUT WE FOUND SOME!!
WE WANT TO SHARE THEM WITH YOU, SHAL-LOT.
DRIP!
!
STOP!
WHAT?
What's the matter, Shallot?!
JUST STOP IT!!
DON'T HANG OUT WITH ME ANY-MORE!!!

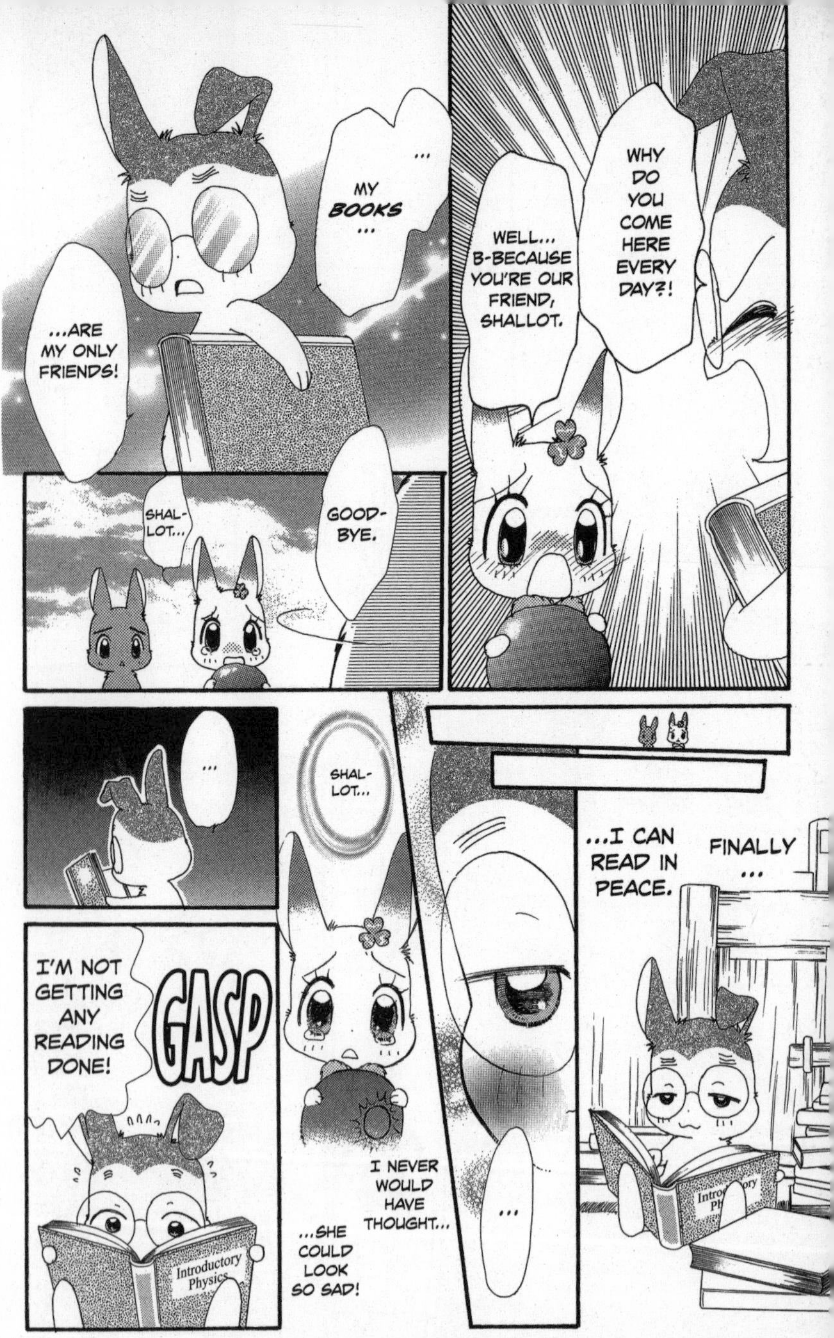
WHY DO YOU COME HERE EVERY DAY?!
WELL... B-BECAUSE YOU'RE OUR FRIEND, SHALLOT.
...
MY BOOKS ...
...ARE MY ONLY FRIENDS!
GOOD-BYE.
SHAL-LOT...
FINALLY ...
...I CAN READ IN PEACE.
...
SHAL-LOT...
I NEVER WOULD HAVE THOUGHT...
...SHE COULD LOOK SO SAD!
...
GASP
I'M NOT GETTING ANY READING DONE!
Introductory Physics

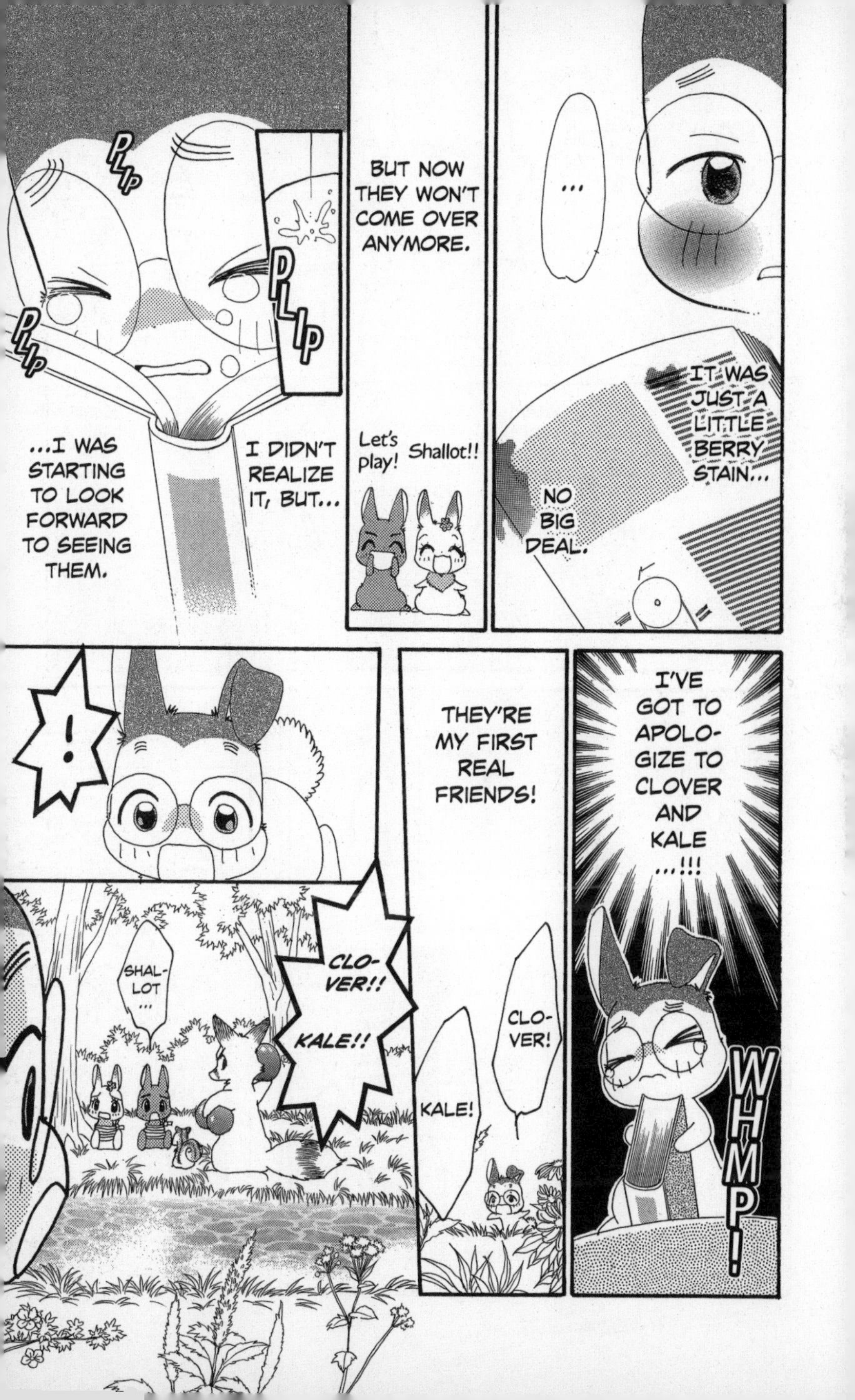
...
IT WAS JUST A LITTLE BERRY STAIN...
NO BIG DEAL.
BUT NOW THEY WON'T COME OVER ANYMORE.
Shallot!!
Let's play!
PLIP
PLIP
PLIP
I DIDN'T REALIZE IT, BUT...
...I WAS STARTING TO LOOK FORWARD TO SEEING THEM.
I'VE GOT TO APOLOGIZE TO CLOVER AND KALE ...!!!
WHMP!
THEY'RE MY FIRST REAL FRIENDS!
CLOVER!
KALE!
!
CLOVER!!
KALE!!
SHALLOT ...

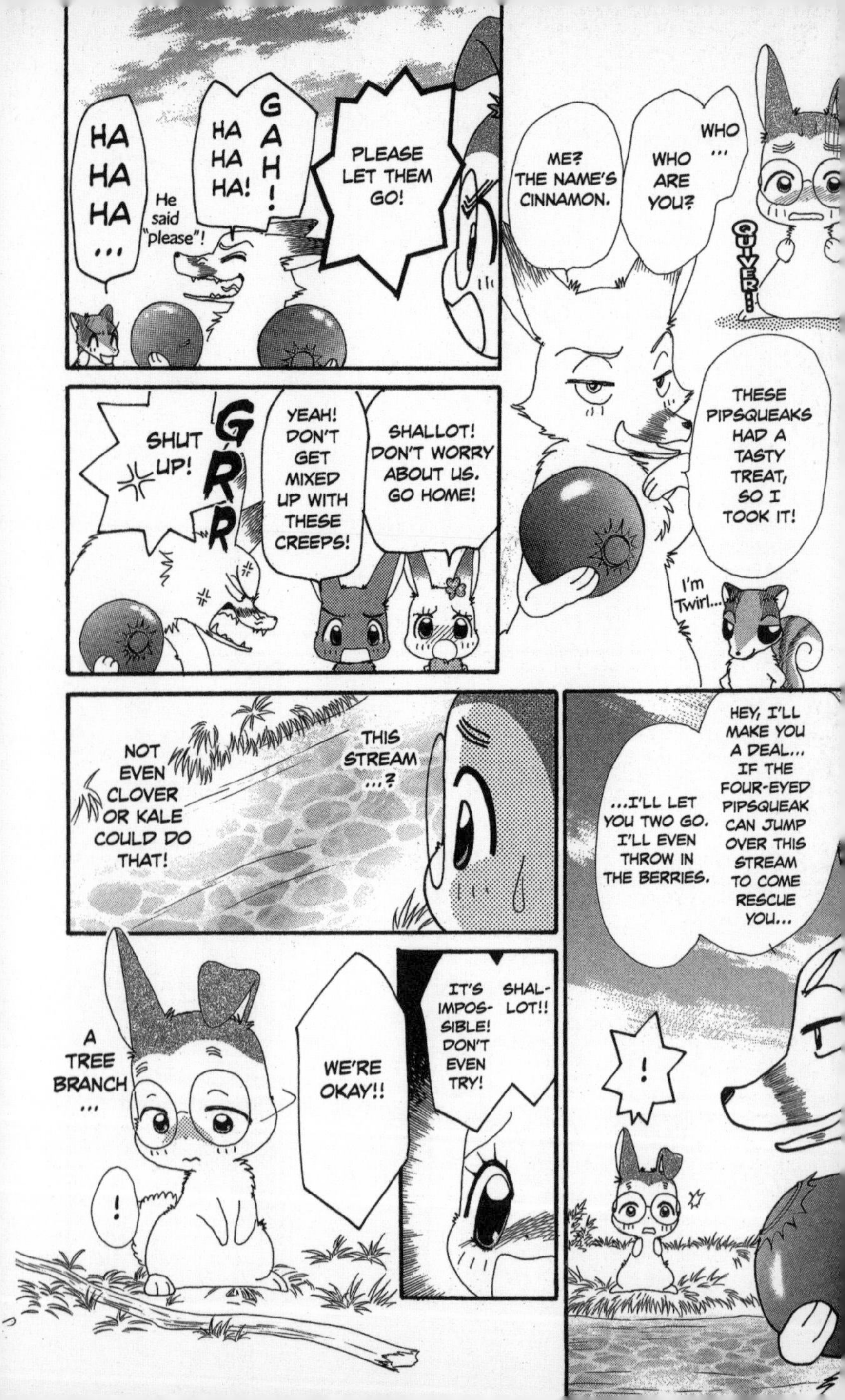
WHO ...
WHO ARE YOU?
QUIVER!!
ME? THE NAME'S CINNAMON.
THESE PIPSQUEAKS HAD A TASTY TREAT, SO I TOOK IT!
I'm Twirl...
PLEASE LET THEM GO!
GAH!
HA HA HA!
He said "please"!
HA HA HA ...
SHALLOT! DON'T WORRY ABOUT US. GO HOME!
YEAH! DON'T GET MIXED UP WITH THESE CREEPS!
GRRR
SHUT UP!
HEY, I'LL MAKE YOU A DEAL... IF THE FOUR-EYED PIPSQUEAK CAN JUMP OVER THIS STREAM TO COME RESCUE YOU...
...I'LL LET YOU TWO GO. I'LL EVEN THROW IN THE BERRIES.
!
THIS STREAM ...?
NOT EVEN CLOVER OR KALE COULD DO THAT!
SHAL-LOT!!
IT'S IMPOS-SIBLE! DON'T EVEN TRY!
WE'RE OKAY!!
A TREE BRANCH ...
!

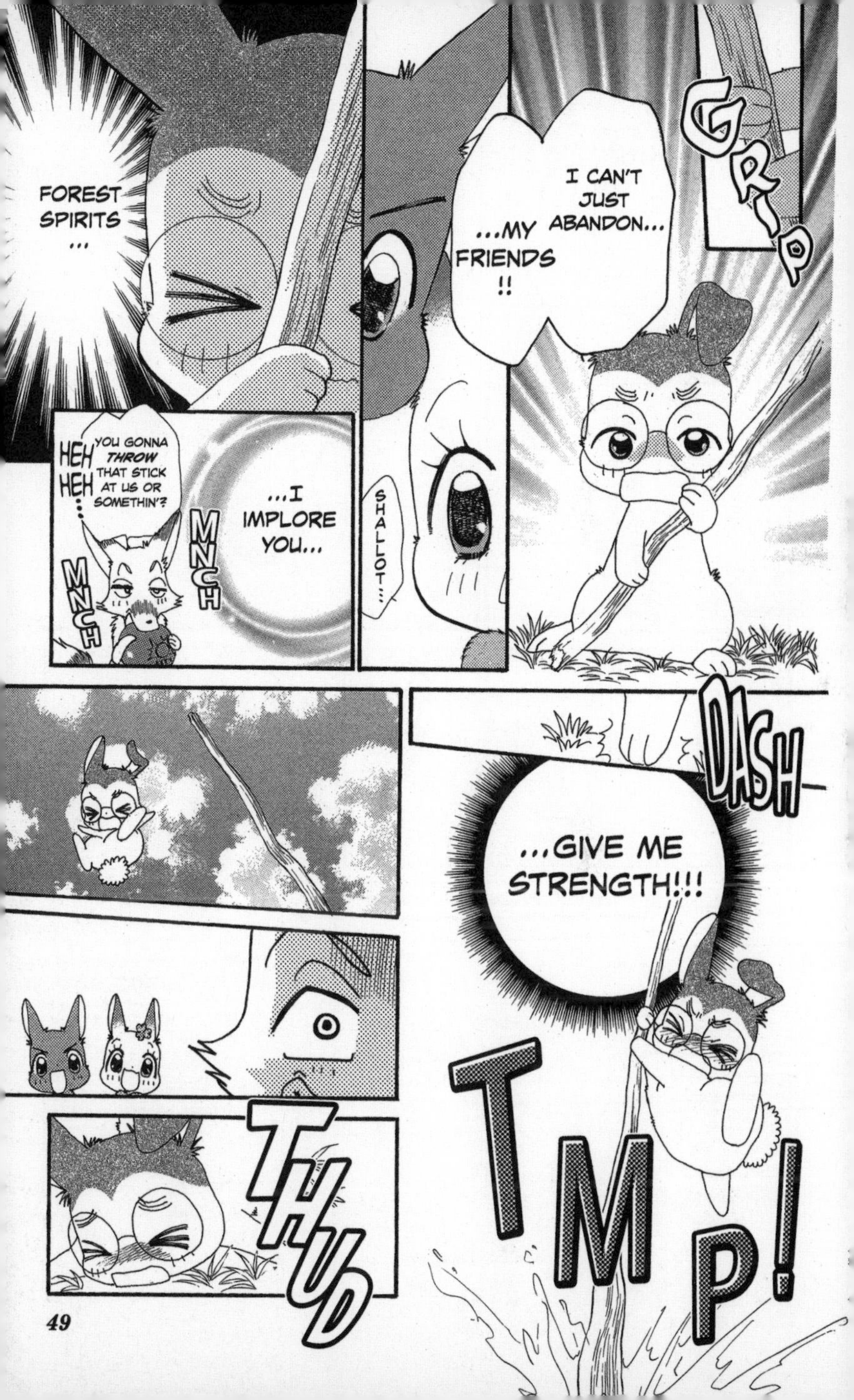
GRIP
I CAN'T JUST ABANDON...
...MY FRIENDS !!
SHALLOT...
FOREST SPIRITS ...
...I IMPLORE YOU...
HEH HEH...
YOU GONNA *THROW* THAT STICK AT US OR SOMETHIN'?
MNCH
MNCH
DASH
...GIVE ME STRENGTH!!!
TMP!
THUD

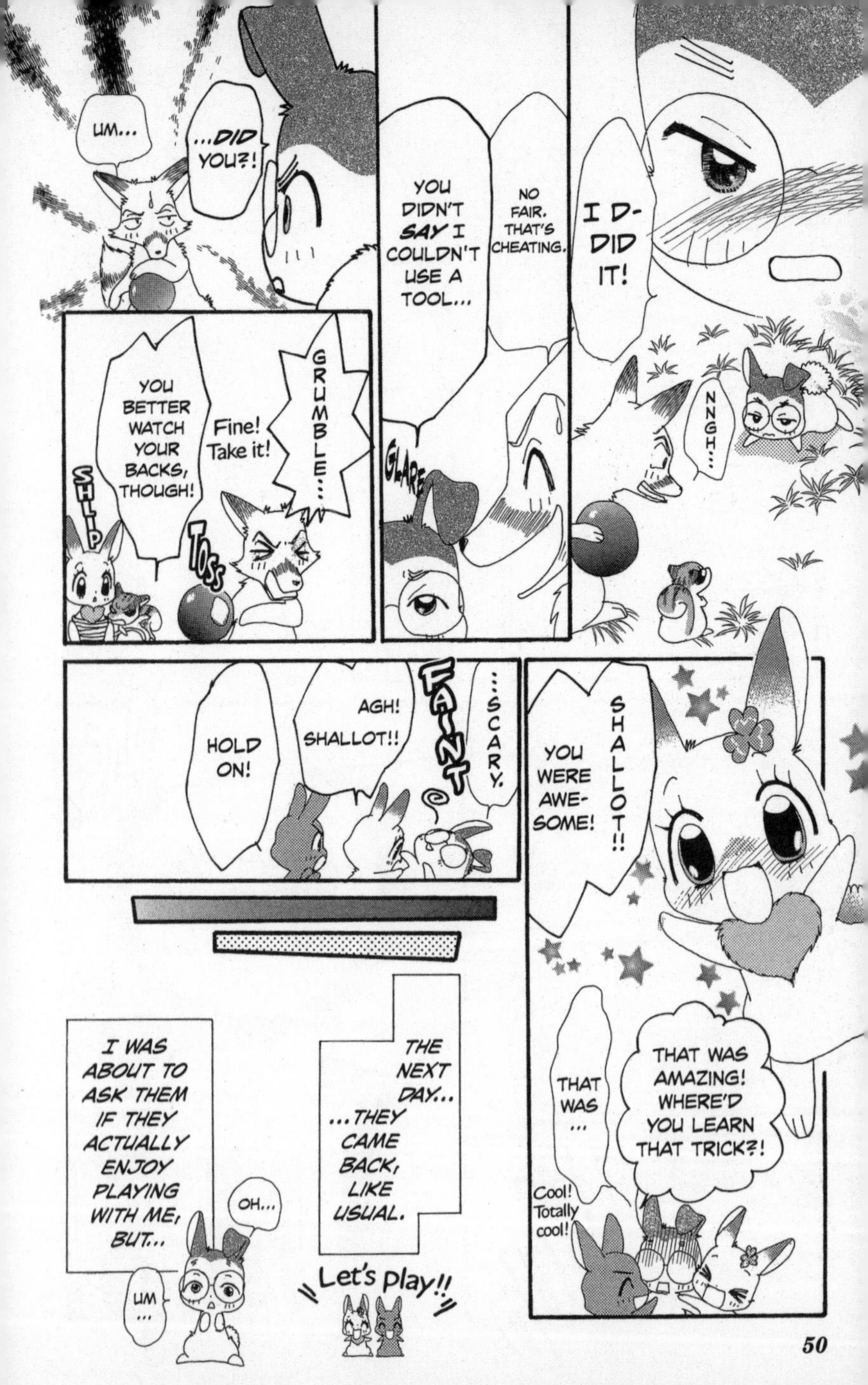
I D-DID IT!
NNGH...
NO FAIR. THAT'S CHEATING.
YOU DIDN'T SAY I COULDN'T USE A TOOL...
GLARE
...DID YOU?!
UM...
GRUMBLE...
Fine! Take it!
YOU BETTER WATCH YOUR BACKS, THOUGH!
TOSS
SHLIP
SHALLOT!!
YOU WERE AWESOME!
THAT WAS AMAZING! WHERE'D YOU LEARN THAT TRICK?!
THAT WAS...
Cool! Totally cool!
...SCARY.
FAINT
AGH! SHALLOT!!
HOLD ON!
THE NEXT DAY...
...THEY CAME BACK, LIKE USUAL.
Let's play!!
I WAS ABOUT TO ASK THEM IF THEY ACTUALLY ENJOY PLAYING WITH ME, BUT...
OH...
UM...

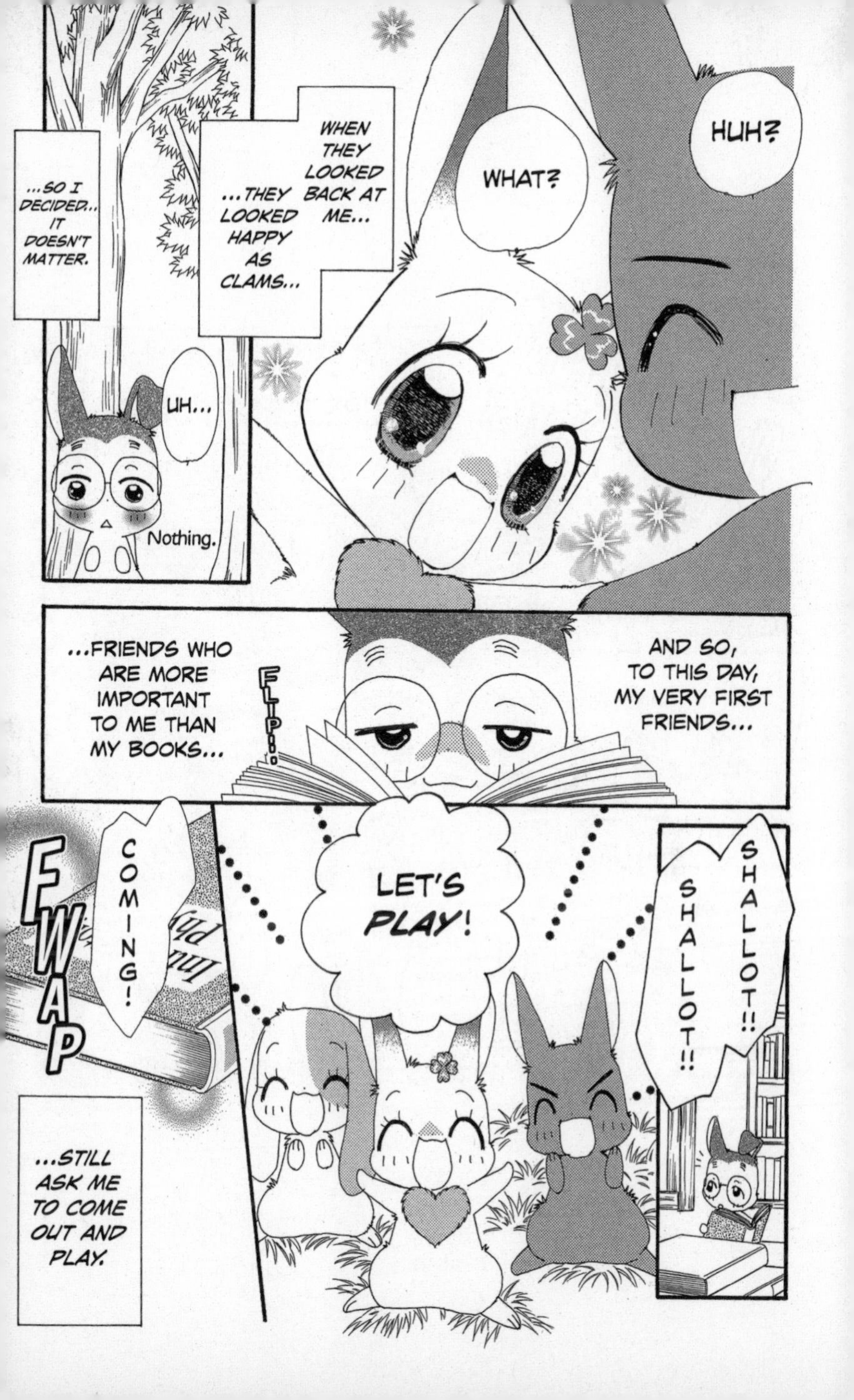
HUH?
WHAT?
WHEN THEY LOOKED BACK AT ME...
...THEY LOOKED HAPPY AS CLAMS...
...SO I DECIDED... IT DOESN'T MATTER.
UH...
Nothing.
AND SO, TO THIS DAY, MY VERY FIRST FRIENDS...
FLIP!!
...FRIENDS WHO ARE MORE IMPORTANT TO ME THAN MY BOOKS...
SHALLOT!!
SHALLOT!!
LET'S PLAY!
COMING!
FWAP
...STILL ASK ME TO COME OUT AND PLAY.

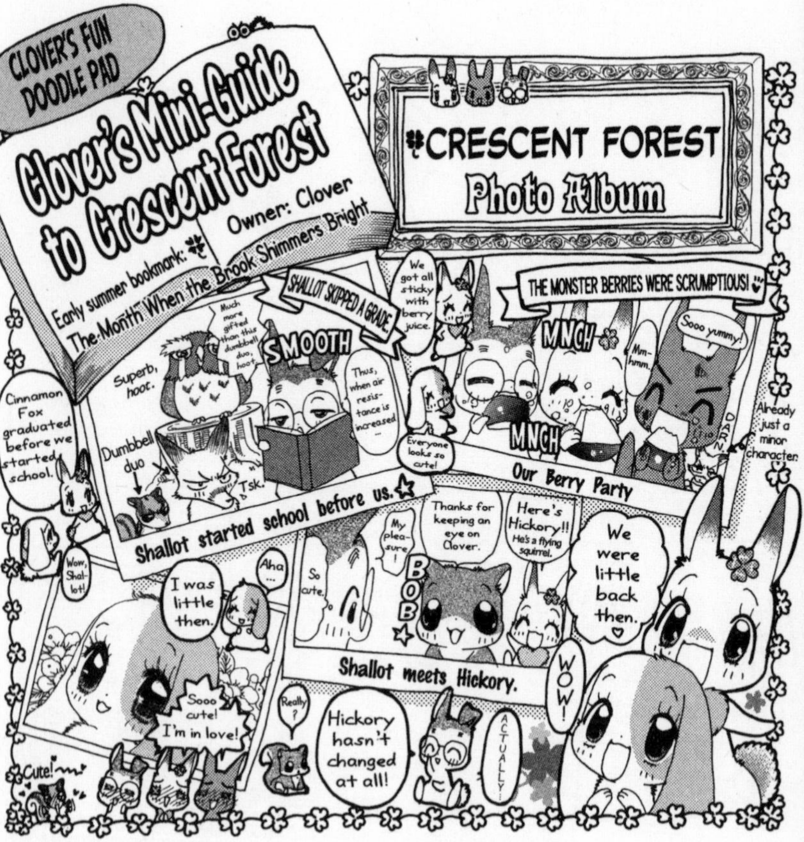
CRESCENT FOREST Photo Album
CLOVER'S FUN DOODLE PAD
Clover's Mini-Guide to Crescent Forest
Owner: Clover
Early summer bookmark:
The Month When the Brook Shimmers Bright
THE MONSTER BERRIES WERE SCRUMPTIOUS!
Sooo yummy!
Mm-hmm.
MNCH
MNCH
DARN.
Already just a minor character.
We got all sticky with berry juice.
Everyone looks so cute!
Our Berry Party
SHALLOT SKIPPED A GRADE.
Much more gifted than this dumbbell duo, hoot.
SMOOTH
Thus, when air resistance is increased...
Superb, hoot.
Dumbbell duo
Tsk.
Shallot started school before us.
Cinnamon Fox graduated before we started school.
We were little back then.
Here's Hickory!! He's a flying squirrel.
Thanks for keeping an eye on Clover.
My pleasure!
So cute.
BOB
Shallot meets Hickory.
Aha...
I was little then.
Wow, Shallot!
WOW!
ACTUALLY...
Hickory hasn't changed at all!
Really?
Sooo cute! I'm in love!
Cute!

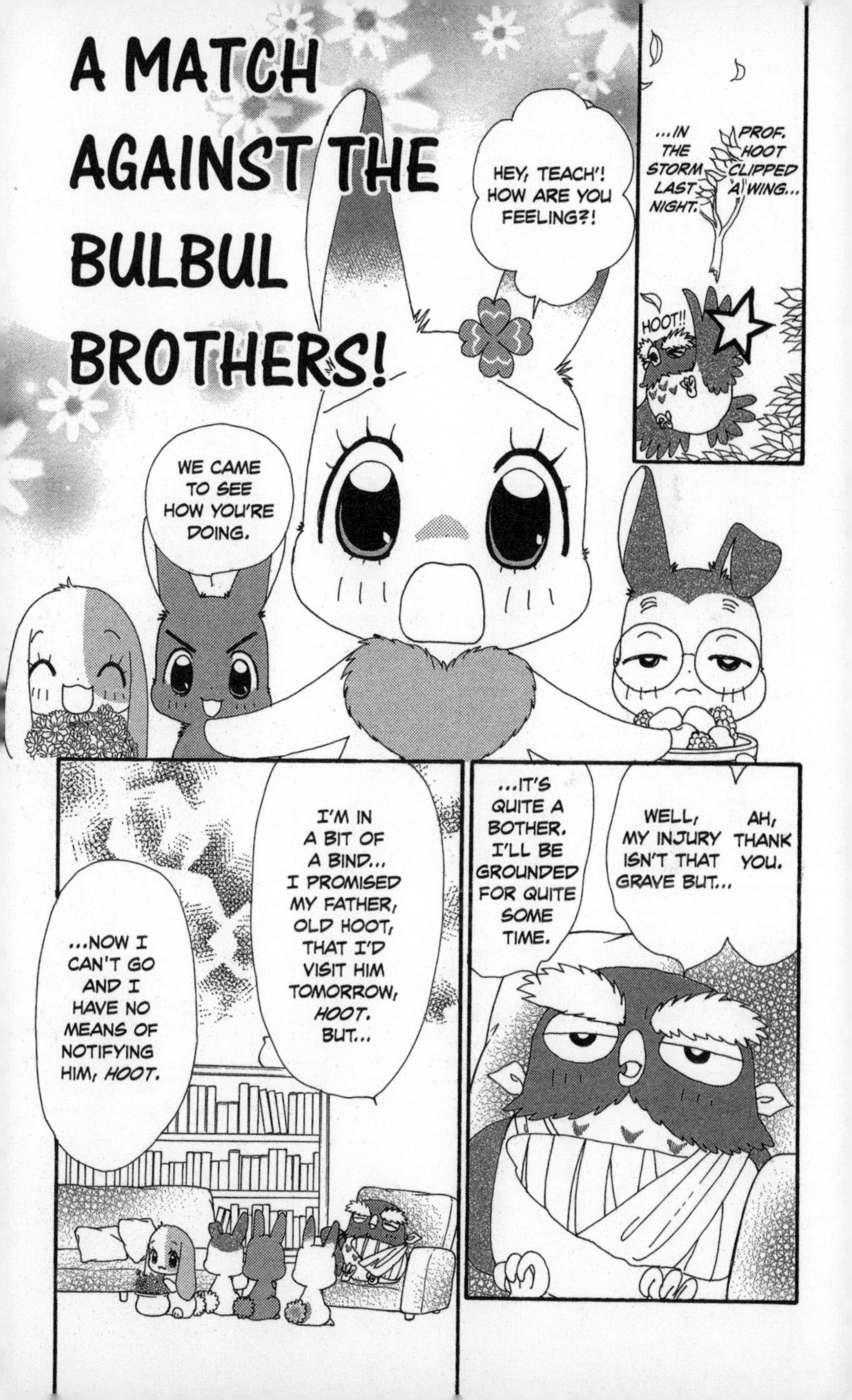

PROF. HOOT CLIPPED A WING...
...IN THE STORM LAST NIGHT.
HOOT!!
A MATCH AGAINST THE BULBUL BROTHERS!
HEY, TEACH'! HOW ARE YOU FEELING?!
WE CAME TO SEE HOW YOU'RE DOING.
AH, THANK YOU.
WELL, MY INJURY ISN'T THAT GRAVE BUT...
...IT'S QUITE A BOTHER. I'LL BE GROUNDED FOR QUITE SOME TIME.
I'M IN A BIT OF A BIND... I PROMISED MY FATHER, OLD HOOT, THAT I'D VISIT HIM TOMORROW, *HOOT*. BUT...
...NOW I CAN'T GO AND I HAVE NO MEANS OF NOTIFYING HIM, *HOOT*.

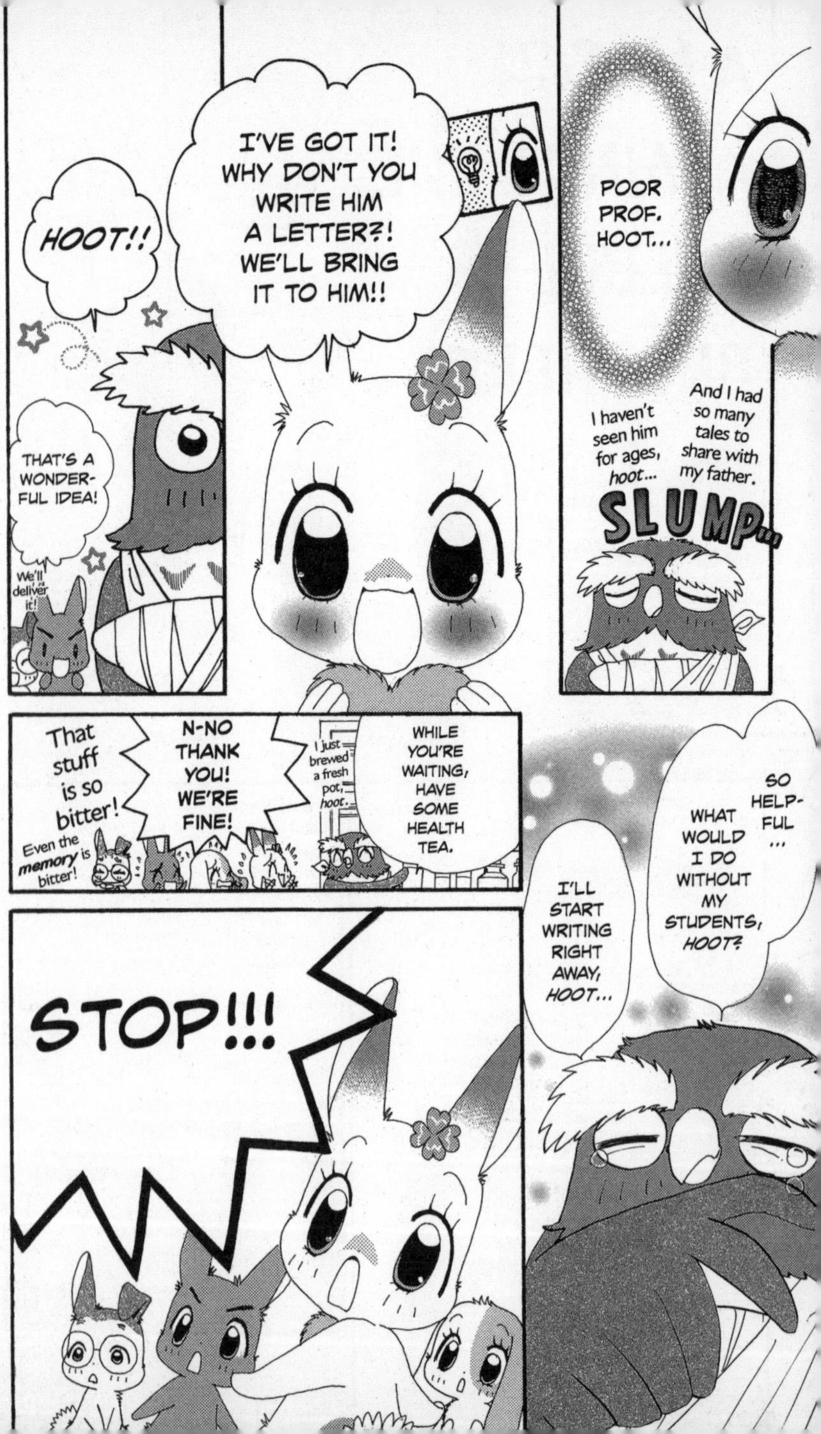
POOR PROF. HOOT...
And I had so many tales to share with my father.
I haven't seen him for ages, *hoot*...
SLUMP...
I'VE GOT IT! WHY DON'T YOU WRITE HIM A LETTER?! WE'LL BRING IT TO HIM!!
HOOT!!
THAT'S A WONDERFUL IDEA!
We'll deliver it!
SO HELPFUL...
WHAT WOULD I DO WITHOUT MY STUDENTS, *HOOT*?
I'LL START WRITING RIGHT AWAY, *HOOT*...
WHILE YOU'RE WAITING, HAVE SOME HEALTH TEA.
I just brewed a fresh pot, *hoot*.
N-NO THANK YOU! WE'RE FINE!
That stuff is so bitter!
Even the **memory** is bitter!
STOP!!!

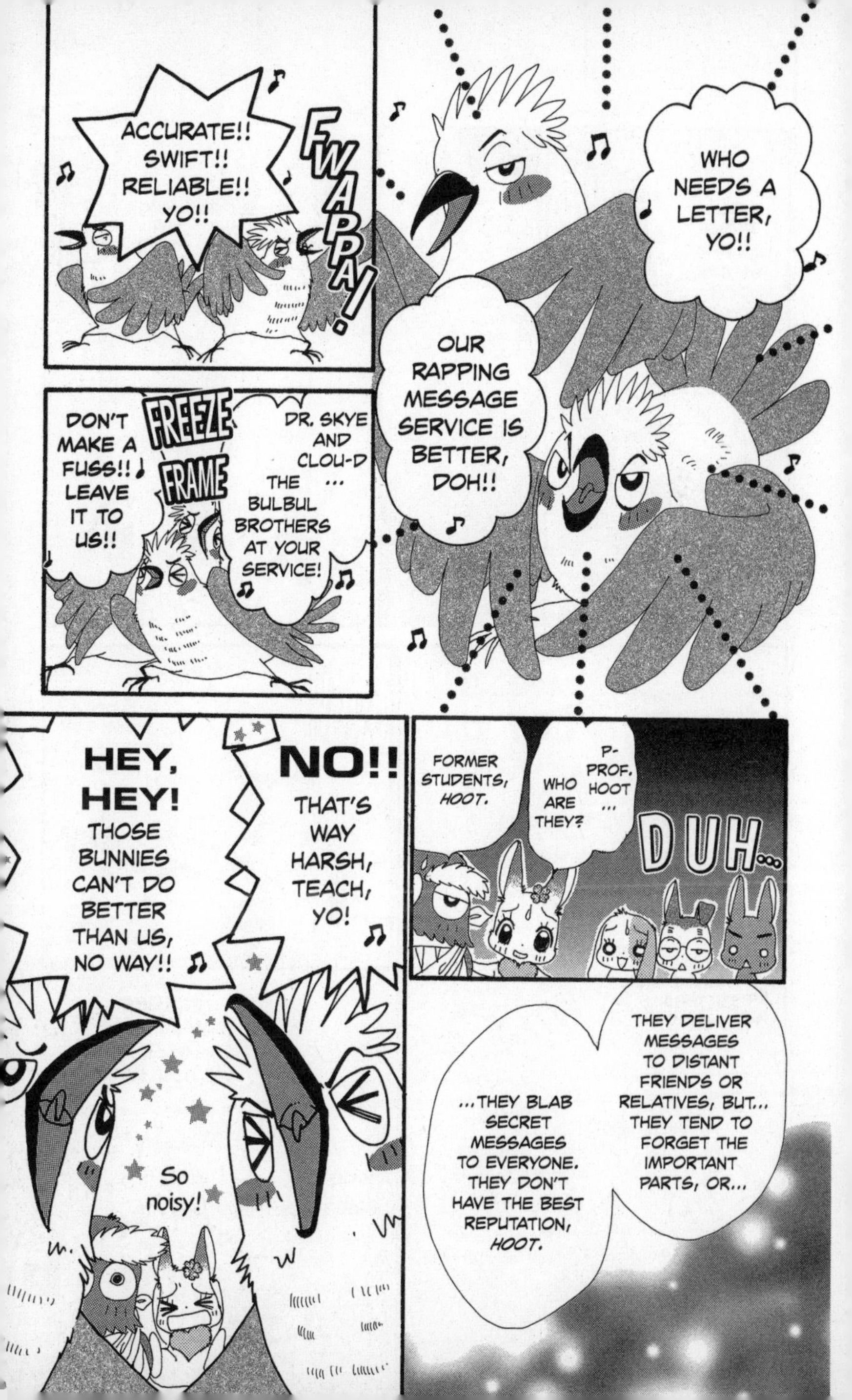

WHO NEEDS A LETTER, YO!!
OUR RAPPING MESSAGE SERVICE IS BETTER, DOH!!
FWAPPA!
ACCURATE!! SWIFT!! RELIABLE!! YO!!
DR. SKYE AND CLOU-D ... THE BULBUL BROTHERS AT YOUR SERVICE!
FREEZE FRAME
DON'T MAKE A FUSS!! LEAVE IT TO US!!
P-PROF. HOOT ...
WHO ARE THEY?
FORMER STUDENTS, HOOT.
DUH...
THEY DELIVER MESSAGES TO DISTANT FRIENDS OR RELATIVES, BUT... THEY TEND TO FORGET THE IMPORTANT PARTS, OR...
...THEY BLAB SECRET MESSAGES TO EVERYONE. THEY DON'T HAVE THE BEST REPUTATION, HOOT.
NO!! THAT'S WAY HARSH, TEACH, YO!
HEY, HEY! THOSE BUNNIES CAN'T DO BETTER THAN US, NO WAY!!
So noisy!

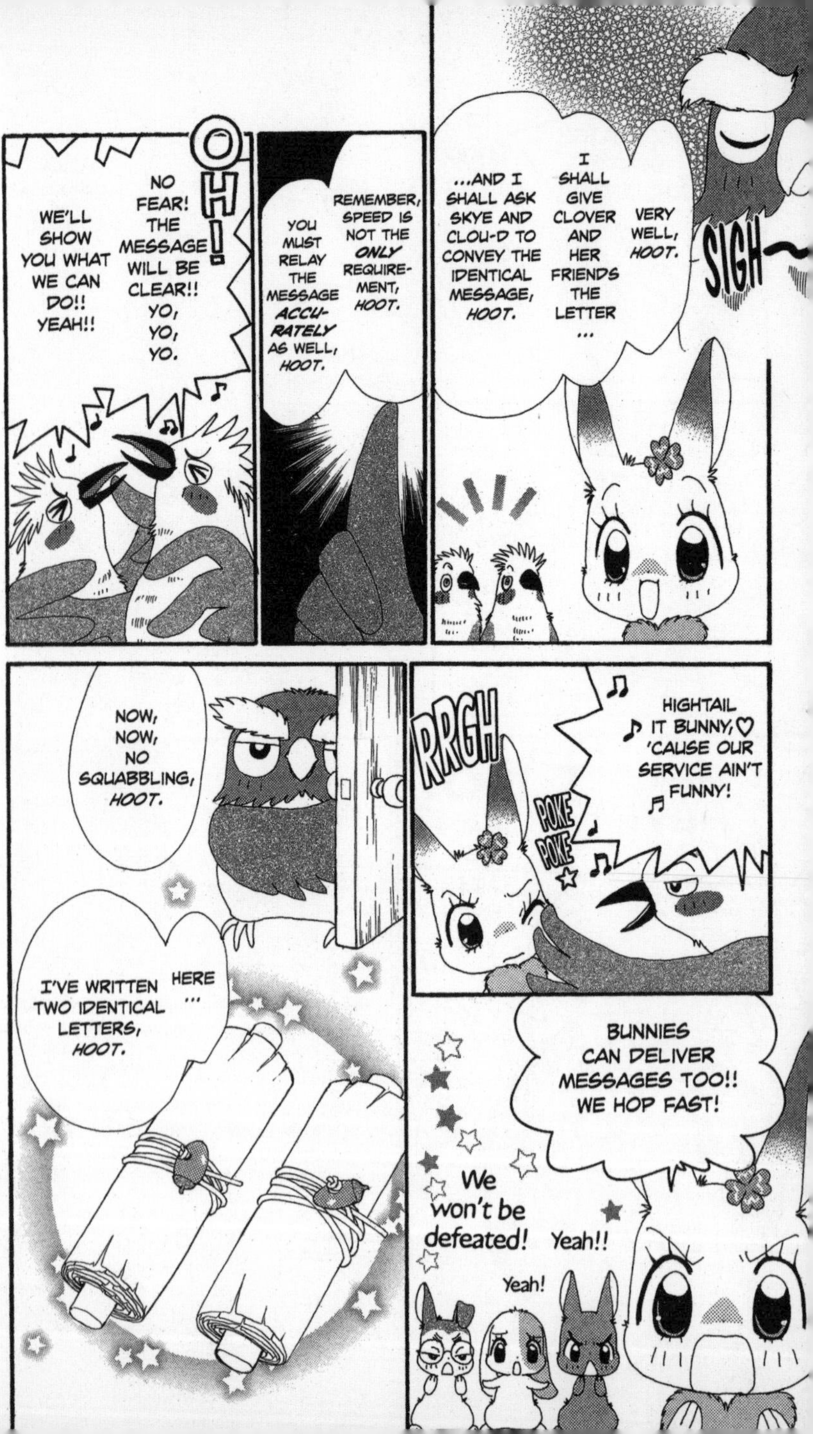
SIGH~
VERY WELL, HOOT.
I SHALL GIVE CLOVER AND HER FRIENDS THE LETTER ...
...AND I SHALL ASK SKYE AND CLOU-D TO CONVEY THE IDENTICAL MESSAGE, HOOT.
REMEMBER, SPEED IS NOT THE ONLY REQUIREMENT, HOOT.
YOU MUST RELAY THE MESSAGE ACCURATELY AS WELL, HOOT.
OH!
NO FEAR! THE MESSAGE WILL BE CLEAR!! YO, YO, YO.
WE'LL SHOW YOU WHAT WE CAN DO!! YEAH!!
HIGHTAIL IT BUNNY, ♡ 'CAUSE OUR SERVICE AIN'T FUNNY!
RRGH
POKE POKE
BUNNIES CAN DELIVER MESSAGES TOO!! WE HOP FAST!
Yeah!!
We won't be defeated!
Yeah!
NOW, NOW, NO SQUABBLING, HOOT.
HERE ...
I'VE WRITTEN TWO IDENTICAL LETTERS, HOOT.

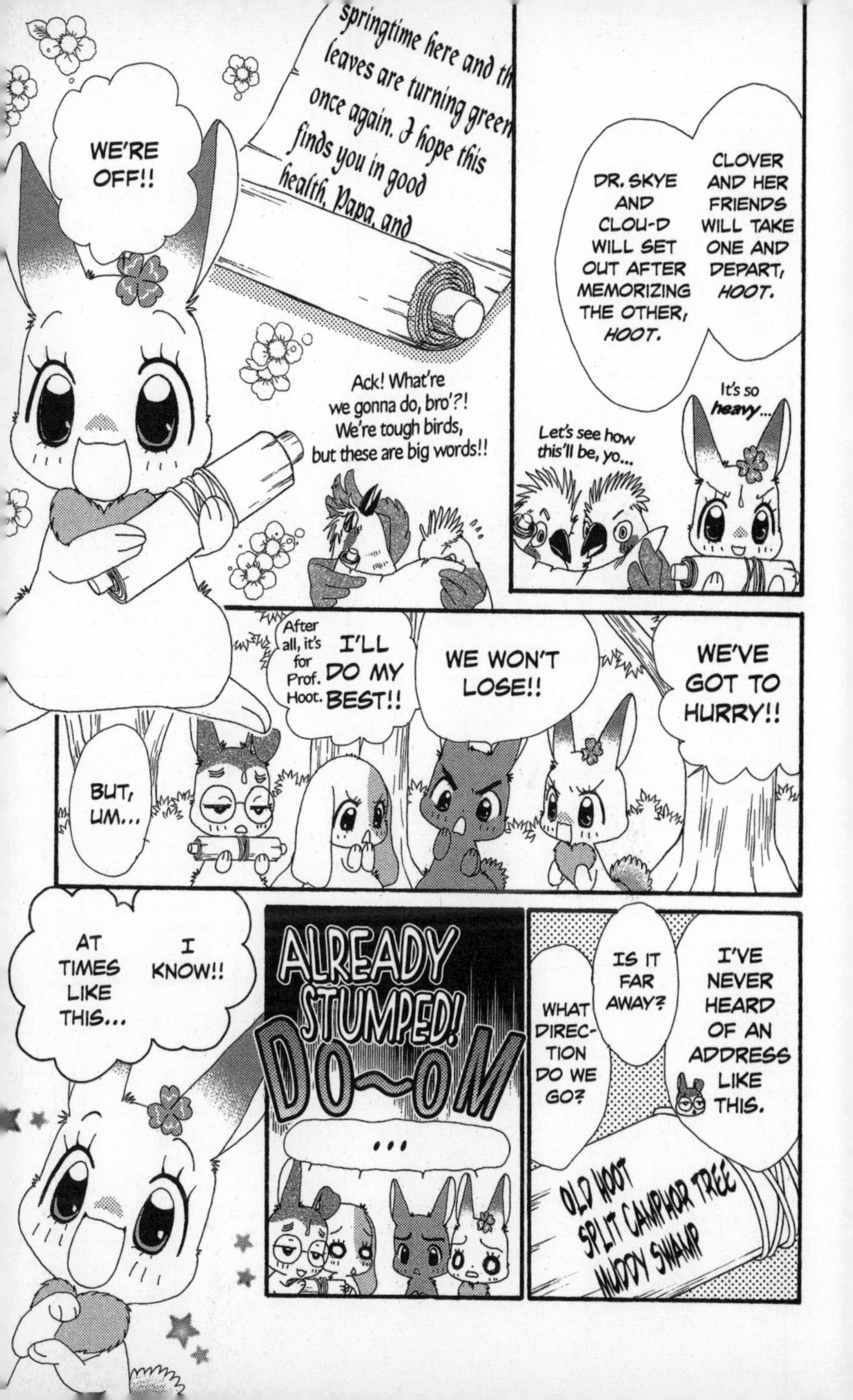
CLOVER AND HER FRIENDS WILL TAKE ONE AND DEPART, *HOOT*.
DR. SKYE AND CLOU-D WILL SET OUT AFTER MEMORIZING THE OTHER, *HOOT*.
It's so **heavy**...
Let's see how this'll be, yo...
springtime here and th leaves are turning green once again. I hope this finds you in good health, Papa, and
Ack! What're we gonna do, bro'?! We're tough birds, but these are big words!!
WE'RE OFF!!
WE'VE GOT TO HURRY!!
WE WON'T LOSE!!
I'LL DO MY BEST!!
After all, it's for Prof. Hoot.
BUT, UM...
I'VE NEVER HEARD OF AN ADDRESS LIKE THIS.
IS IT FAR AWAY?
WHAT DIRECTION DO WE GO?
OLD HOOT
SPLIT CAMPHOR TREE
MUDDY SWAMP
ALREADY STUMPED!
DO~OM
...
I KNOW!!
AT TIMES LIKE THIS...

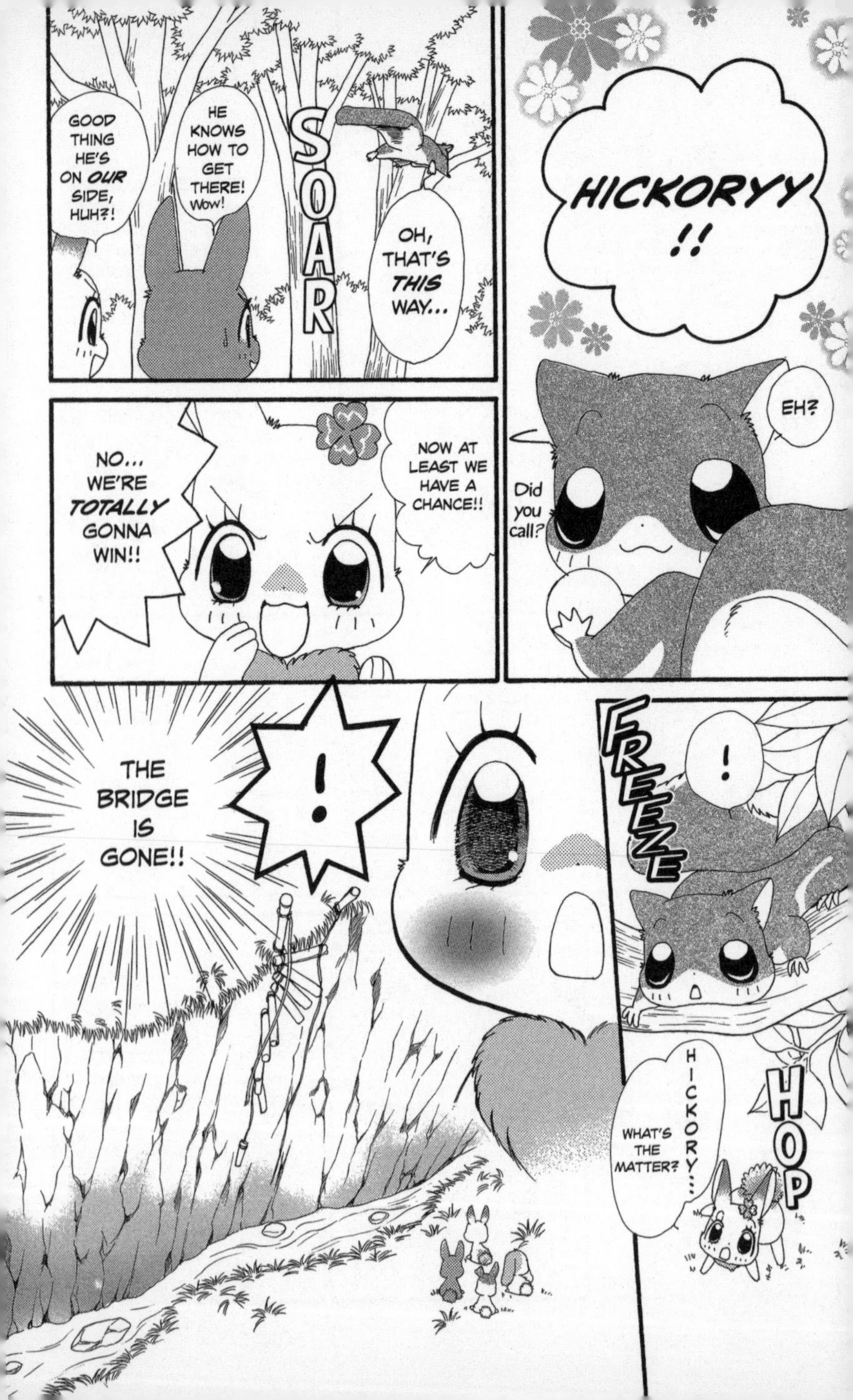
HICKORYY !!
SOAR
OH, THAT'S THIS WAY...
HE KNOWS HOW TO GET THERE! Wow!
GOOD THING HE'S ON OUR SIDE, HUH?!
EH?
Did you call?
NOW AT LEAST WE HAVE A CHANCE!!
NO... WE'RE TOTALLY GONNA WIN!!
FREEZE
!
HOP
HICKORY...
WHAT'S THE MATTER?
!
THE BRIDGE IS GONE!!

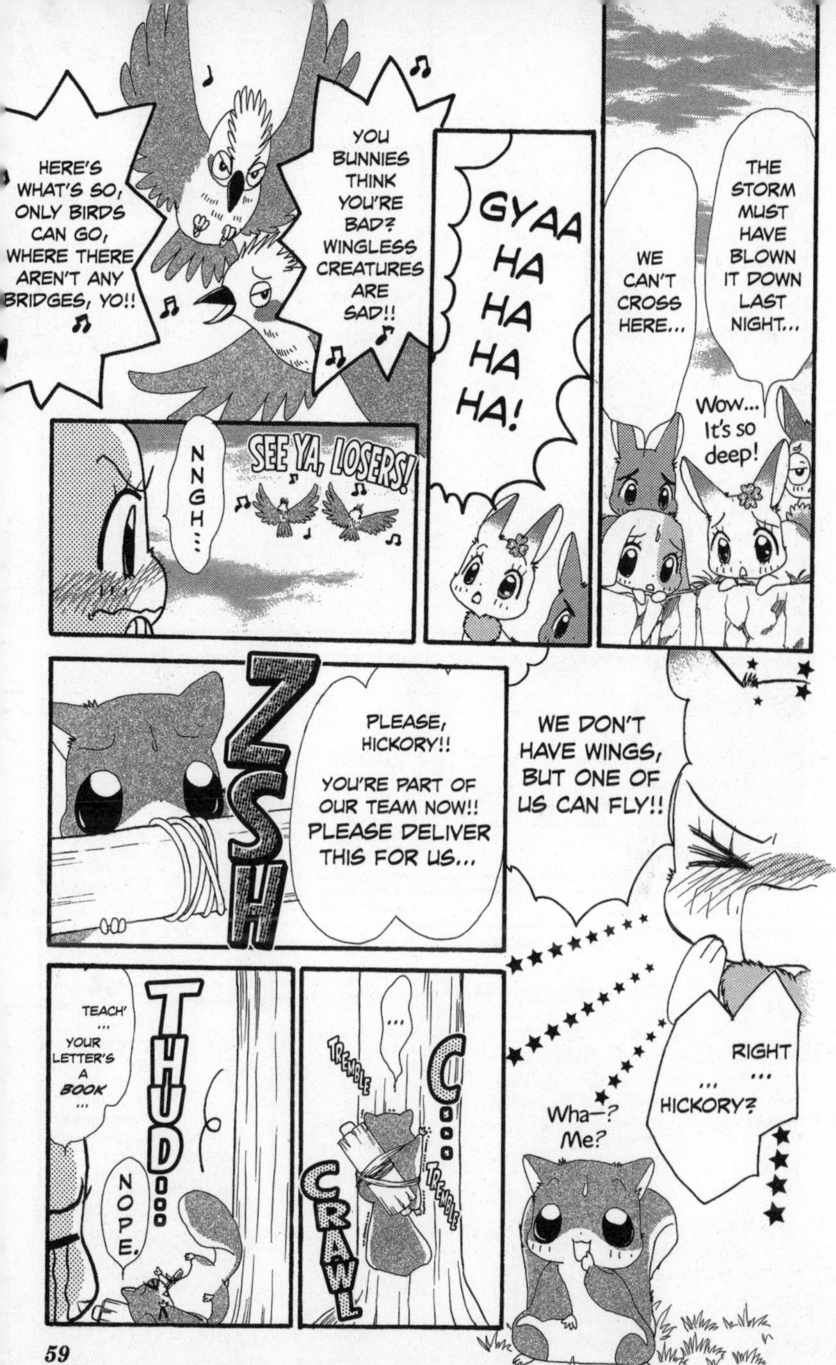
THE STORM MUST HAVE BLOWN IT DOWN LAST NIGHT...
WE CAN'T CROSS HERE...
Wow... It's so deep!
GYAA HA HA HA HA HA!
YOU BUNNIES THINK YOU'RE BAD? WINGLESS CREATURES ARE SAD!!
HERE'S WHAT'S SO, ONLY BIRDS CAN GO, WHERE THERE AREN'T ANY BRIDGES, YO!!
SEE YA, LOSERS!
NNGH...
WE DON'T HAVE WINGS, BUT ONE OF US CAN FLY!!
RIGHT ... ... HICKORY?
Wha-? Me?
ZSH
PLEASE, HICKORY!! YOU'RE PART OF OUR TEAM NOW!! PLEASE DELIVER THIS FOR US...
...
TREMBLE
COOO
TREMBLE
CRAWL
TEACH' ... YOUR LETTER'S A *BOOK* ...
THUDOOO
NOPE.

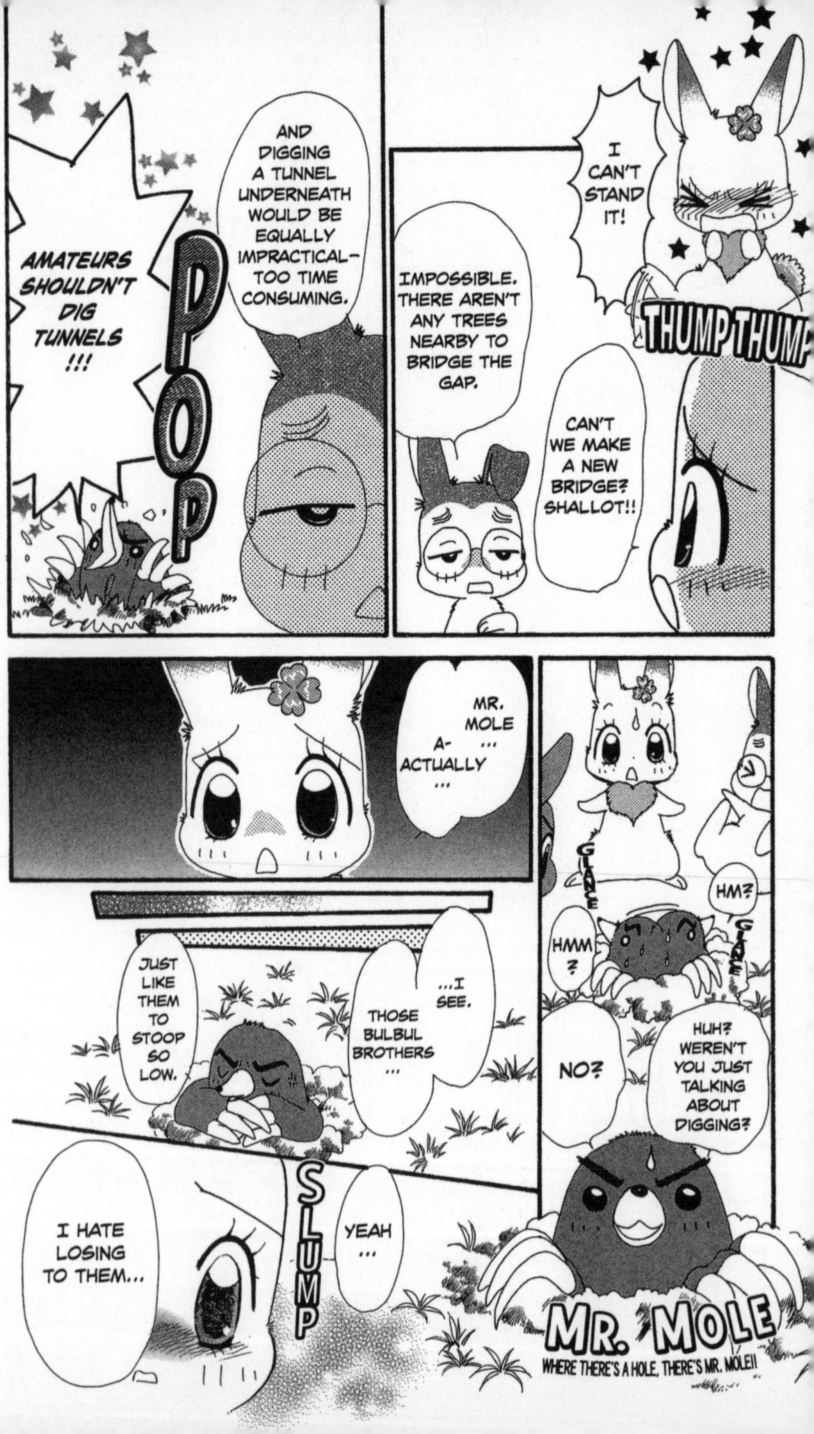
I CAN'T STAND IT!
THUMP THUMP
CAN'T WE MAKE A NEW BRIDGE? SHALLOT!!
IMPOSSIBLE. THERE AREN'T ANY TREES NEARBY TO BRIDGE THE GAP.
AND DIGGING A TUNNEL UNDERNEATH WOULD BE EQUALLY IMPRACTICAL— TOO TIME CONSUMING.
POP
AMATEURS SHOULDN'T DIG TUNNELS !!!
GLANCE
HM?
GLANCE
HMM ?
HUH? WEREN'T YOU JUST TALKING ABOUT DIGGING?
NO?
MR. MOLE
WHERE THERE'S A HOLE, THERE'S MR. MOLE!!
MR. MOLE ... A- ACTUALLY ...
...I SEE.
THOSE BULBUL BROTHERS ...
JUST LIKE THEM TO STOOP SO LOW.
SLUMP
YEAH ...
I HATE LOSING TO THEM...

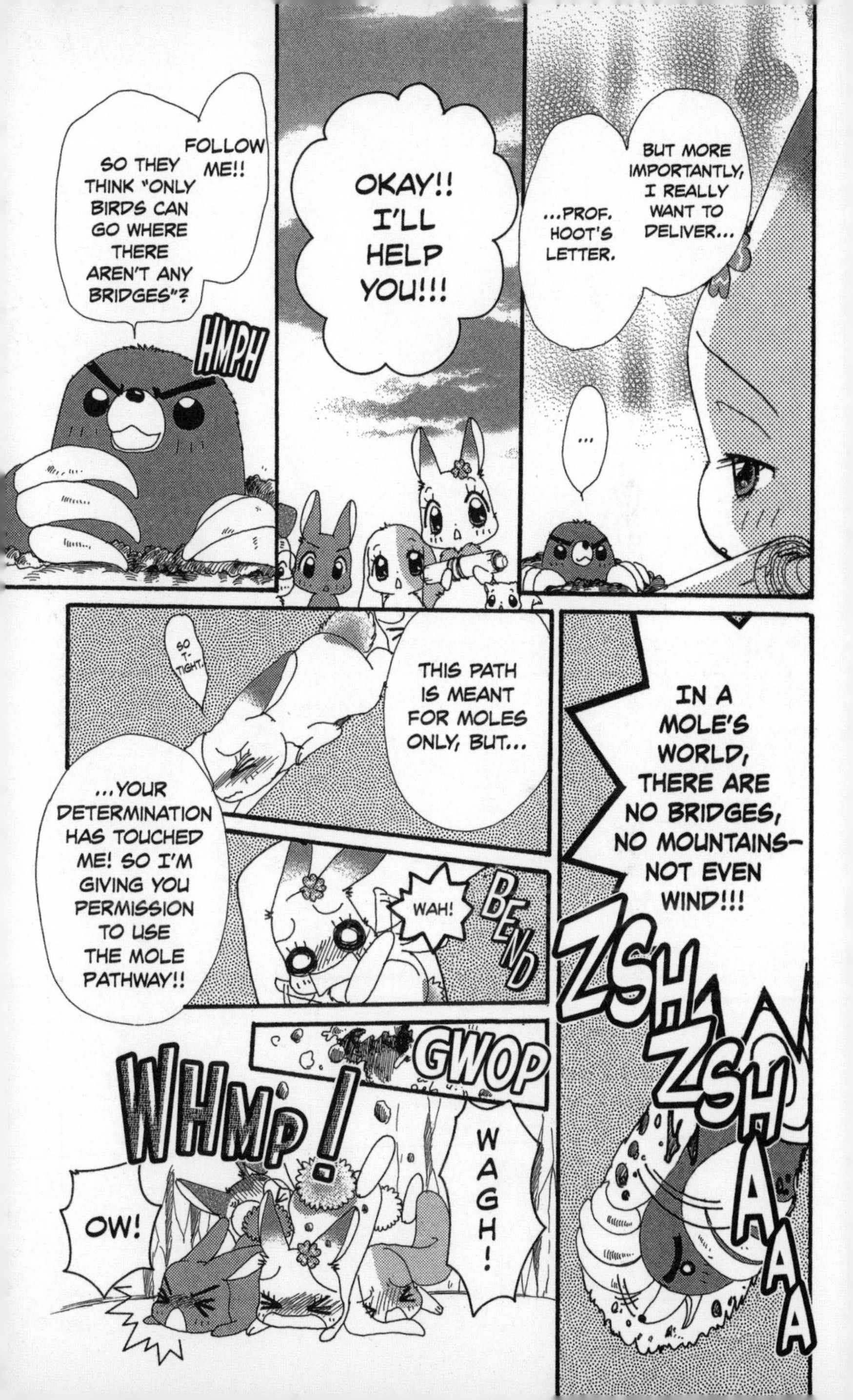
BUT MORE IMPORTANTLY, I REALLY WANT TO DELIVER...
...PROF. HOOT'S LETTER.
...
OKAY!! I'LL HELP YOU!!!
FOLLOW ME!!
SO THEY THINK "ONLY BIRDS CAN GO WHERE THERE AREN'T ANY BRIDGES"?
HMPH
IN A MOLE'S WORLD, THERE ARE NO BRIDGES, NO MOUNTAINS— NOT EVEN WIND!!!
ZSH
ZSH
HAAAA
THIS PATH IS MEANT FOR MOLES ONLY, BUT...
SO T-TIGHT.
...YOUR DETERMINATION HAS TOUCHED ME! SO I'M GIVING YOU PERMISSION TO USE THE MOLE PATHWAY!!
BEND
WAH!
GWOP
WAGH!
WHMP!
OW!

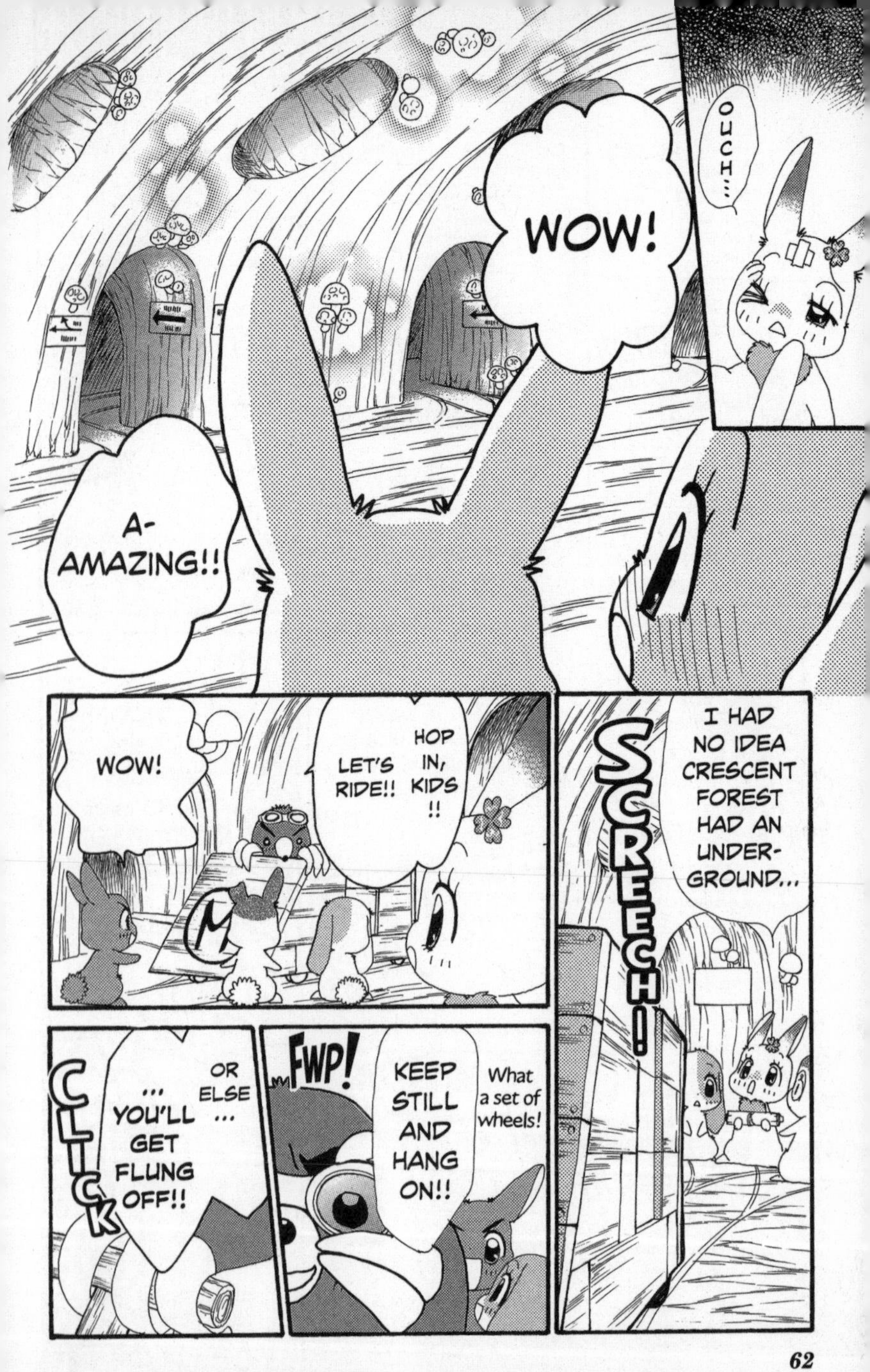
OUCH...
WOW!
A-AMAZING!!
I HAD NO IDEA CRESCENT FOREST HAD AN UNDERGROUND...
SCREECH!
HOP IN, KIDS!!
LET'S RIDE!!
WOW!
What a set of wheels!
KEEP STILL AND HANG ON!!
FWP!
OR ELSE...
... YOU'LL GET FLUNG OFF!!
CLICK

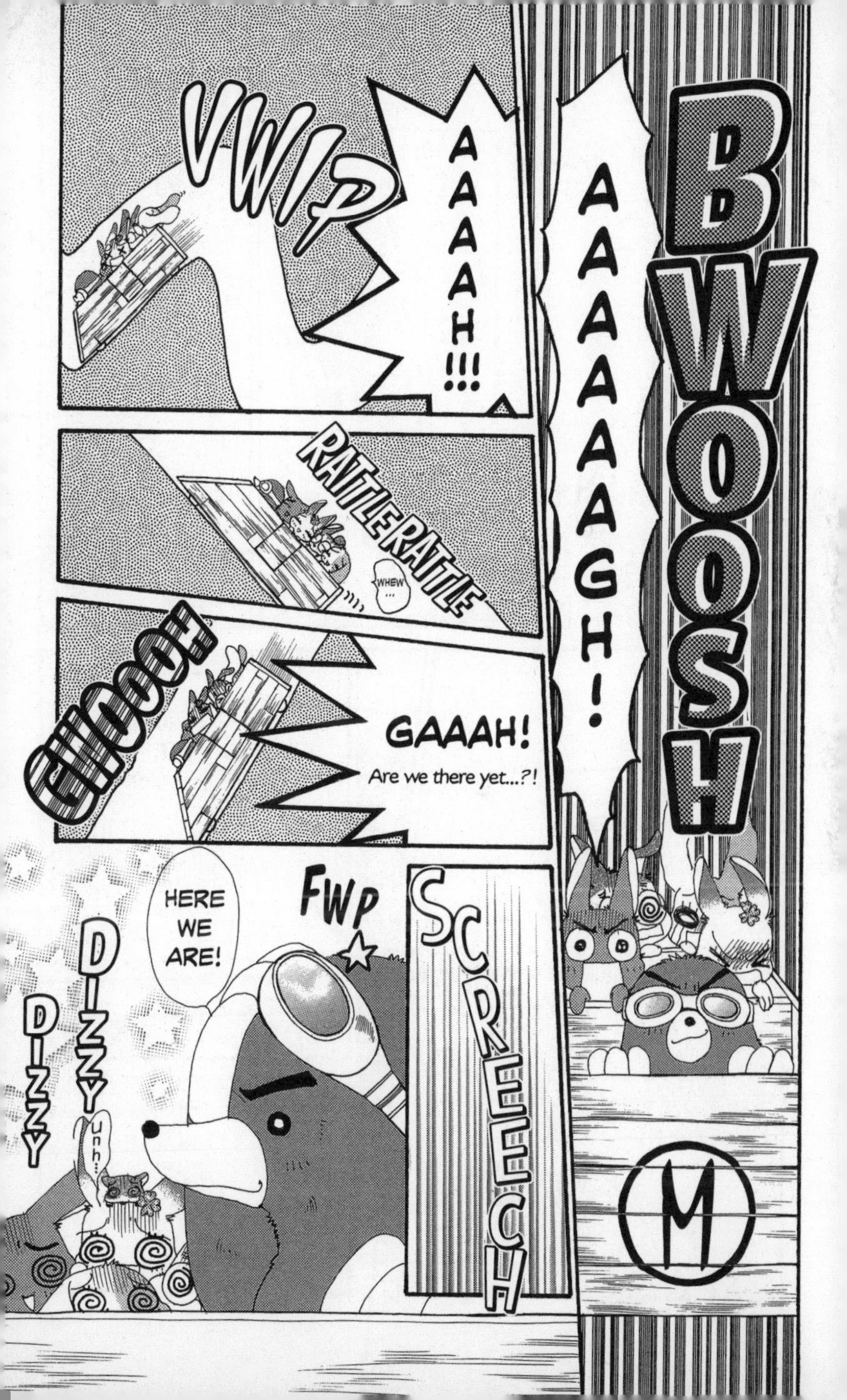

BWOOSH
AAAAAAAAGH!
AAAAAH!!!
VWIP
RATTLE RATTLE
WHEW...
GAAAH!
Are we there yet...?!
CHOOOH
SCREECH
FWP
HERE WE ARE!
DIZZY
DIZZY
Unh...
M

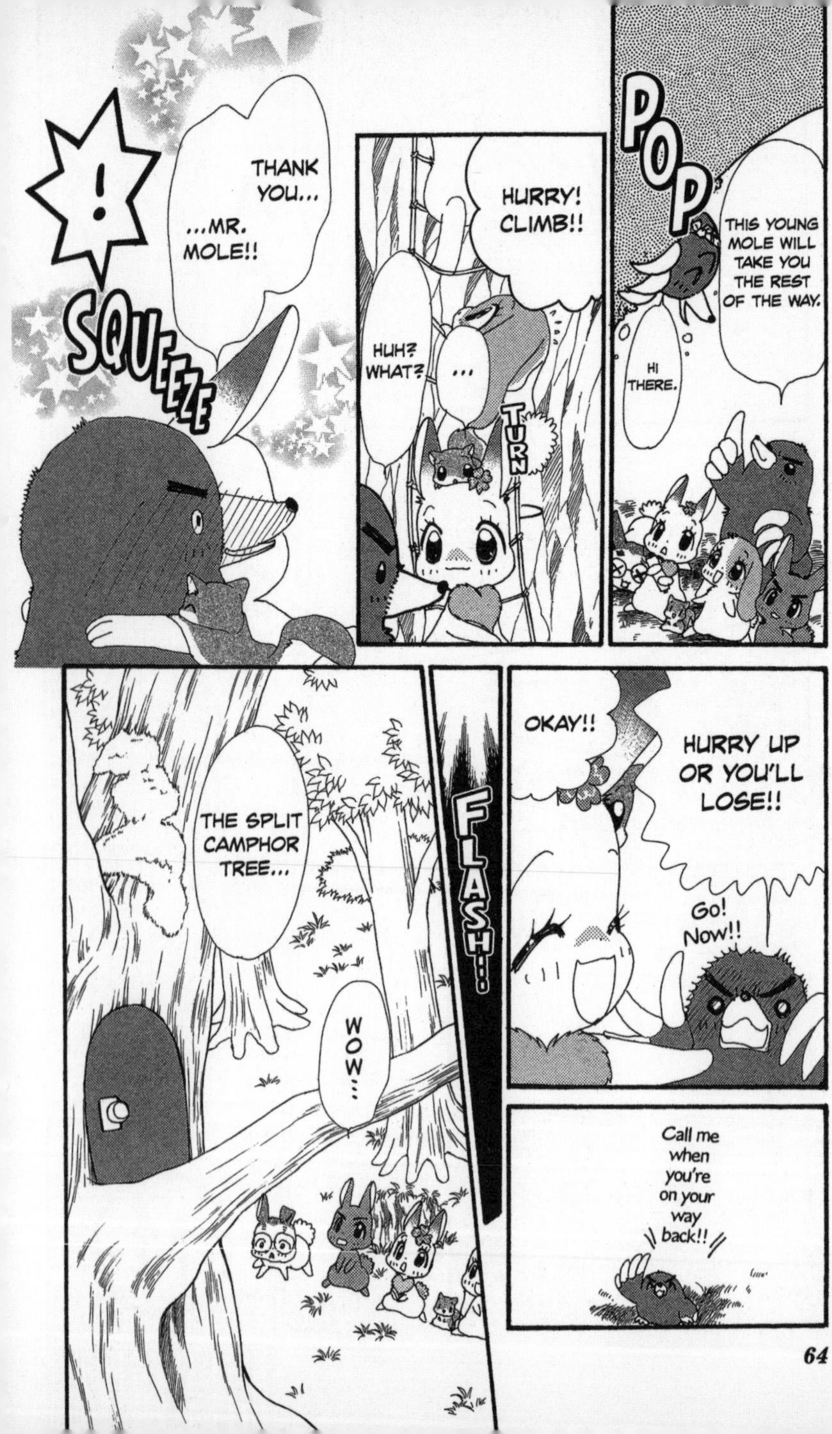
POP
THIS YOUNG MOLE WILL TAKE YOU THE REST OF THE WAY.
HI THERE.
HURRY! CLIMB!!
HUH? WHAT?
...
TURN
THANK YOU...
...MR. MOLE!!
!
SQUEEZE
HURRY UP OR YOU'LL LOSE!!
OKAY!!
Go! Now!!
Call me when you're on your way back!!
FLASH!!
THE SPLIT CAMPHOR TREE...
WOW...

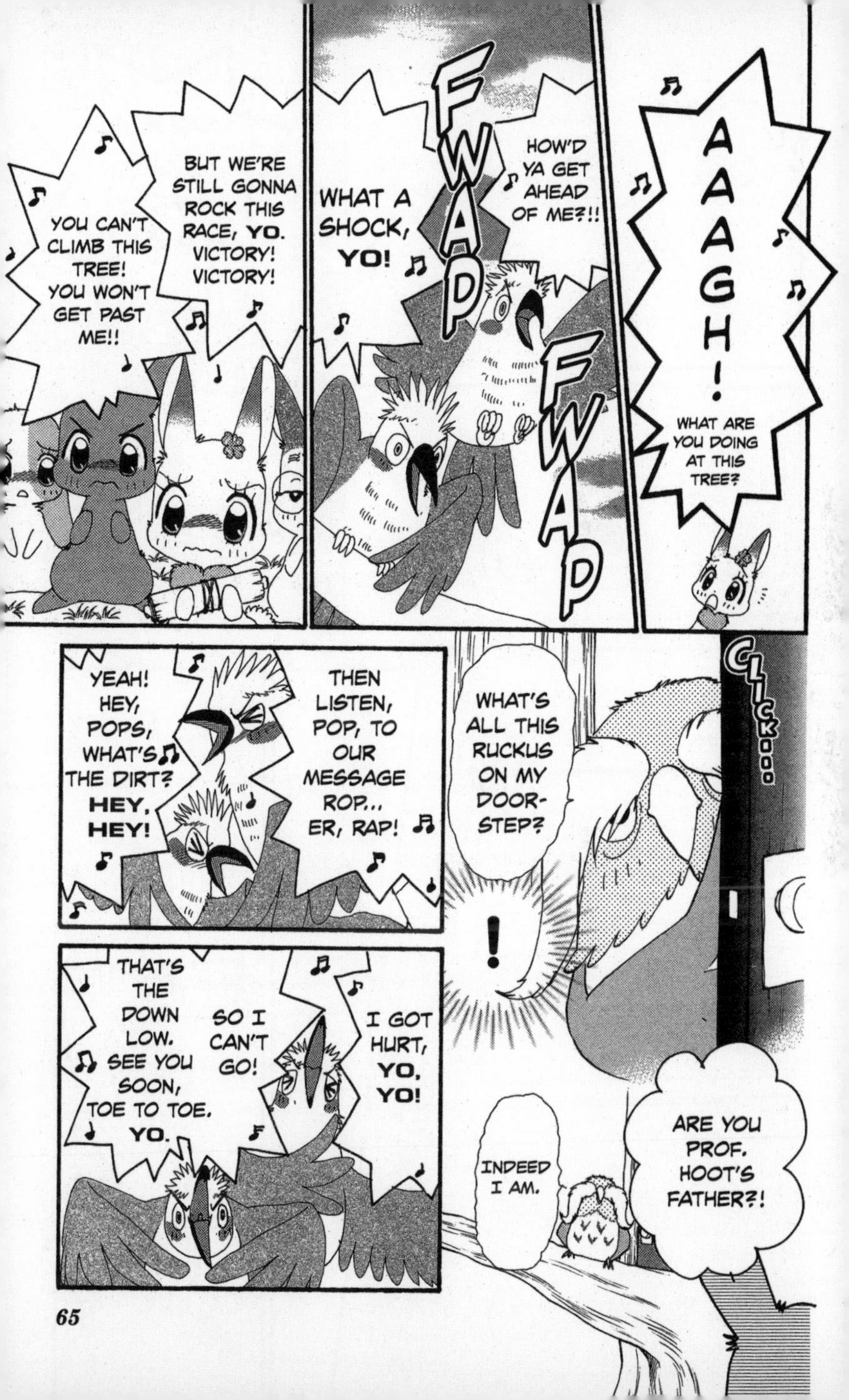
AAAGH!
WHAT ARE YOU DOING AT THIS TREE?
FWAP
FWAP
HOW'D YA GET AHEAD OF ME?!!
WHAT A SHOCK, YO!
BUT WE'RE STILL GONNA ROCK THIS RACE, YO. VICTORY! VICTORY!
YOU CAN'T CLIMB THIS TREE! YOU WON'T GET PAST ME!!
CLICK...
WHAT'S ALL THIS RUCKUS ON MY DOOR-STEP?
!
ARE YOU PROF. HOOT'S FATHER?!
INDEED I AM.
THEN LISTEN, POP, TO OUR MESSAGE ROP... ER, RAP!
YEAH! HEY, POPS, WHAT'S THE DIRT? HEY, HEY!
I GOT HURT, YO, YO!
SO I CAN'T GO!
THAT'S THE DOWN LOW. SEE YOU SOON, TOE TO TOE. YO.

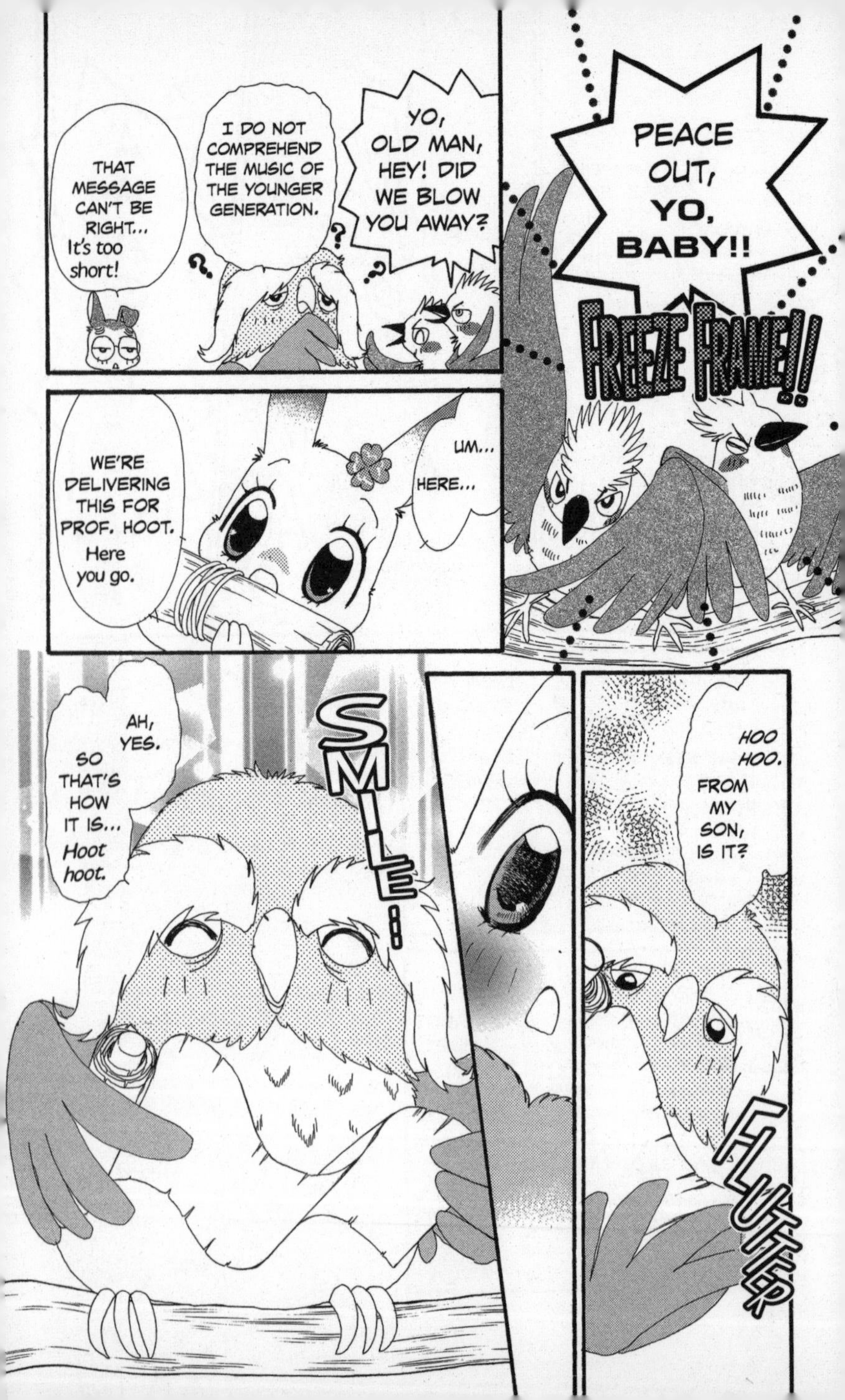

PEACE OUT, YO, BABY!!
FREEZE FRAME!!
YO, OLD MAN, HEY! DID WE BLOW YOU AWAY?
I DO NOT COMPREHEND THE MUSIC OF THE YOUNGER GENERATION.
THAT MESSAGE CAN'T BE RIGHT... It's too short!
UM... HERE...
WE'RE DELIVERING THIS FOR PROF. HOOT. Here you go.
HOO HOO. FROM MY SON, IS IT?
FLUTTER
SMILE!!
AH, YES. SO THAT'S HOW IT IS... Hoot hoot.

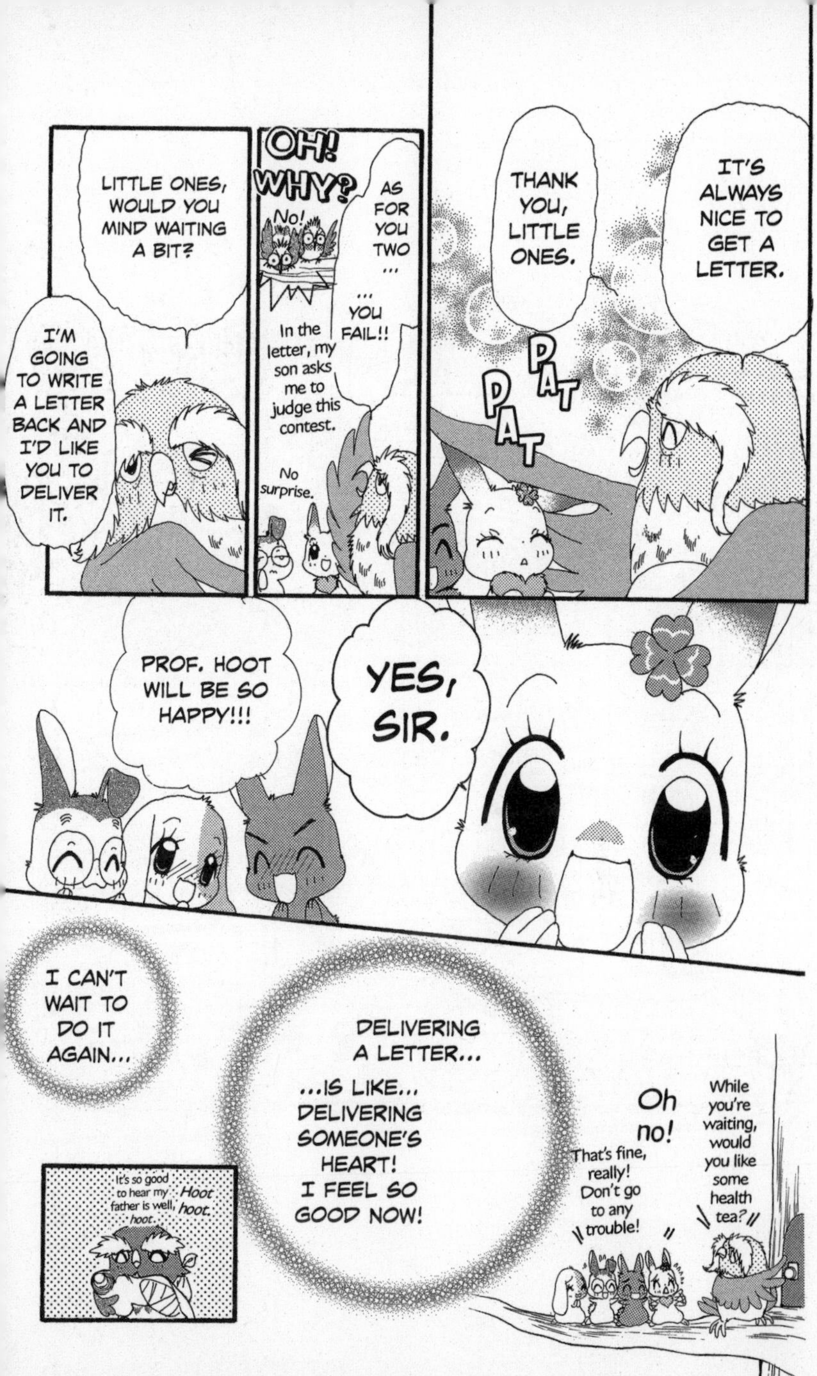
IT'S ALWAYS NICE TO GET A LETTER.
THANK YOU, LITTLE ONES.
PAT PAT
AS FOR YOU TWO ...
... YOU FAIL!!
OH! WHY?
No!
In the letter, my son asks me to judge this contest.
No surprise.
LITTLE ONES, WOULD YOU MIND WAITING A BIT?
I'M GOING TO WRITE A LETTER BACK AND I'D LIKE YOU TO DELIVER IT.
YES, SIR.
PROF. HOOT WILL BE SO HAPPY!!!
While you're waiting, would you like some health tea?
Oh no!
That's fine, really! Don't go to any trouble!
DELIVERING A LETTER...
...IS LIKE... DELIVERING SOMEONE'S HEART! I FEEL SO GOOD NOW!
I CAN'T WAIT TO DO IT AGAIN...
It's so good to hear my father is well, hoot.
Hoot hoot.

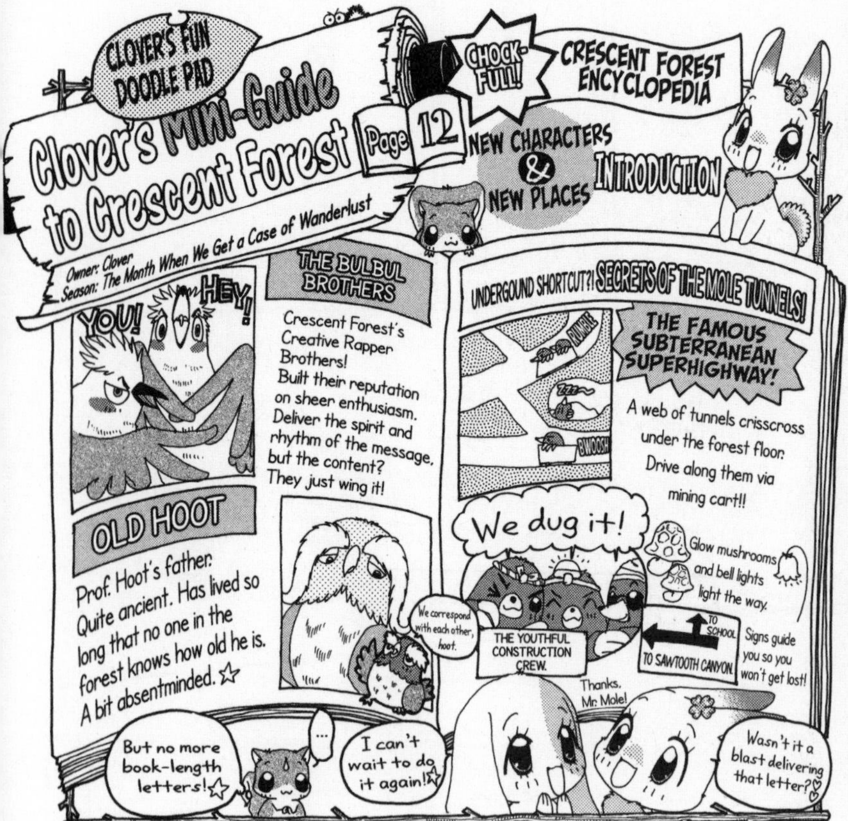
CRESCENT FOREST ENCYCLOPEDIA
CHOCK-FULL!
CLOVER'S FUN DOODLE PAD
Clover's Mini-Guide to Crescent Forest
Page 12
NEW CHARACTERS & NEW PLACES INTRODUCTION
The Month When We Get a Case of Wanderlust
Owner: Clover
Season: The Month When We Get a Case of Wanderlust
UNDERGOUND SHORTCUT?! SECRETS OF THE MOLE TUNNELS!
THE FAMOUS SUBTERRANEAN SUPERHIGHWAY!
RUMBLE
ZZZ~
BWOOSH
A web of tunnels crisscross under the forest floor. Drive along them via mining cart!!
We dug it!
Glow mushrooms and bell lights light the way.
THE YOUTHFUL CONSTRUCTION CREW.
TO SCHOOL
TO SAWTOOTH CANYON
Signs guide you so you won't get lost!
THE BULBUL BROTHERS
HEY!
YOU!
Crescent Forest's Creative Rapper Brothers! Built their reputation on sheer enthusiasm. Deliver the spirit and rhythm of the message, but the content? They just wing it!
OLD HOOT
Prof. Hoot's father. Quite ancient. Has lived so long that no one in the forest knows how old he is. A bit absentminded. ☆
We correspond with each other, hoot.
Wasn't it a blast delivering that letter?♡
Thanks, Mr. Mole!
I can't wait to do it again!☆
...
But no more book-length letters!☆

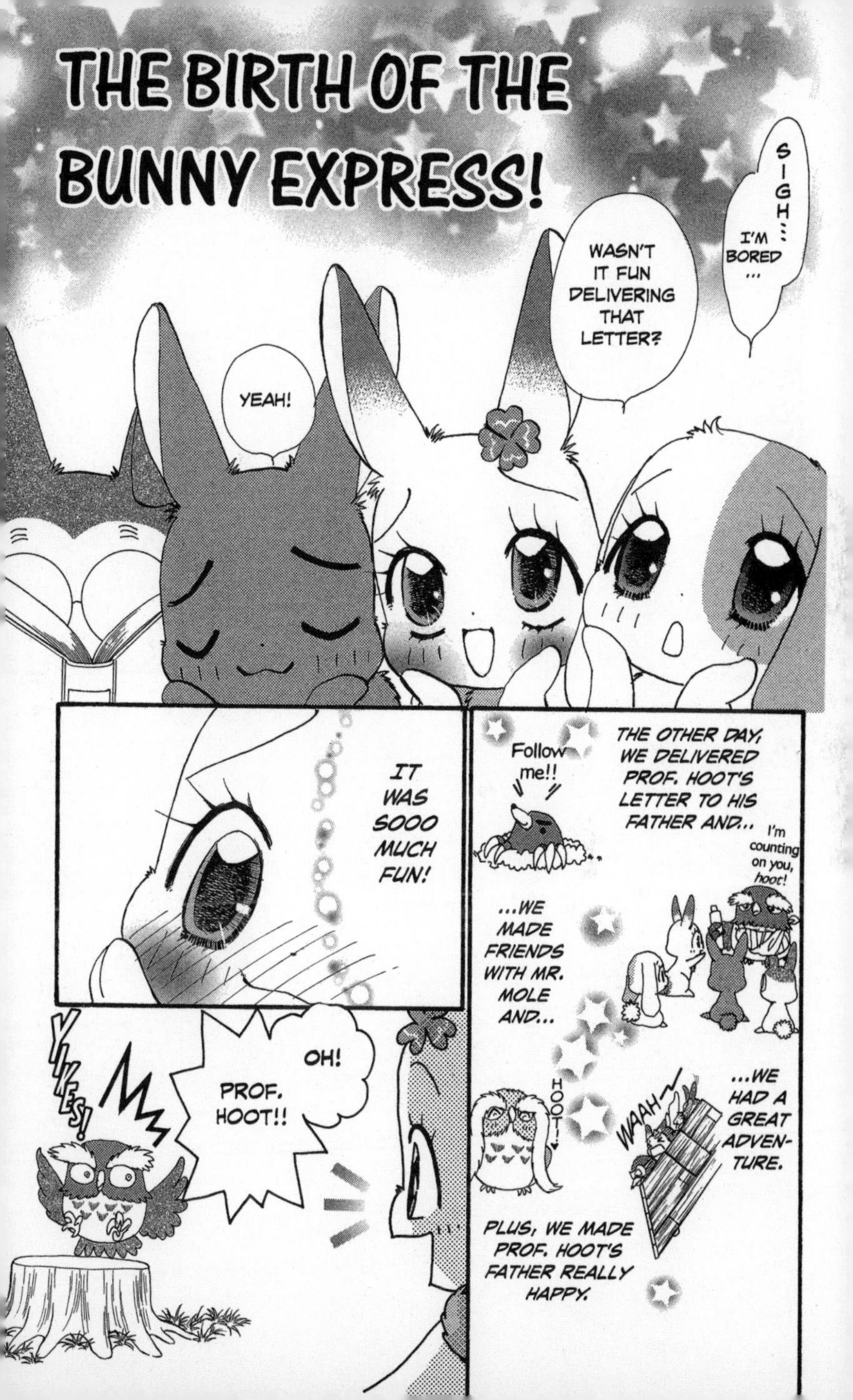
THE BIRTH OF THE BUNNY EXPRESS!
SIGH... I'M BORED...
WASN'T IT FUN DELIVERING THAT LETTER?
YEAH!
THE OTHER DAY, WE DELIVERED PROF. HOOT'S LETTER TO HIS FATHER AND...
Follow me!!
...WE MADE FRIENDS WITH MR. MOLE AND...
I'm counting on you, hoot!
...WE HAD A GREAT ADVENTURE.
WAAH
HOOT!
PLUS, WE MADE PROF. HOOT'S FATHER REALLY HAPPY.
IT WAS SOOO MUCH FUN!
OH!
PROF. HOOT!!
YIKES!

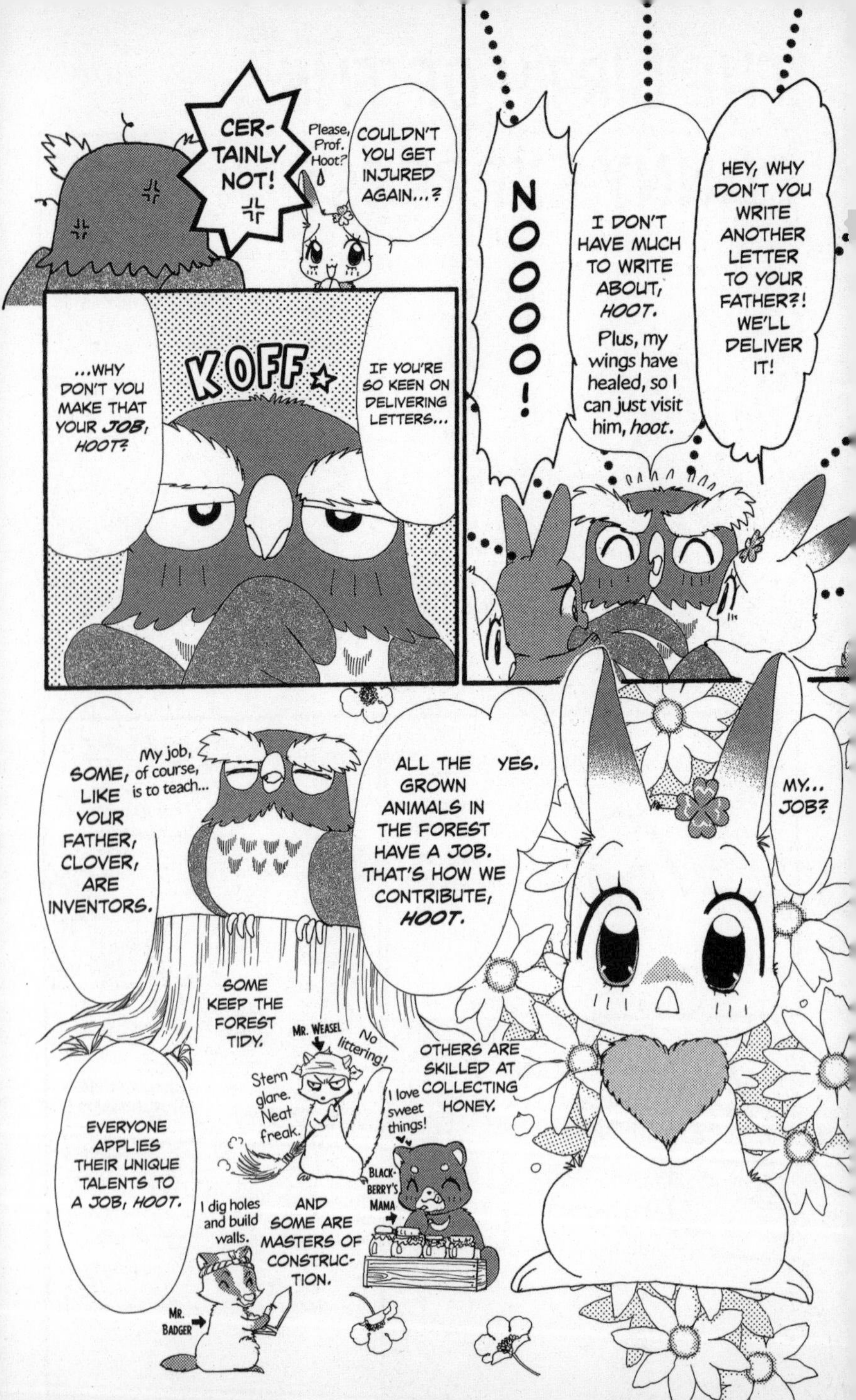
HEY, WHY DON'T YOU WRITE ANOTHER LETTER TO YOUR FATHER?! WE'LL DELIVER IT!
I DON'T HAVE MUCH TO WRITE ABOUT, HOOT. Plus, my wings have healed, so I can just visit him, hoot.
NOOOO!
COULDN'T YOU GET INJURED AGAIN...?
Please, Prof. Hoot?
CER-TAINLY NOT!
IF YOU'RE SO KEEN ON DELIVERING LETTERS...
KOFF
...WHY DON'T YOU MAKE THAT YOUR JOB, HOOT?
MY... JOB?
YES.
ALL THE GROWN ANIMALS IN THE FOREST HAVE A JOB. THAT'S HOW WE CONTRIBUTE, HOOT.
My job, of course, is to teach...
SOME, LIKE YOUR FATHER, CLOVER, ARE INVENTORS.
OTHERS ARE SKILLED AT COLLECTING HONEY.
I love sweet things!
BLACK-BERRY'S MAMA
SOME KEEP THE FOREST TIDY.
MR. WEASEL
No littering!
Stern glare. Neat freak.
AND SOME ARE MASTERS OF CONSTRUC-TION.
I dig holes and build walls.
MR. BADGER
EVERYONE APPLIES THEIR UNIQUE TALENTS TO A JOB, HOOT.

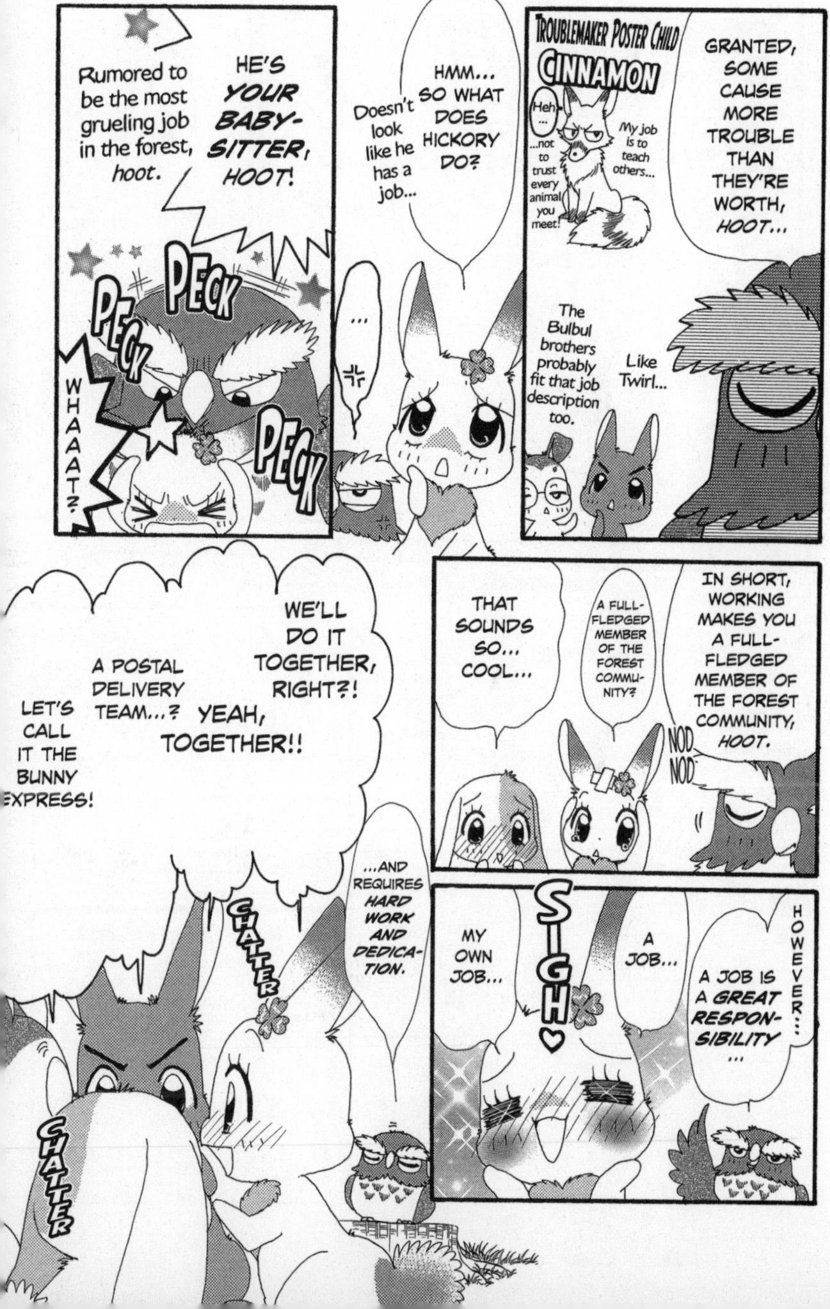
GRANTED, SOME CAUSE MORE TROUBLE THAN THEY'RE WORTH, *HOOT*...
TROUBLEMAKER POSTER CHILD
CINNAMON
My job is to teach others...
Heh... ...not to trust every animal you meet!
The Bulbul brothers probably fit that job description too.
Like Twirl...
HMM... SO WHAT DOES HICKORY DO?
Doesn't look like he has a job...
...
HE'S *YOUR BABY-SITTER*, *HOOT*!
Rumored to be the most grueling job in the forest, *hoot*.
PECK
PECK
PECK
WHAAAAT?
IN SHORT, WORKING MAKES YOU A FULL-FLEDGED MEMBER OF THE FOREST COMMUNITY, *HOOT*.
NOD NOD
A FULL-FLEDGED MEMBER OF THE FOREST COMMUNITY?
THAT SOUNDS SO... COOL...
HOWEVER...
A JOB IS A *GREAT RESPONSIBILITY*...
A JOB...
SIGH
MY OWN JOB...
...AND REQUIRES *HARD WORK AND DEDICATION*.
WE'LL DO IT TOGETHER, RIGHT?!
YEAH, TOGETHER!!
A POSTAL DELIVERY TEAM...?
LET'S CALL IT THE BUNNY EXPRESS!
CHATTER
CHATTER

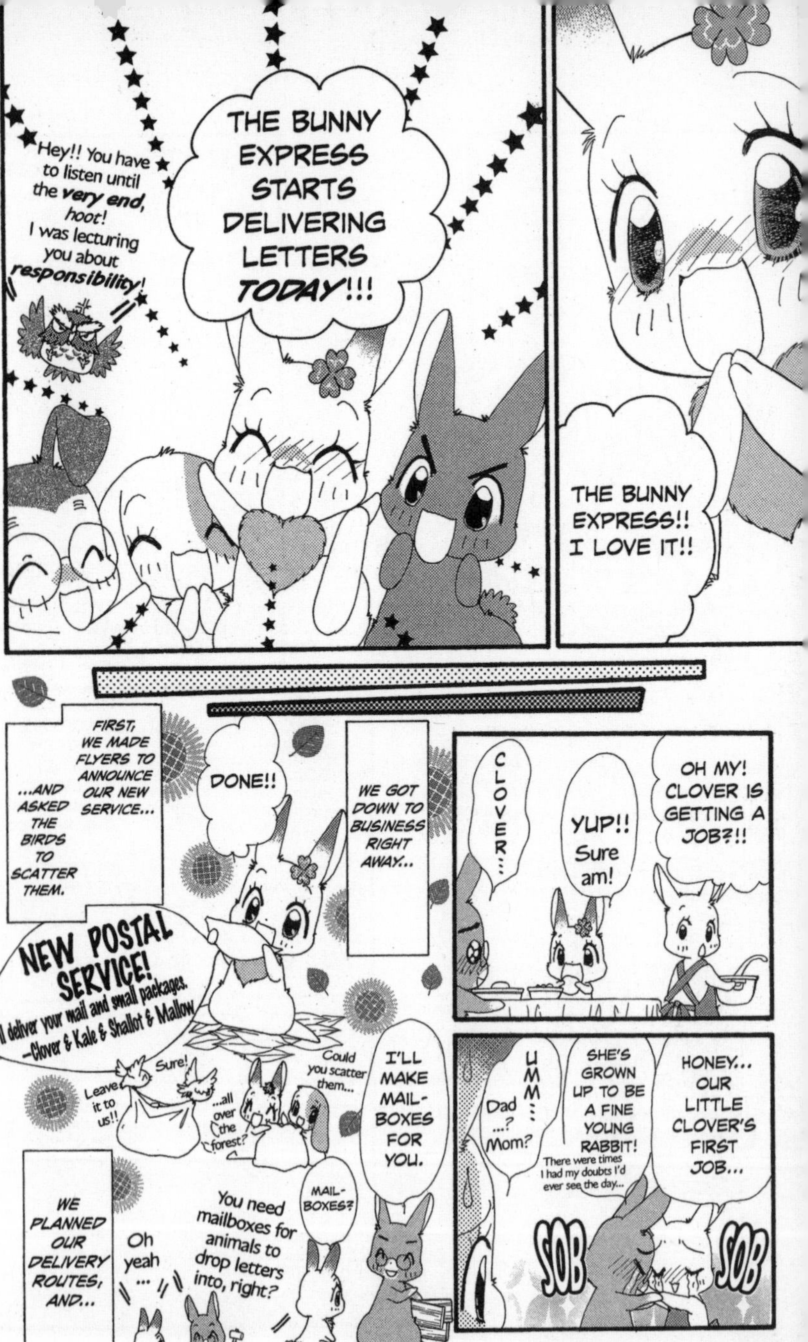
THE BUNNY EXPRESS!! I LOVE IT!!
THE BUNNY EXPRESS STARTS DELIVERING LETTERS TODAY!!!
Hey!! You have to listen until the very end, hoot! I was lecturing you about responsibility!
OH MY! CLOVER IS GETTING A JOB?!!
YUP!! Sure am!
CLOVER...
HONEY... OUR LITTLE CLOVER'S FIRST JOB...
SHE'S GROWN UP TO BE A FINE YOUNG RABBIT!
There were times I had my doubts I'd ever see the day...
UMM...
Dad ...? Mom?
SOB
SOB
WE GOT DOWN TO BUSINESS RIGHT AWAY...
DONE!!
FIRST, WE MADE FLYERS TO ANNOUNCE OUR NEW SERVICE...
...AND ASKED THE BIRDS TO SCATTER THEM.
NEW POSTAL SERVICE!
We'll deliver your mail and small packages.
-Clover & Kale & Shallot & Mallow
Could you scatter them...
...all over the forest?
Sure!
Leave it to us!!
I'LL MAKE MAIL-BOXES FOR YOU.
MAIL-BOXES?
You need mailboxes for animals to drop letters into, right?
Oh yeah ...
WE PLANNED OUR DELIVERY ROUTES, AND...

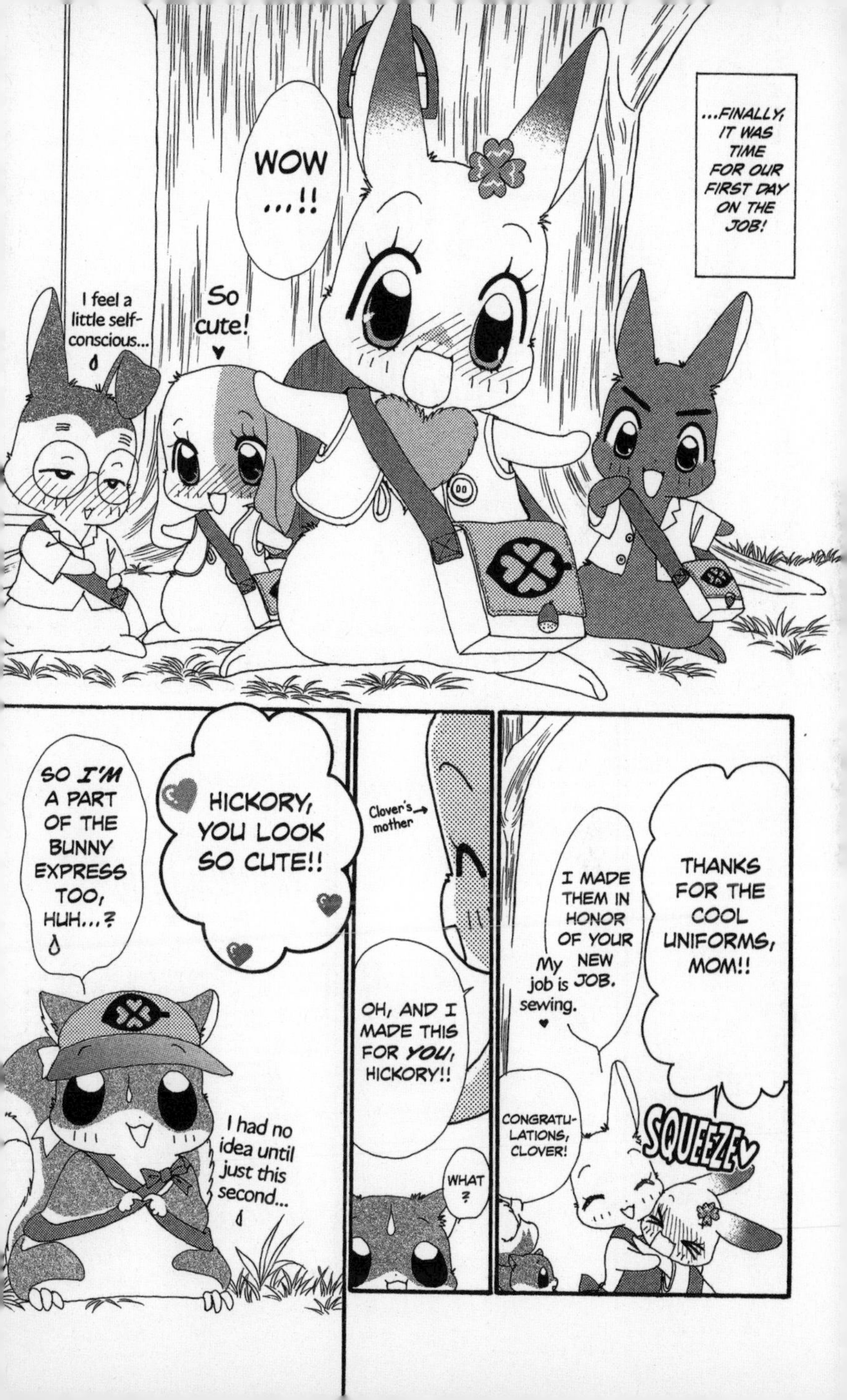
...FINALLY, IT WAS TIME FOR OUR FIRST DAY ON THE JOB!
WOW ...!!
So cute!
I feel a little self-conscious...
THANKS FOR THE COOL UNIFORMS, MOM!!
SQUEEZE
I MADE THEM IN HONOR OF YOUR NEW JOB.
My job is sewing.
CONGRATULATIONS, CLOVER!
Clover's mother
OH, AND I MADE THIS FOR YOU, HICKORY!!
WHAT?
HICKORY, YOU LOOK SO CUTE!!
SO I'M A PART OF THE BUNNY EXPRESS TOO, HUH...?
I had no idea until just this second...

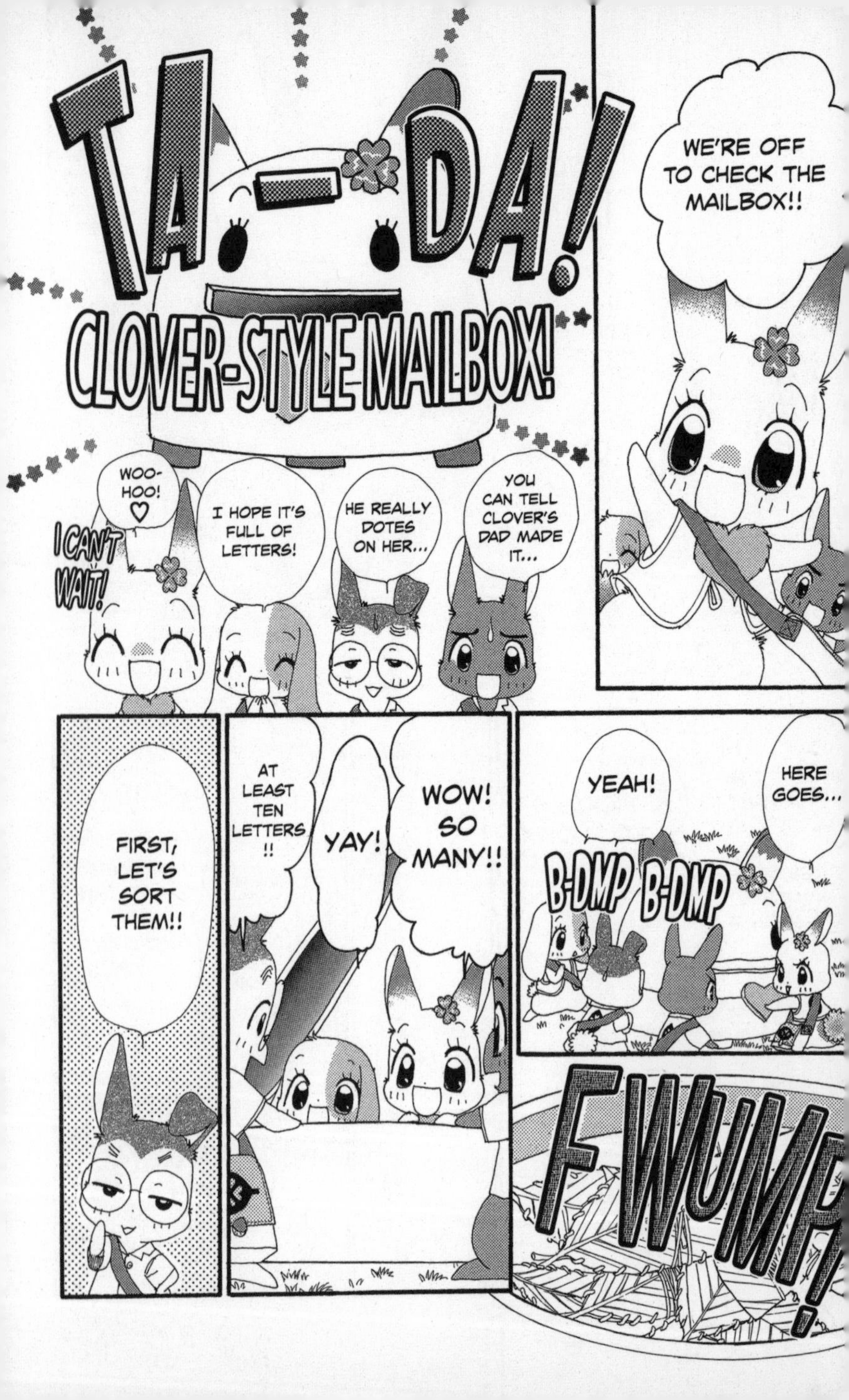
WE'RE OFF TO CHECK THE MAILBOX!!
TA-DA!
CLOVER-STYLE MAILBOX!
YOU CAN TELL CLOVER'S DAD MADE IT...
HE REALLY DOTES ON HER...
I HOPE IT'S FULL OF LETTERS!
WOO-HOO! ♡
I CAN'T WAIT!
HERE GOES...
YEAH!
B-DMP B-DMP
FWUMP!
WOW! SO MANY!!
YAY!
AT LEAST TEN LETTERS !!
FIRST, LET'S SORT THEM!!

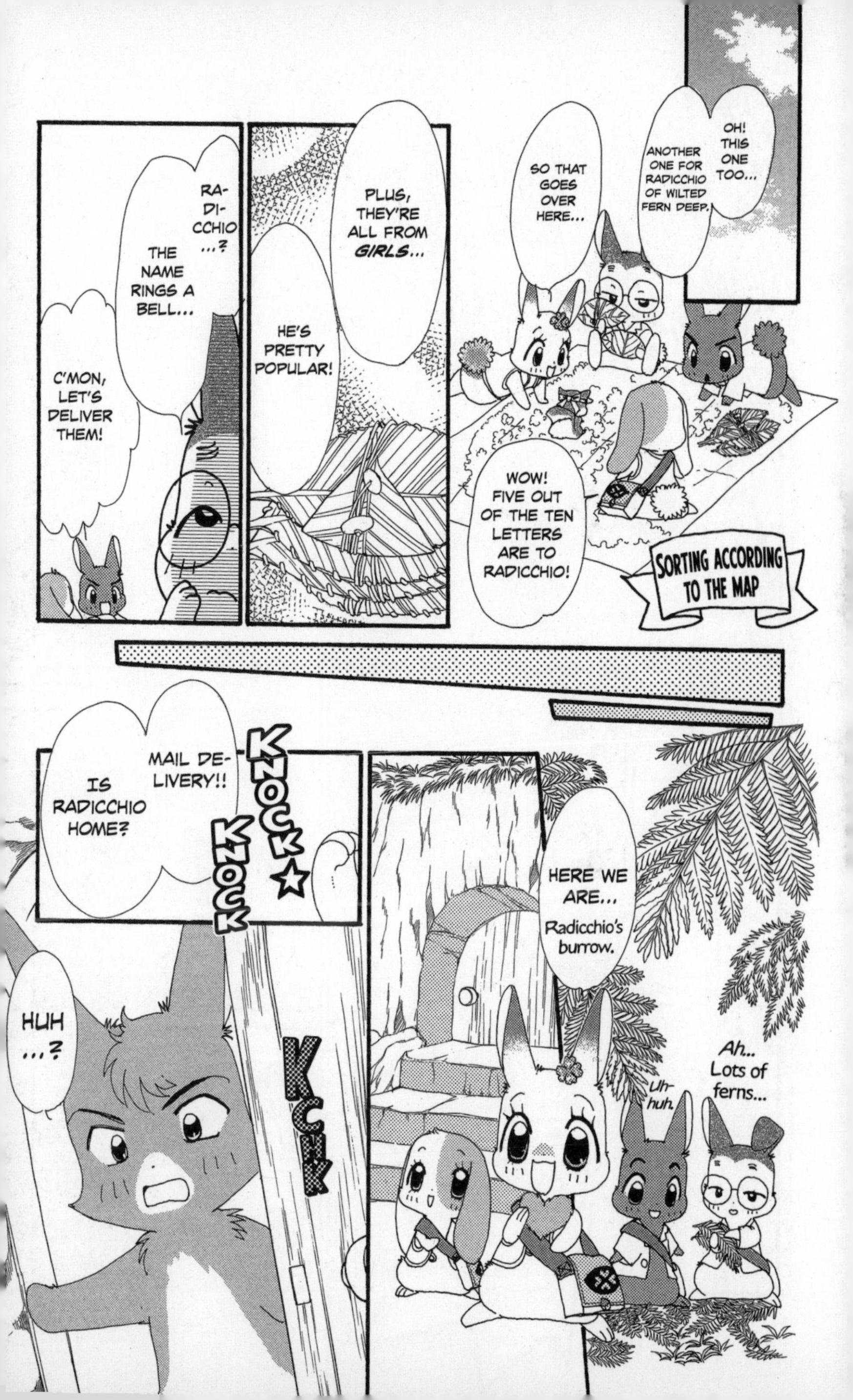
OH! THIS ONE TOO...
ANOTHER ONE FOR RADICCHIO OF WILTED FERN DEEP.
SO THAT GOES OVER HERE...
WOW! FIVE OUT OF THE TEN LETTERS ARE TO RADICCHIO!
SORTING ACCORDING TO THE MAP
PLUS, THEY'RE ALL FROM *GIRLS*...
HE'S PRETTY POPULAR!
RA-DI-CCHIO ...?
THE NAME RINGS A BELL...
C'MON, LET'S DELIVER THEM!
HERE WE ARE... Radicchio's burrow.
Ah... Lots of ferns...
Uh huh.
MAIL DE-LIVERY!!
IS RADICCHIO HOME?
KNOCK☆
KNOCK KNOCK
KCHK
HUH ...?

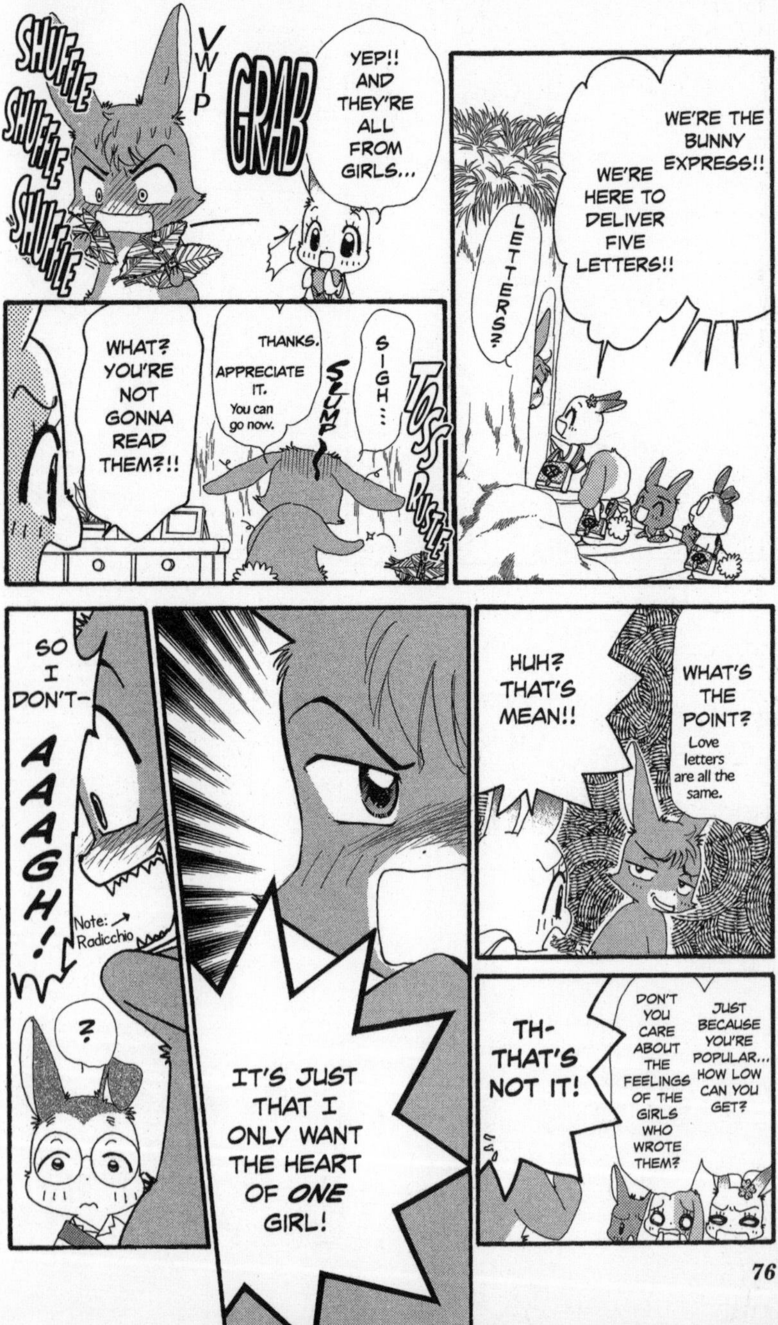
WE'RE THE BUNNY EXPRESS!!
WE'RE HERE TO DELIVER FIVE LETTERS!!
LETTERS?
YEP!! AND THEY'RE ALL FROM GIRLS...
GRAB
VWIP
SHUFFLE SHUFFLE SHUFFLE
TOSS RUSTLE
SIGH...
SLUMP
THANKS. APPRECIATE IT. You can go now.
WHAT? YOU'RE NOT GONNA READ THEM?!!
WHAT'S THE POINT? Love letters are all the same.
HUH? THAT'S MEAN!!
JUST BECAUSE YOU'RE POPULAR... HOW LOW CAN YOU GET?
DON'T YOU CARE ABOUT THE FEELINGS OF THE GIRLS WHO WROTE THEM?
TH- THAT'S NOT IT!
IT'S JUST THAT I ONLY WANT THE HEART OF ONE GIRL!
SO I DON'T-
AAAGH!
Note: Radicchio
?

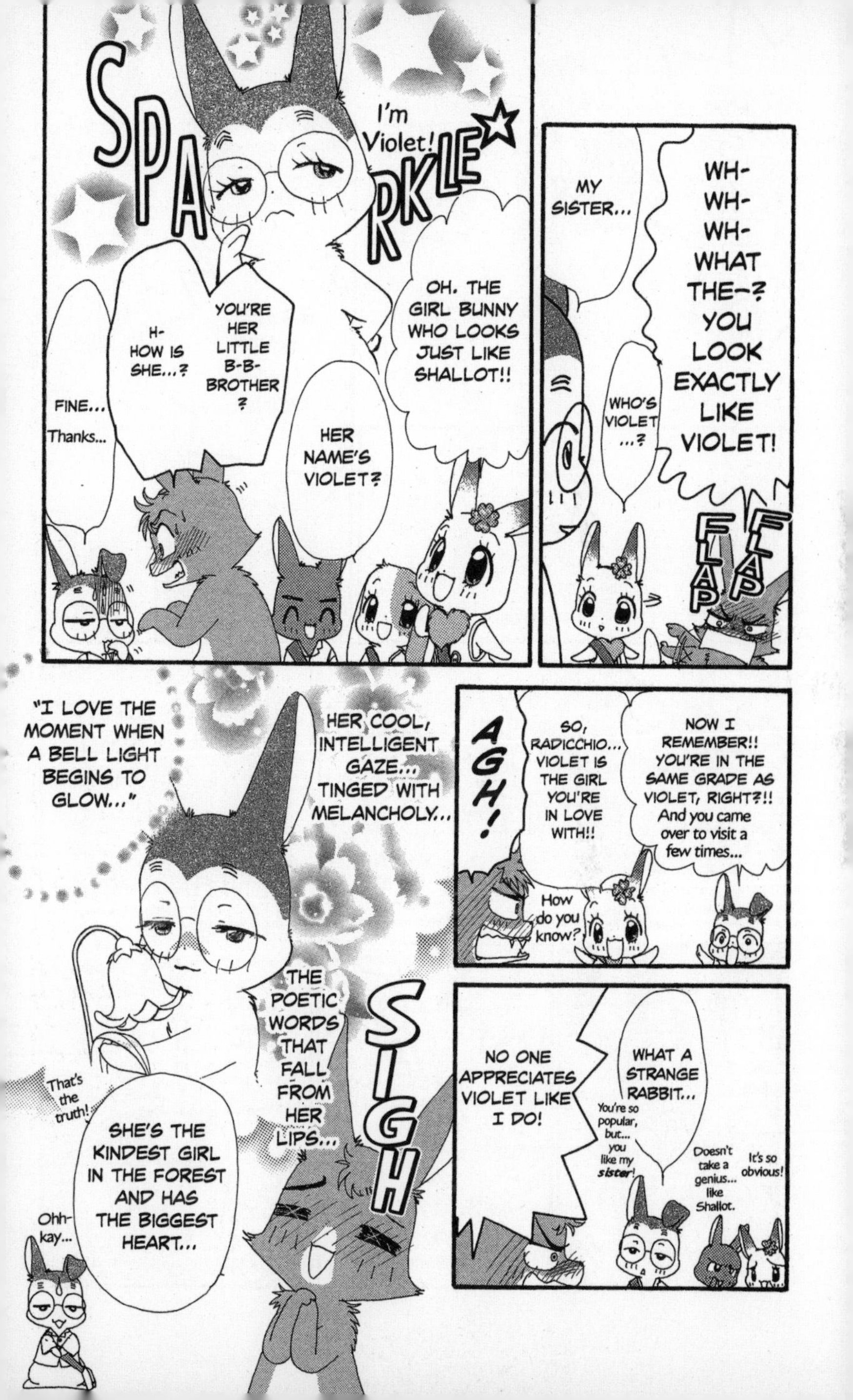
WH-WH-WH-WHAT THE--? YOU LOOK EXACTLY LIKE VIOLET!
MY SISTER...
WHO'S VIOLET...?
FLAP FLAP
I'm Violet!
SPARKLE☆
OH. THE GIRL BUNNY WHO LOOKS JUST LIKE SHALLOT!!
HER NAME'S VIOLET?
YOU'RE HER LITTLE B-B-BROTHER?
H-HOW IS SHE...?
FINE...
Thanks...
NOW I REMEMBER!! YOU'RE IN THE SAME GRADE AS VIOLET, RIGHT?!! And you came over to visit a few times...
SO, RADICCHIO... VIOLET IS THE GIRL YOU'RE IN LOVE WITH!!
AGH!
How do you know?
WHAT A STRANGE RABBIT...
NO ONE APPRECIATES VIOLET LIKE I DO!
You're so popular, but... you like my *sister*!
It's so obvious!
Doesn't take a genius... like Shallot.
HER COOL, INTELLIGENT GAZE... TINGED WITH MELANCHOLY...
"I LOVE THE MOMENT WHEN A BELL LIGHT BEGINS TO GLOW..."
THE POETIC WORDS THAT FALL FROM HER LIPS...
SIGH
That's the truth!
SHE'S THE KINDEST GIRL IN THE FOREST AND HAS THE BIGGEST HEART...
Ohh-kay...

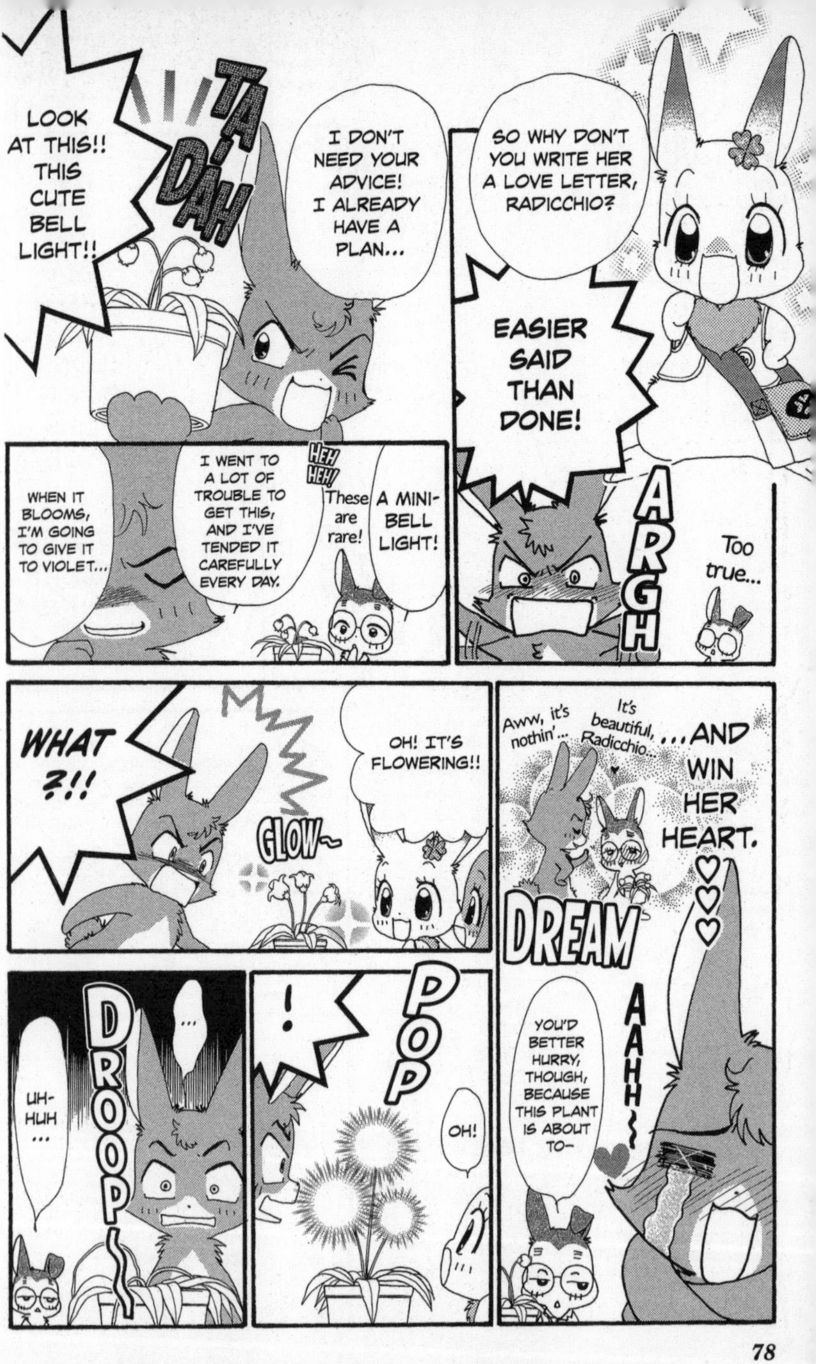
SO WHY DON'T YOU WRITE HER A LOVE LETTER, RADICCHIO?
EASIER SAID THAN DONE!
ARGH
Too true...
I DON'T NEED YOUR ADVICE! I ALREADY HAVE A PLAN...
TA-DAH
LOOK AT THIS!! THIS CUTE BELL LIGHT!!
A MINI-BELL LIGHT!
These are rare!
HEH HEH!
I WENT TO A LOT OF TROUBLE TO GET THIS, AND I'VE TENDED IT CAREFULLY EVERY DAY.
WHEN IT BLOOMS, I'M GOING TO GIVE IT TO VIOLET...
...AND WIN HER HEART.
It's beautiful, Radicchio...
Aww, it's nothin'...
DREAM
AAHH~
YOU'D BETTER HURRY, THOUGH, BECAUSE THIS PLANT IS ABOUT TO–
OH! IT'S FLOWERING!!
GLOW~
WHAT ?!!
POP
!
OH!
DROOP~
...
UH-HUH...

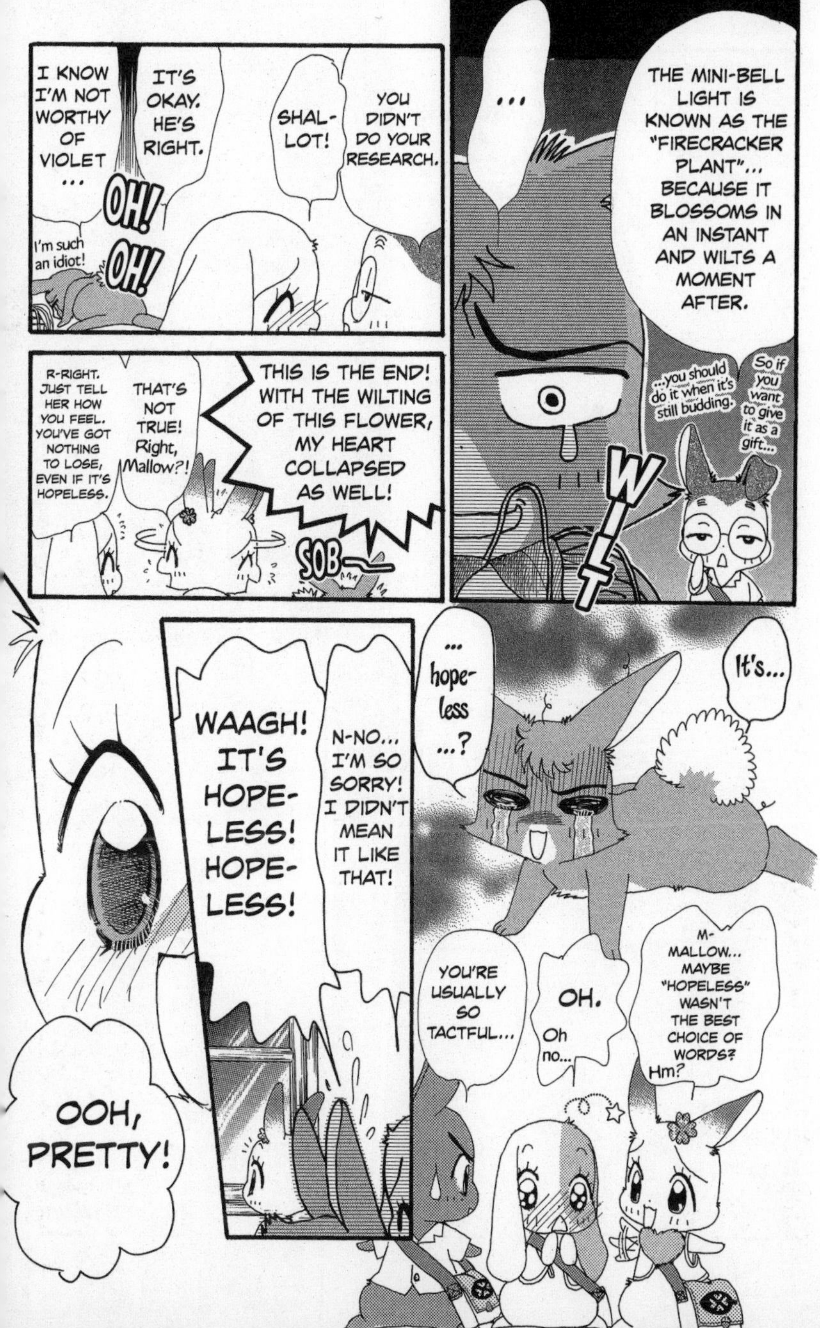

THE MINI-BELL LIGHT IS KNOWN AS THE "FIRECRACKER PLANT"... BECAUSE IT BLOSSOMS IN AN INSTANT AND WILTS A MOMENT AFTER.
...
So if you want to give it as a gift...
...you should do it when it's still budding.
WILT
YOU DIDN'T DO YOUR RESEARCH.
SHAL-LOT!
IT'S OKAY. HE'S RIGHT.
I KNOW I'M NOT WORTHY OF VIOLET...
OH! OH!
I'm such an idiot!
THIS IS THE END! WITH THE WILTING OF THIS FLOWER, MY HEART COLLAPSED AS WELL!
SOB
THAT'S NOT TRUE! Right, Mallow?!
R-RIGHT. JUST TELL HER HOW YOU FEEL. YOU'VE GOT NOTHING TO LOSE, EVEN IF IT'S HOPELESS.
It's...
...hopeless...?
M-MALLOW... MAYBE "HOPELESS" WASN'T THE BEST CHOICE OF WORDS?
Hm?
OH.
Oh no...
YOU'RE USUALLY SO TACTFUL...
N-NO... I'M SO SORRY! I DIDN'T MEAN IT LIKE THAT!
WAAGH! IT'S HOPELESS! HOPELESS!
OOH, PRETTY!

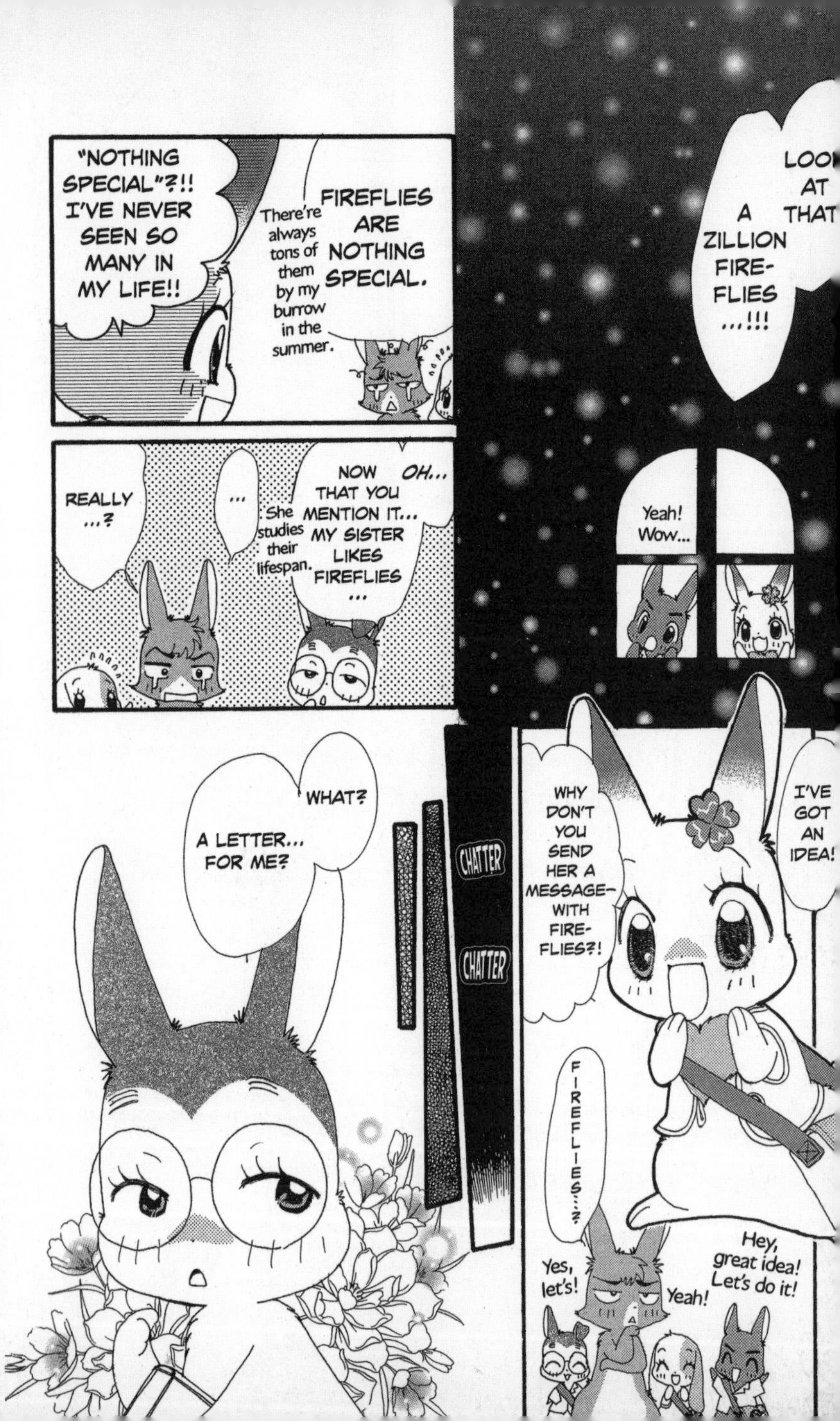
LOOK AT THAT A ZILLION FIRE-FLIES ...!!!
Yeah! Wow...
FIREFLIES ARE NOTHING SPECIAL.
There're always tons of them by my burrow in the summer.
"NOTHING SPECIAL"?!! I'VE NEVER SEEN SO MANY IN MY LIFE!!
OH... NOW THAT YOU MENTION IT... MY SISTER LIKES FIREFLIES ...
She studies their lifespan.
...
REALLY ...?
I'VE GOT AN IDEA!
WHY DON'T YOU SEND HER A MESSAGE—WITH FIRE-FLIES?!
FIREFLIES...?
Hey, great idea! Let's do it!
Yeah!
Yes, let's!
CHATTER
CHATTER
WHAT?
A LETTER... FOR ME?

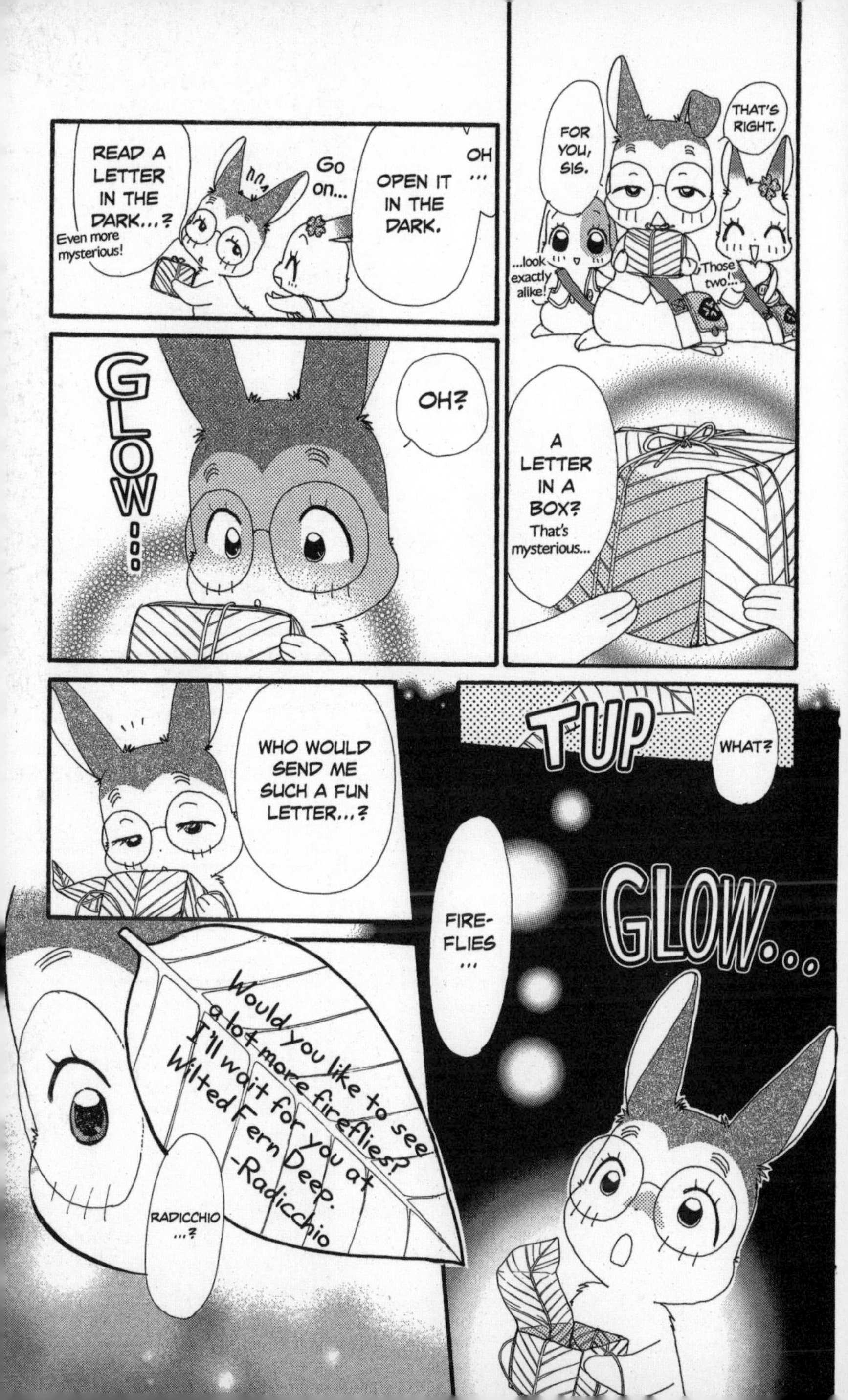
THAT'S RIGHT.
FOR YOU, SIS.
Those two...
...look exactly alike!
OH ...
OPEN IT IN THE DARK.
Go on...
READ A LETTER IN THE DARK...?
Even more mysterious!
A LETTER IN A BOX?
That's mysterious...
OH?
GLOW...
TUP
WHAT?
GLOW...
FIRE-FLIES ...
WHO WOULD SEND ME SUCH A FUN LETTER...?
Would you like to see a lot more fireflies? I'll wait for you at Wilted Fern Deep. -Radicchio
RADICCHIO ...?

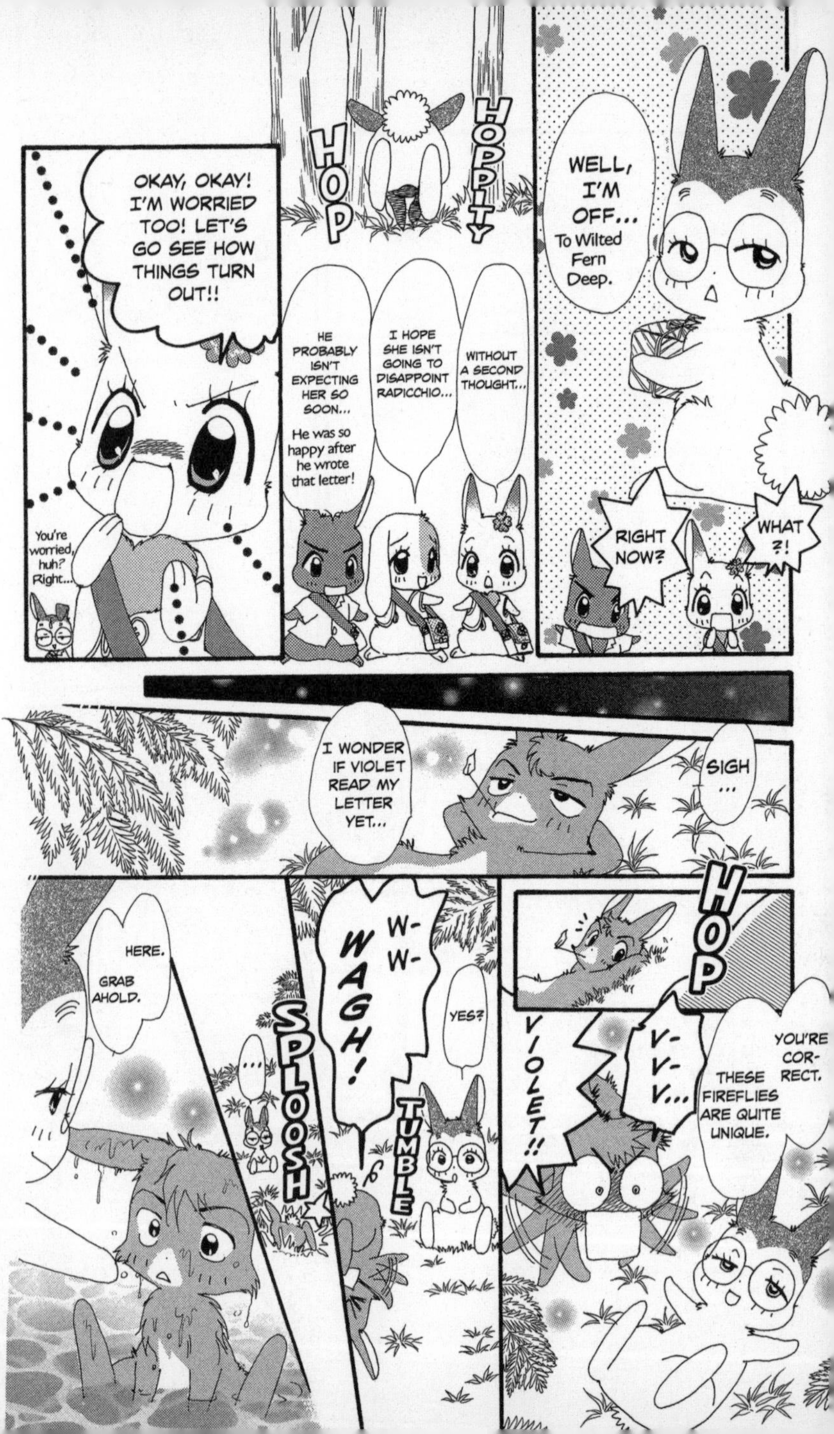
WELL, I'M OFF... To Wilted Fern Deep.
WHAT?!
RIGHT NOW?
HOPPITY
HOP
WITHOUT A SECOND THOUGHT...
I HOPE SHE ISN'T GOING TO DISAPPOINT RADICCHIO...
HE PROBABLY ISN'T EXPECTING HER SO SOON...
He was so happy after he wrote that letter!
OKAY, OKAY! I'M WORRIED TOO! LET'S GO SEE HOW THINGS TURN OUT!!
You're worried, huh? Right...
SIGH...
I WONDER IF VIOLET READ MY LETTER YET...
HOP
YOU'RE CORRECT. THESE FIREFLIES ARE QUITE UNIQUE.
V-V-V...
VIOLET!!
YES?
W-W-WAGH!
TUMBLE
SPLOOSH
...
HERE. GRAB AHOLD.

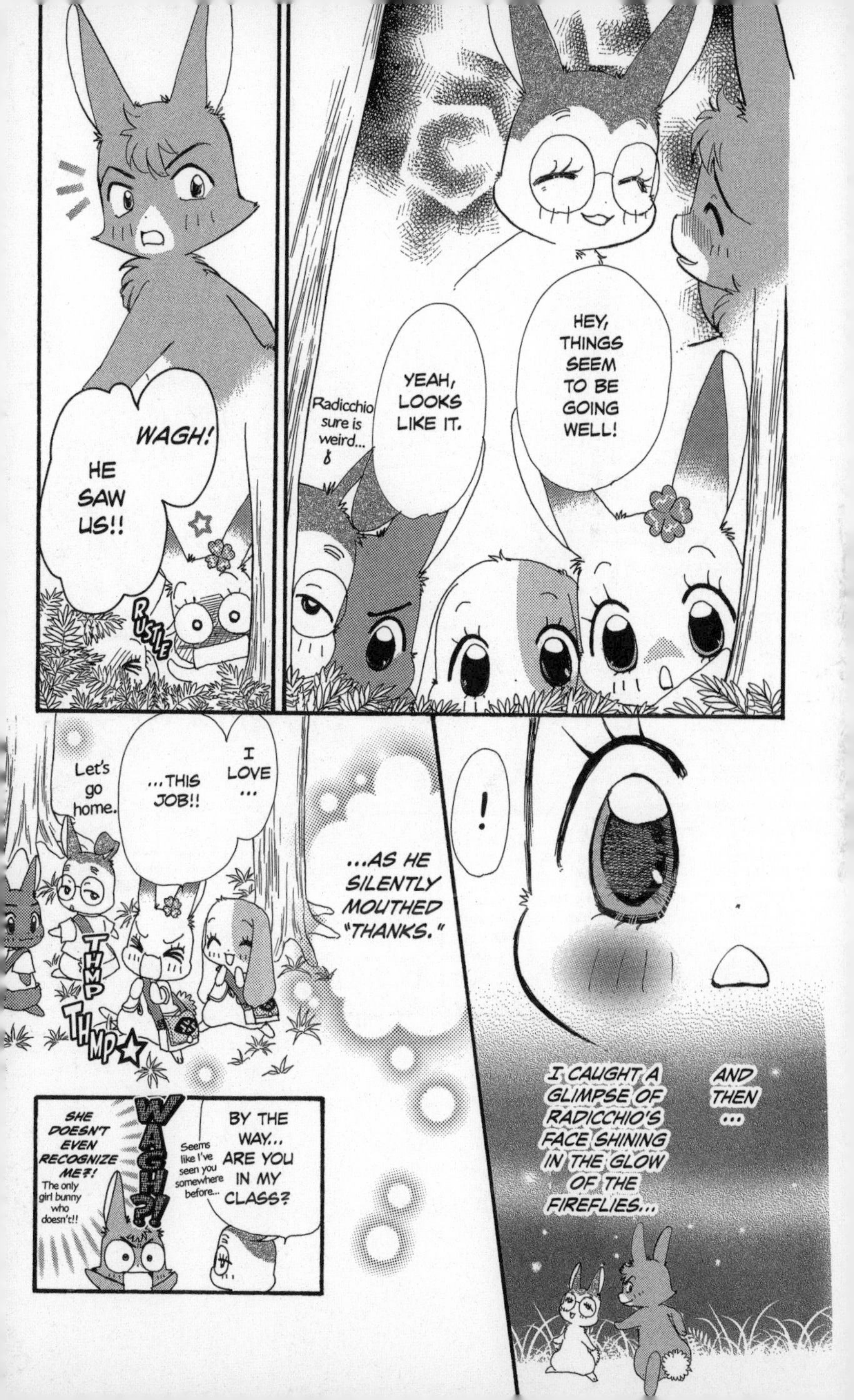
HEY, THINGS SEEM TO BE GOING WELL!
YEAH, LOOKS LIKE IT.
Radicchio sure is weird...
WAGH!
HE SAW US!!
RUSTLE
!
AND THEN...
I CAUGHT A GLIMPSE OF RADICCHIO'S FACE SHINING IN THE GLOW OF THE FIREFLIES...
...AS HE SILENTLY MOUTHED "THANKS."
I LOVE...
...THIS JOB!!
Let's go home.
THMP
THMP
BY THE WAY... ARE YOU IN MY CLASS?
Seems like I've seen you somewhere before...
WAGH?!
SHE DOESN'T EVEN RECOGNIZE ME?!
The only girl bunny who doesn't!!

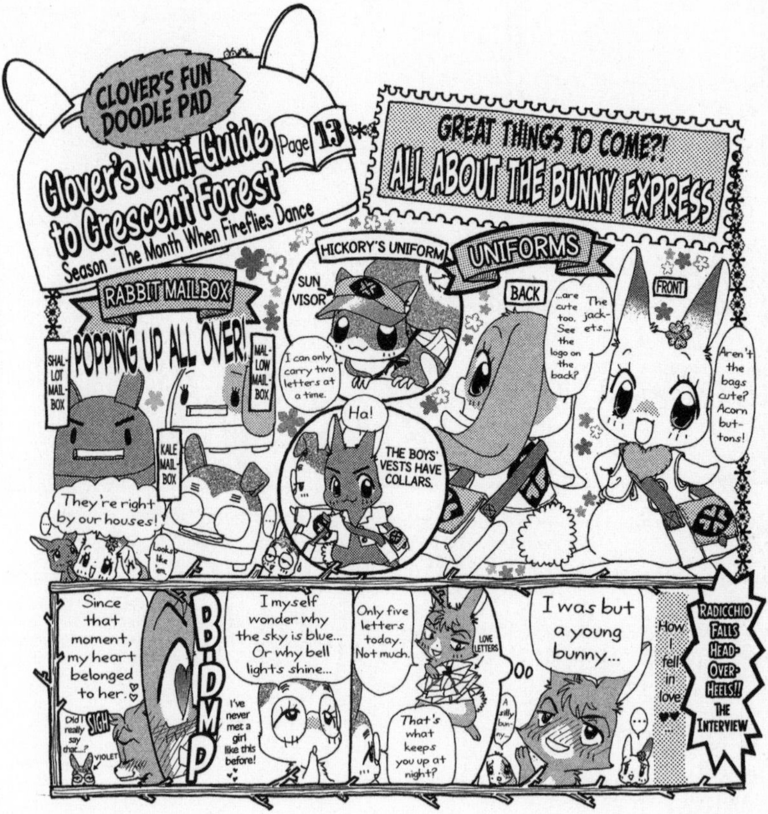
GREAT THINGS TO COME?!
ALL ABOUT THE BUNNY EXPRESS
CLOVER'S FUN DOODLE PAD
Page 13
Clover's Mini-Guide to Crescent Forest
Season - The Month When Fireflies Dance
UNIFORMS
FRONT
Aren't the bags cute? Acorn but-tons!
BACK
The jack-ets...
...are cute too. See the logo on the back?
HICKORY'S UNIFORM
SUN VISOR
I can only carry two letters at a time.
Ha!
THE BOYS' VESTS HAVE COLLARS.
RABBIT MAILBOX
POPPING UP ALL OVER!
MAL-LOW MAIL-BOX
SHAL-LOT MAIL-BOX
KALE MAIL-BOX
They're right by our houses!
Looks like 'em.
RADICCHIO FALLS HEAD-OVER-HEELS!! THE INTERVIEW
How I fell in love
I was but a young bunny...
A silly bun-ny...
Only five letters today. Not much.
LOVE LETTERS
That's what keeps you up at night?
I myself wonder why the sky is blue... Or why bell lights shine...
I've never met a girl like this before!
BDMP
Since that moment, my heart belonged to her.
SIGH
Did I really say that...?
VIOLET

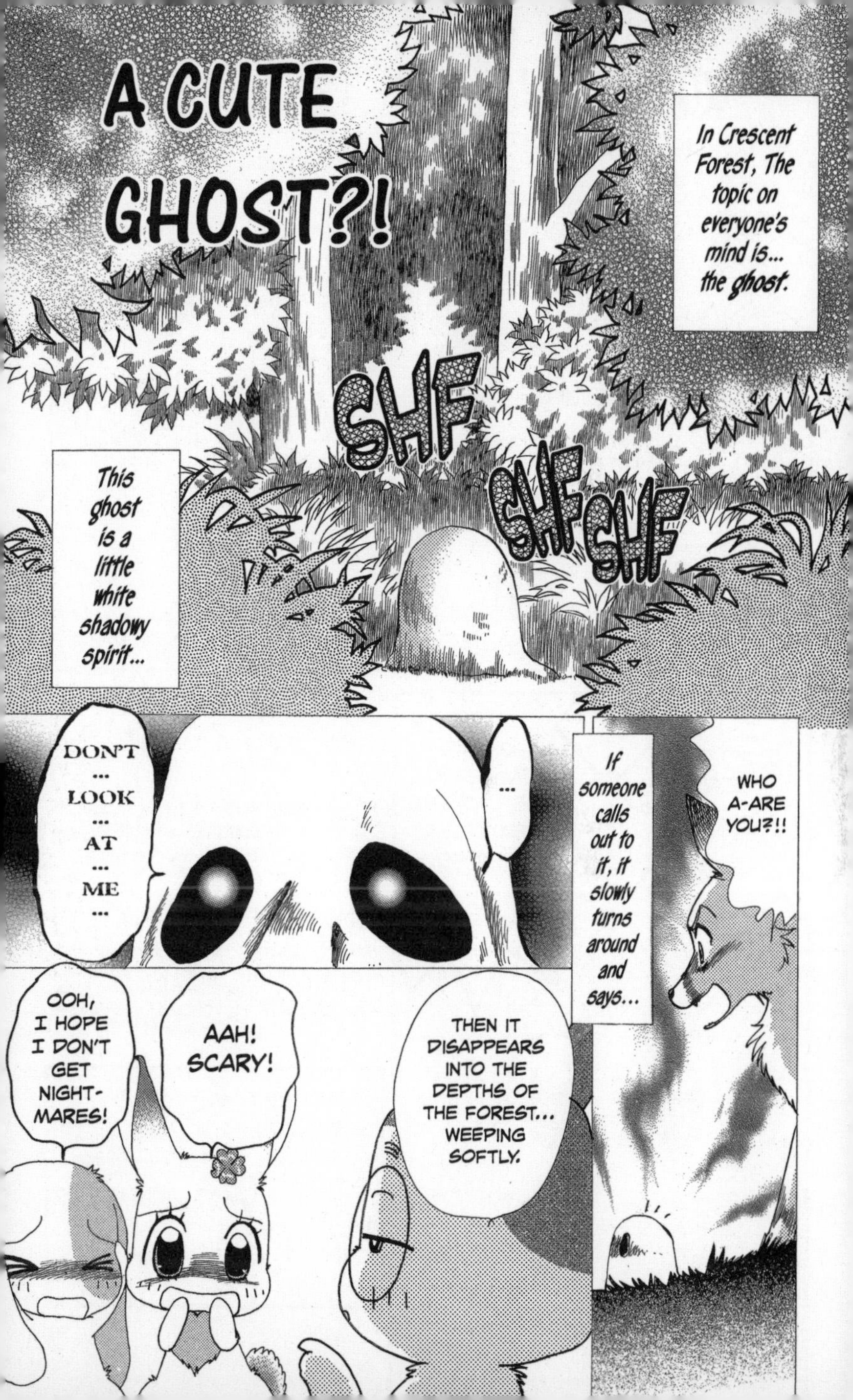
In Crescent Forest, The topic on everyone's mind is... the ghost.
A CUTE GHOST?!
SHF
SHF SHF
This ghost is a little white shadowy spirit...
If someone calls out to it, it slowly turns around and says...
WHO A-ARE YOU?!!
...
DON'T ... LOOK ... AT ... ME ...
THEN IT DISAPPEARS INTO THE DEPTHS OF THE FOREST... WEEPING SOFTLY.
AAH! SCARY!
OOH, I HOPE I DON'T GET NIGHT-MARES!

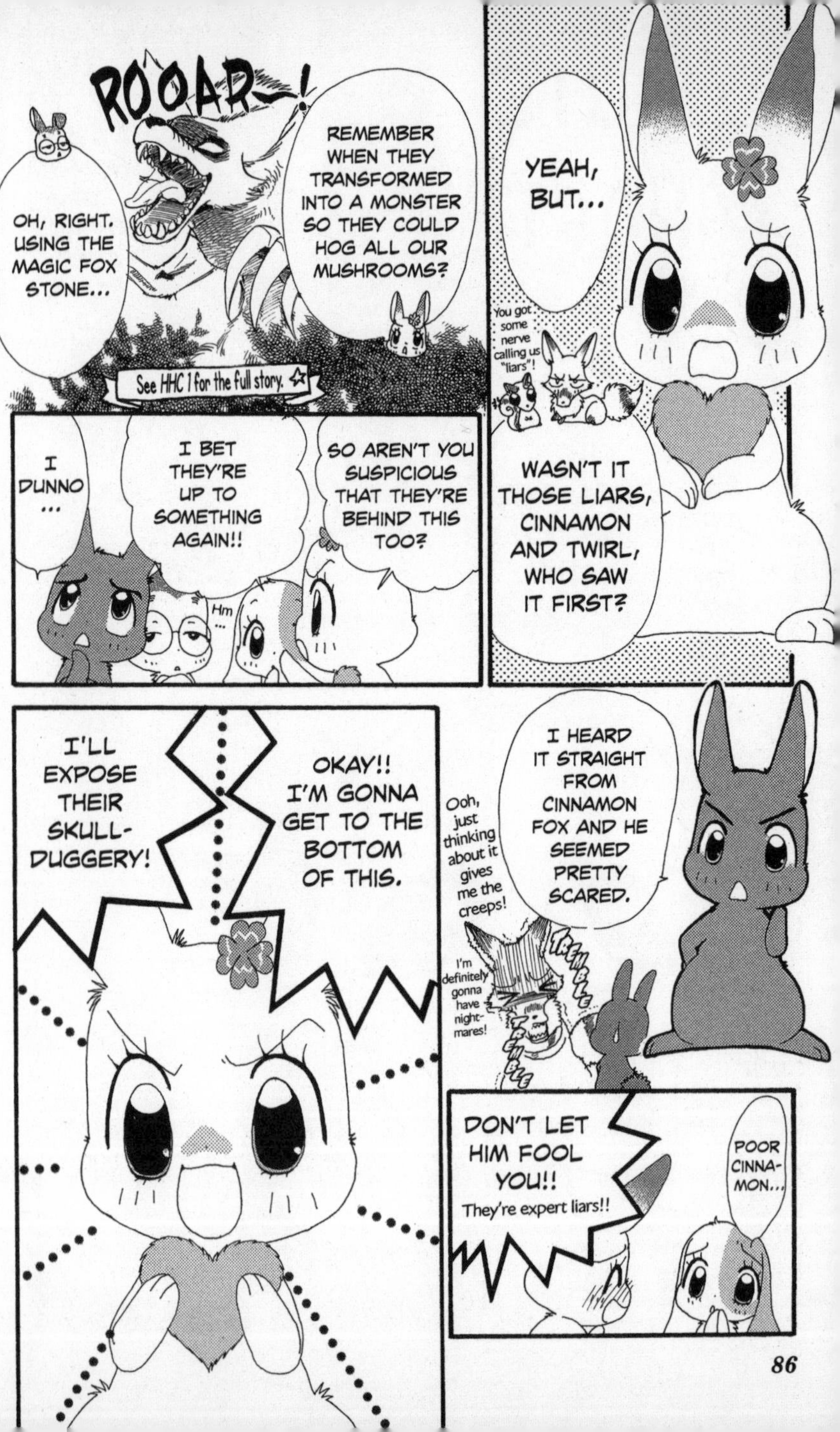
YEAH, BUT...
WASN'T IT THOSE LIARS, CINNAMON AND TWIRL, WHO SAW IT FIRST?
You got some nerve calling us "liars"!
ROOAR—!
REMEMBER WHEN THEY TRANSFORMED INTO A MONSTER SO THEY COULD HOG ALL OUR MUSHROOMS?
OH, RIGHT. USING THE MAGIC FOX STONE...
See HHC 1 for the full story.
SO AREN'T YOU SUSPICIOUS THAT THEY'RE BEHIND THIS TOO?
Hm...
I BET THEY'RE UP TO SOMETHING AGAIN!!
I DUNNO...
I HEARD IT STRAIGHT FROM CINNAMON FOX AND HE SEEMED PRETTY SCARED.
Ooh, just thinking about it gives me the creeps!
TREMBLE
I'm definitely gonna have night-mares!
DON'T LET HIM FOOL YOU!!
They're expert liars!!
POOR CINNA-MON...
OKAY!! I'M GONNA GET TO THE BOTTOM OF THIS.
I'LL EXPOSE THEIR SKULL-DUGGERY!

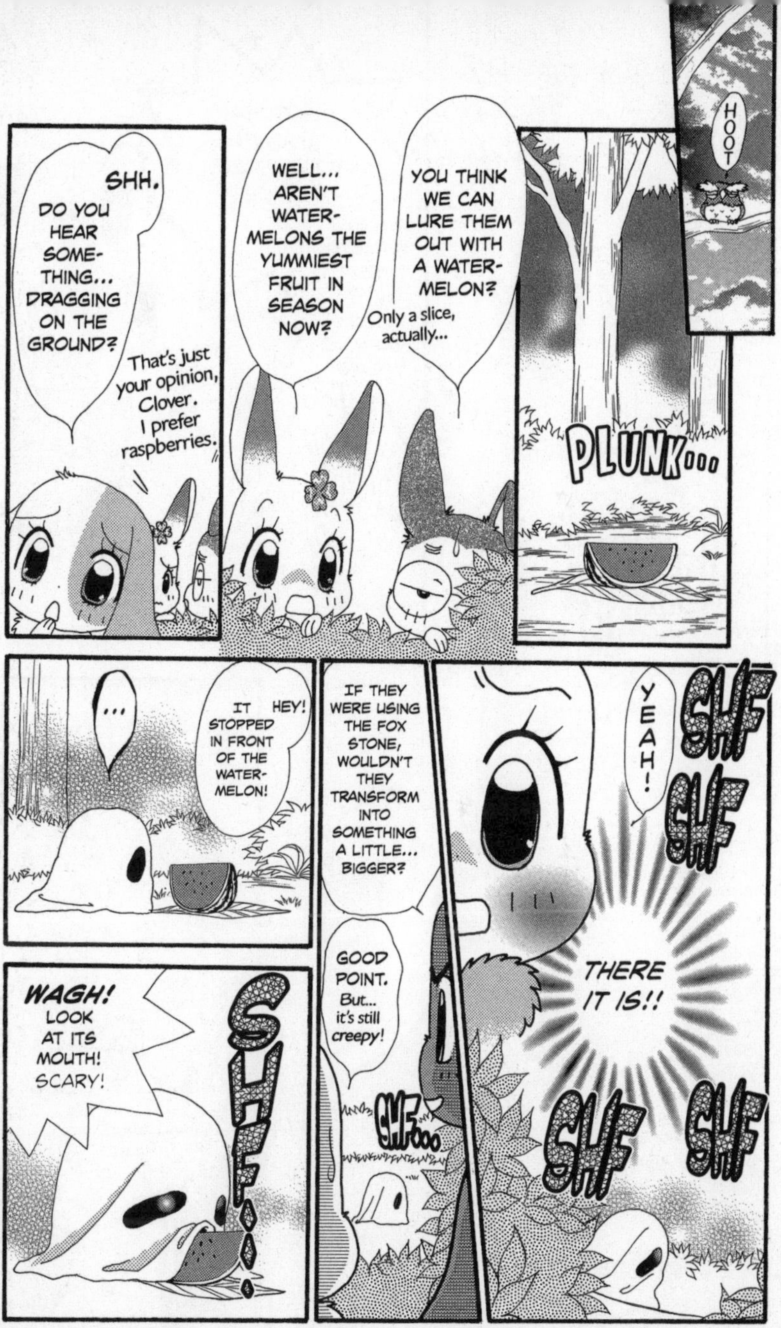
HOOT
PLUNK...
YOU THINK WE CAN LURE THEM OUT WITH A WATERMELON?
Only a slice, actually...
WELL... AREN'T WATERMELONS THE YUMMIEST FRUIT IN SEASON NOW?
SHH.
DO YOU HEAR SOMETHING... DRAGGING ON THE GROUND?
That's just your opinion, Clover. I prefer raspberries.
YEAH!
SHF SHF
THERE IT IS!!
SHF SHF
IF THEY WERE USING THE FOX STONE, WOULDN'T THEY TRANSFORM INTO SOMETHING A LITTLE... BIGGER?
GOOD POINT. But... it's still creepy!
SHF...
HEY! IT STOPPED IN FRONT OF THE WATERMELON!
...
WAGH! LOOK AT ITS MOUTH! SCARY!
SHHF...

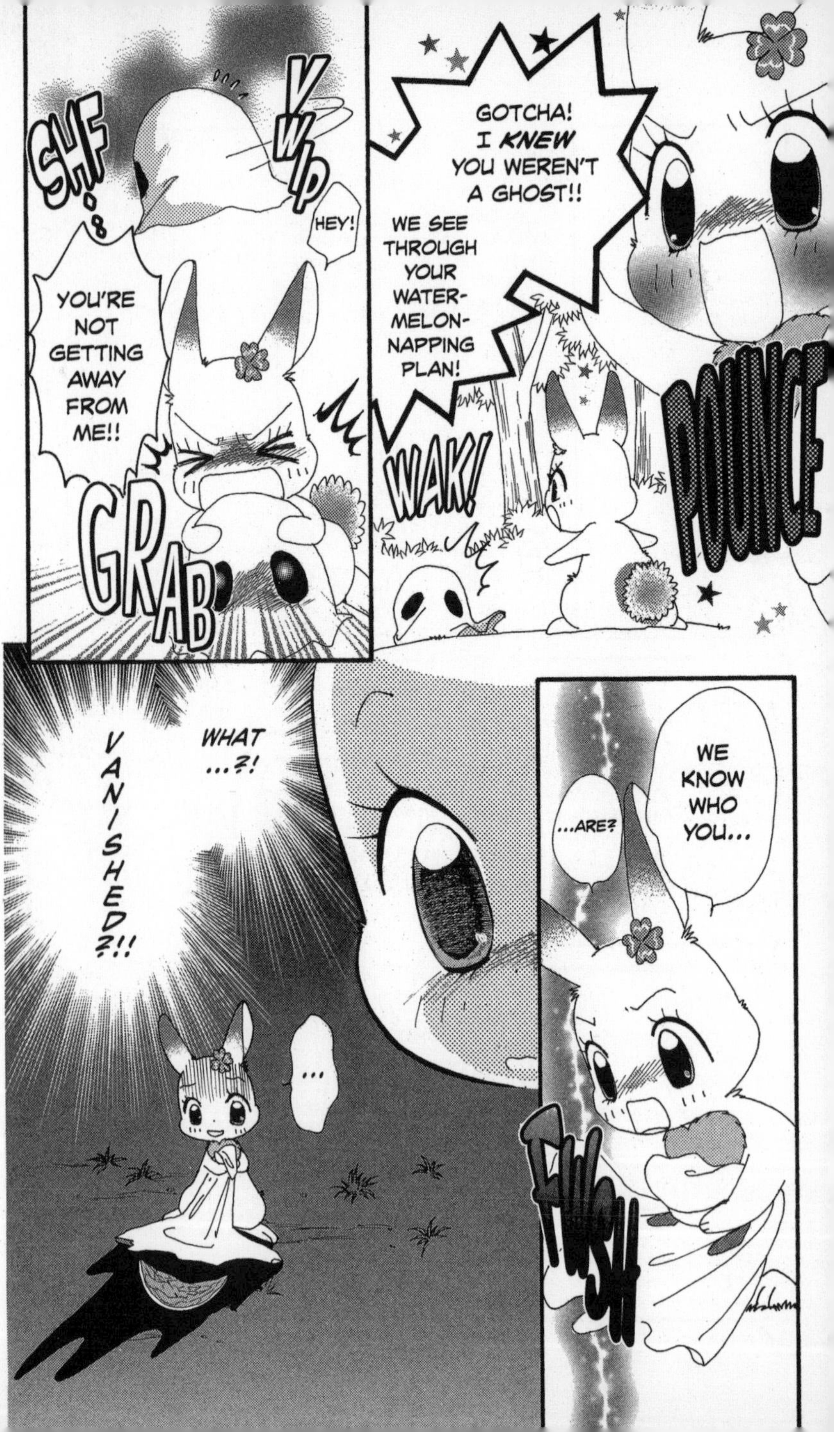

GOTCHA! I *KNEW* YOU WEREN'T A GHOST!!
POUNCE
WE SEE THROUGH YOUR WATER-MELON-NAPPING PLAN!
WAK!
VWIP
HEY!
SHF
YOU'RE NOT GETTING AWAY FROM ME!!
GRAB
WE KNOW WHO YOU...
...ARE?
FWISH
VANISHED?!!
WHAT ...?!
...

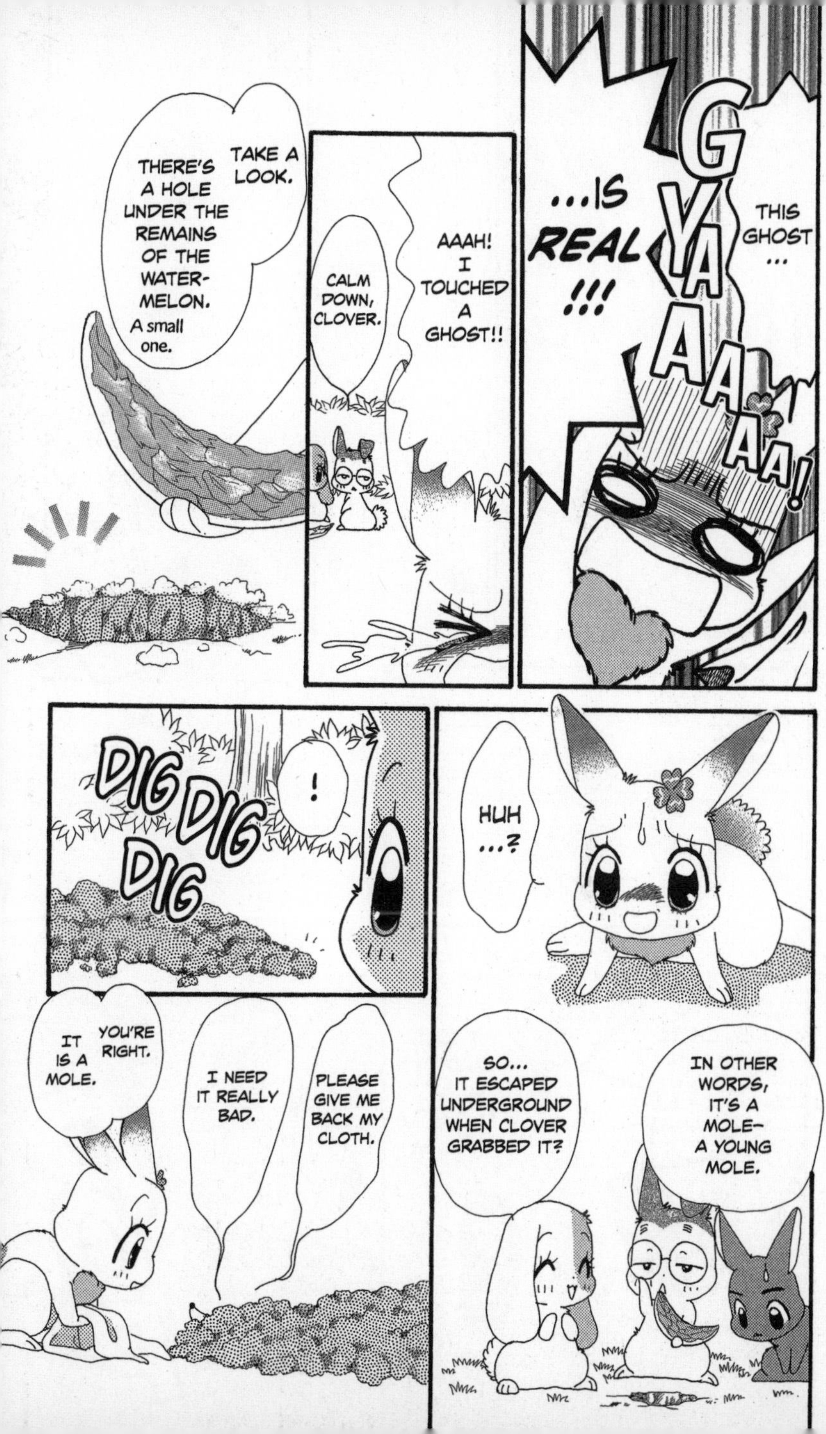
THIS GHOST...
...IS REAL!!!
GYAAAAAA!
AAAH! I TOUCHED A GHOST!!
CALM DOWN, CLOVER.
TAKE A LOOK.
THERE'S A HOLE UNDER THE REMAINS OF THE WATER-MELON.
A small one.
HUH...?
!
DIG DIG DIG
IN OTHER WORDS, IT'S A MOLE— A YOUNG MOLE.
SO... IT ESCAPED UNDERGROUND WHEN CLOVER GRABBED IT?
PLEASE GIVE ME BACK MY CLOTH.
I NEED IT REALLY BAD.
YOU'RE RIGHT.
IT IS A MOLE.

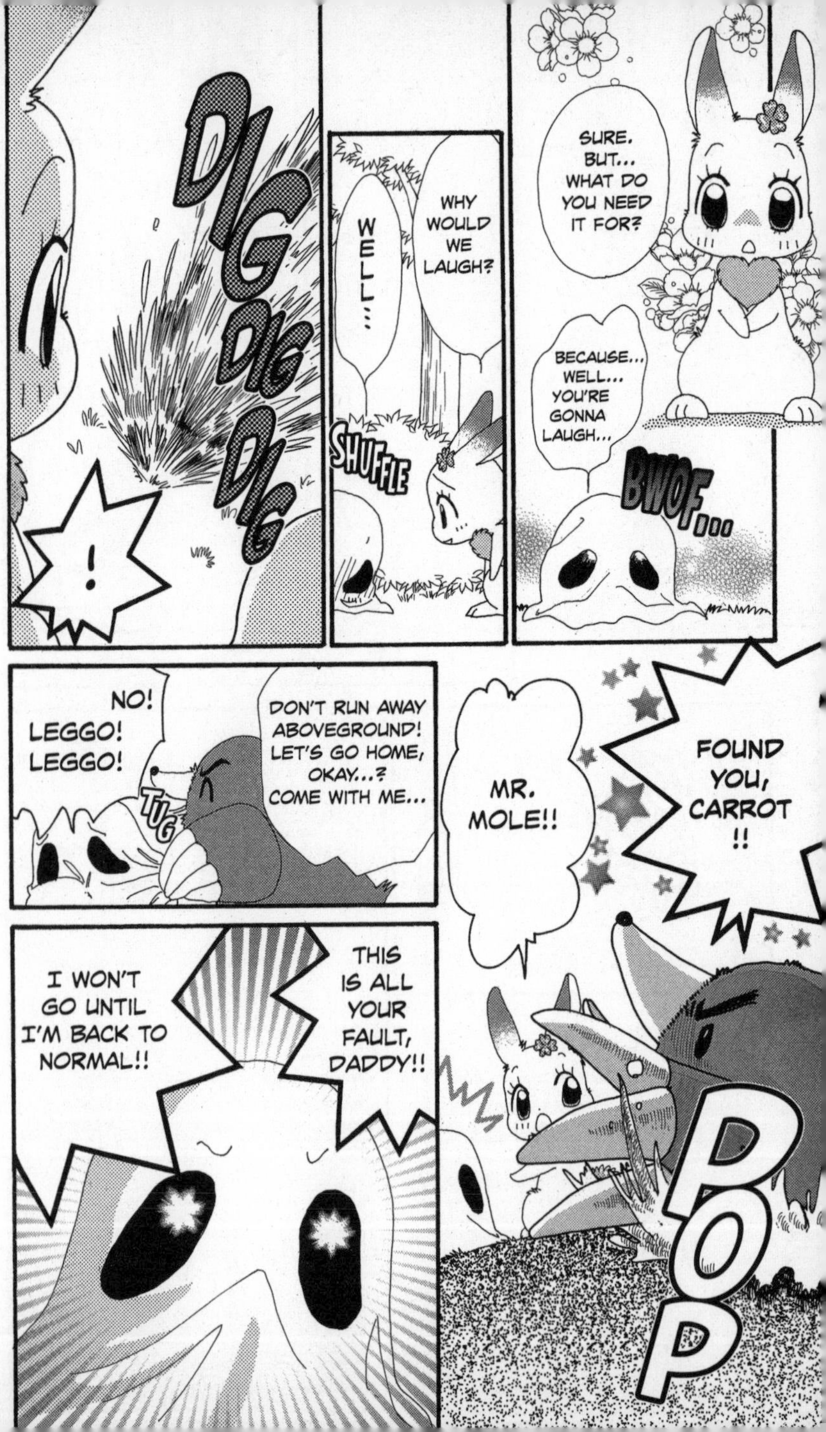
SURE. BUT... WHAT DO YOU NEED IT FOR?
BECAUSE... WELL... YOU'RE GONNA LAUGH...
BWOF...
WHY WOULD WE LAUGH?
WELL...
SHUFFLE
DIG DIG DIG
!
FOUND YOU, CARROT!!
MR. MOLE!!
POP
DON'T RUN AWAY ABOVEGROUND! LET'S GO HOME, OKAY...? COME WITH ME...
NO! LEGGO! LEGGO!
TUG
THIS IS ALL YOUR FAULT, DADDY!!
I WON'T GO UNTIL I'M BACK TO NORMAL!!

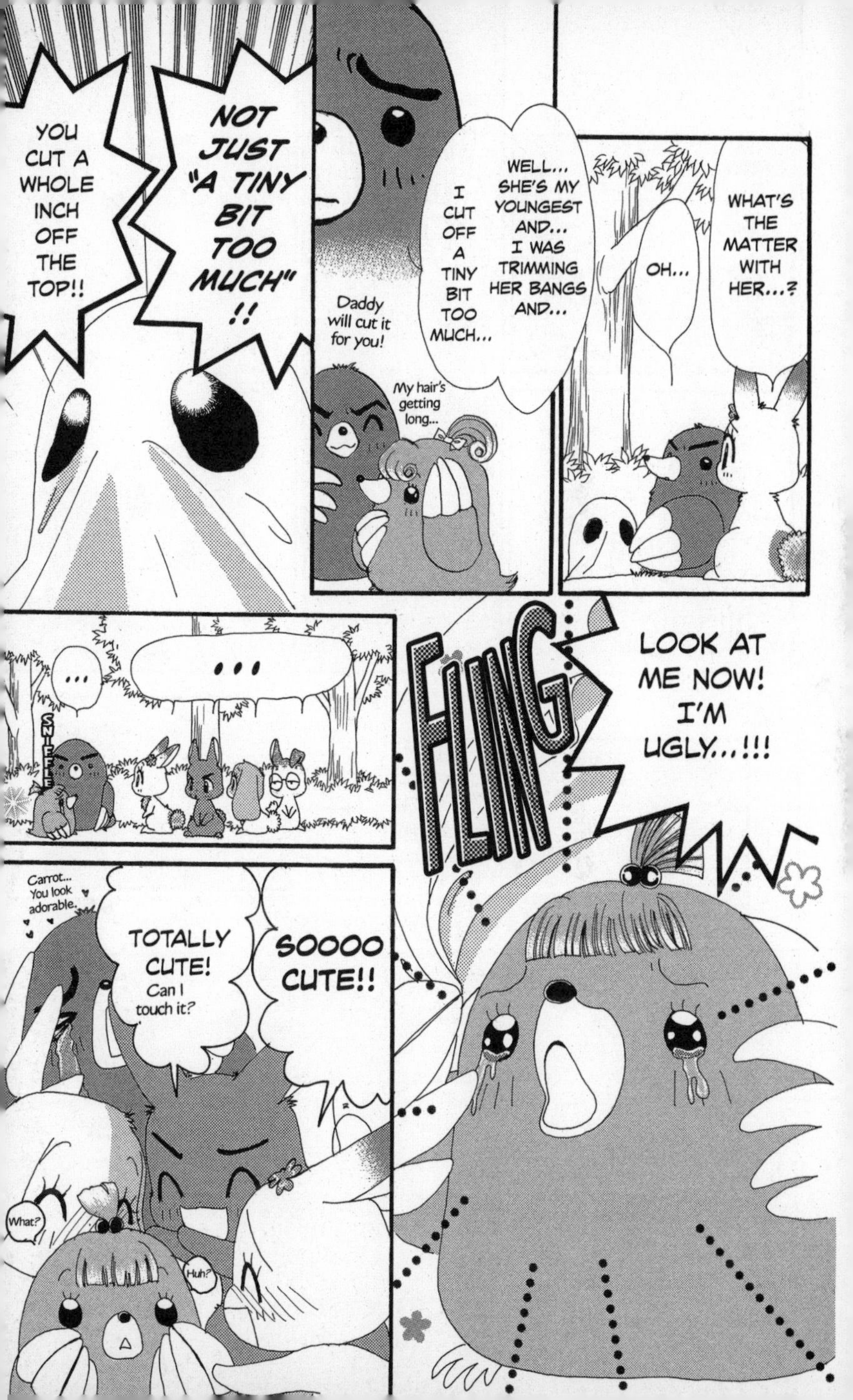
WHAT'S THE MATTER WITH HER...?
OH...
WELL... SHE'S MY YOUNGEST AND... I WAS TRIMMING HER BANGS AND...
I CUT OFF A TINY BIT TOO MUCH...
Daddy will cut it for you!
My hair's getting long...
NOT JUST "A TINY BIT TOO MUCH"!!
YOU CUT A WHOLE INCH OFF THE TOP!!
LOOK AT ME NOW! I'M UGLY...!!!
FLING
...
...
SNIFFLE
SOOOO CUTE!!
TOTALLY CUTE! Can I touch it?
Carrot... You look adorable.
What?
Huh?

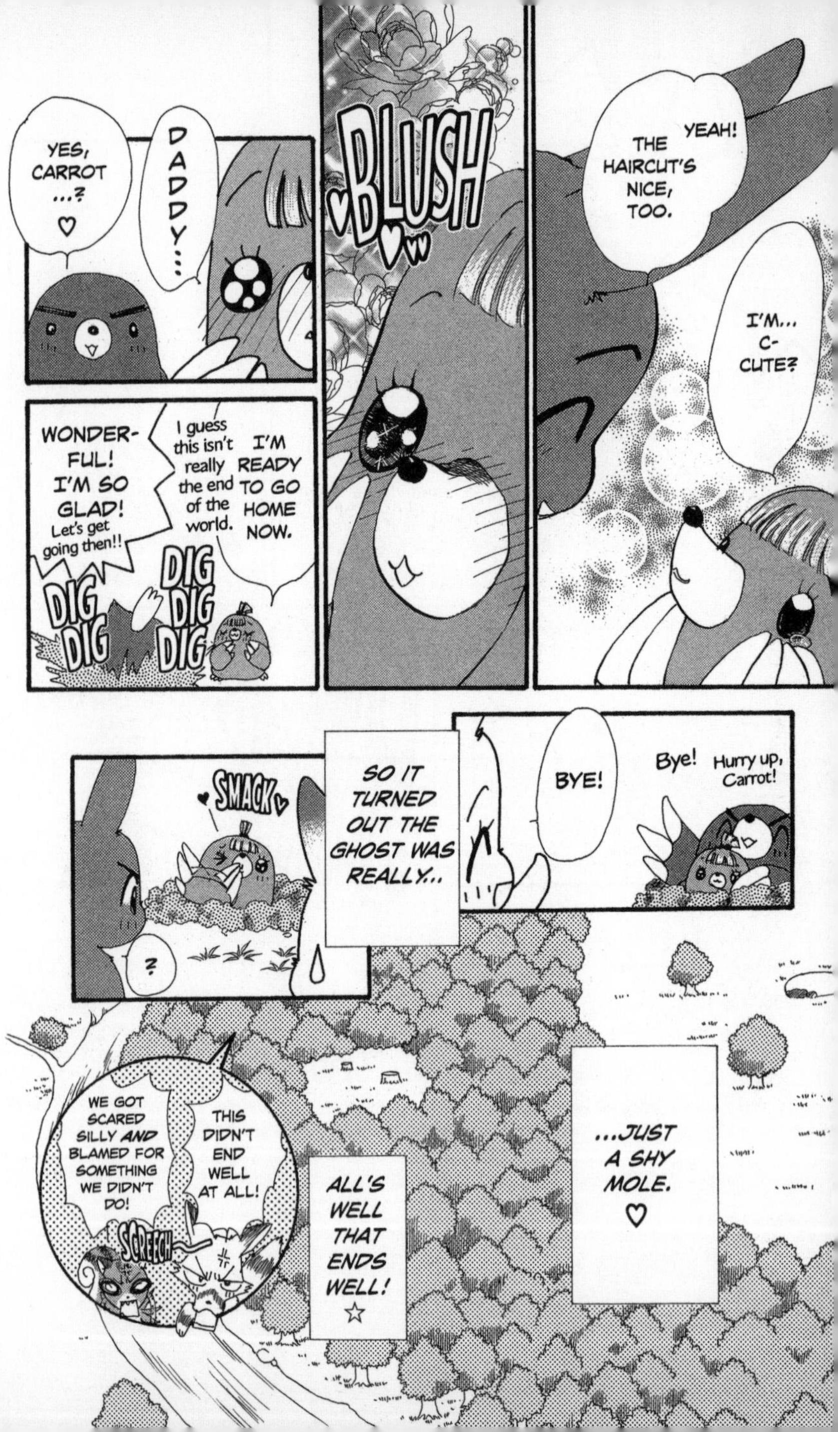

YEAH! THE HAIRCUT'S NICE, TOO.
I'M... C-CUTE?
BLUSH
DADDY...
YES, CARROT...? ♡
I'M READY TO GO HOME NOW.
I guess this isn't really the end of the world.
WONDERFUL! I'M SO GLAD! Let's get going then!!
DIG DIG DIG
DIG DIG
Hurry up, Carrot!
Bye!
BYE!
SO IT TURNED OUT THE GHOST WAS REALLY...
SMACK
?
...JUST A SHY MOLE. ♡
ALL'S WELL THAT ENDS WELL! ☆
THIS DIDN'T END WELL AT ALL!
WE GOT SCARED SILLY AND BLAMED FOR SOMETHING WE DIDN'T DO!
SCREECH

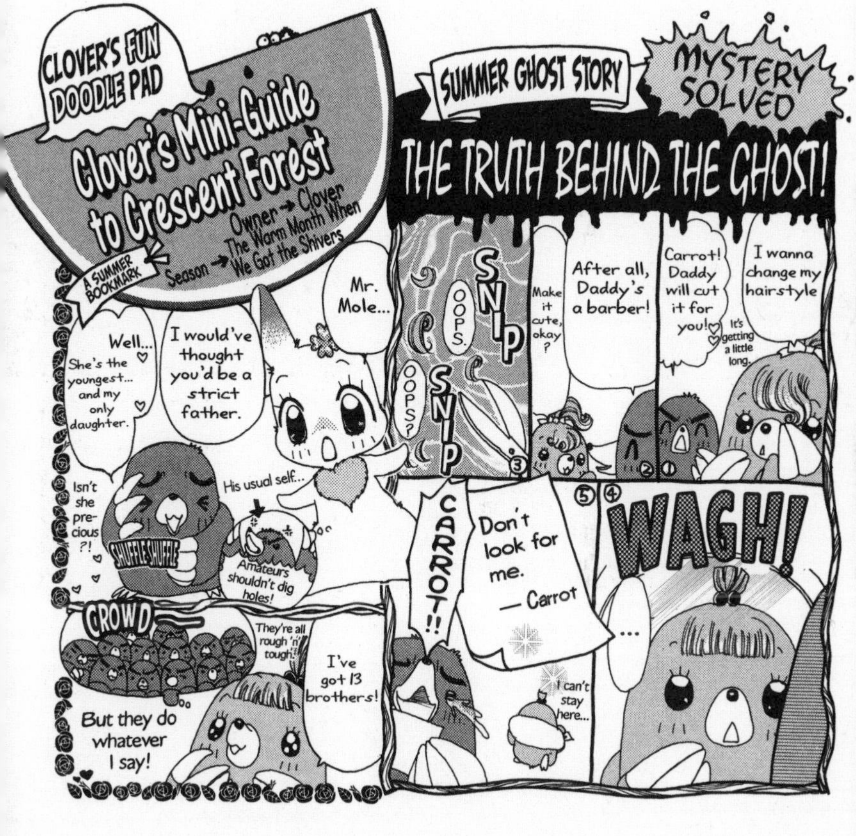
SUMMER GHOST STORY
MYSTERY SOLVED
THE TRUTH BEHIND THE GHOST!
I wanna change my hairstyle
It's getting a little long.
Carrot! Daddy will cut it for you!
After all, Daddy's a barber!
Make it cute, okay?
SNIP
OOPS.
SNIP
OOPS?
WAGH!
...
Don't look for me. — Carrot
CARROT!!
I can't stay here...
CLOVER'S FUN DOODLE PAD
Clover's Mini-Guide to Crescent Forest
Owner → Clover
Season → The Warm Month When We Got the Shivers
A SUMMER BOOKMARK
Mr. Mole...
I would've thought you'd be a strict father.
Well... She's the youngest... and my only daughter.
Isn't she precious?!
SHUFFLE SHUFFLE
His usual self...
Amateurs shouldn't dig holes!
CROWD
They're all rough 'n' tough!
I've got 13 brothers!
But they do whatever I say!

SNIFF
SNIFF

Clover, drawn a bit more realistically. Smelling the wind...

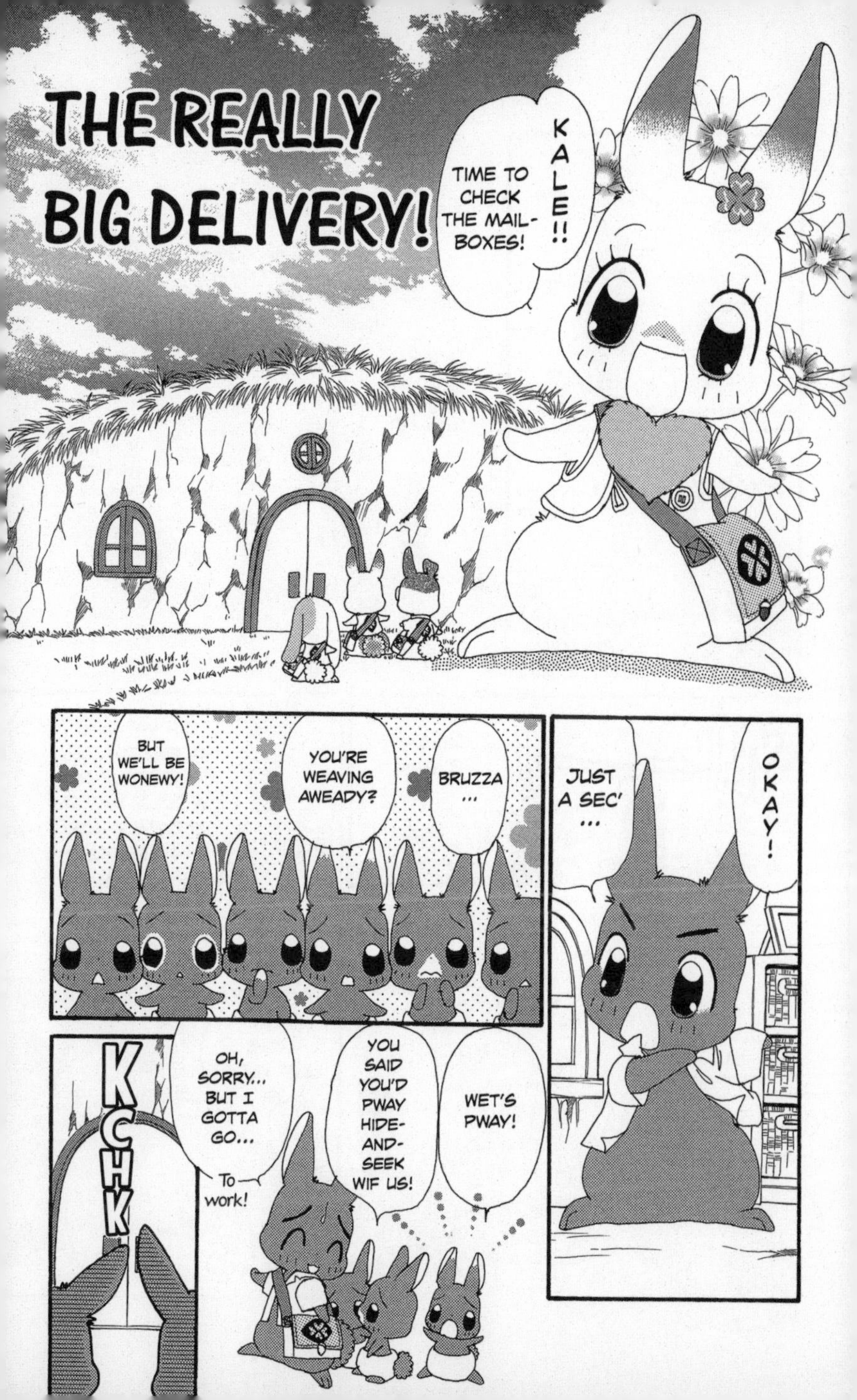
THE REALLY BIG DELIVERY!
KALE!!
TIME TO CHECK THE MAIL-BOXES!
OKAY!
JUST A SEC' ...
BRUZZA ...
YOU'RE WEAVING AWEADY?
BUT WE'LL BE WONEWY!
WET'S PWAY!
YOU SAID YOU'D PWAY HIDE-AND-SEEK WIF US!
OH, SORRY... BUT I GOTTA GO...
To work!
KCHK

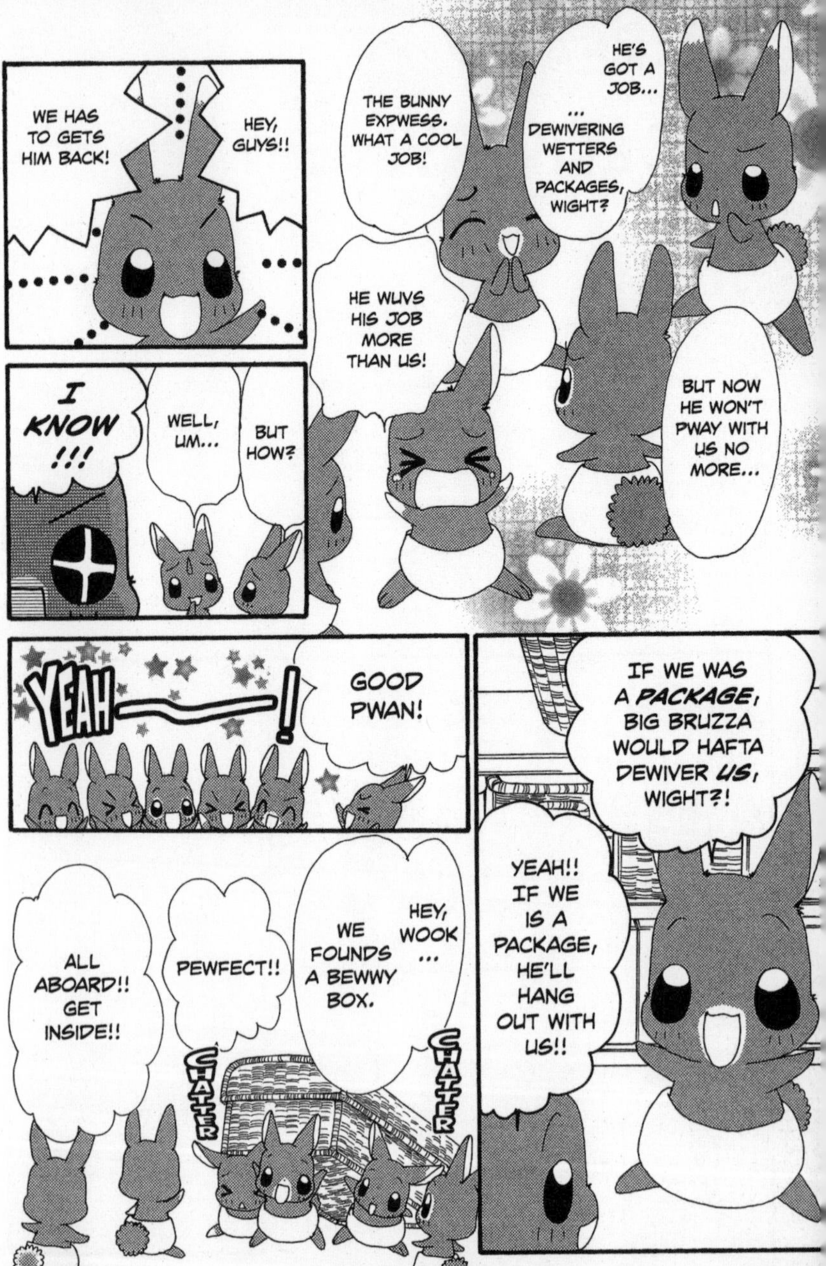
HE'S GOT A JOB...
...DEWIVERING WETTERS AND PACKAGES, WIGHT?
THE BUNNY EXPWESS. WHAT A COOL JOB!
HE WUVS HIS JOB MORE THAN US!
BUT NOW HE WON'T PWAY WITH US NO MORE...
HEY, GUYS!!
WE HAS TO GETS HIM BACK!
BUT HOW?
WELL, UM...
I KNOW!!!
IF WE WAS A *PACKAGE*, BIG BRUZZA WOULD HAFTA DEWIVER *US*, WIGHT?!
YEAH!! IF WE IS A PACKAGE, HE'LL HANG OUT WITH US!!
GOOD PWAN!
YEAH—!
HEY, WOOK...
WE FOUNDS A BEWWY BOX.
CHATTER
CHATTER
PEWFECT!!
ALL ABOARD!! GET INSIDE!!

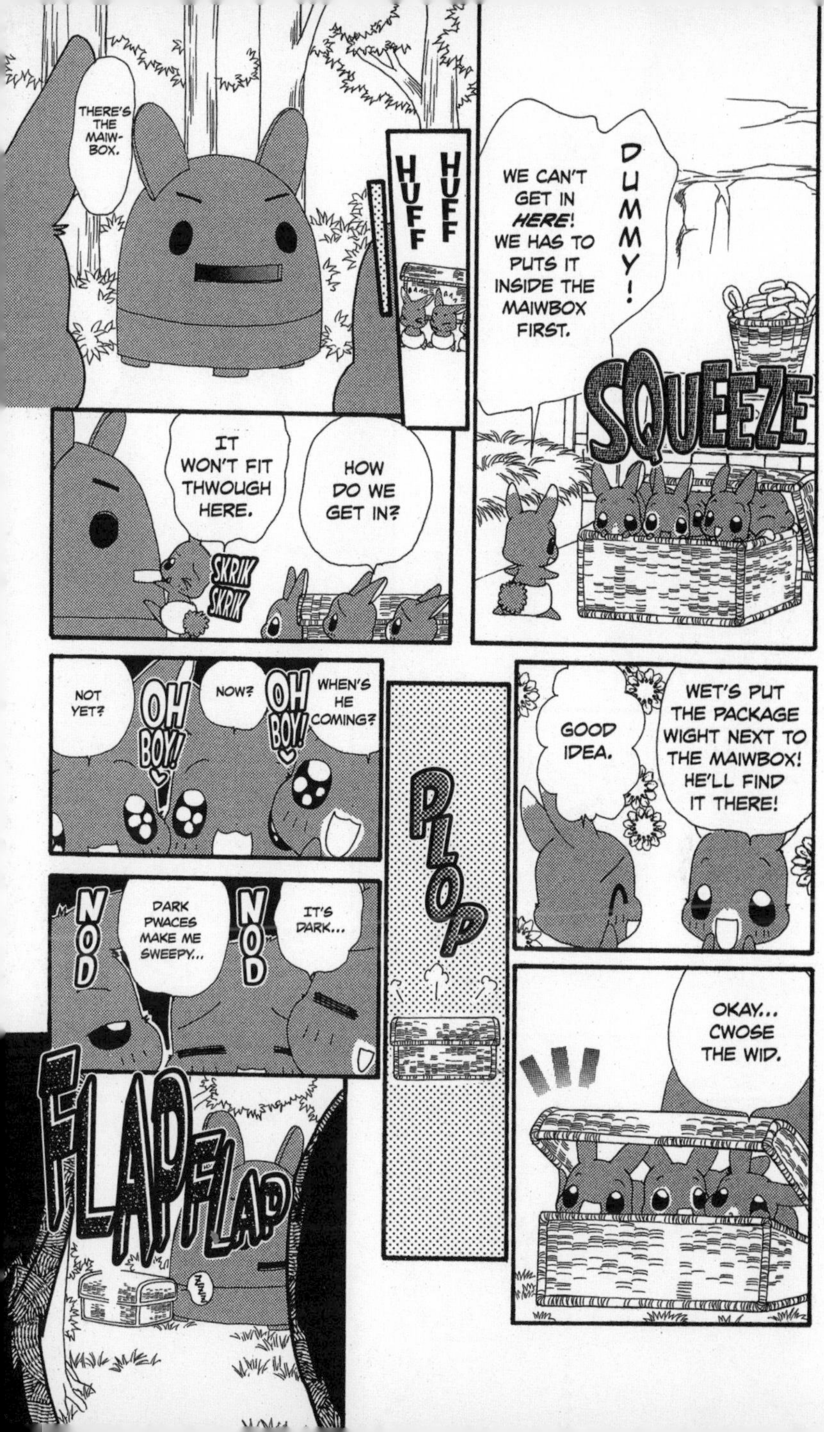
DUMMY!
WE CAN'T GET IN HERE! WE HAS TO PUTS IT INSIDE THE MAIWBOX FIRST.
SQUEEZE
HUFF HUFF
THERE'S THE MAIW-BOX.
HOW DO WE GET IN?
IT WON'T FIT THWOUGH HERE.
SKRIK SKRIK
WET'S PUT THE PACKAGE WIGHT NEXT TO THE MAIWBOX! HE'LL FIND IT THERE!
GOOD IDEA.
OKAY... CWOSE THE WID.
PLOP
WHEN'S HE COMING?
OH BOY!
NOW?
OH BOY!
NOT YET?
IT'S DARK...
NOD
DARK PWACES MAKE ME SWEEPY...
NOD
FLAP FLAP

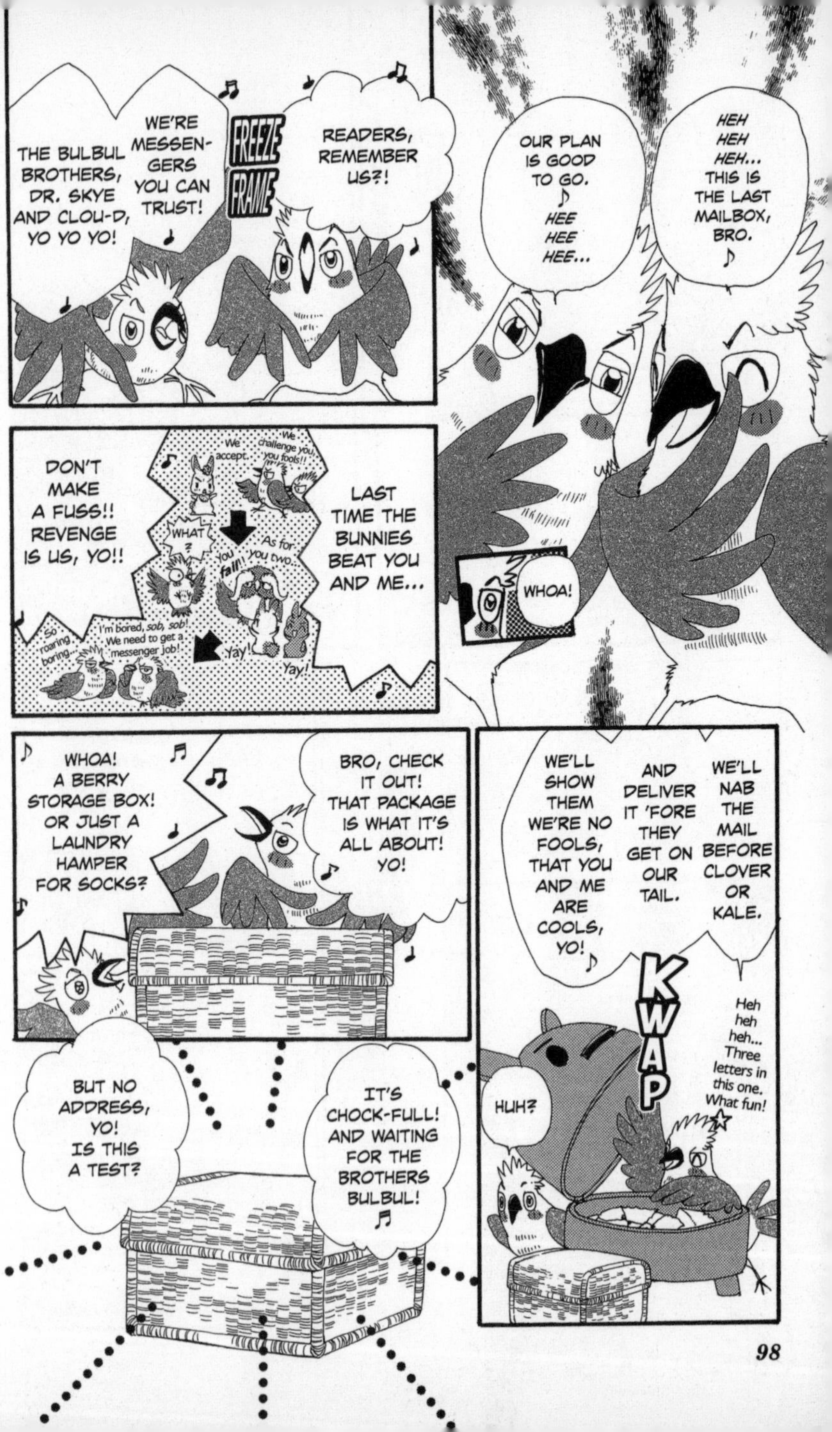
HEH HEH HEH... THIS IS THE LAST MAILBOX, BRO. ♪
OUR PLAN IS GOOD TO GO. ♪ HEE HEE HEE...
WHOA!
READERS, REMEMBER US?!
FREEZE FRAME
WE'RE MESSENGERS YOU CAN TRUST!
THE BULBUL BROTHERS, DR. SKYE AND CLOU-D, YO YO YO!
LAST TIME THE BUNNIES BEAT YOU AND ME...
We challenge you, you fools!!
We accept.
WHAT?
As for you two...
You fail!!
Yay!
Yay!
I'm bored, sob, sob! We need to get a messenger job!
So roaring boring...
DON'T MAKE A FUSS!! REVENGE IS US, YO!!
WE'LL NAB THE MAIL BEFORE CLOVER OR KALE.
AND DELIVER IT 'FORE THEY GET ON OUR TAIL.
WE'LL SHOW THEM WE'RE NO FOOLS, THAT YOU AND ME ARE COOLS, YO! ♪
Heh heh heh... Three letters in this one. What fun!
KWAP
HUH?
BRO, CHECK IT OUT! THAT PACKAGE IS WHAT IT'S ALL ABOUT! YO!
WHOA! A BERRY STORAGE BOX! OR JUST A LAUNDRY HAMPER FOR SOCKS?
IT'S CHOCK-FULL! AND WAITING FOR THE BROTHERS BULBUL! ♬
BUT NO ADDRESS, YO! IS THIS A TEST?

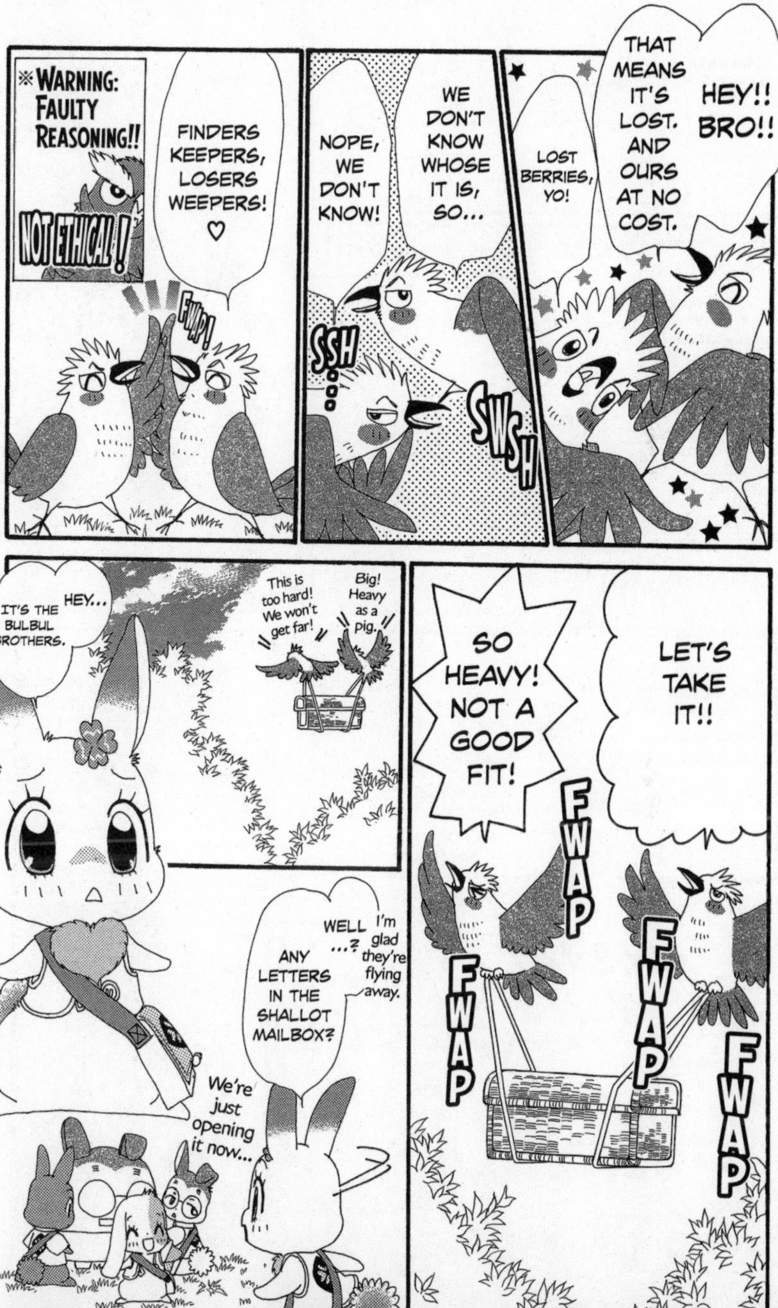
HEY!! BRO!!
THAT MEANS IT'S LOST. AND OURS AT NO COST.
LOST BERRIES, YO!
WE DON'T KNOW WHOSE IT IS, SO...
NOPE, WE DON'T KNOW!
SSH
SWSH
FINDERS KEEPERS, LOSERS WEEPERS! ♡
FWP!
※WARNING: FAULTY REASONING!!
NOT ETHICAL!
LET'S TAKE IT!!
SO HEAVY! NOT A GOOD FIT!
FWAP
FWAP
FWAP
FWAP
Big! Heavy as a pig.
This is too hard! We won't get far!
HEY...
IT'S THE BULBUL BROTHERS.
I'm glad they're flying away.
WELL ...?
ANY LETTERS IN THE SHALLOT MAILBOX?
We're just opening it now...

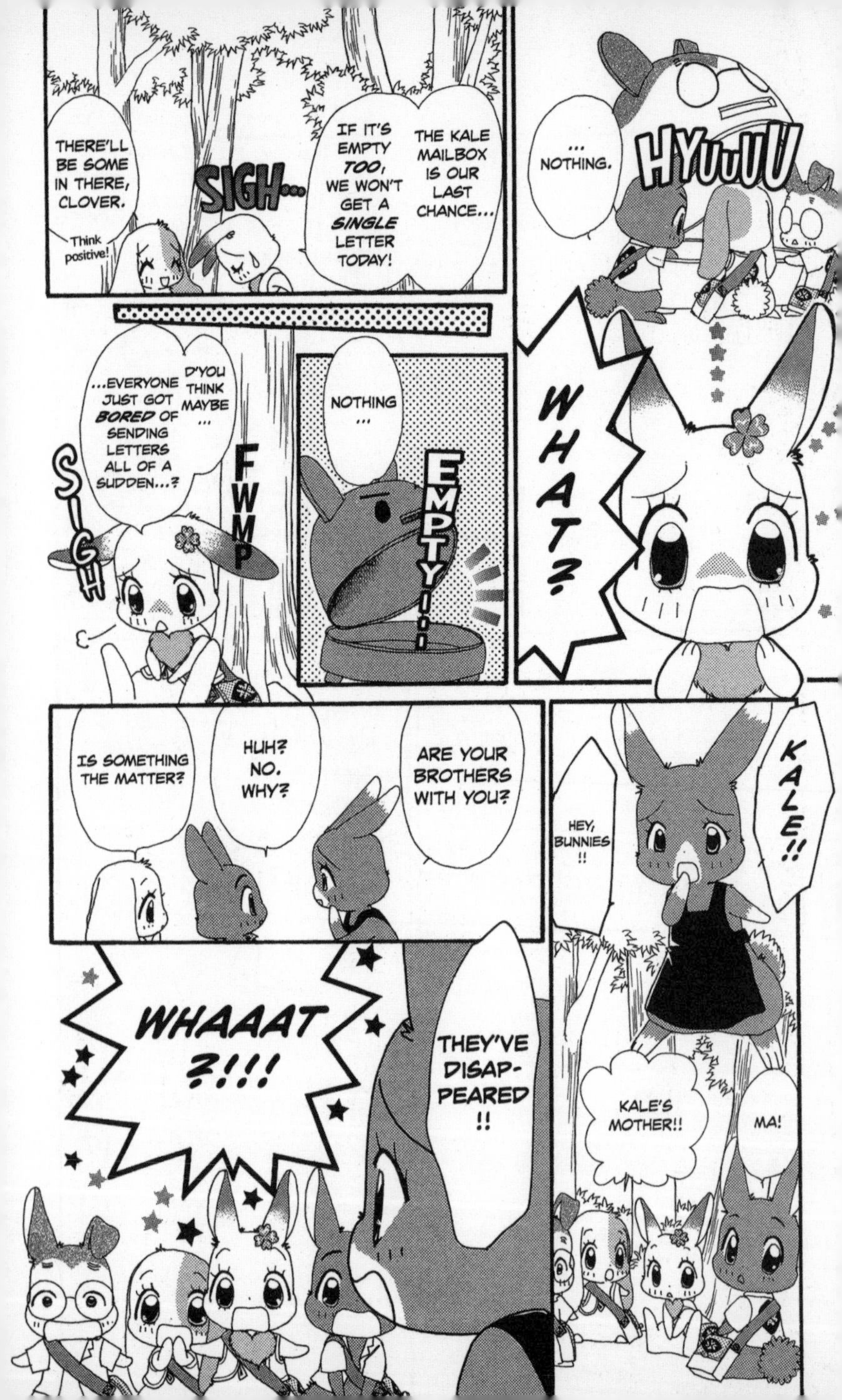
... NOTHING.
HYUUUU
THE KALE MAILBOX IS OUR LAST CHANCE...
IF IT'S EMPTY *TOO*, WE WON'T GET A *SINGLE* LETTER TODAY!
SIGH...
THERE'LL BE SOME IN THERE, CLOVER.
Think positive!
WHAT?
NOTHING...
EMPTY!!!
D'YOU THINK MAYBE...
...EVERYONE JUST GOT *BORED* OF SENDING LETTERS ALL OF A SUDDEN...?
FWMP
SIGH
KALE!!
HEY, BUNNIES!!
MA!
KALE'S MOTHER!!
ARE YOUR BROTHERS WITH YOU?
HUH? NO. WHY?
IS SOMETHING THE MATTER?
THEY'VE DISAP-PEARED!!
WHAAAT?!!!

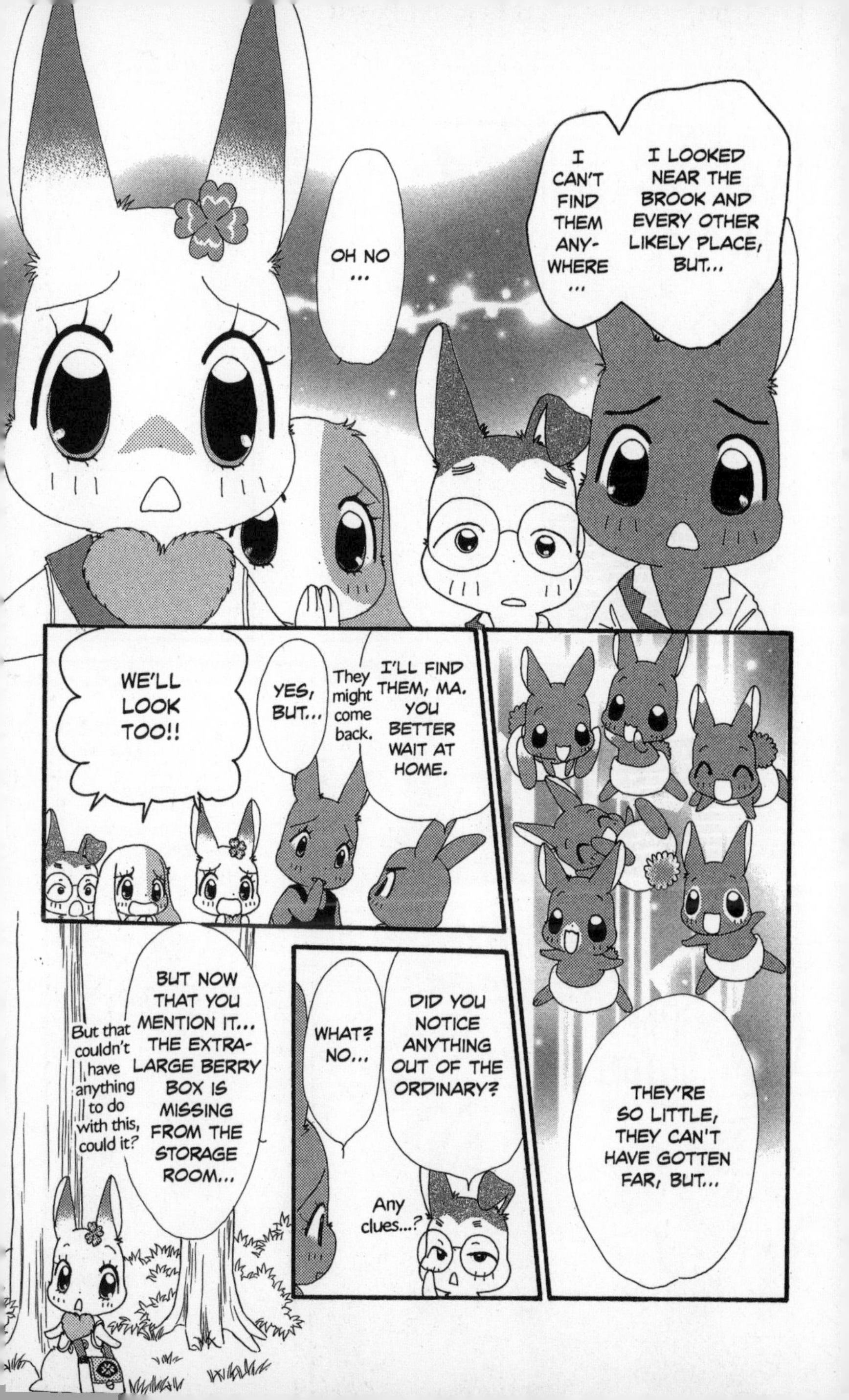
I LOOKED NEAR THE BROOK AND EVERY OTHER LIKELY PLACE, BUT...
I CAN'T FIND THEM ANY-WHERE...
OH NO...
THEY'RE SO LITTLE, THEY CAN'T HAVE GOTTEN FAR, BUT...
I'LL FIND THEM, MA. YOU BETTER WAIT AT HOME.
They might come back.
YES, BUT...
WE'LL LOOK TOO!!
DID YOU NOTICE ANYTHING OUT OF THE ORDINARY?
WHAT? NO...
Any clues...?
BUT NOW THAT YOU MENTION IT... THE EXTRA-LARGE BERRY BOX IS MISSING FROM THE STORAGE ROOM...
But that couldn't have anything to do with this, could it?

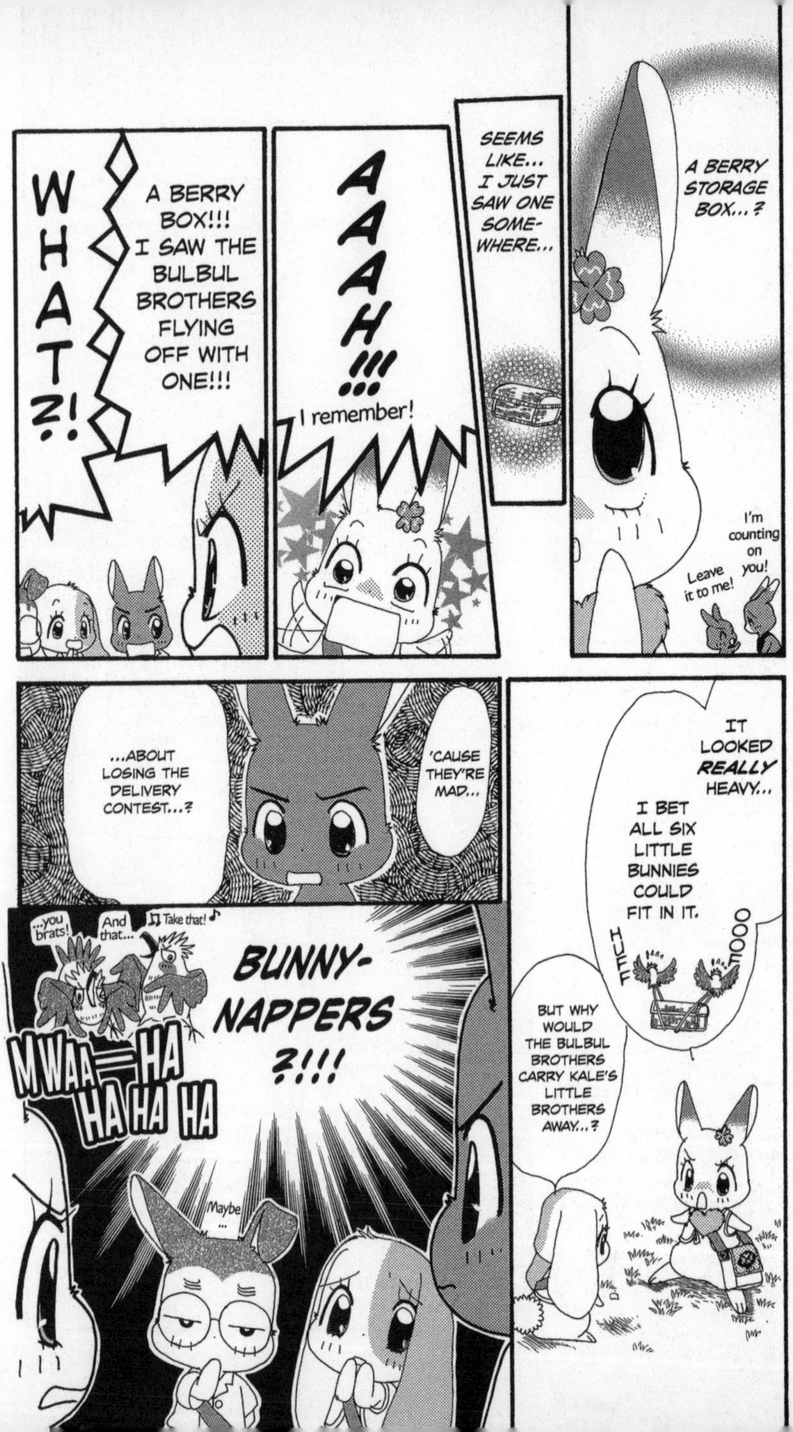

A BERRY STORAGE BOX...?
I'm counting on you!
Leave it to me!
SEEMS LIKE... I JUST SAW ONE SOME-WHERE...
AAAH!!!
I remember!
WHAT?!
A BERRY BOX!!! I SAW THE BULBUL BROTHERS FLYING OFF WITH ONE!!!
IT LOOKED REALLY HEAVY...
I BET ALL SIX LITTLE BUNNIES COULD FIT IN IT.
HUFF
OOOF
BUT WHY WOULD THE BULBUL BROTHERS CARRY KALE'S LITTLE BROTHERS AWAY...?
'CAUSE THEY'RE MAD...
...ABOUT LOSING THE DELIVERY CONTEST...?
BUNNY-NAPPERS?!!!
Take that!
And that...
...you brats!
MWAA—HA HA HA HA
Maybe...

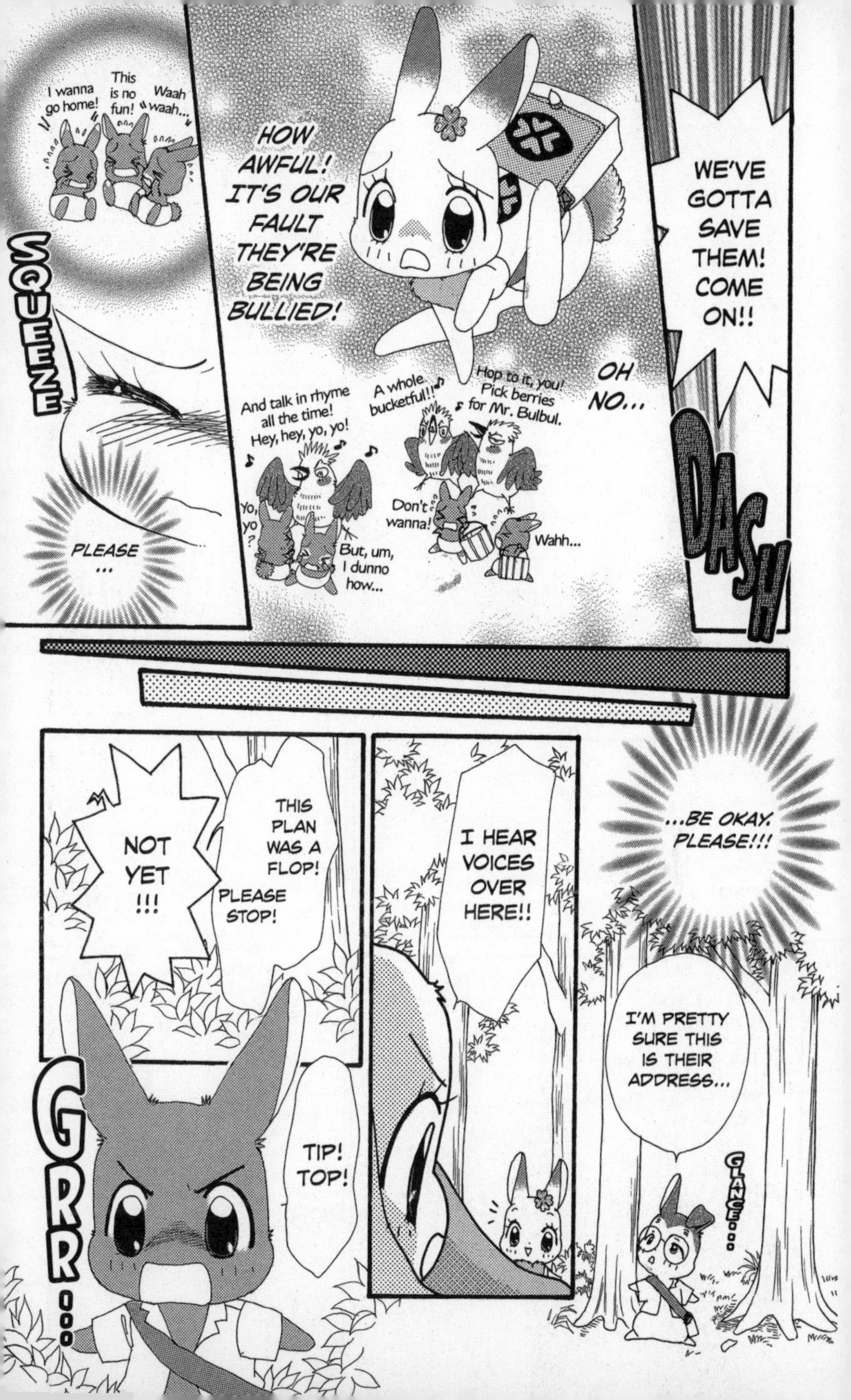
WE'VE GOTTA SAVE THEM! COME ON!!
DASH
OH NO...
HOW AWFUL! IT'S OUR FAULT THEY'RE BEING BULLIED!
Hop to it, you! Pick berries for Mr. Bulbul.
A whole bucketful!!
And talk in rhyme all the time! Hey, hey, yo, yo!
Wahh...
Don't wanna!
But, um, I dunno how...
Yo, yo?
Waah waah...
This is no fun!
I wanna go home!
SQUEEZE
PLEASE ...
...BE OKAY. PLEASE!!!
I'M PRETTY SURE THIS IS THEIR ADDRESS...
GLANCE...
I HEAR VOICES OVER HERE!!
THIS PLAN WAS A FLOP! PLEASE STOP!
NOT YET!!!
TIP! TOP!
GRRR...

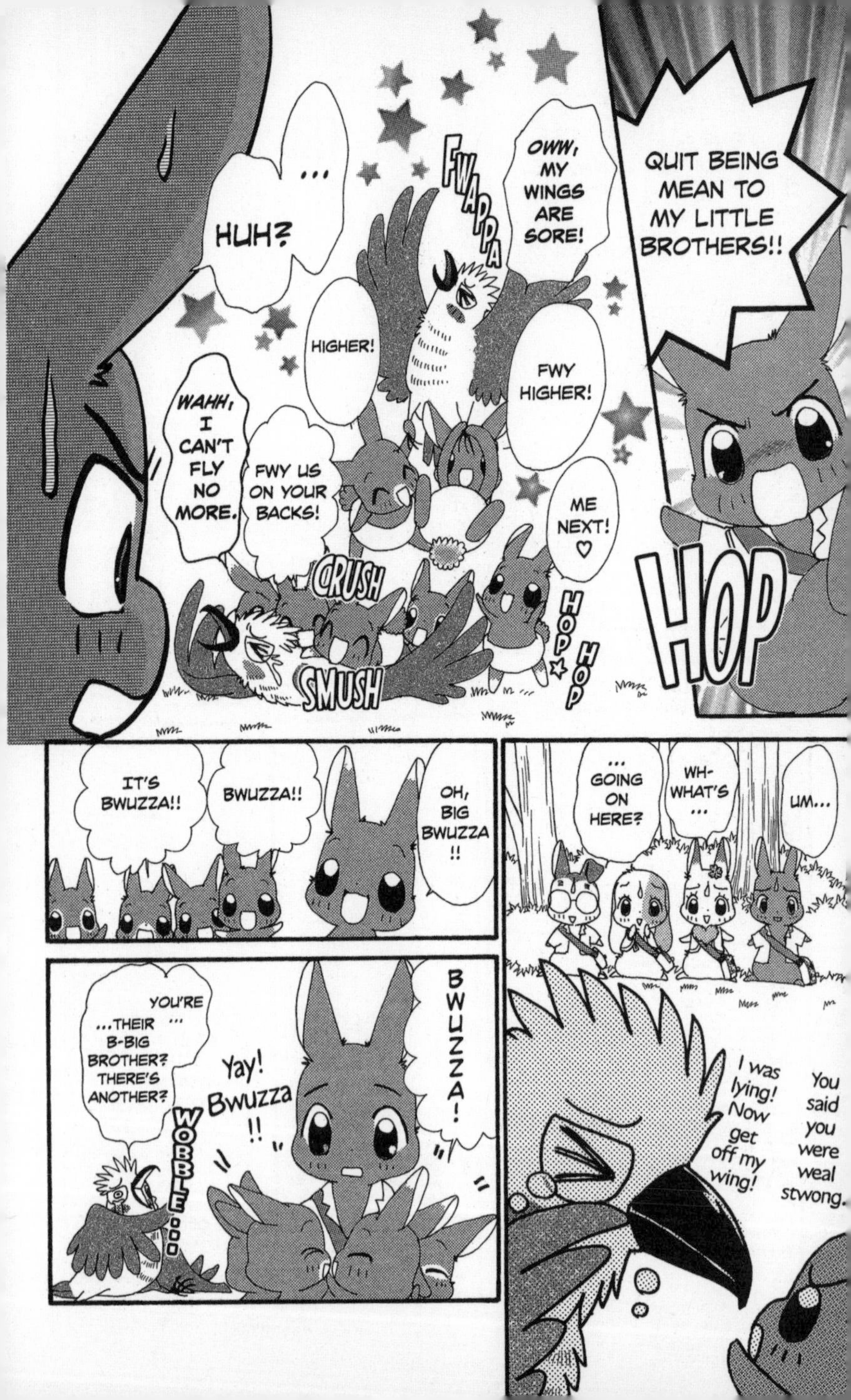
QUIT BEING MEAN TO MY LITTLE BROTHERS!!
HOP
OWW, MY WINGS ARE SORE!
FWAPPA
... HUH?
FWY HIGHER!
HIGHER!
ME NEXT! ♡
HOP HOP HOP
FWY US ON YOUR BACKS!
WAHH, I CAN'T FLY NO MORE.
CRUSH
SMUSH
UM...
WH-WHAT'S ...
... GOING ON HERE?
OH, BIG BWUZZA!!
BWUZZA!!
IT'S BWUZZA!!
You said you were weal stwong.
I was lying! Now get off my wing!
BWUZZA!
Yay! Bwuzza!!
YOU'RE ... ...THEIR B-BIG BROTHER? THERE'S ANOTHER?
WOBBLE...

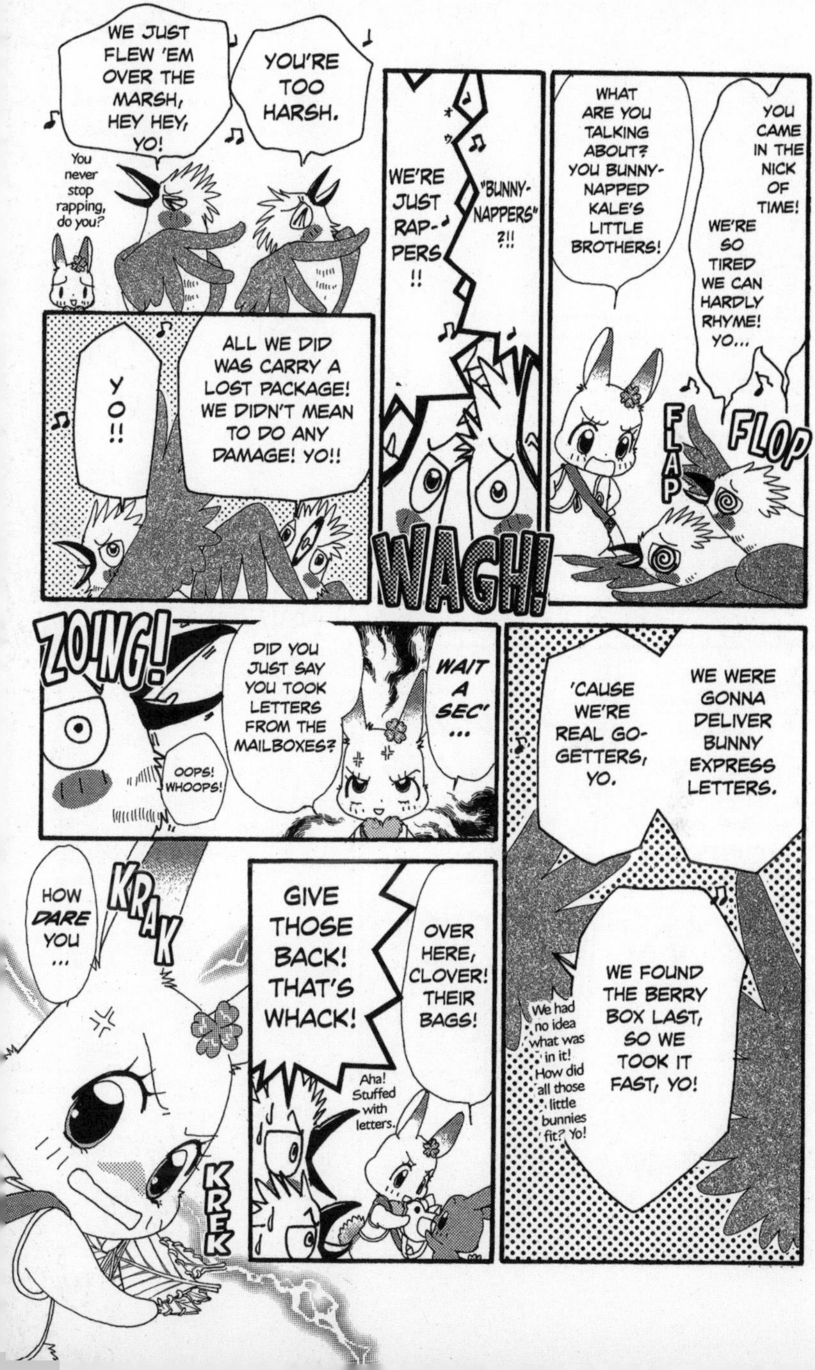
YOU CAME IN THE NICK OF TIME!
WE'RE SO TIRED WE CAN HARDLY RHYME! YO...
WHAT ARE YOU TALKING ABOUT? YOU BUNNY-NAPPED KALE'S LITTLE BROTHERS!
FLOP
FLAP
"BUNNY-NAPPERS"?!!
WE'RE JUST RAP-PERS!!
WAGH!
YOU'RE TOO HARSH.
WE JUST FLEW 'EM OVER THE MARSH, HEY HEY, YO!
You never stop rapping, do you?
ALL WE DID WAS CARRY A LOST PACKAGE! WE DIDN'T MEAN TO DO ANY DAMAGE! YO!!
YO!!
WE WERE GONNA DELIVER BUNNY EXPRESS LETTERS.
'CAUSE WE'RE REAL GO-GETTERS, YO.
WE FOUND THE BERRY BOX LAST, SO WE TOOK IT FAST, YO!
We had no idea what was in it! How did all those little bunnies fit? Yo!
WAIT A SEC'...
DID YOU JUST SAY YOU TOOK LETTERS FROM THE MAILBOXES?
OOPS! WHOOPS!
ZOING!
OVER HERE, CLOVER! THEIR BAGS!
GIVE THOSE BACK! THAT'S WHACK!
Aha! Stuffed with letters.
KRAK
HOW DARE YOU...
KREK

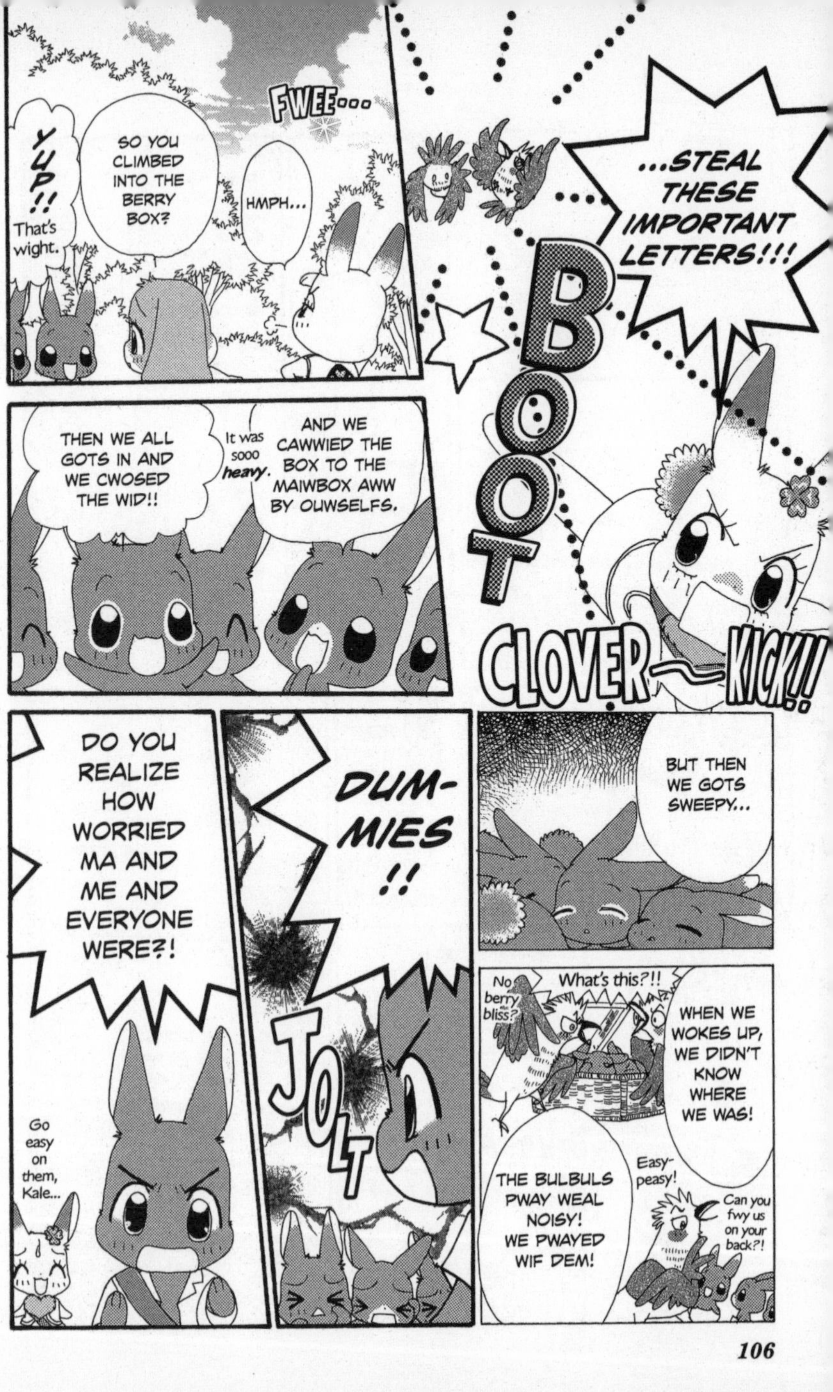

...STEAL THESE IMPORTANT LETTERS!!!
BOOT
CLOVER~KICK!!
FWEE...
HMPH...
SO YOU CLIMBED INTO THE BERRY BOX?
YUP!! That's wight.
AND WE CAWWIED THE BOX TO THE MAIWBOX AWW BY OUWSELFS.
It was sooo heavy.
THEN WE ALL GOTS IN AND WE CWOSED THE WID!!
BUT THEN WE GOTS SWEEPY...
WHEN WE WOKES UP, WE DIDN'T KNOW WHERE WE WAS!
What's this?!!
No berry bliss?
Can you fwy us on your back?!
Easy-peasy!
THE BULBULS PWAY WEAL NOISY! WE PWAYED WIF DEM!
DUM-MIES!!
JOLT
DO YOU REALIZE HOW WORRIED MA AND ME AND EVERYONE WERE?!
Go easy on them, Kale...

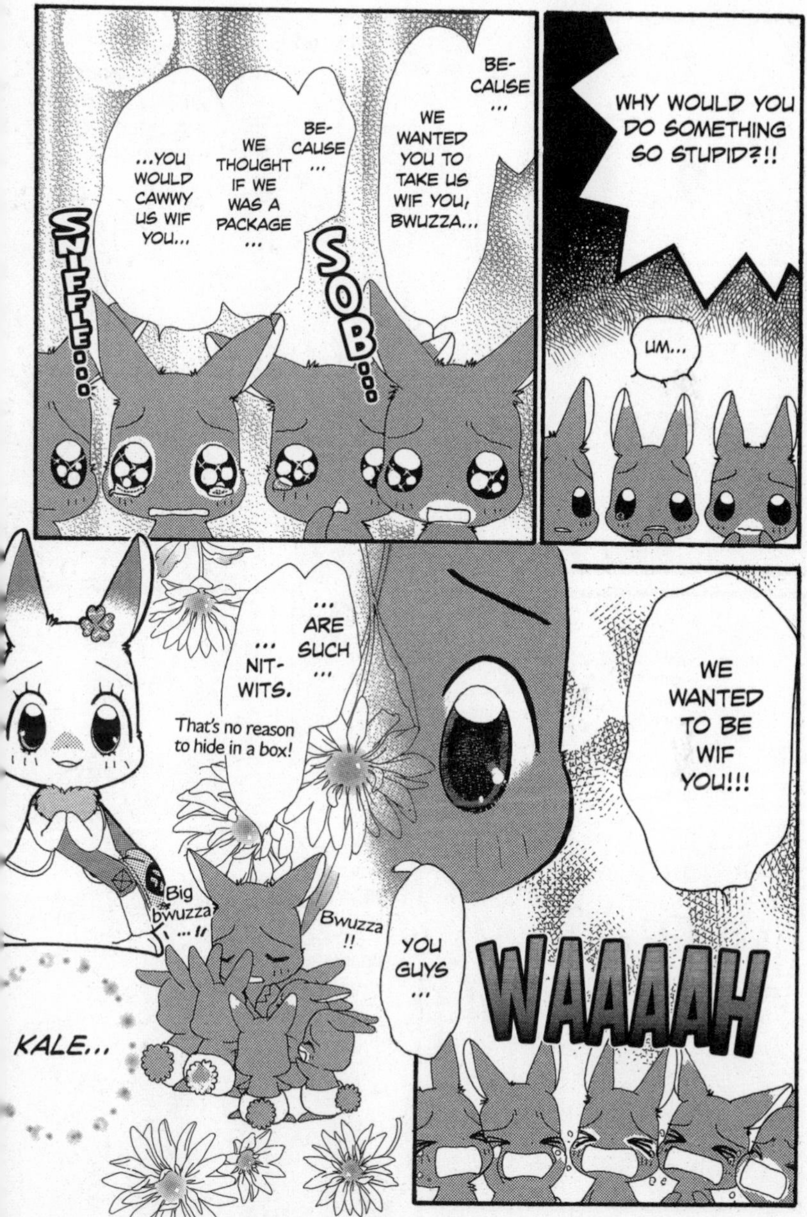
WHY WOULD YOU DO SOMETHING SO STUPID?!!
UM...
BE-CAUSE ...
WE WANTED YOU TO TAKE US WIF YOU, BWUZZA...
SOB...
BE-CAUSE ...
WE THOUGHT IF WE WAS A PACKAGE ...
...YOU WOULD CAWWY US WIF YOU...
SNIFFLE...
WE WANTED TO BE WIF YOU!!!
WAAAAH
... ARE SUCH ...
... NIT-WITS.
That's no reason to hide in a box!
YOU GUYS ...
Bwuzza !!
Big bwuzza ...!!
KALE...

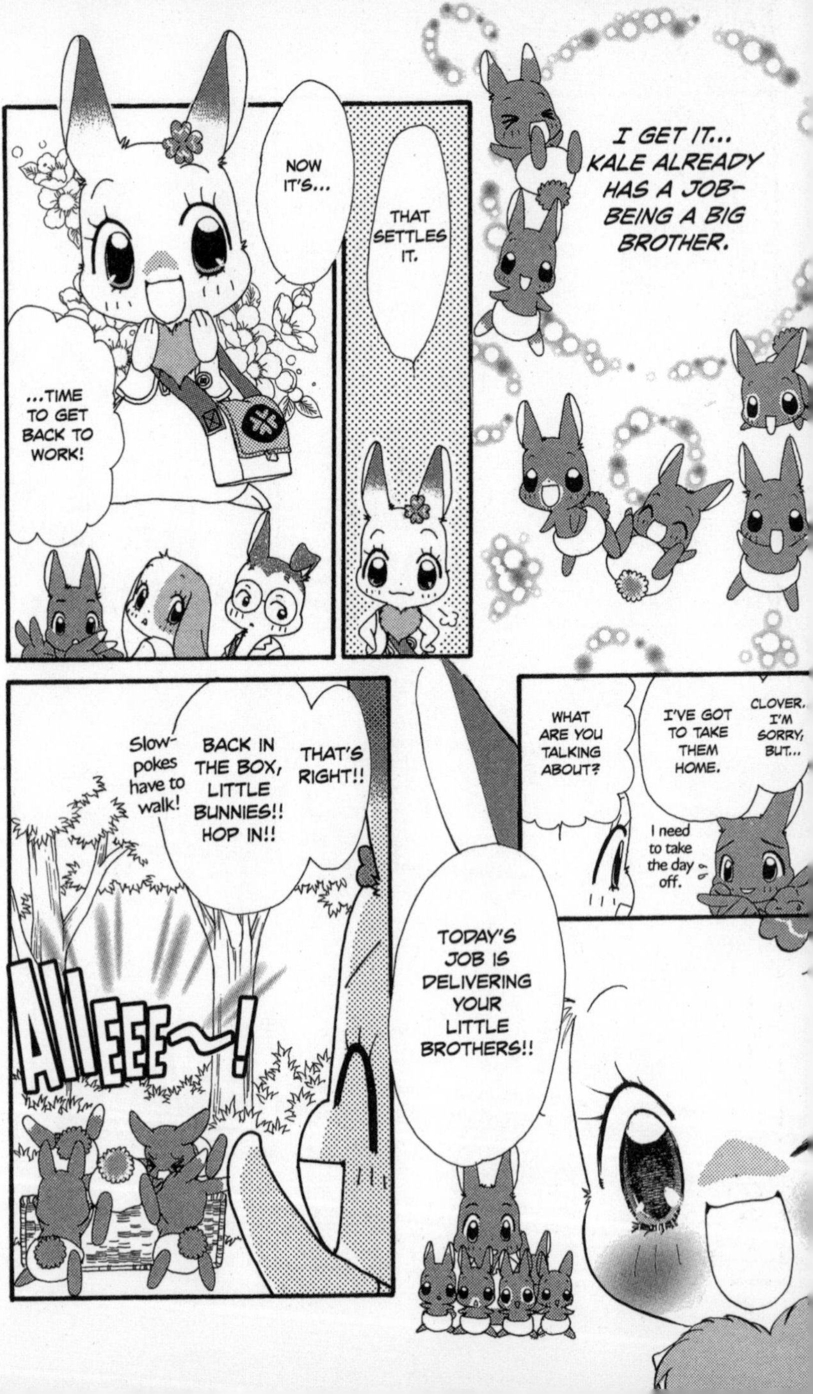
I GET IT... KALE ALREADY HAS A JOB- BEING A BIG BROTHER.
THAT SETTLES IT.
NOW IT'S...
...TIME TO GET BACK TO WORK!
CLOVER. I'M SORRY, BUT...
I'VE GOT TO TAKE THEM HOME.
I need to take the day off.
WHAT ARE YOU TALKING ABOUT?
TODAY'S JOB IS DELIVERING YOUR LITTLE BROTHERS!!
THAT'S RIGHT!!
BACK IN THE BOX, LITTLE BUNNIES!! HOP IN!!
Slow-pokes have to walk!
AIIEEE~!

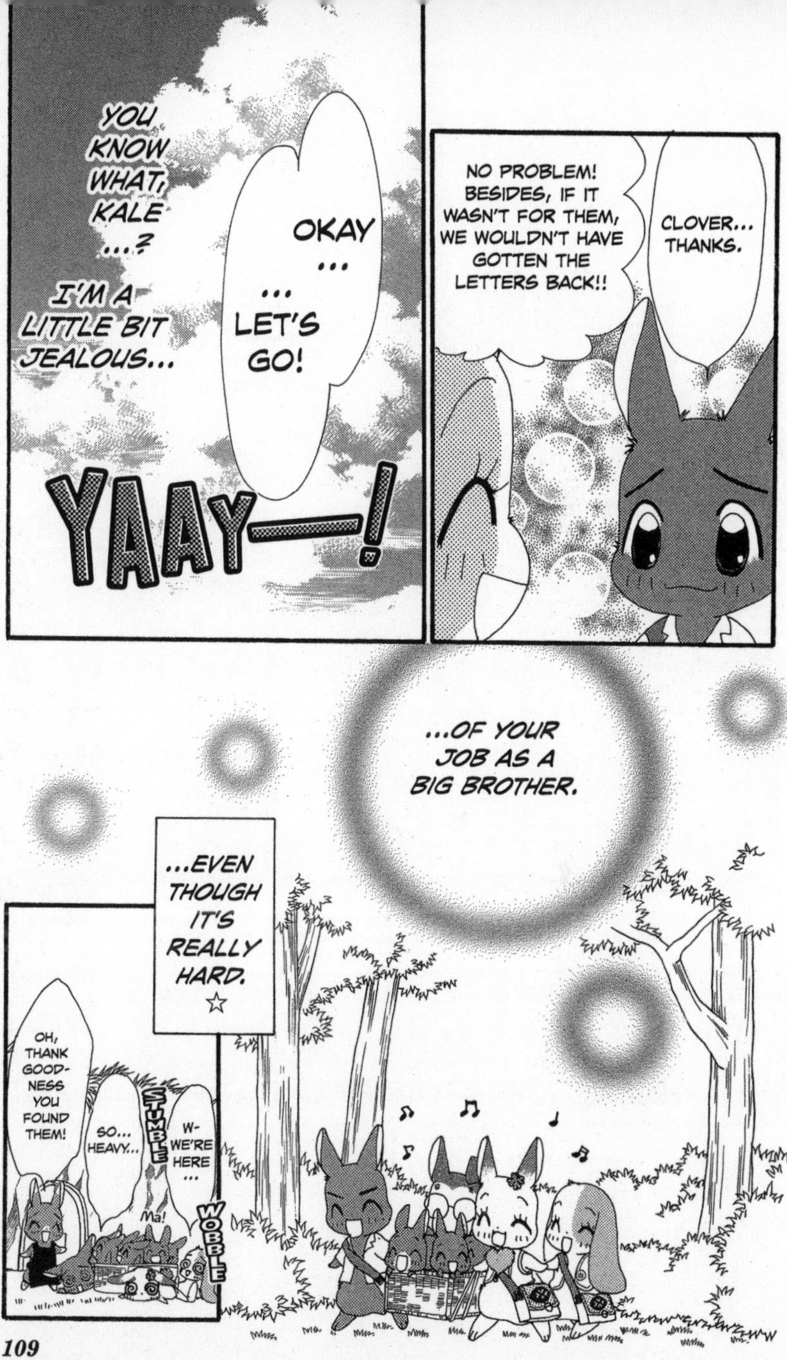
CLOVER... THANKS.
NO PROBLEM! BESIDES, IF IT WASN'T FOR THEM, WE WOULDN'T HAVE GOTTEN THE LETTERS BACK!!
OKAY ... ... LET'S GO!
YOU KNOW WHAT, KALE ...?
I'M A LITTLE BIT JEALOUS...
YAAY—!
...OF YOUR JOB AS A BIG BROTHER.
...EVEN THOUGH IT'S REALLY HARD. ☆
W-WE'RE HERE ...
STUMBLE
SO... HEAVY...
OH, THANK GOODNESS YOU FOUND THEM!
Ma!
WOBBLE

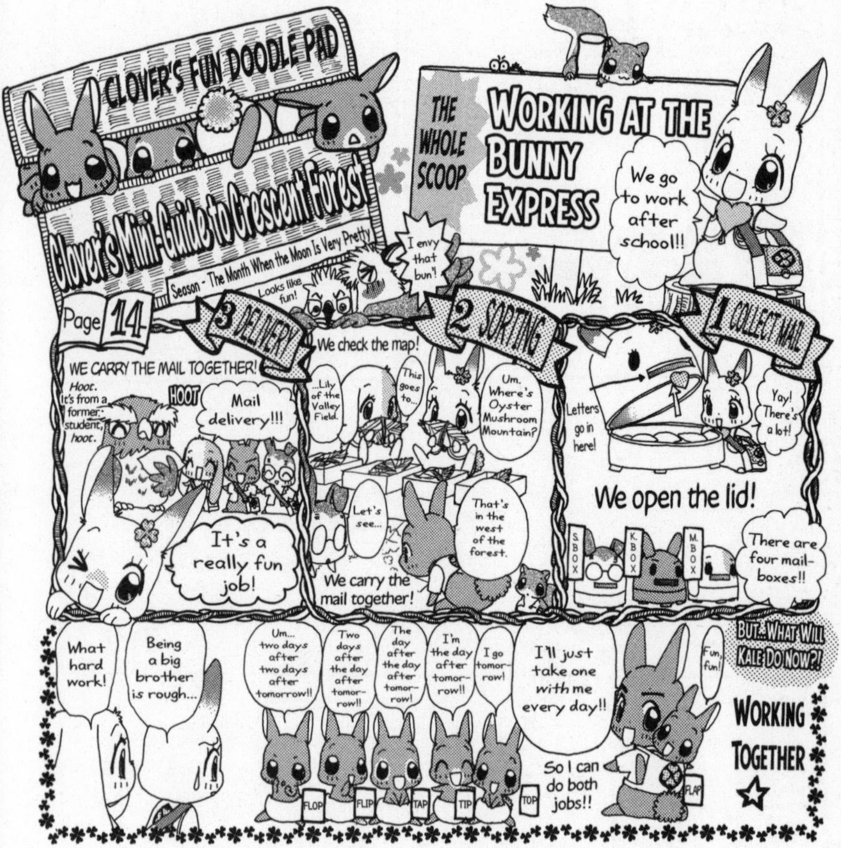
THE WHOLE SCOOP
WORKING AT THE BUNNY EXPRESS
We go to work after school!!
CLOVER'S FUN DOODLE PAD
Clover's Mini-Guide to Crescent Forest
Season - The Month When the Moon Is Very Pretty
Page 14
I envy that bun!
Looks like fun!
1 COLLECT MAIL
Yay! There's a lot!
Letters go in here!
We open the lid!
There are four mail-boxes!!
S. BOX
K. BOX
M. BOX
2 SORTING
We check the map!
Um. Where's Oyster Mushroom Mountain?
This goes to...
...Lily of the Valley Field.
That's in the west of the forest.
Let's see...
We carry the mail together!
3 DELIVERY
WE CARRY THE MAIL TOGETHER!
HOOT
Mail delivery!!!
Hoot. It's from a former student, hoot.
It's a really fun job!
BUT... WHAT WILL KALE DO NOW?!
WORKING TOGETHER ☆
Fun, fun!
I'll just take one with me every day!!
So I can do both jobs!!
FLAP
I go tomorrow!
TOP
I'm the day after tomorrow!!
TIP
The day after the day after tomorrow!
TAP
Two days after the day after tomorrow!!
FLIP
Um... two days after two days after tomorrow!!
FLOP
Being a big brother is rough...
What hard work!

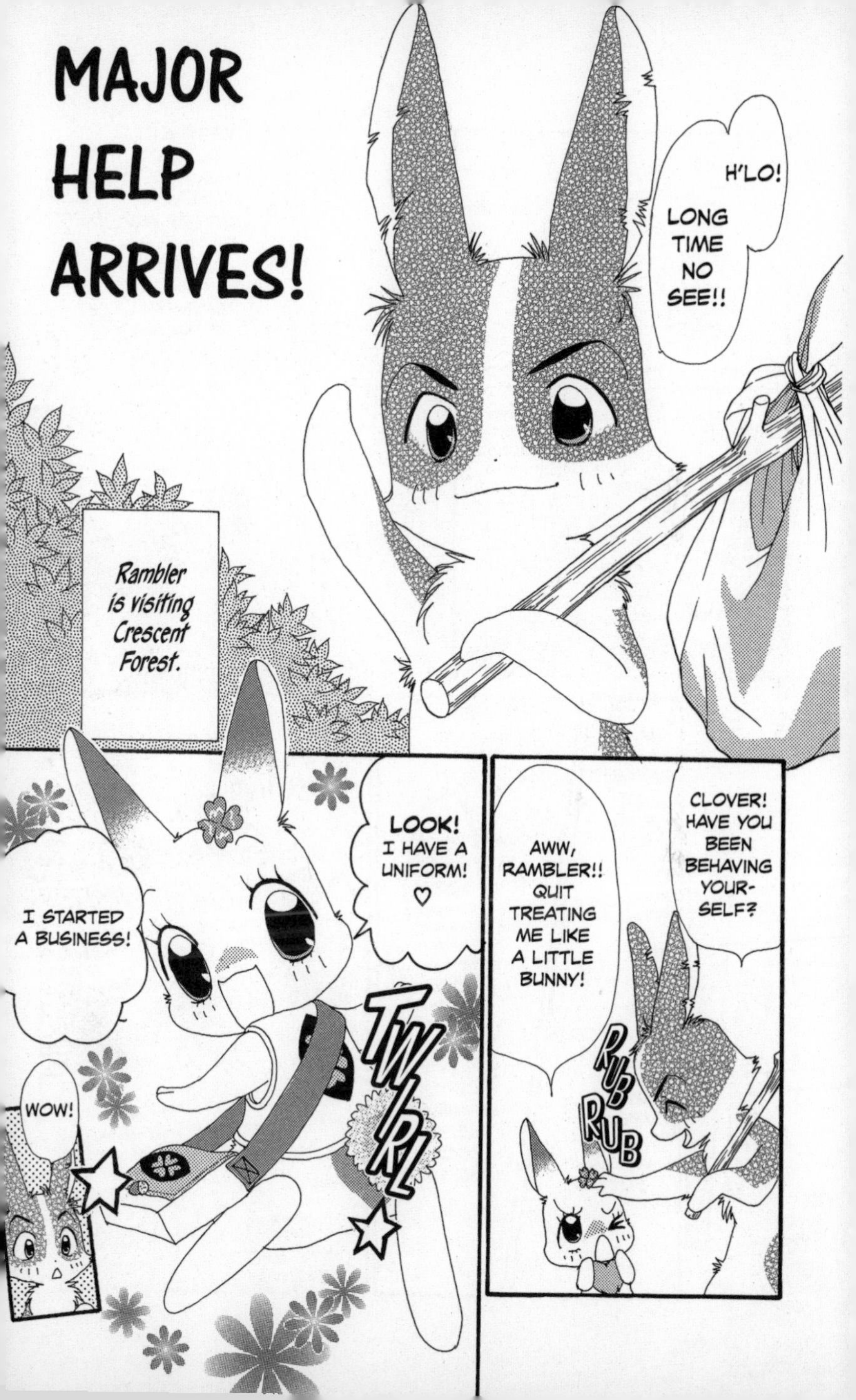
MAJOR HELP ARRIVES!
H'LO! LONG TIME NO SEE!!
Rambler is visiting Crescent Forest.
CLOVER! HAVE YOU BEEN BEHAVING YOURSELF?
AWW, RAMBLER!! QUIT TREATING ME LIKE A LITTLE BUNNY!
RUB RUB
LOOK! I HAVE A UNIFORM! ♡
I STARTED A BUSINESS!
TWIRL
WOW!

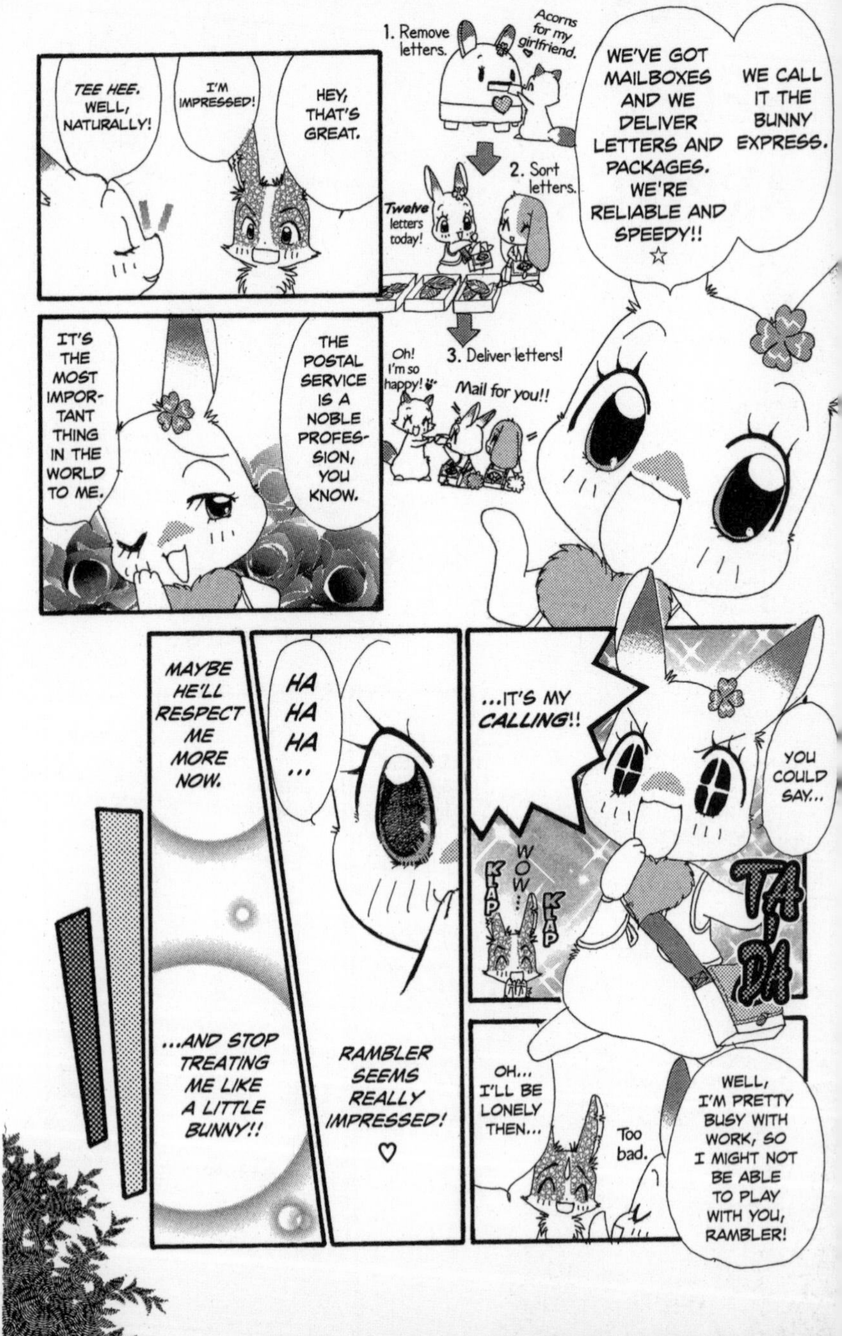
WE CALL IT THE BUNNY EXPRESS.
WE'VE GOT MAILBOXES AND WE DELIVER LETTERS AND PACKAGES. WE'RE RELIABLE AND SPEEDY!! ☆
1. Remove letters.
Acorns for my girlfriend.
2. Sort letters.
Twelve letters today!
3. Deliver letters!
Mail for you!!
Oh! I'm so happy!
HEY, THAT'S GREAT.
I'M IMPRESSED!
TEE HEE. WELL, NATURALLY!
THE POSTAL SERVICE IS A NOBLE PROFESSION, YOU KNOW.
IT'S THE MOST IMPORTANT THING IN THE WORLD TO ME.
YOU COULD SAY...
...IT'S MY CALLING!!
TA DA
WOW...
KLAP KLAP
WELL, I'M PRETTY BUSY WITH WORK, SO I MIGHT NOT BE ABLE TO PLAY WITH YOU, RAMBLER!
Too bad.
OH... I'LL BE LONELY THEN...
HA HA HA...
RAMBLER SEEMS REALLY IMPRESSED! ♡
MAYBE HE'LL RESPECT ME MORE NOW.
...AND STOP TREATING ME LIKE A LITTLE BUNNY!!

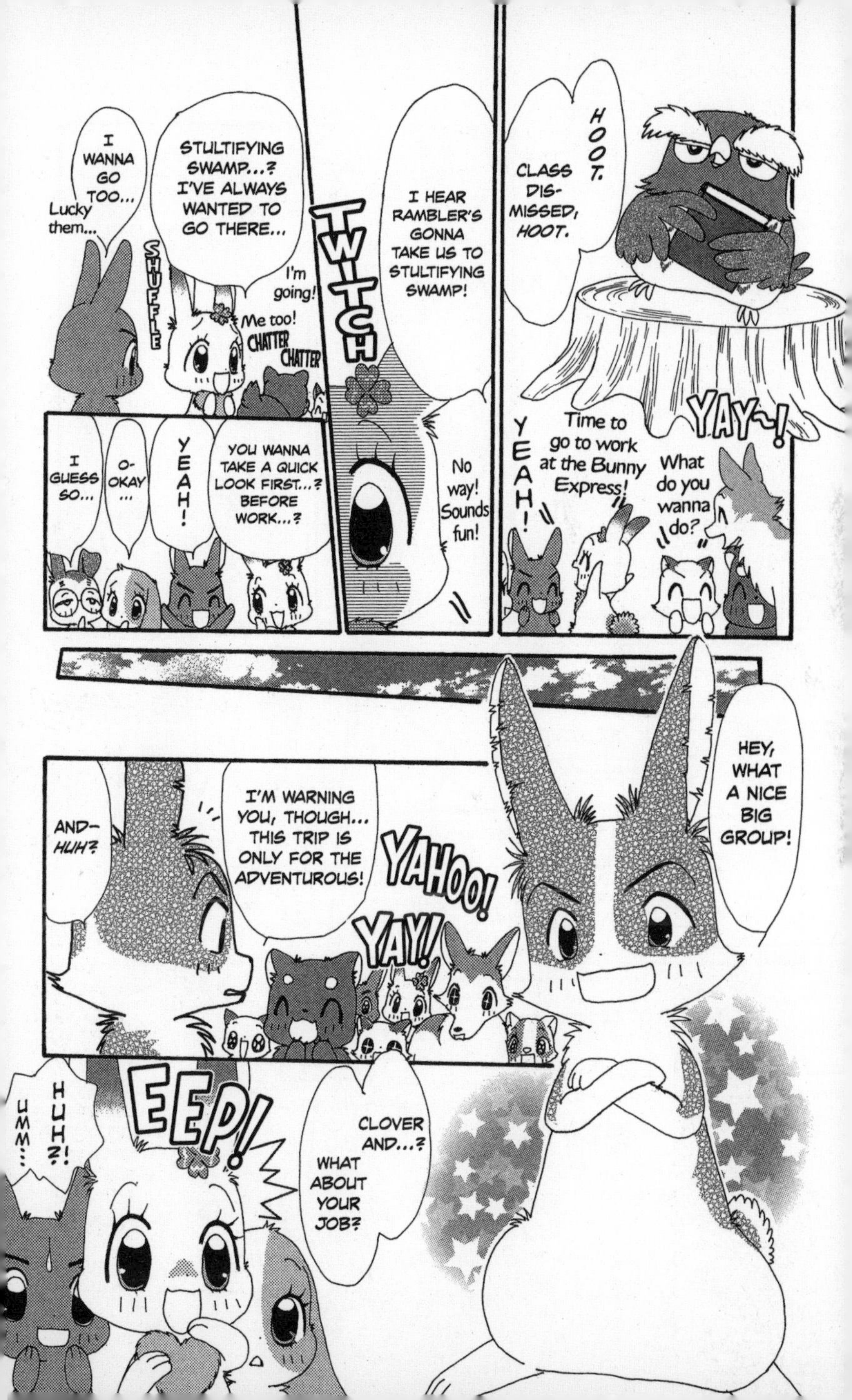
HOOT.
CLASS DIS-MISSED, HOOT.
YAY~!
What do you wanna do?
Time to go to work at the Bunny Express!
YEAH!
I HEAR RAMBLER'S GONNA TAKE US TO STULTIFYING SWAMP!
TWITCH
No way! Sounds fun!
STULTIFYING SWAMP...? I'VE ALWAYS WANTED TO GO THERE...
I WANNA GO TOO...
Lucky them...
SHUFFLE
I'm going!
Me too!
CHATTER CHATTER
YOU WANNA TAKE A QUICK LOOK FIRST...? BEFORE WORK...?
YEAH!
O-OKAY...
I GUESS SO...
HEY, WHAT A NICE BIG GROUP!
YAHOO!
YAY!
I'M WARNING YOU, THOUGH... THIS TRIP IS ONLY FOR THE ADVENTUROUS!
AND— HUH?
CLOVER AND...? WHAT ABOUT YOUR JOB?
EEP!
HUH?!
UMM...

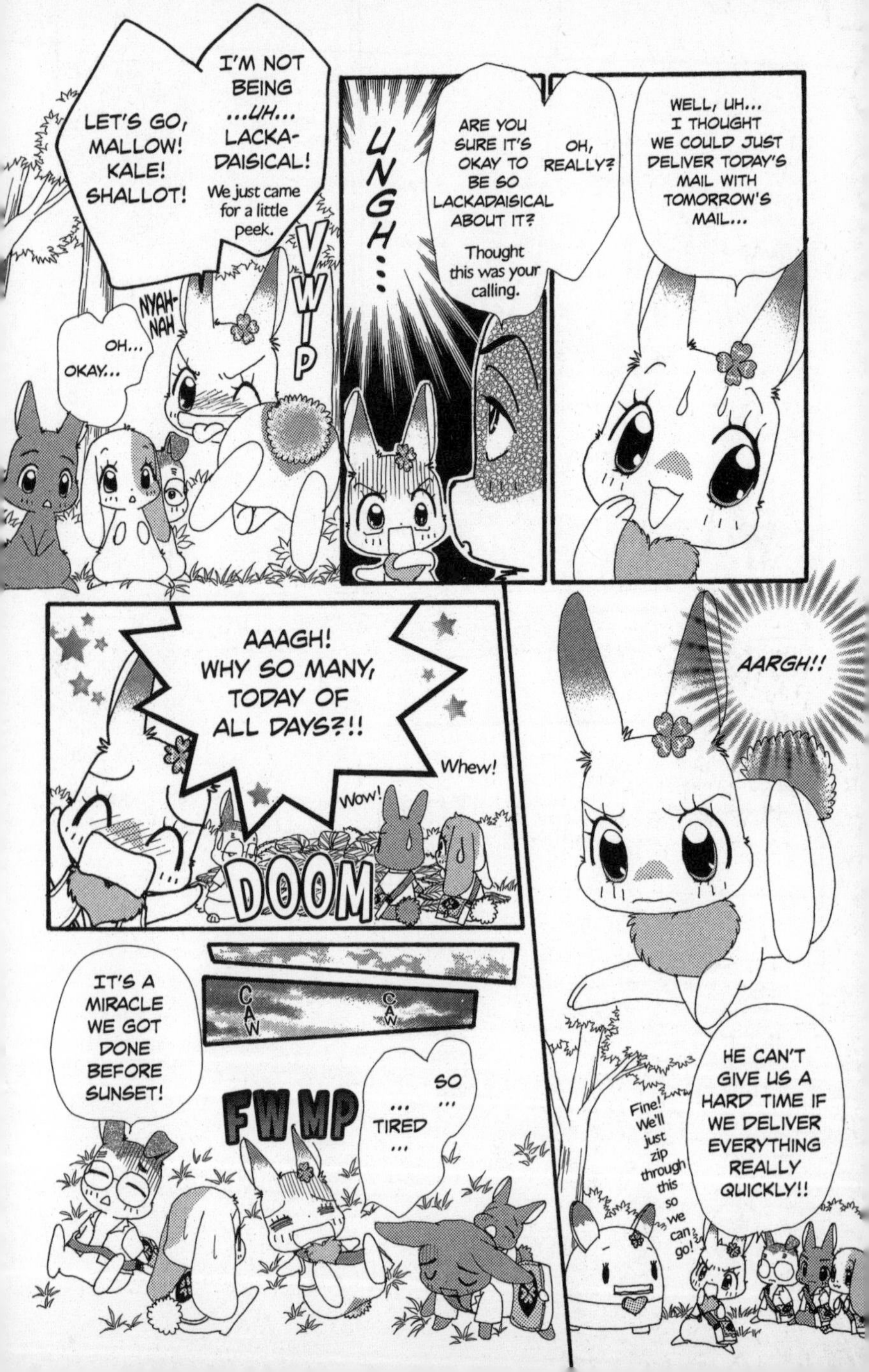
WELL, UH... I THOUGHT WE COULD JUST DELIVER TODAY'S MAIL WITH TOMORROW'S MAIL...
OH, REALLY?
ARE YOU SURE IT'S OKAY TO BE SO LACKADAISICAL ABOUT IT?
Thought this was your calling.
UNGH...
I'M NOT BEING ...UH... LACKA-DAISICAL!
We just came for a little peek.
VWIP
LET'S GO, MALLOW! KALE! SHALLOT!
NYAH-NAH
OH... OKAY...
AARGH!!
HE CAN'T GIVE US A HARD TIME IF WE DELIVER EVERYTHING REALLY QUICKLY!!
Fine! We'll just zip through this so we can go!
AAAGH! WHY SO MANY, TODAY OF ALL DAYS?!!
Whew!
Wow!
DOOM
CAW
CAW
SO ... TIRED ...
FWMP
IT'S A MIRACLE WE GOT DONE BEFORE SUNSET!

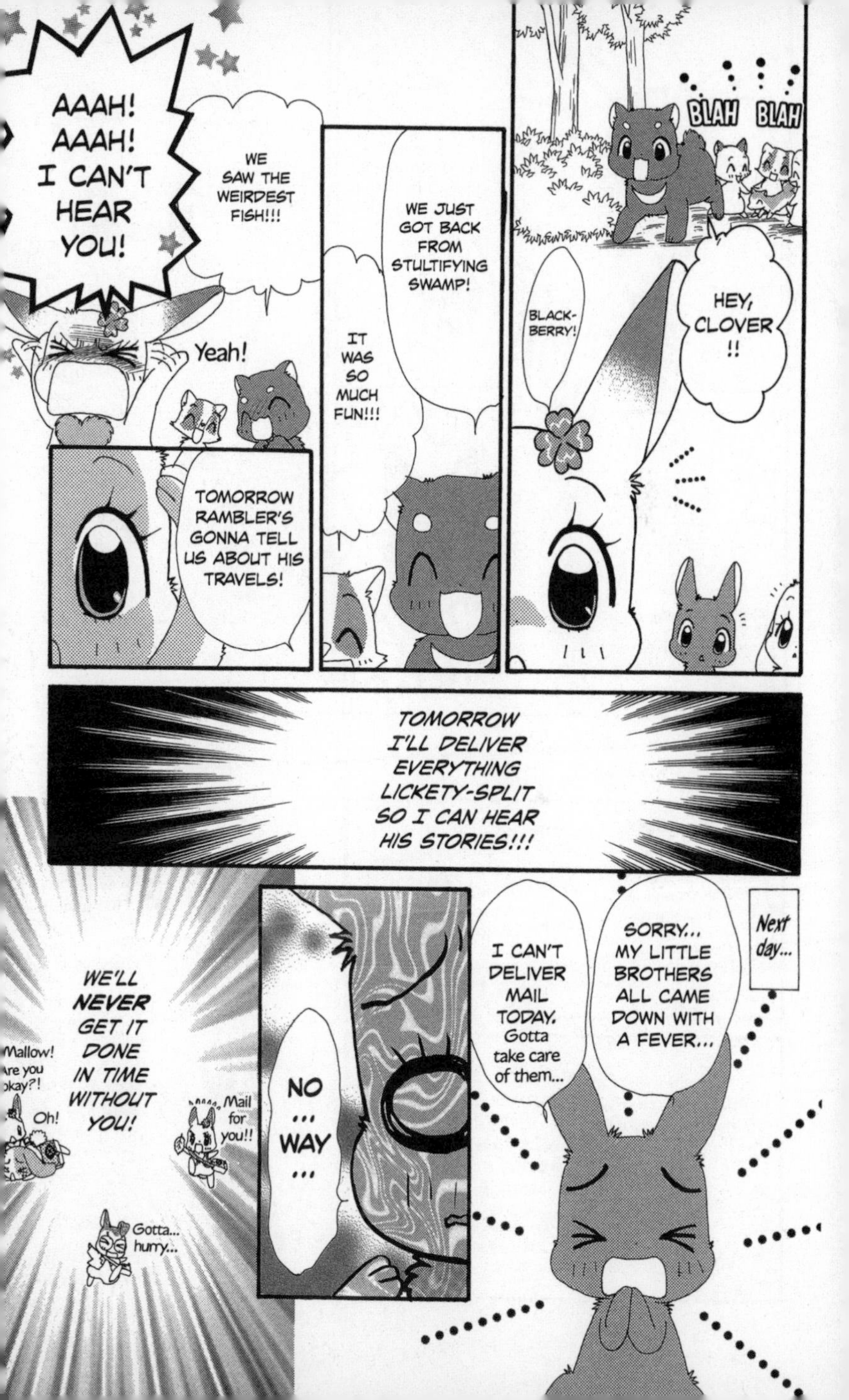
BLAH BLAH
HEY, CLOVER!!
BLACK-BERRY!
......
WE JUST GOT BACK FROM STULTIFYING SWAMP!
IT WAS SO MUCH FUN!!!
WE SAW THE WEIRDEST FISH!!!
AAAH! AAAH! I CAN'T HEAR YOU!
Yeah!
TOMORROW RAMBLER'S GONNA TELL US ABOUT HIS TRAVELS!
TOMORROW I'LL DELIVER EVERYTHING LICKETY-SPLIT SO I CAN HEAR HIS STORIES!!!
Next day...
SORRY... MY LITTLE BROTHERS ALL CAME DOWN WITH A FEVER...
I CAN'T DELIVER MAIL TODAY. Gotta take care of them...
NO ... WAY ...
Mail for you!!
WE'LL NEVER GET IT DONE IN TIME WITHOUT YOU!
Mallow!
Oh!
Gotta... hurry...

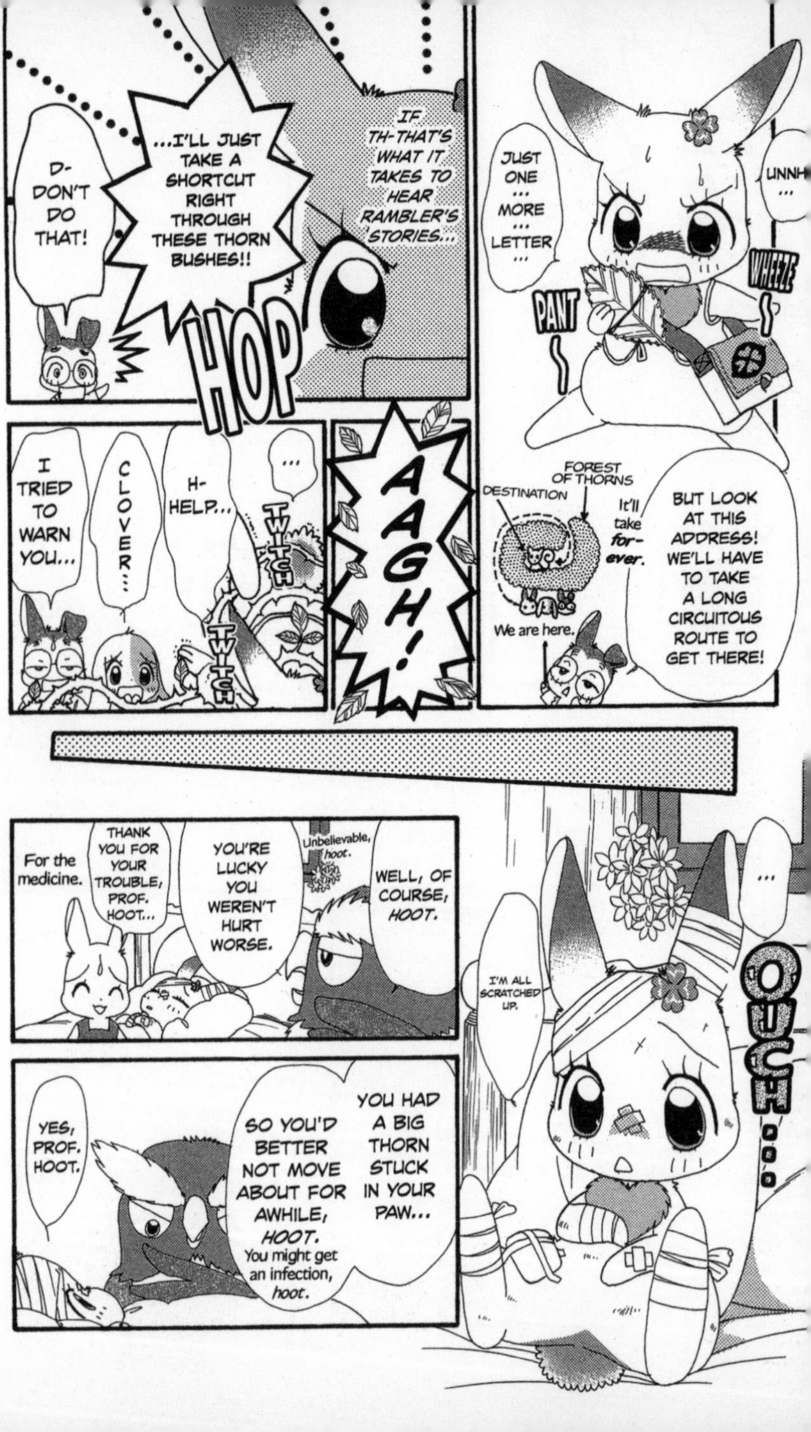
UNNH...
JUST ONE ... MORE ... LETTER ...
WHEEZE
PANT
FOREST OF THORNS
DESTINATION
We are here.
It'll take *for-ever*.
BUT LOOK AT THIS ADDRESS! WE'LL HAVE TO TAKE A LONG CIRCUITOUS ROUTE TO GET THERE!
IF TH-THAT'S WHAT IT TAKES TO HEAR RAMBLER'S STORIES...
...I'LL JUST TAKE A SHORTCUT RIGHT THROUGH THESE THORN BUSHES!!
D-DON'T DO THAT!
HOP
AAGH!
...
TWITCH
TWITCH
H-HELP...
CLOVER...
I TRIED TO WARN YOU...
...
OUCH...
I'M ALL SCRATCHED UP.
WELL, OF COURSE, *HOOT*.
Unbelievable, *hoot*.
YOU'RE LUCKY YOU WEREN'T HURT WORSE.
THANK YOU FOR YOUR TROUBLE, PROF. HOOT...
For the medicine.
YOU HAD A BIG THORN STUCK IN YOUR PAW...
SO YOU'D BETTER NOT MOVE ABOUT FOR AWHILE, *HOOT*.
You might get an infection, *hoot*.
YES, PROF. HOOT.

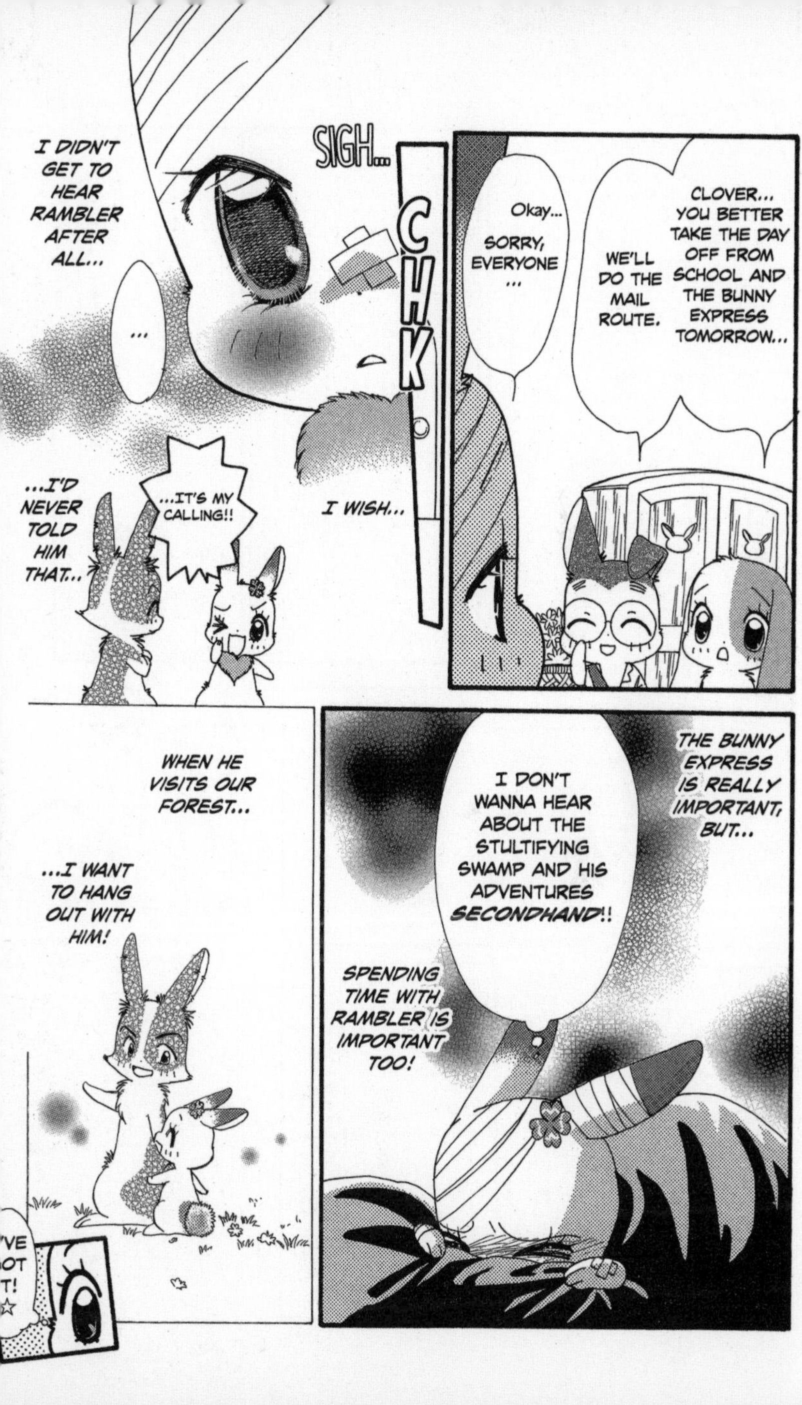
CLOVER... YOU BETTER TAKE THE DAY OFF FROM SCHOOL AND THE BUNNY EXPRESS TOMORROW...
WE'LL DO THE MAIL ROUTE.
Okay... SORRY, EVERYONE ...
SIGH...
CHK
I DIDN'T GET TO HEAR RAMBLER AFTER ALL...
...
I WISH...
...I'D NEVER TOLD HIM THAT...
...IT'S MY CALLING!!
THE BUNNY EXPRESS IS REALLY IMPORTANT, BUT...
I DON'T WANNA HEAR ABOUT THE STULTIFYING SWAMP AND HIS ADVENTURES SECONDHAND!!
SPENDING TIME WITH RAMBLER IS IMPORTANT TOO!
WHEN HE VISITS OUR FOREST...
...I WANT TO HANG OUT WITH HIM!

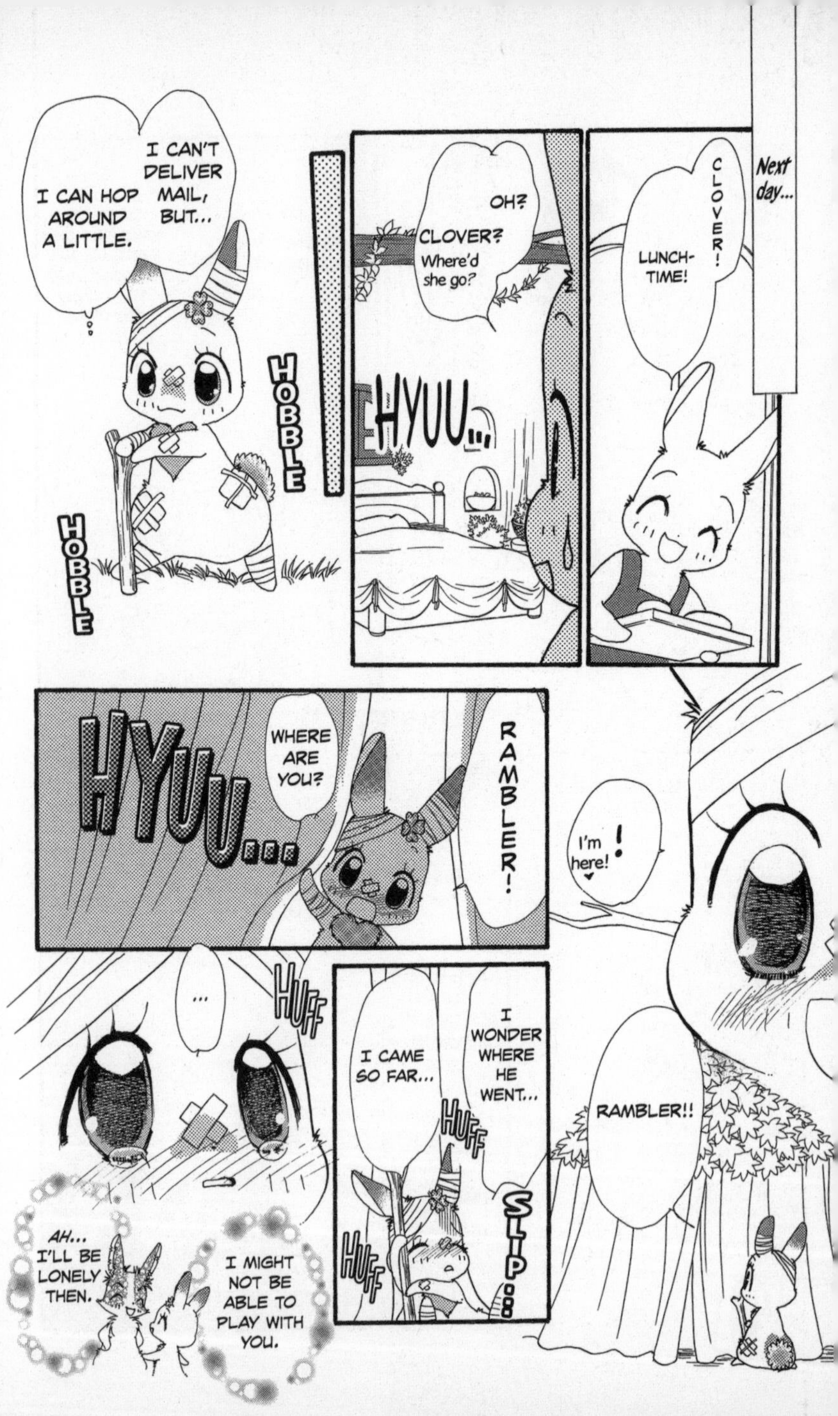
Next day...
CLOVER!
LUNCH-TIME!
OH?
CLOVER? Where'd she go?
HYUU...
I CAN'T DELIVER MAIL, BUT...
I CAN HOP AROUND A LITTLE.
HOBBLE
HOBBLE
I'm here!
RAMBLER!!
RAMBLER!
WHERE ARE YOU?
HYUU...
I WONDER WHERE HE WENT...
I CAME SO FAR...
HUFF
SLIP
HUFF
...
HUFF
AH... I'LL BE LONELY THEN.
I MIGHT NOT BE ABLE TO PLAY WITH YOU.

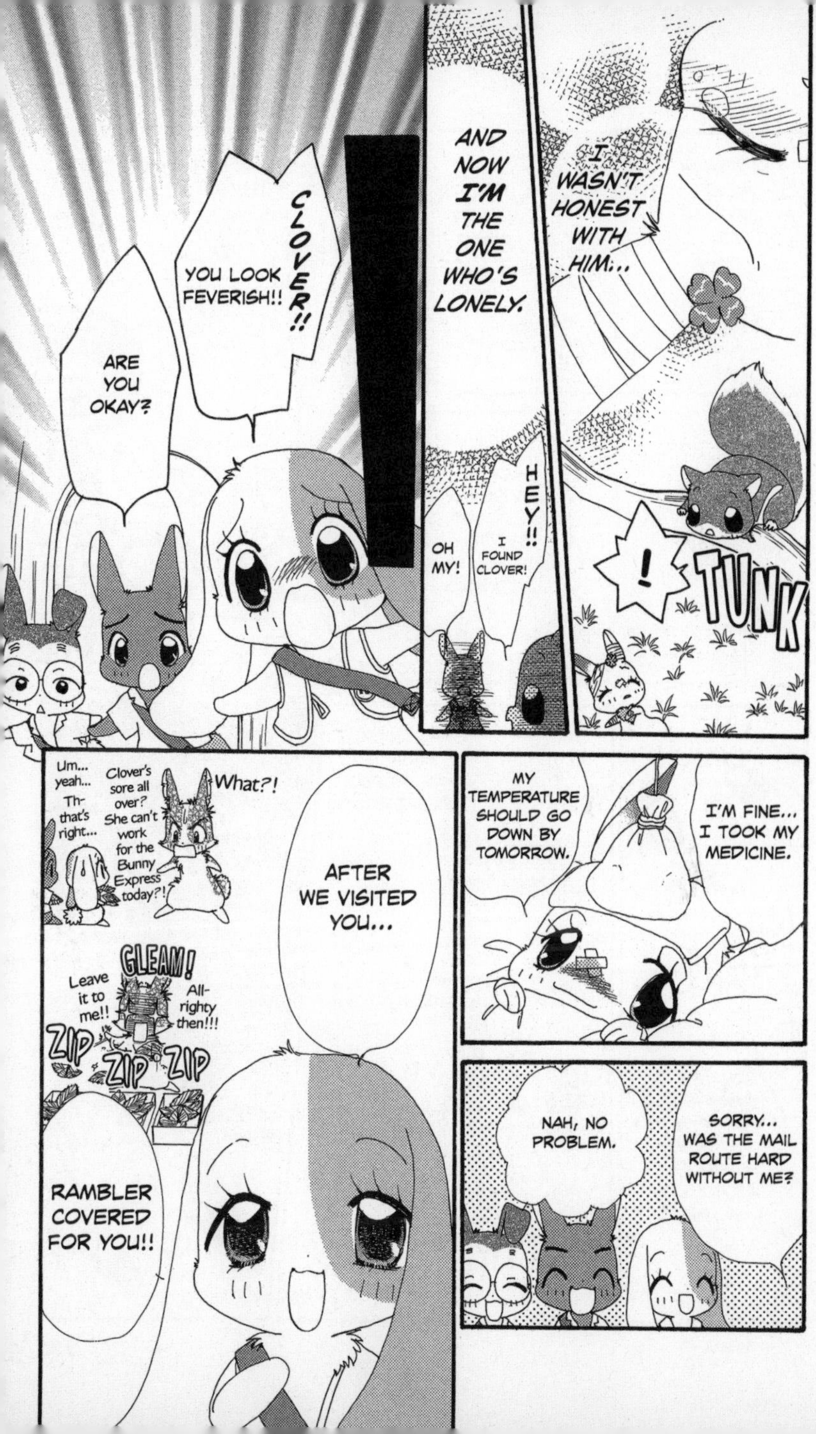
I WASN'T HONEST WITH HIM...
!
TUNK
AND NOW I'M THE ONE WHO'S LONELY.
HEY!!
I FOUND CLOVER!
OH MY!
CLOVER!!
YOU LOOK FEVERISH!!
ARE YOU OKAY?
I'M FINE... I TOOK MY MEDICINE.
MY TEMPERATURE SHOULD GO DOWN BY TOMORROW.
SORRY... WAS THE MAIL ROUTE HARD WITHOUT ME?
NAH, NO PROBLEM.
AFTER WE VISITED YOU...
What?!
Clover's sore all over? She can't work for the Bunny Express today?!
Um... yeah... Th-that's right...
GLEAM!
All-righty then!!!
Leave it to me!!
ZIP
ZIP
ZIP
RAMBLER COVERED FOR YOU!!

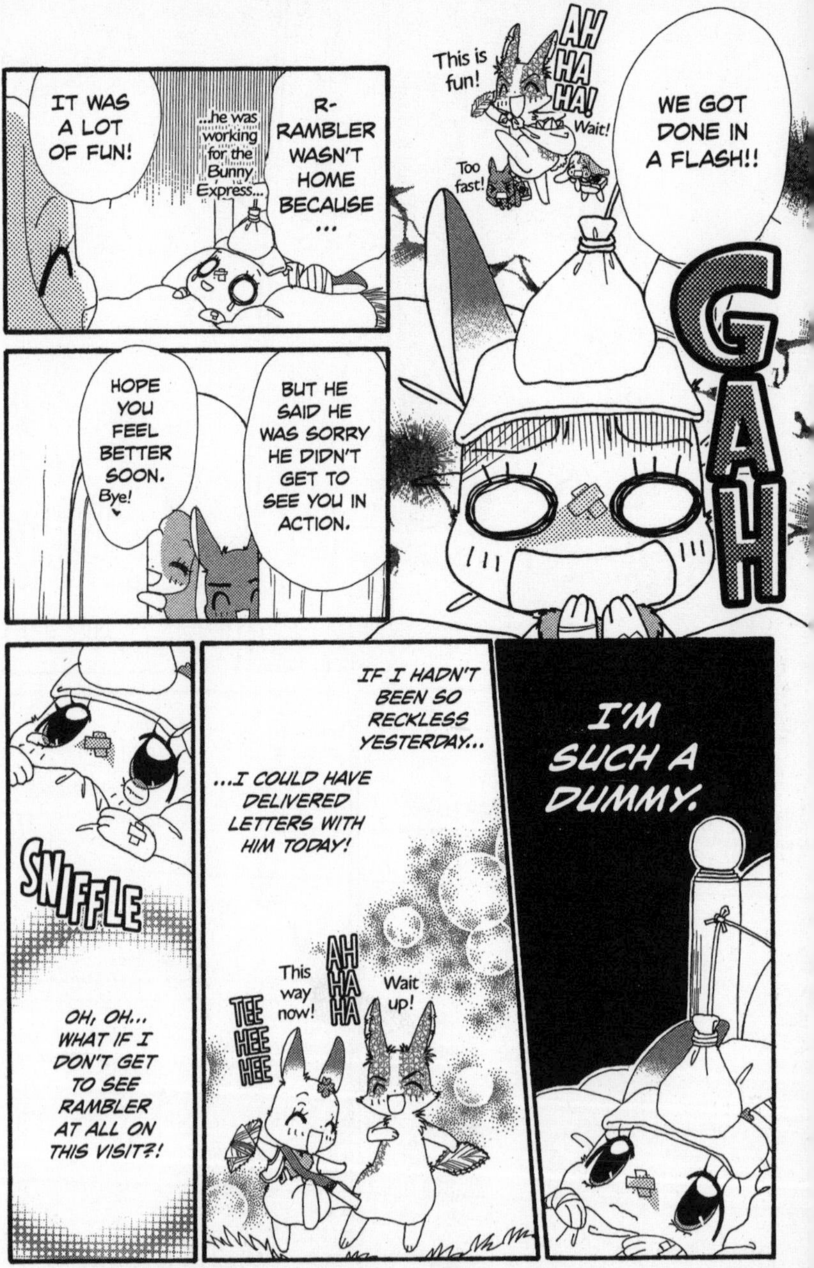
WE GOT DONE IN A FLASH!!
AH HA HA!
This is fun!
Wait!
Too fast!
GAH
R-RAMBLER WASN'T HOME BECAUSE...
...he was working for the Bunny Express...
IT WAS A LOT OF FUN!
BUT HE SAID HE WAS SORRY HE DIDN'T GET TO SEE YOU IN ACTION.
HOPE YOU FEEL BETTER SOON.
Bye!
I'M SUCH A DUMMY.
IF I HADN'T BEEN SO RECKLESS YESTERDAY...
...I COULD HAVE DELIVERED LETTERS WITH HIM TODAY!
Wait up!
AH HA HA
This way now!
TEE HEE HEE
SNIFFLE
OH, OH... WHAT IF I DON'T GET TO SEE RAMBLER AT ALL ON THIS VISIT?!

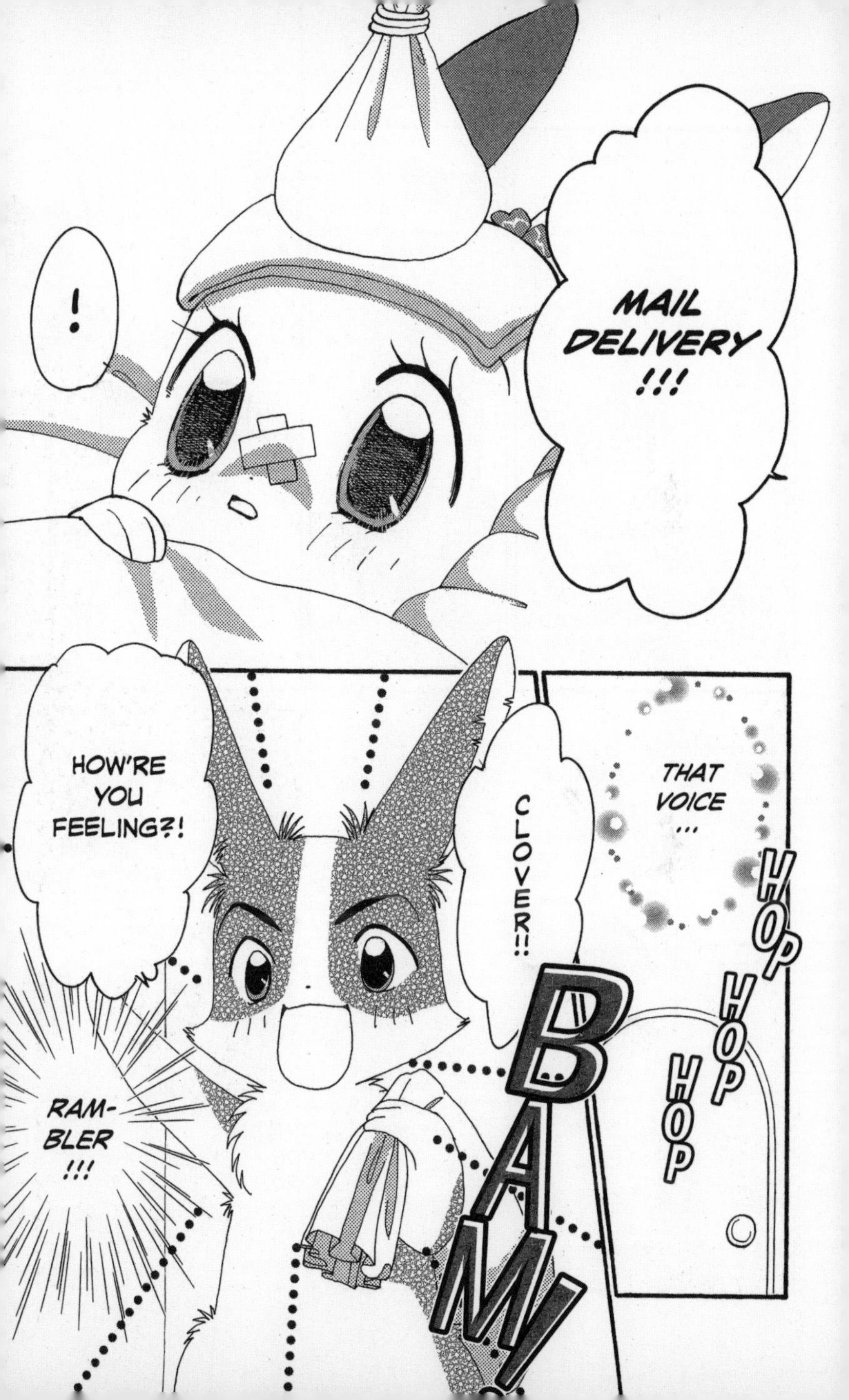
MAIL DELIVERY !!!
!
THAT VOICE ...
HOP HOP HOP
CLOVER!!
HOW'RE YOU FEELING?!
BAM!
RAMBLER !!!

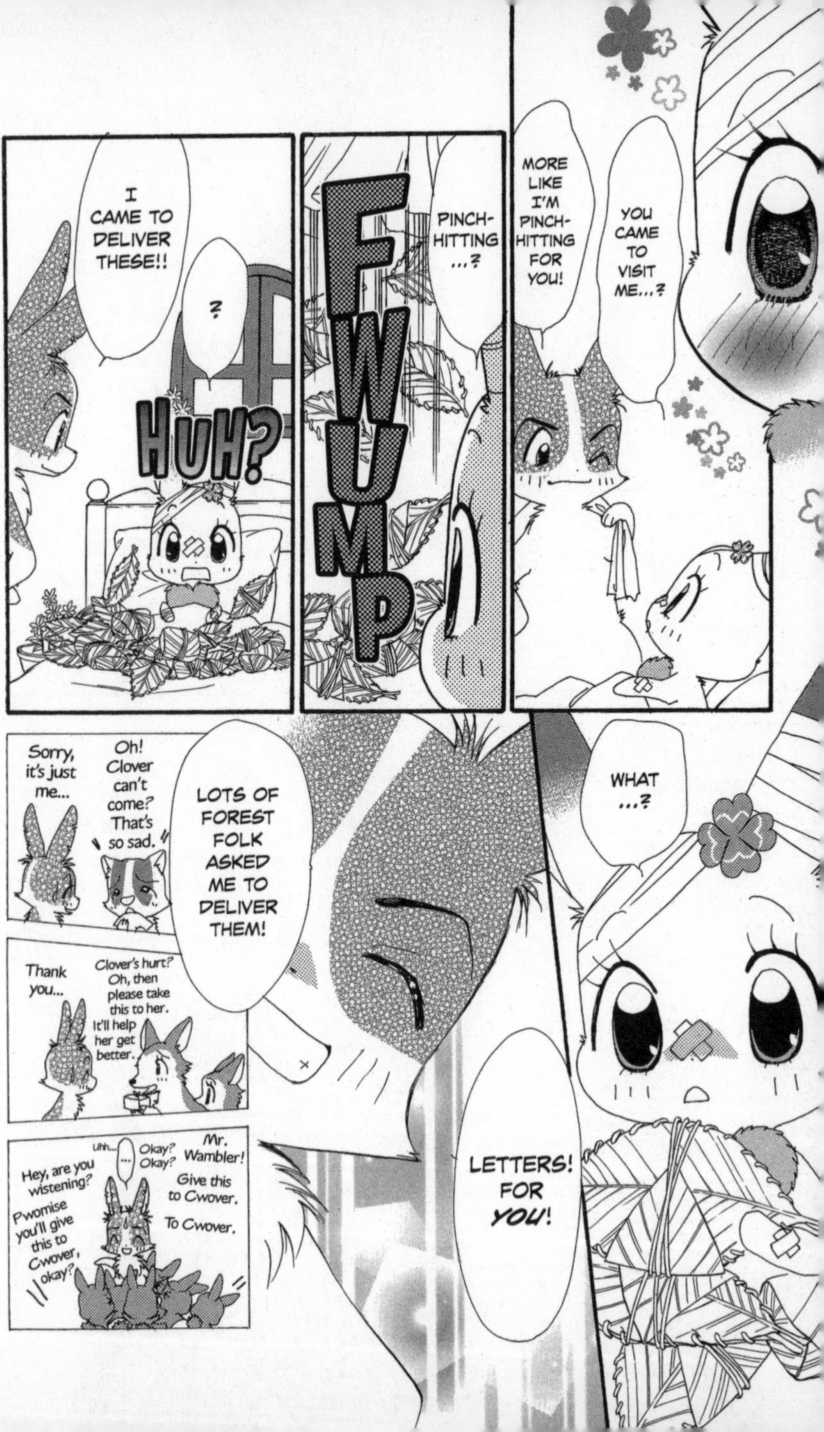
YOU CAME TO VISIT ME...?
MORE LIKE I'M PINCH-HITTING FOR YOU!
PINCH-HITTING...?
FWUMP
I CAME TO DELIVER THESE!!
?
HUH?
WHAT...?
LETTERS! FOR YOU!
LOTS OF FOREST FOLK ASKED ME TO DELIVER THEM!
Oh! Clover can't come? That's so sad.
Sorry, it's just me...
Clover's hurt? Oh, then please take this to her. It'll help her get better.
Thank you...
Mr. Wambler!
Give this to Cwover.
To Cwover.
Okay? Okay?
Uhh...
...
Hey, are you wistening?
Pwomise you'll give this to Cwover, okay?

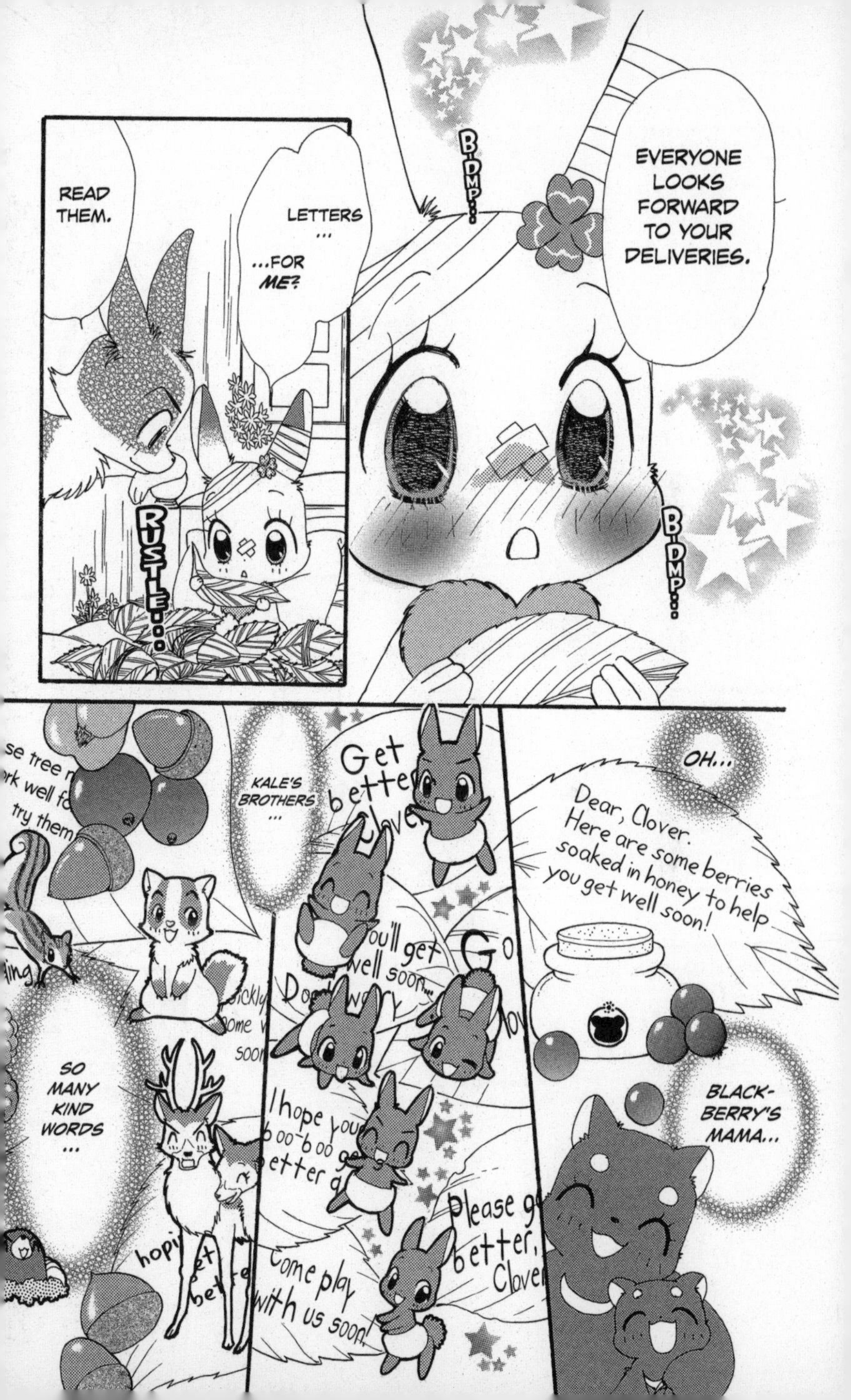
B-DMP...
EVERYONE LOOKS FORWARD TO YOUR DELIVERIES.
B-DMP...
LETTERS...
...FOR ME?
READ THEM.
RUSTLE...
OH...
Dear, Clover. Here are some berries soaked in honey to help you get well soon!
BLACK-BERRY'S MAMA...
KALE'S BROTHERS...
Get better
Come play with us soon!
SO MANY KIND WORDS...

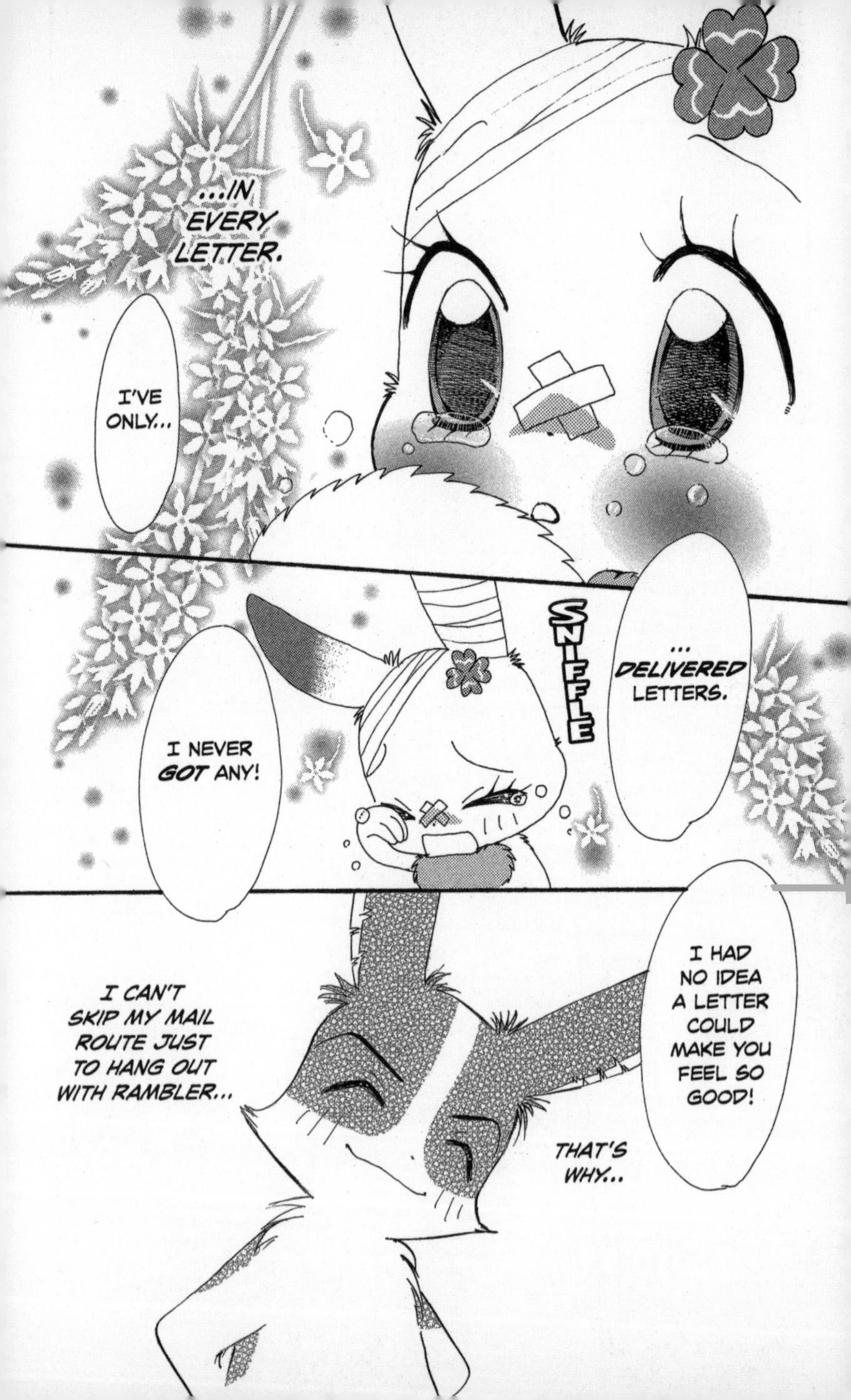
...IN EVERY LETTER.
I'VE ONLY...
...DELIVERED LETTERS.
SNIFFLE
I NEVER GOT ANY!
I HAD NO IDEA A LETTER COULD MAKE YOU FEEL SO GOOD!
THAT'S WHY...
I CAN'T SKIP MY MAIL ROUTE JUST TO HANG OUT WITH RAMBLER...

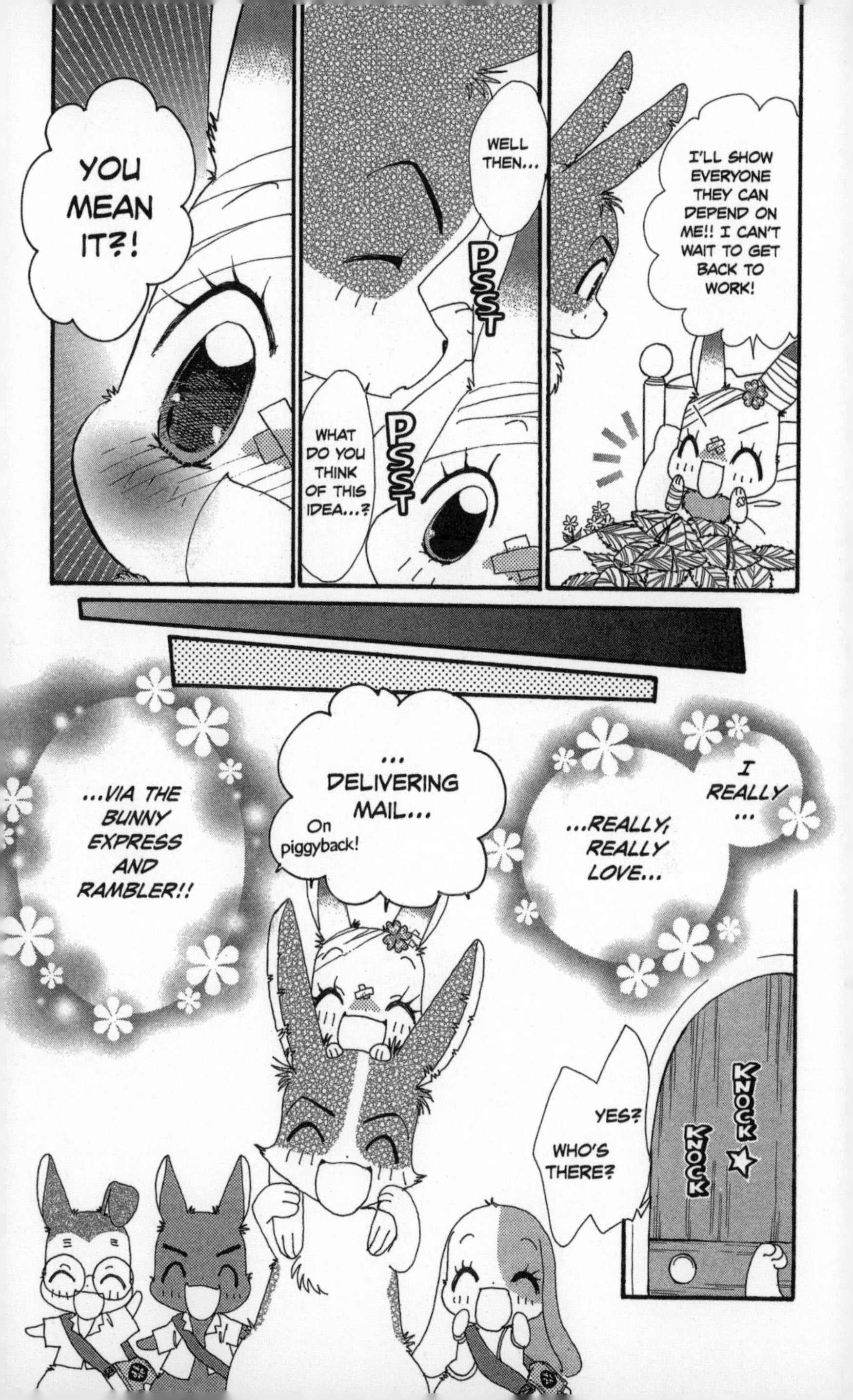
I'LL SHOW EVERYONE THEY CAN DEPEND ON ME!! I CAN'T WAIT TO GET BACK TO WORK!
WELL THEN...
PSST
WHAT DO YOU THINK OF THIS IDEA...?
PSST
YOU MEAN IT?!
I REALLY...
...REALLY, REALLY LOVE...
...DELIVERING MAIL...
On piggyback!
...VIA THE BUNNY EXPRESS AND RAMBLER!!
KNOCK☆KNOCK
YES? WHO'S THERE?

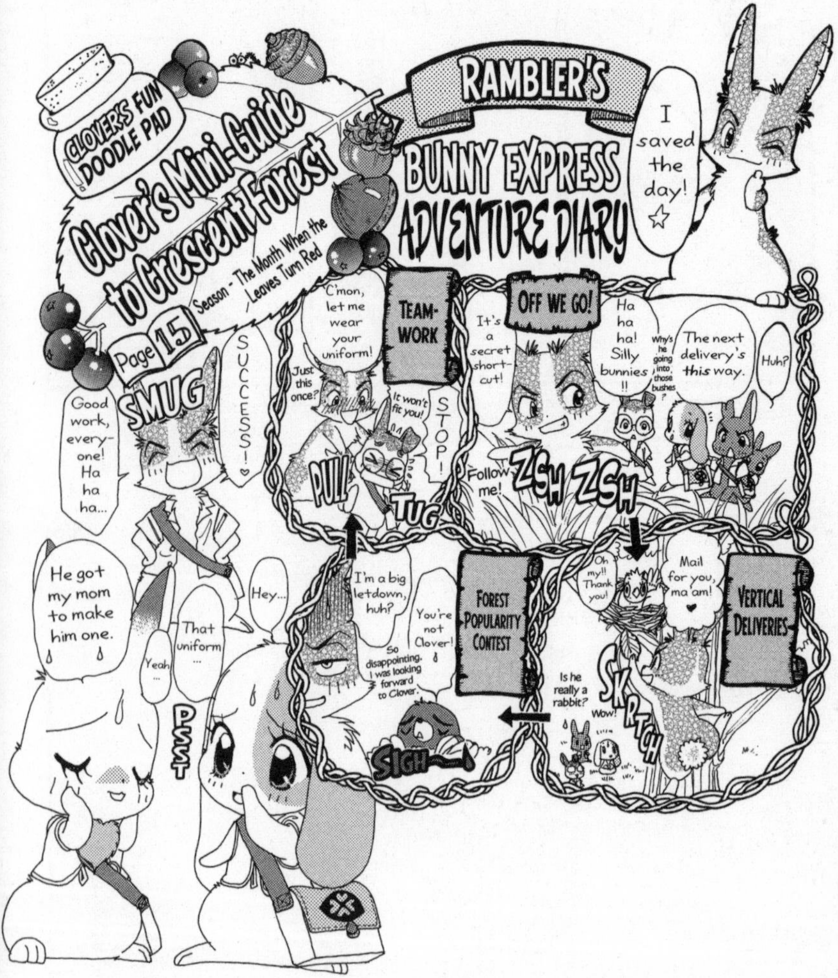
RAMBLER'S
BUNNY EXPRESS ADVENTURE DIARY
I saved the day! ☆
CLOVER'S FUN DOODLE PAD
Clover's Mini-Guide to Crescent Forest
Season - The Month When the Leaves Turn Red
Page 15
OFF WE GO!
The next delivery's this way.
Huh?
Why's he going into those bushes?
Ha ha ha! Silly bunnies!!
It's a secret short-cut!
Follow me!
ZSH ZSH
TEAM-WORK
C'mon, let me wear your uniform!
Just this once?
It won't fit you!
STOP!
PULL
TUG
VERTICAL DELIVERIES
Mail for you, ma'am! ♥
Oh my!! Thank you!
SKRTCH
Is he really a rabbit?
Wow!
FOREST POPULARITY CONTEST
You're not Clover!
So disappointing. I was looking forward to Clover.
I'm a big letdown, huh?
SIGH
SUCCESS! ♥
SMUG
Good work, every-one! Ha ha ha...
Hey...
That uniform...
Yeah...
He got my mom to make him one.
PSST

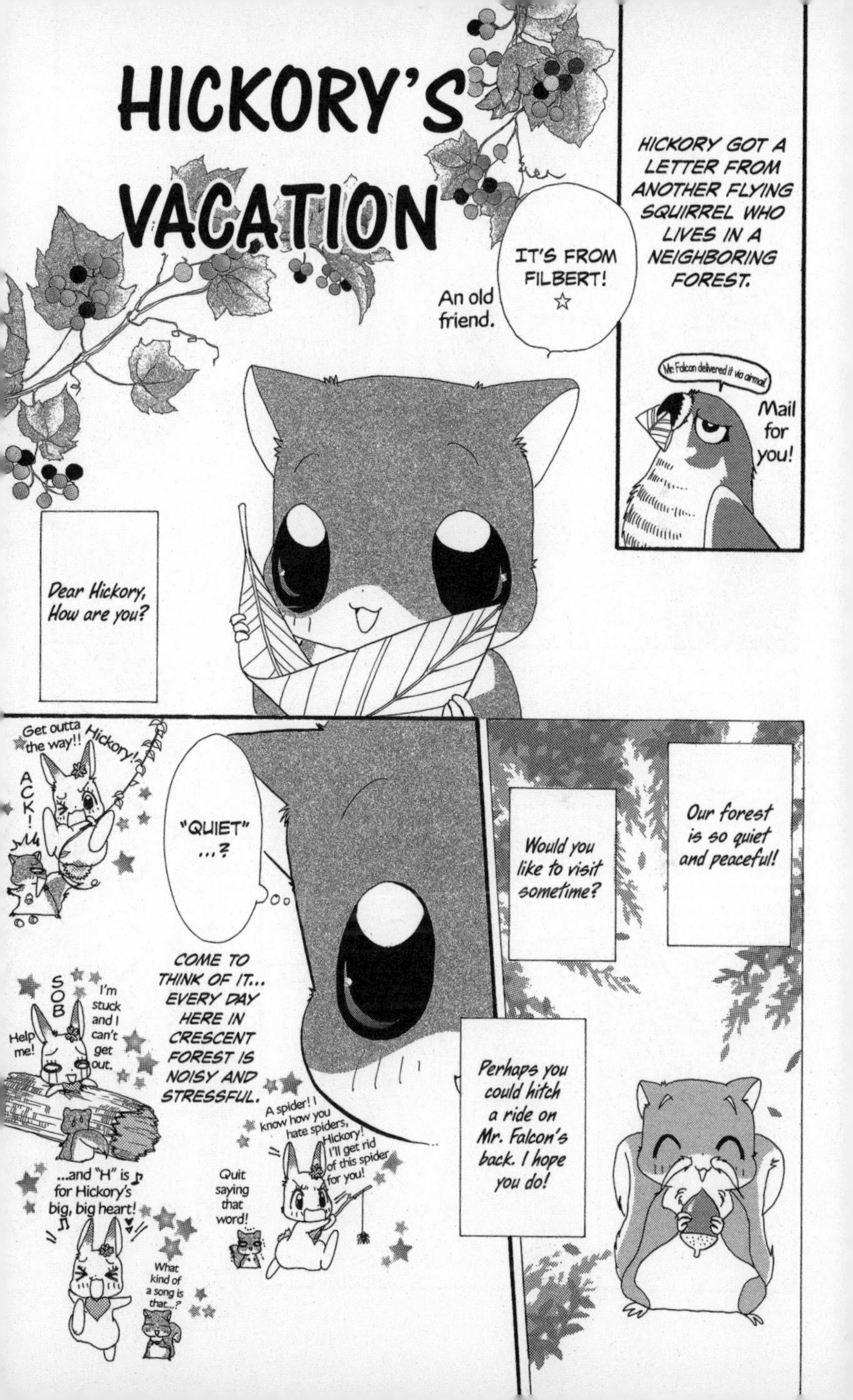
HICKORY GOT A LETTER FROM ANOTHER FLYING SQUIRREL WHO LIVES IN A NEIGHBORING FOREST.
Mr. Falcon delivered it via airmail
Mail for you!
HICKORY'S VACATION
IT'S FROM FILBERT! ☆
An old friend.
Dear Hickory, How are you?
Our forest is so quiet and peaceful!
Would you like to visit sometime?
Perhaps you could hitch a ride on Mr. Falcon's back. I hope you do!
"QUIET" ...?
COME TO THINK OF IT... EVERY DAY HERE IN CRESCENT FOREST IS NOISY AND STRESSFUL.
Hickory!
Get outta the way!!
ACK!
SOB
I'm stuck and I can't get out.
Help me!
A spider! I know how you hate spiders, Hickory! I'll get rid of this spider for you!
Quit saying that word!
...and "H" is for Hickory's big, big heart!
What kind of a song is that...?

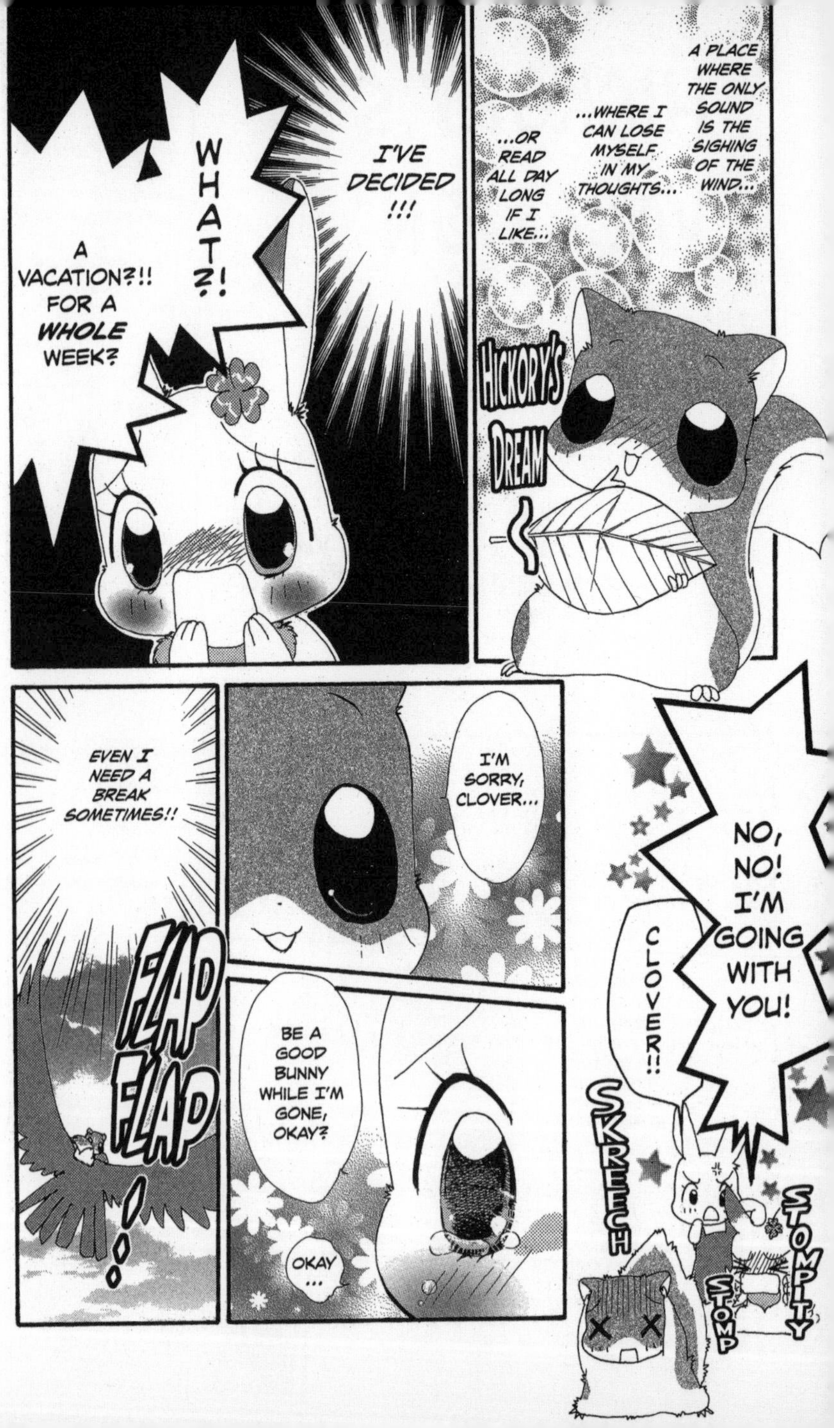
A PLACE WHERE THE ONLY SOUND IS THE SIGHING OF THE WIND...
...WHERE I CAN LOSE MYSELF IN MY THOUGHTS...
...OR READ ALL DAY LONG IF I LIKE...
HICKORY'S DREAM
I'VE DECIDED!!!
WHAT?!
A VACATION?!! FOR A WHOLE WEEK?
NO, NO! I'M GOING WITH YOU!
CLOVER!!
SKREECH
STOMPITY
STOMP
I'M SORRY, CLOVER...
BE A GOOD BUNNY WHILE I'M GONE, OKAY?
OKAY...
EVEN I NEED A BREAK SOMETIMES!!
FLAP FLAP
...

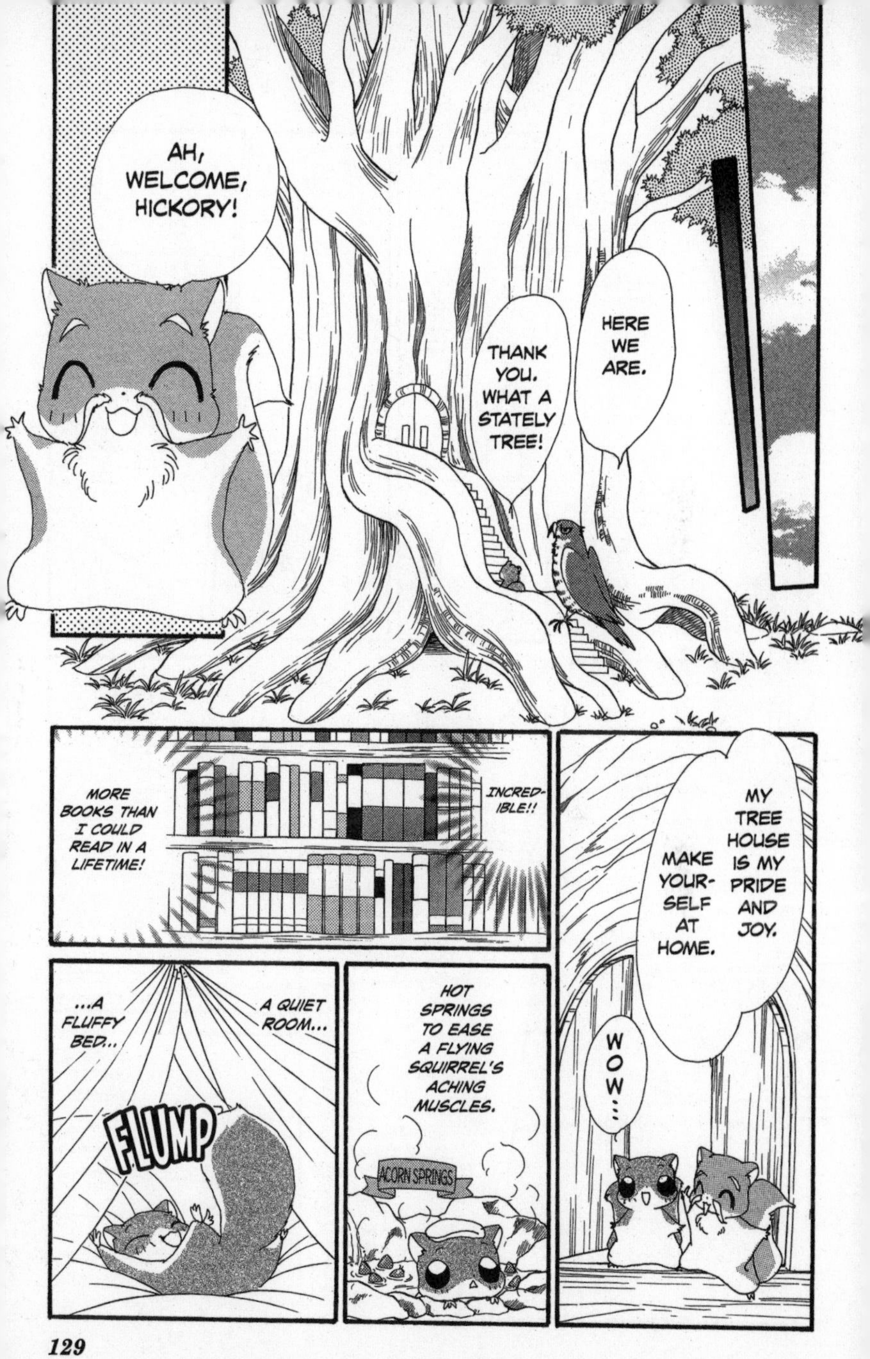
HERE WE ARE.
THANK YOU. WHAT A STATELY TREE!
AH, WELCOME, HICKORY!
MY TREE HOUSE IS MY PRIDE AND JOY.
MAKE YOURSELF AT HOME.
WOW...
INCREDIBLE!!
MORE BOOKS THAN I COULD READ IN A LIFETIME!
HOT SPRINGS TO EASE A FLYING SQUIRREL'S ACHING MUSCLES.
ACORN SPRINGS
A QUIET ROOM...
...A FLUFFY BED...
FLUMP

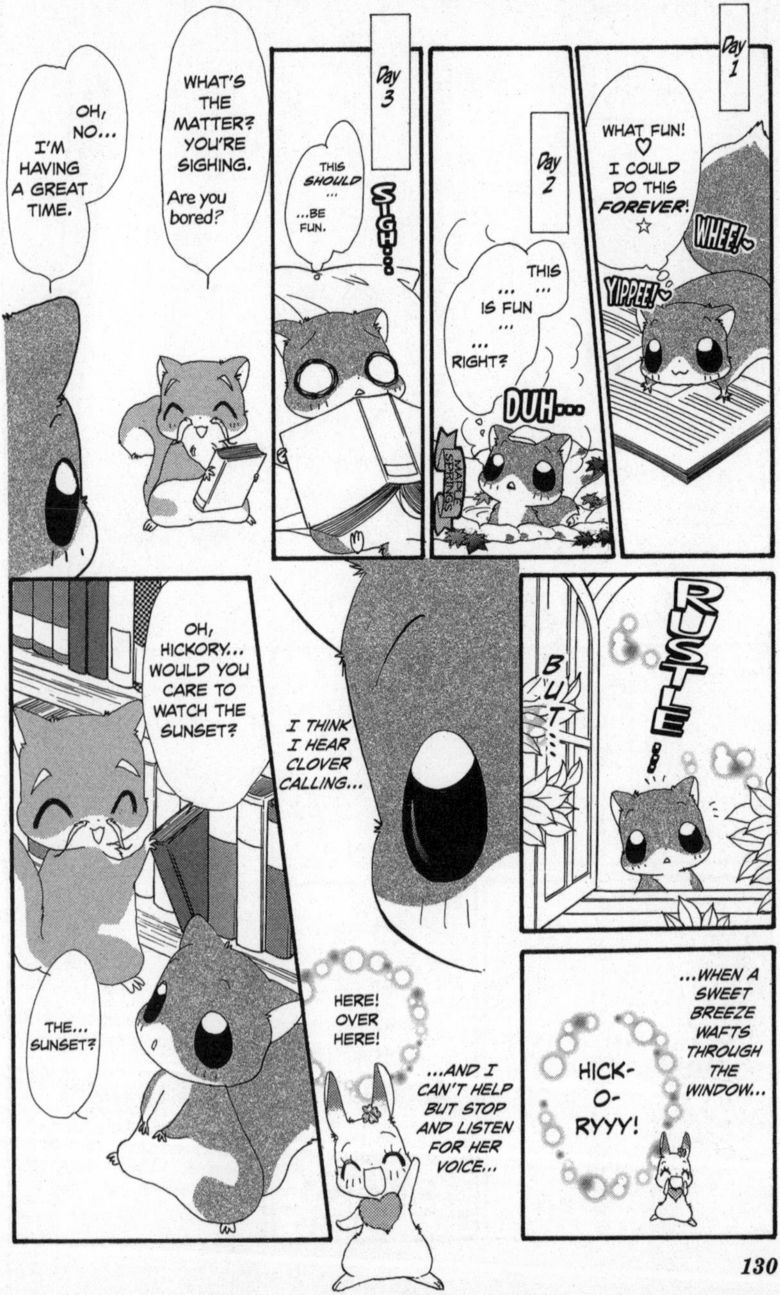
Day 1
WHAT FUN! ♡ I COULD DO THIS FOREVER! ☆
WHEE!
YIPPEE!
Day 2
THIS ... ... IS FUN ... ... RIGHT?
DUH...
MAPLE SPRINGS
Day 3
THIS SHOULD ... ...BE FUN.
SIGH...
WHAT'S THE MATTER? YOU'RE SIGHING. Are you bored?
OH, NO... I'M HAVING A GREAT TIME.
RUSTLE...
BUT...
...WHEN A SWEET BREEZE WAFTS THROUGH THE WINDOW...
HICK-O-RYYY!
I THINK I HEAR CLOVER CALLING...
HERE! OVER HERE!
...AND I CAN'T HELP BUT STOP AND LISTEN FOR HER VOICE...
OH, HICKORY... WOULD YOU CARE TO WATCH THE SUNSET?
THE... SUNSET?

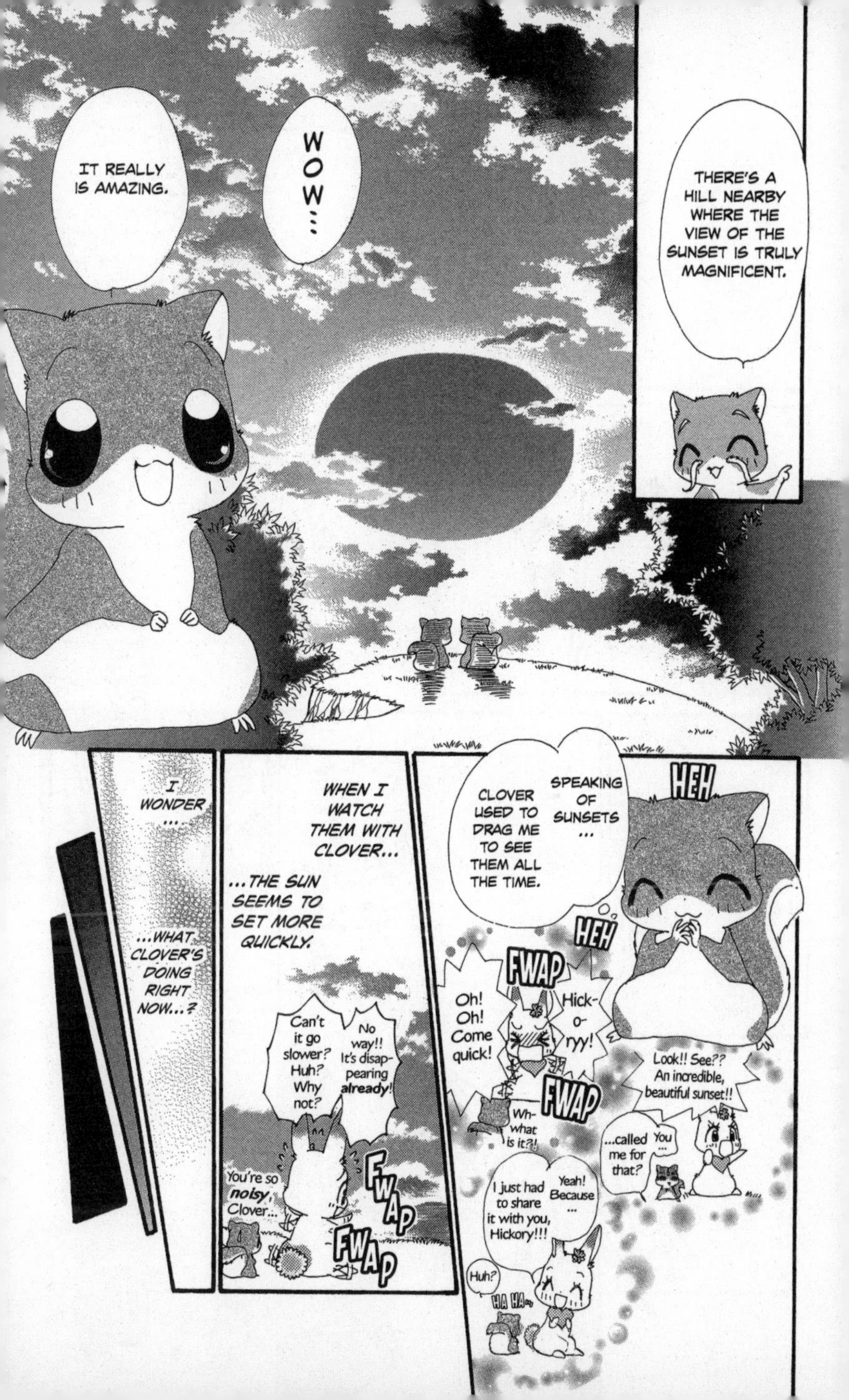
THERE'S A HILL NEARBY WHERE THE VIEW OF THE SUNSET IS TRULY MAGNIFICENT.
WOW...
IT REALLY IS AMAZING.
HEH
SPEAKING OF SUNSETS...
CLOVER USED TO DRAG ME TO SEE THEM ALL THE TIME.
HEH
Hick-o-ryyy!
FWAP
Oh! Oh! Come quick!
FWAP
Look!! See?? An incredible, beautiful sunset!!
Wh-what is it?!
You...
...called me for that?
Yeah! Because...
I just had to share it with you, Hickory!!!
Huh?
HA HA
WHEN I WATCH THEM WITH CLOVER...
...THE SUN SEEMS TO SET MORE QUICKLY.
No way!! It's disap-pearing **already**!
Can't it go slower? Huh? Why not?
FWAP
FWAP
You're so **noisy**, Clover...
I WONDER...
...WHAT CLOVER'S DOING RIGHT NOW...?

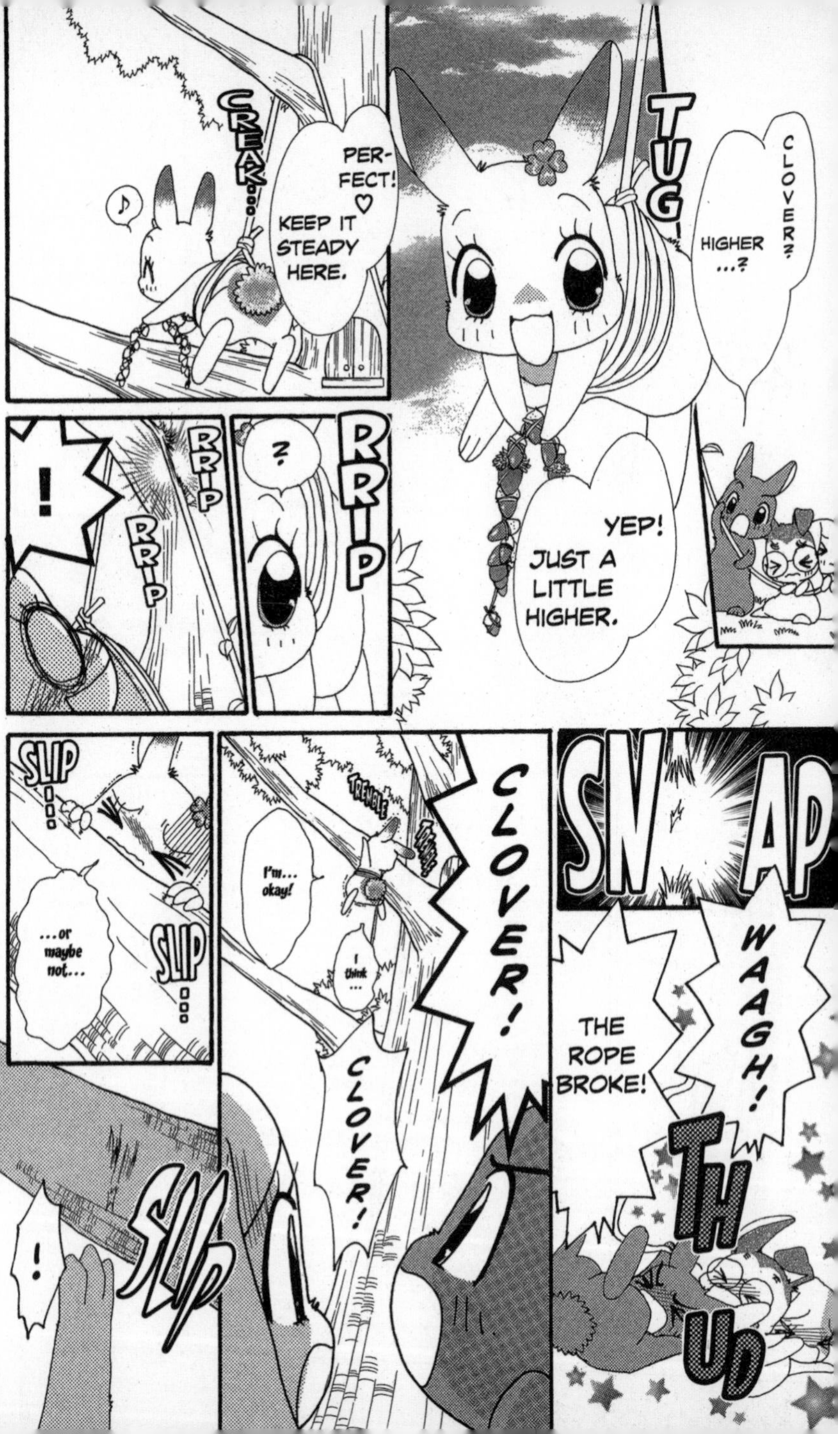
TUG
CLOVER?
HIGHER ...?
YEP! JUST A LITTLE HIGHER.
CREAK...
♪
PER-FECT! ♡ KEEP IT STEADY HERE.
RRIP
?
!
RRIP
RRIP
SNAP
WAAGH!
THE ROPE BROKE!
THUD
CLOVER!
TREMBLE
I'm... okay!
I think...
CLOVER!
SLIP...
...or maybe not...
SLIP...
SLIP
!

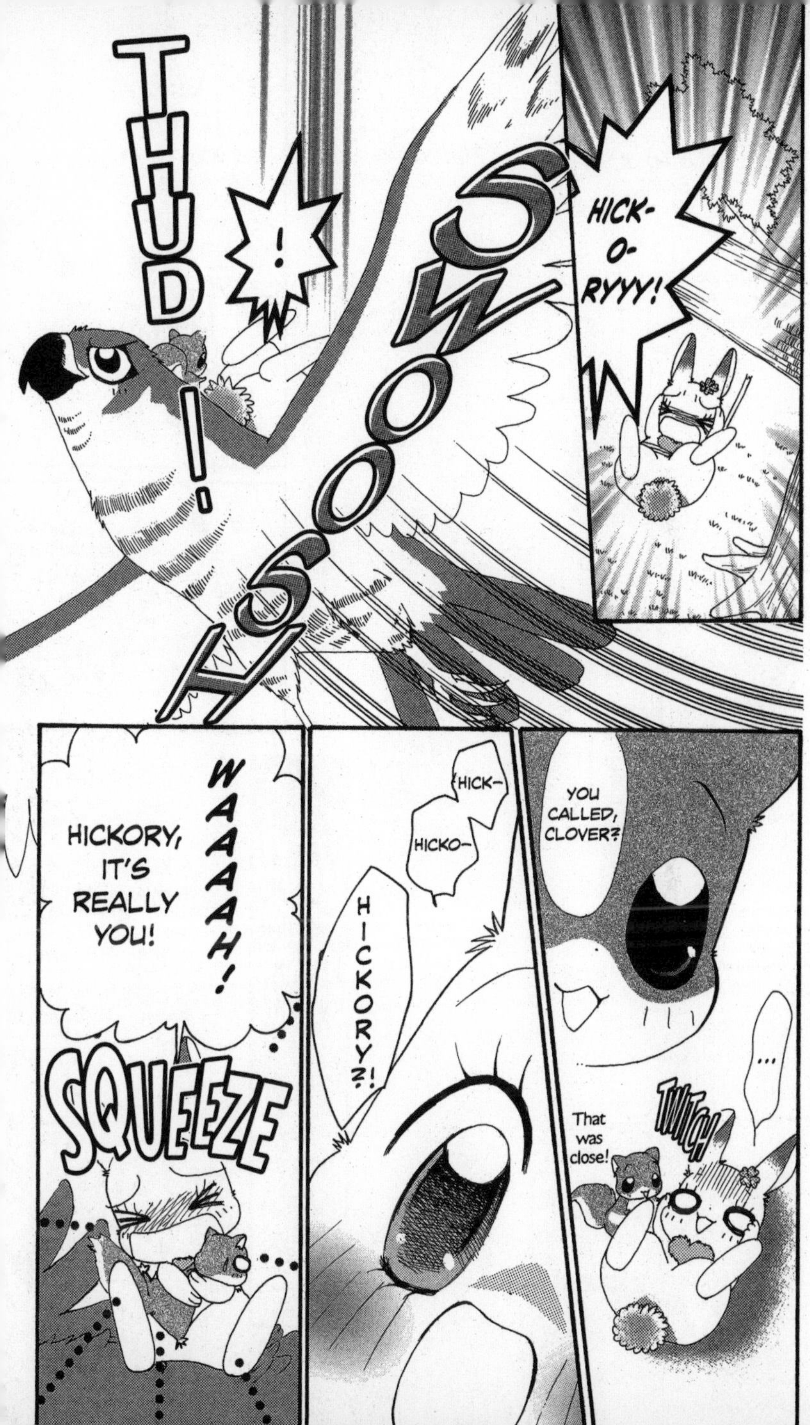
HICK-O-RYYY!
SWOOSH
!
THUD!!
YOU CALLED, CLOVER?
...
...
TWITCH
That was close!
HICK-
HICKO-
HICKORY?!
WAAAAAH!
HICKORY, IT'S REALLY YOU!
SQUEEZE

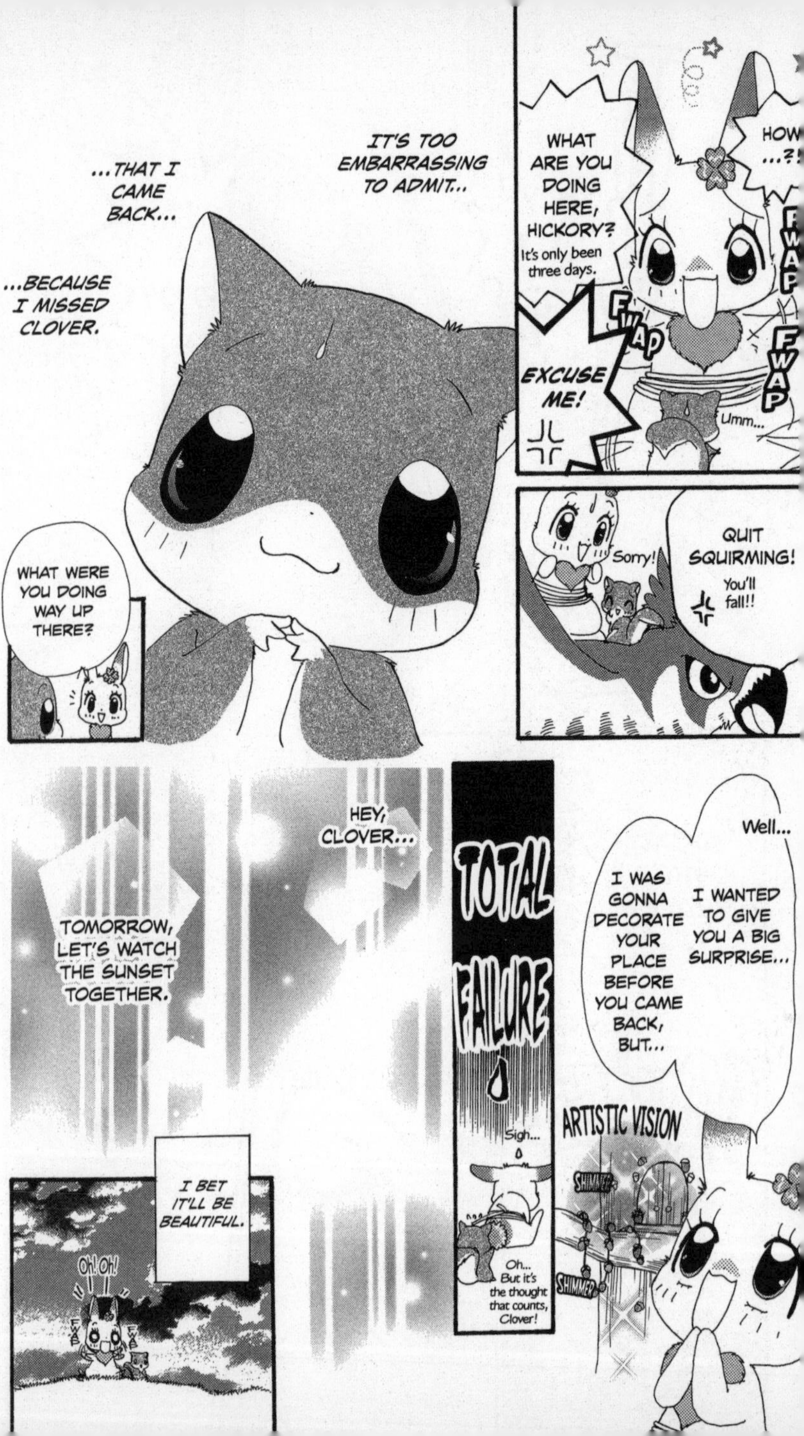
HOW ...?!
WHAT ARE YOU DOING HERE, HICKORY?
It's only been three days.
FWAP
FWAP
FWAP
EXCUSE ME!
Umm...
QUIT SQUIRMING!
You'll fall!!
Sorry!
IT'S TOO EMBARRASSING TO ADMIT...
...THAT I CAME BACK...
...BECAUSE I MISSED CLOVER.
WHAT WERE YOU DOING WAY UP THERE?
Well...
I WANTED TO GIVE YOU A BIG SURPRISE...
I WAS GONNA DECORATE YOUR PLACE BEFORE YOU CAME BACK, BUT...
ARTISTIC VISION
SHIMMER
SHIMMER
TOTAL FAILURE
Sigh...
Oh... But it's the thought that counts, Clover!
HEY, CLOVER...
TOMORROW, LET'S WATCH THE SUNSET TOGETHER.
I BET IT'LL BE BEAUTIFUL.
Oh! Oh!
FWAP
FWAP

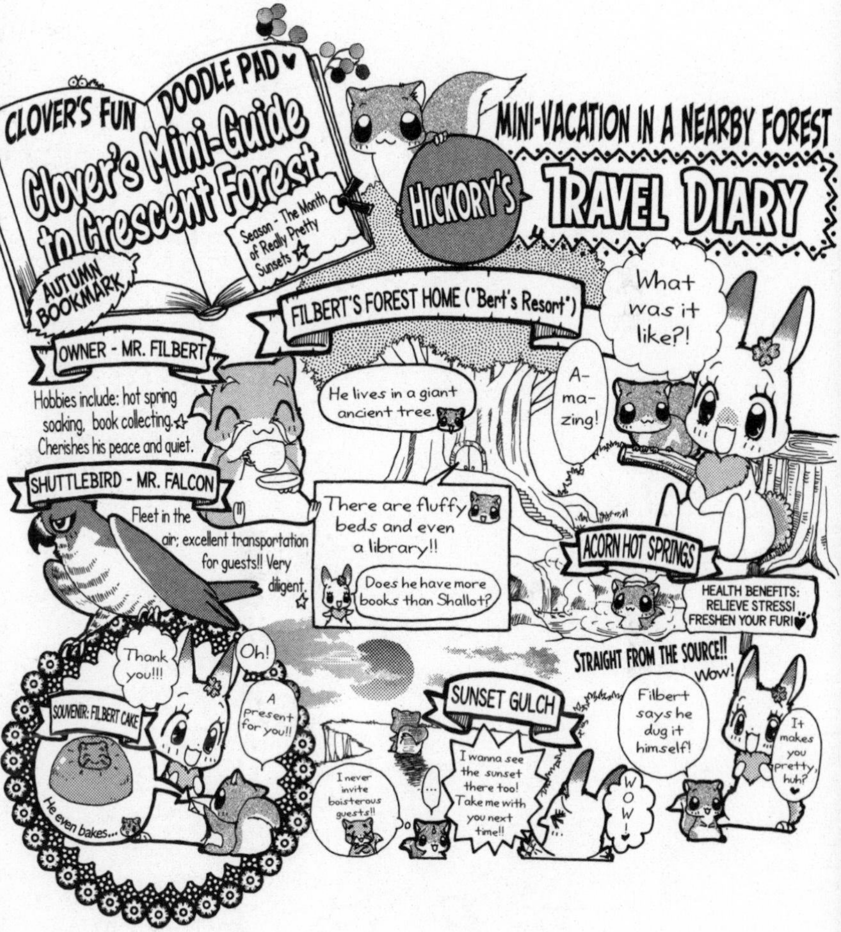
CLOVER'S FUN DOODLE PAD
Clover's Mini-Guide to Crescent Forest
Season - The Month of Really Pretty Sunsets
AUTUMN BOOKMARK
MINI-VACATION IN A NEARBY FOREST
HICKORY'S TRAVEL DIARY
What was it like?!
A-ma-zing!
FILBERT'S FOREST HOME ("Bert's Resort")
He lives in a giant ancient tree.
OWNER - MR. FILBERT
Hobbies include: hot spring soaking, book collecting. Cherishes his peace and quiet.
SHUTTLEBIRD - MR. FALCON
Fleet in the air; excellent transportation for guests!! Very diligent.
There are fluffy beds and even a library!!
Does he have more books than Shallot?
ACORN HOT SPRINGS
HEALTH BENEFITS: RELIEVE STRESS! FRESHEN YOUR FUR!
STRAIGHT FROM THE SOURCE!!
Wow!
Filbert says he dug it himself!
It makes you pretty, huh?
WOW!
SUNSET GULCH
I wanna see the sunset there too! Take me with you next time!!
...
I never invite boisterous guests!!
Oh!
A present for you!!
Thank you!!!
SOUVENIR: FILBERT CAKE
He even bakes...

A semi-realistic
depiction of Hickory.
Looks sleepy…

TEACHER FOR A DAY

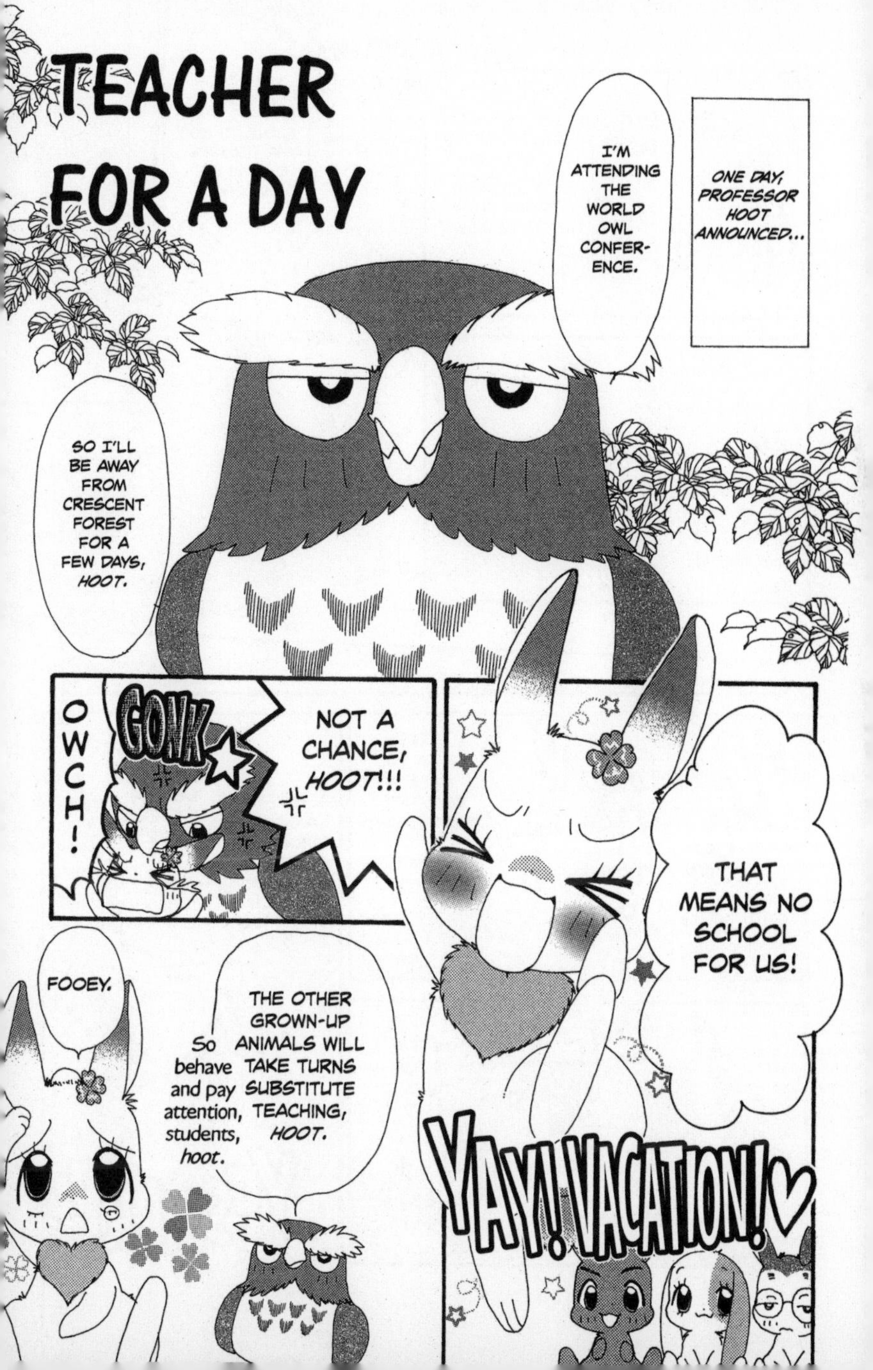
ONE DAY, PROFESSOR HOOT ANNOUNCED...
I'M ATTENDING THE WORLD OWL CONFERENCE.
SO I'LL BE AWAY FROM CRESCENT FOREST FOR A FEW DAYS, HOOT.
THAT MEANS NO SCHOOL FOR US!
YAY! VACATION!♥
NOT A CHANCE, HOOT!!!
GONK
OWCH!
THE OTHER GROWN-UP ANIMALS WILL TAKE TURNS SUBSTITUTE TEACHING, HOOT.
So behave and pay attention, students, hoot.
FOOEY.

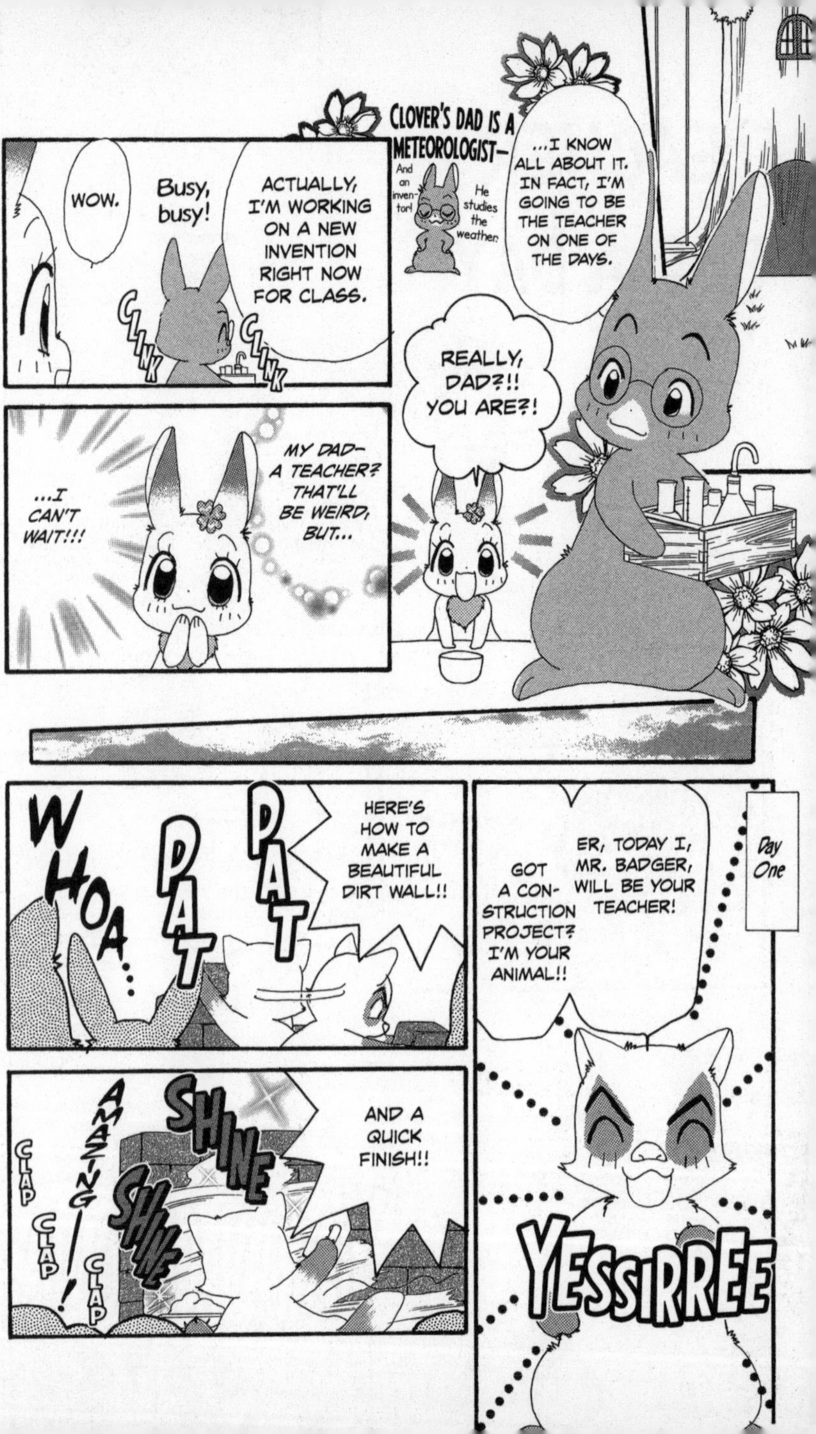
CLOVER'S DAD IS A METEOROLOGIST—
And an inven-tor!
He studies the weather.
...I KNOW ALL ABOUT IT. IN FACT, I'M GOING TO BE THE TEACHER ON ONE OF THE DAYS.
REALLY, DAD?!! YOU ARE?!
ACTUALLY, I'M WORKING ON A NEW INVENTION RIGHT NOW FOR CLASS.
CLINK
CLINK
Busy, busy!
WOW.
MY DAD— A TEACHER? THAT'LL BE WEIRD, BUT...
...I CAN'T WAIT!!!
Day One
ER, TODAY I, MR. BADGER, WILL BE YOUR TEACHER!
GOT A CON-STRUCTION PROJECT? I'M YOUR ANIMAL!!
YESSIRREE
HERE'S HOW TO MAKE A BEAUTIFUL DIRT WALL!!
PAT
PAT
WHOA...
AND A QUICK FINISH!!
SHINE
SHINE
AMAZING!
CLAP
CLAP
CLAP

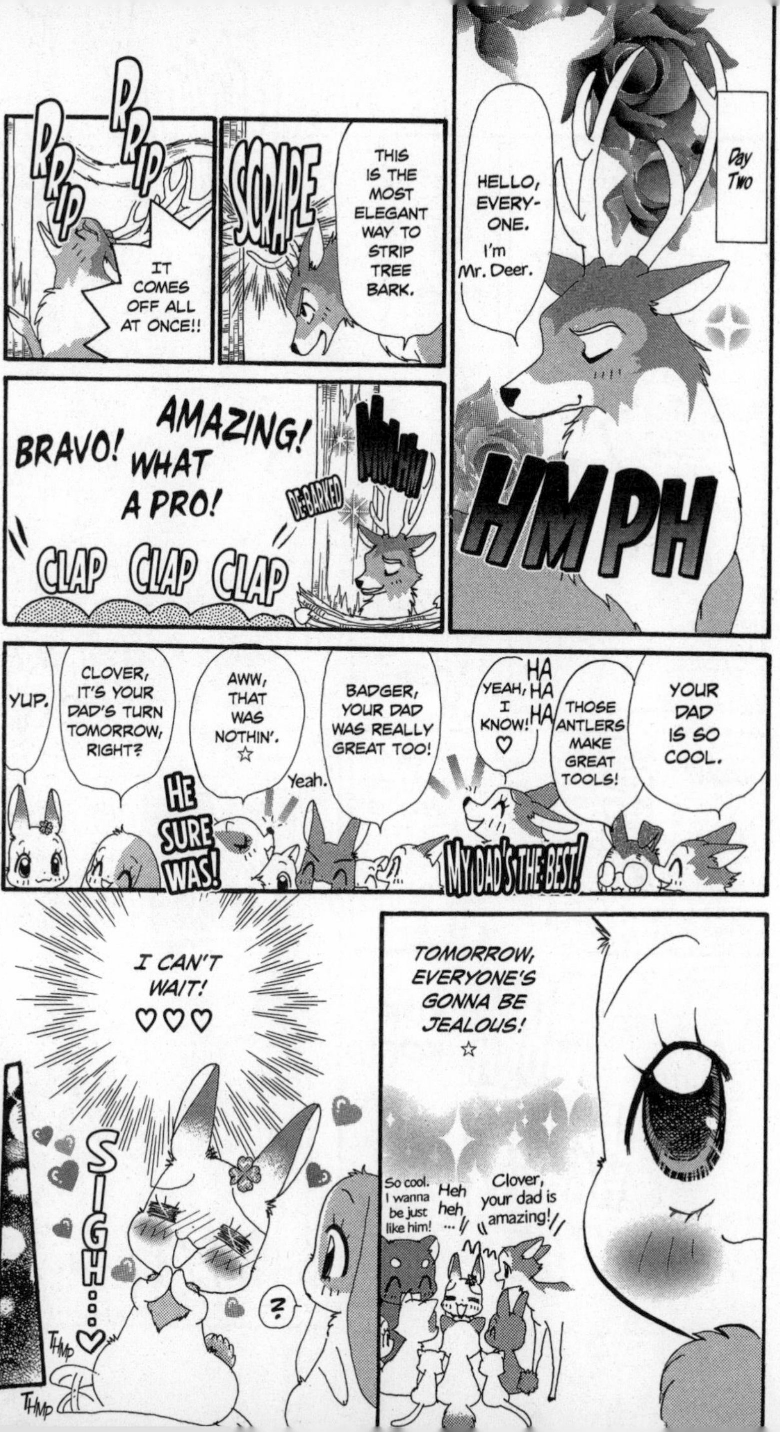
Day Two
HELLO, EVERY-ONE. I'm Mr. Deer.
HMPH
THIS IS THE MOST ELEGANT WAY TO STRIP TREE BARK.
SCRAPE
RRIP RRIP
IT COMES OFF ALL AT ONCE!!
DE-BARKED
AMAZING!
BRAVO!
WHAT A PRO!
CLAP CLAP CLAP
YOUR DAD IS SO COOL.
THOSE ANTLERS MAKE GREAT TOOLS!
HA HA HA
YEAH, I KNOW! ♡
MY DAD'S THE BEST!
BADGER, YOUR DAD WAS REALLY GREAT TOO!
Yeah.
AWW, THAT WAS NOTHIN'. ☆
HE SURE WAS!
CLOVER, IT'S YOUR DAD'S TURN TOMORROW, RIGHT?
YUP.
TOMORROW, EVERYONE'S GONNA BE JEALOUS! ☆
Clover, your dad is amazing!
Heh heh ...
So cool. I wanna be just like him!
I CAN'T WAIT! ♡♡♡
SIGH... ♡
?
THMP
THMP

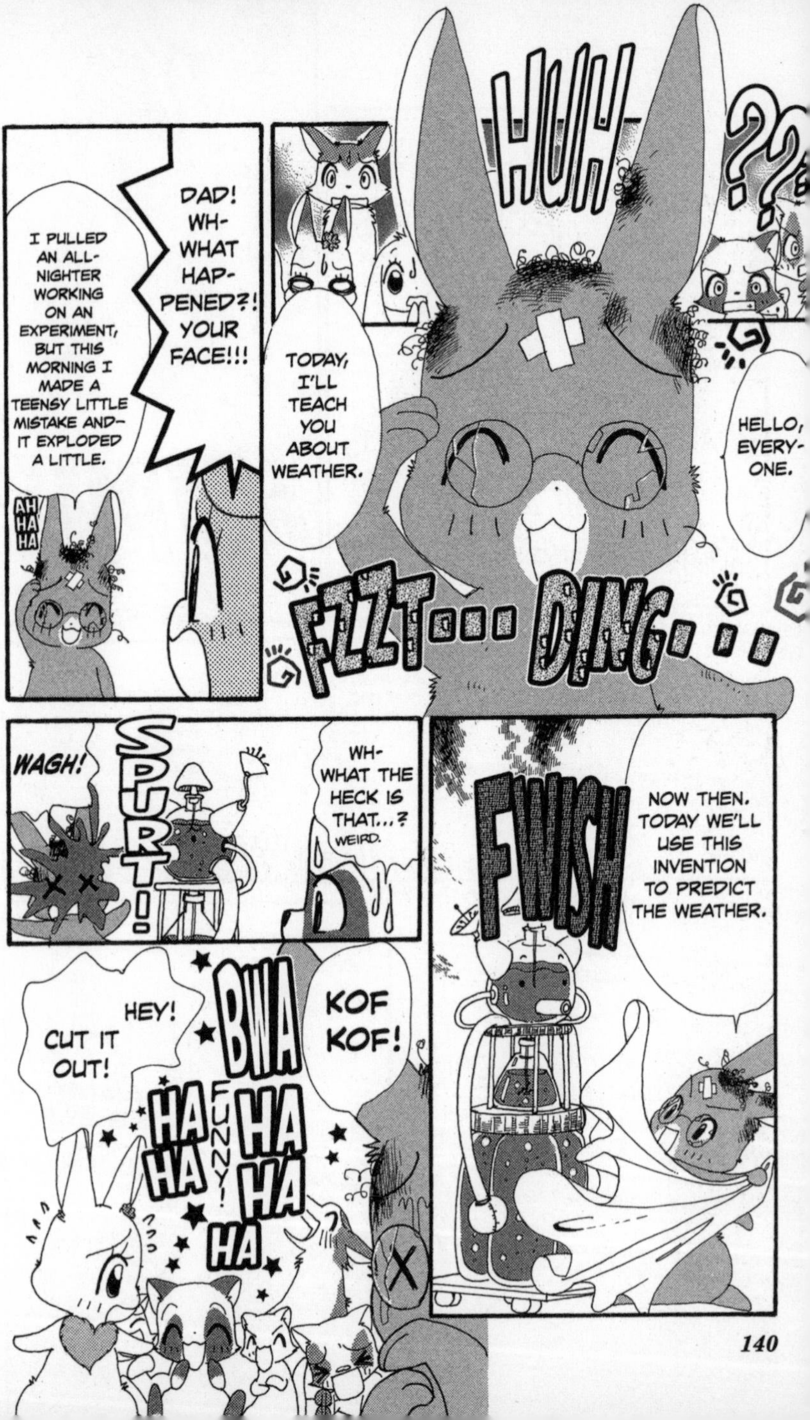
HUH ???
HELLO, EVERYONE.
TODAY, I'LL TEACH YOU ABOUT WEATHER.
FZZT... DING...
DAD! WH-WHAT HAPPENED?! YOUR FACE!!!
I PULLED AN ALL-NIGHTER WORKING ON AN EXPERIMENT, BUT THIS MORNING I MADE A TEENSY LITTLE MISTAKE AND—IT EXPLODED A LITTLE.
AH HA HA
FWISH
NOW THEN. TODAY WE'LL USE THIS INVENTION TO PREDICT THE WEATHER.
WH-WHAT THE HECK IS THAT...?
WEIRD.
SPURT!
WAGH!
KOF KOF!
BWA HA HA HA HA HA
FUNNY!
HEY! CUT IT OUT!
HA HA

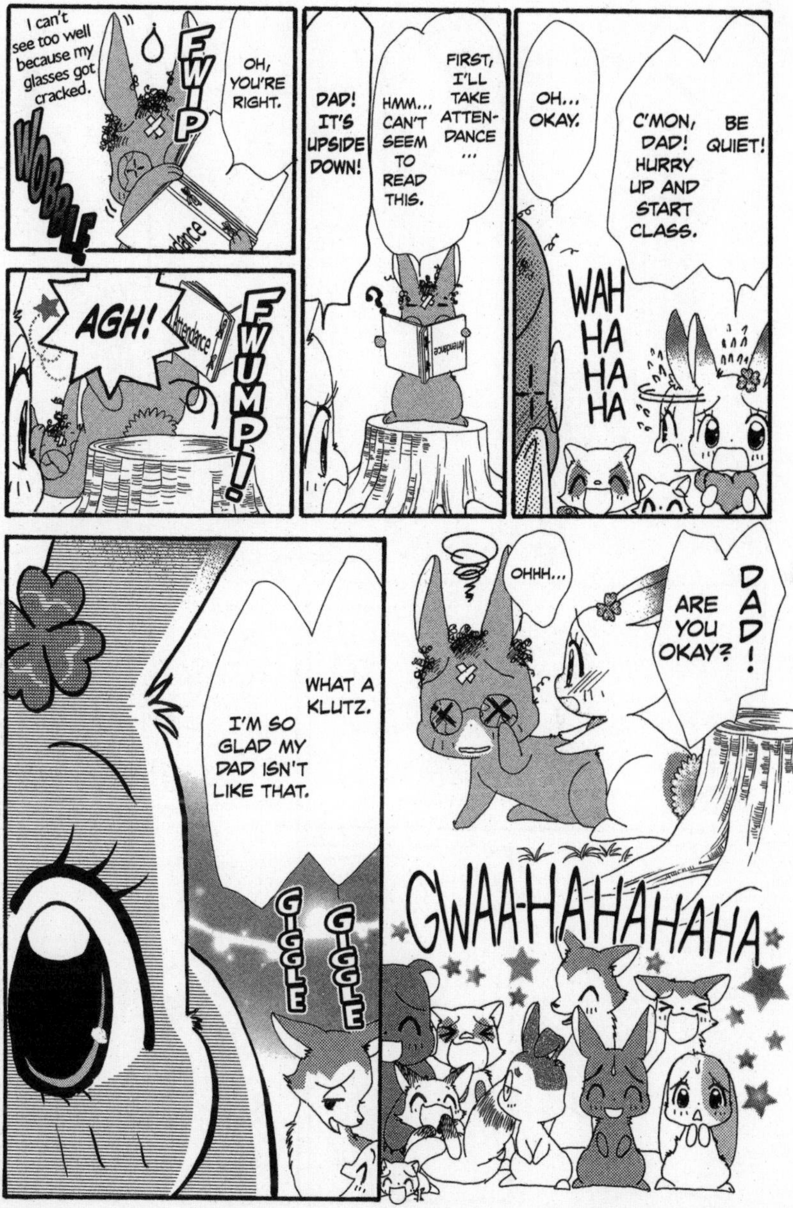
BE QUIET!
C'MON, DAD! HURRY UP AND START CLASS.
OH... OKAY.
WAH HA HA HA
FIRST, I'LL TAKE ATTEN-DANCE...
HMM... CAN'T SEEM TO READ THIS.
DAD! IT'S UPSIDE DOWN!
Attendance
OH, YOU'RE RIGHT.
FWIP
I can't see too well because my glasses got cracked.
WOBBLE
Attendance
FWUMP!
Attendance
AGH!
DAD!
ARE YOU OKAY?
OHHH...
GWAA-HAHAHAHA
WHAT A KLUTZ.
I'M SO GLAD MY DAD ISN'T LIKE THAT.
GIGGLE
GIGGLE

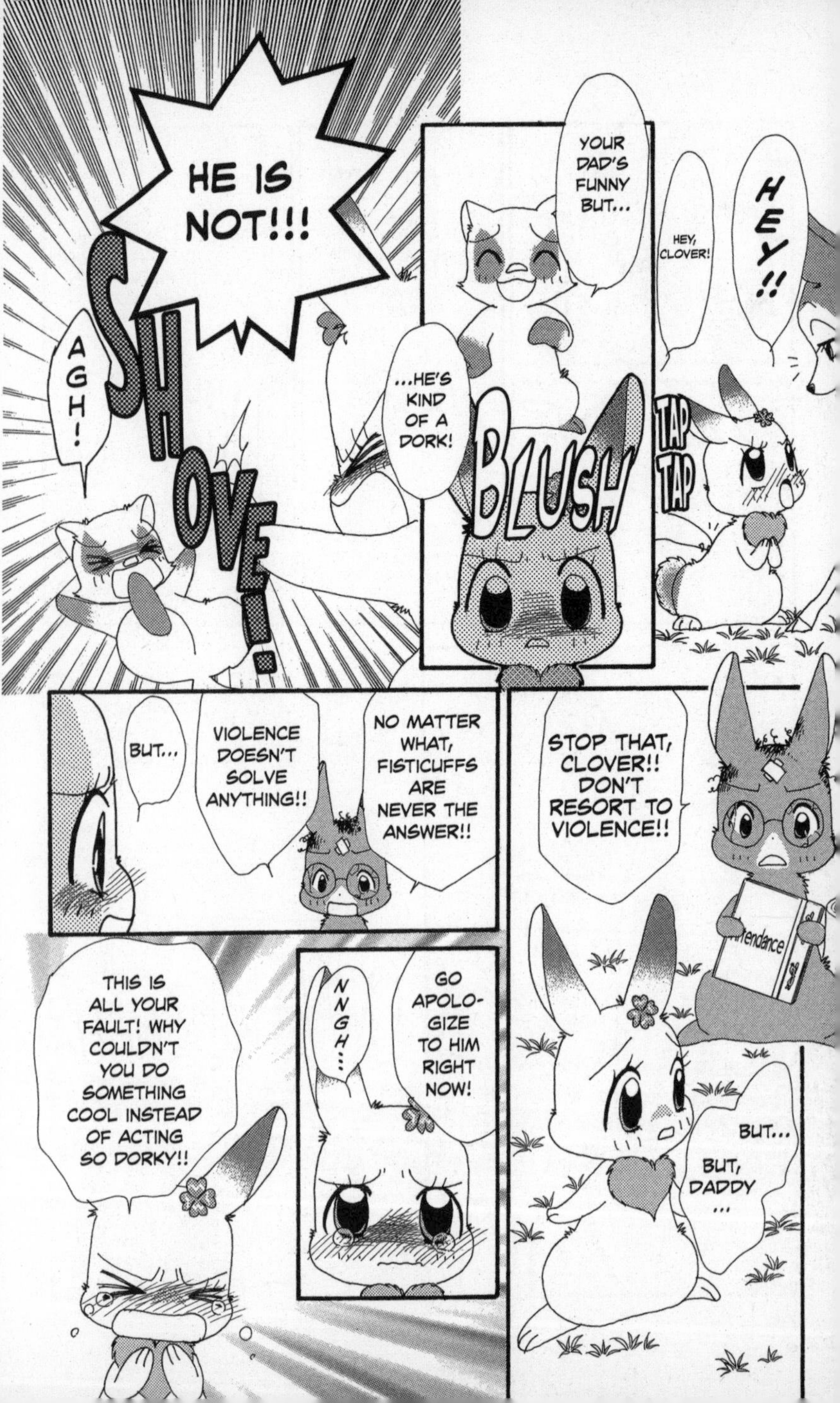
HEY!!
HEY, CLOVER!
TAP TAP
YOUR DAD'S FUNNY BUT...
...HE'S KIND OF A DORK!
BLUSH
HE IS NOT!!!
SHOVE!
AGH!
STOP THAT, CLOVER!! DON'T RESORT TO VIOLENCE!!
NO MATTER WHAT, FISTICUFFS ARE NEVER THE ANSWER!!
VIOLENCE DOESN'T SOLVE ANYTHING!!
BUT...
BUT...
BUT, DADDY ...
GO APOLO-GIZE TO HIM RIGHT NOW!
NNGH...
THIS IS ALL YOUR FAULT! WHY COULDN'T YOU DO SOMETHING COOL INSTEAD OF ACTING SO DORKY!!

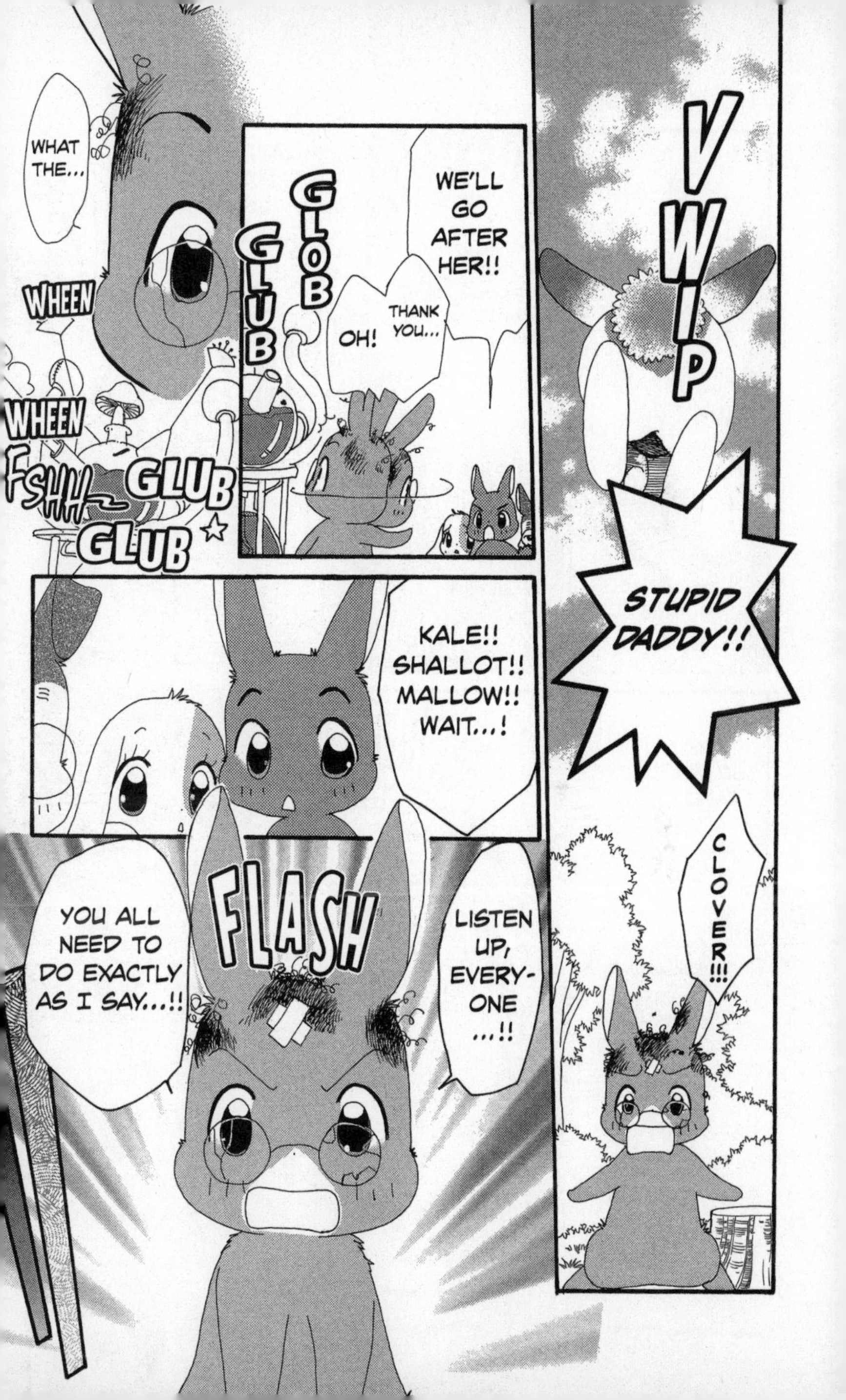

VWIP
STUPID DADDY!!
CLOVER!!!
WE'LL GO AFTER HER!!
THANK YOU...
OH!
GLOB
GLUB
WHAT THE...
WHEEN
WHEEN
FSHH
GLUB
GLUB
KALE!! SHALLOT!! MALLOW!! WAIT...!
LISTEN UP, EVERY-ONE ...!!
FLASH
YOU ALL NEED TO DO EXACTLY AS I SAY...!!

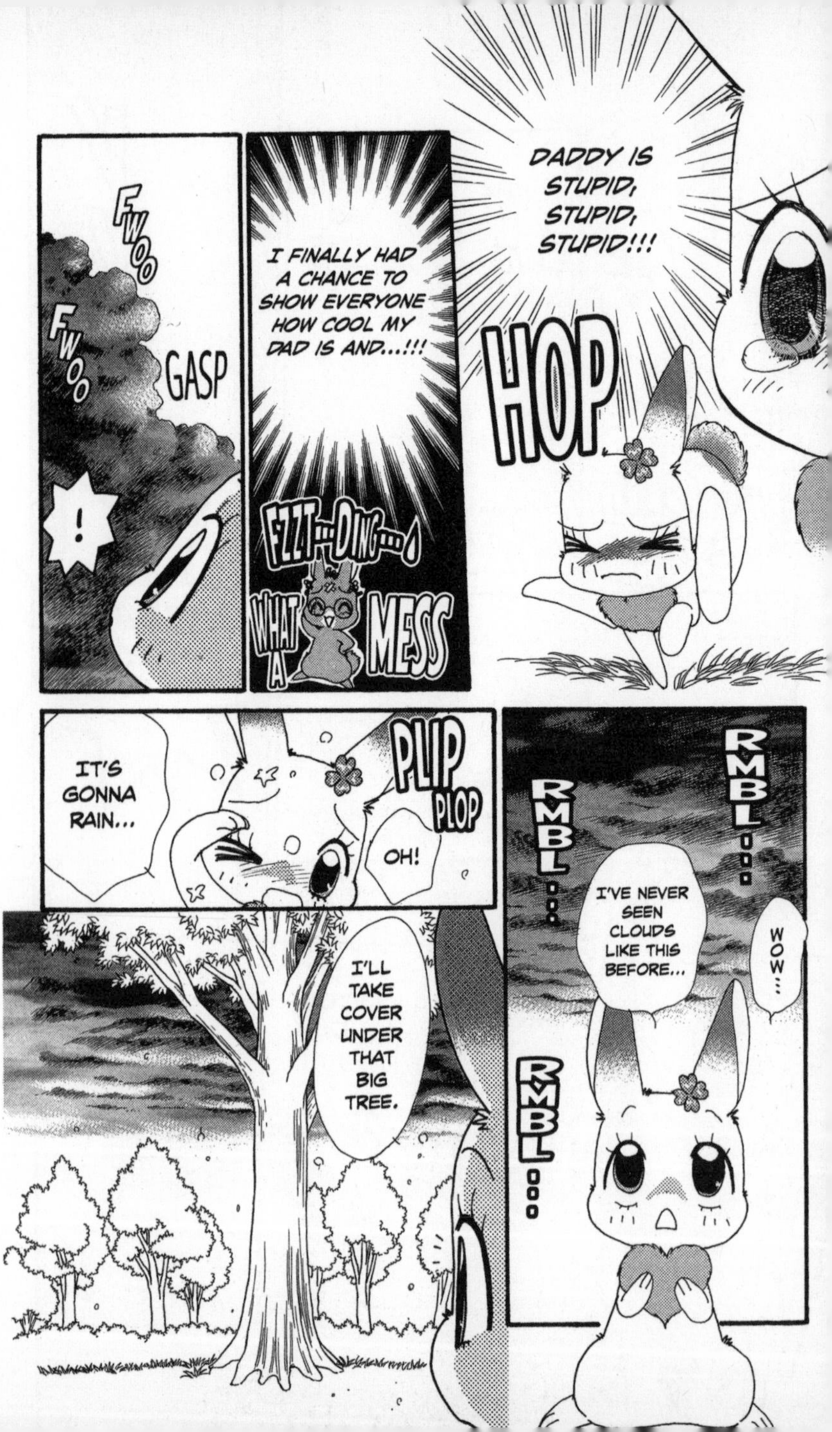
DADDY IS STUPID, STUPID, STUPID!!!
HOP
I FINALLY HAD A CHANCE TO SHOW EVERYONE HOW COOL MY DAD IS AND...!!!
FZZT...DING...
WHAT A MESS
FWOO
FWOO
GASP
!
RMBL...
RMBL...
WOW...
I'VE NEVER SEEN CLOUDS LIKE THIS BEFORE...
RMBL...
PLIP
PLOP
OH!
IT'S GONNA RAIN...
I'LL TAKE COVER UNDER THAT BIG TREE.

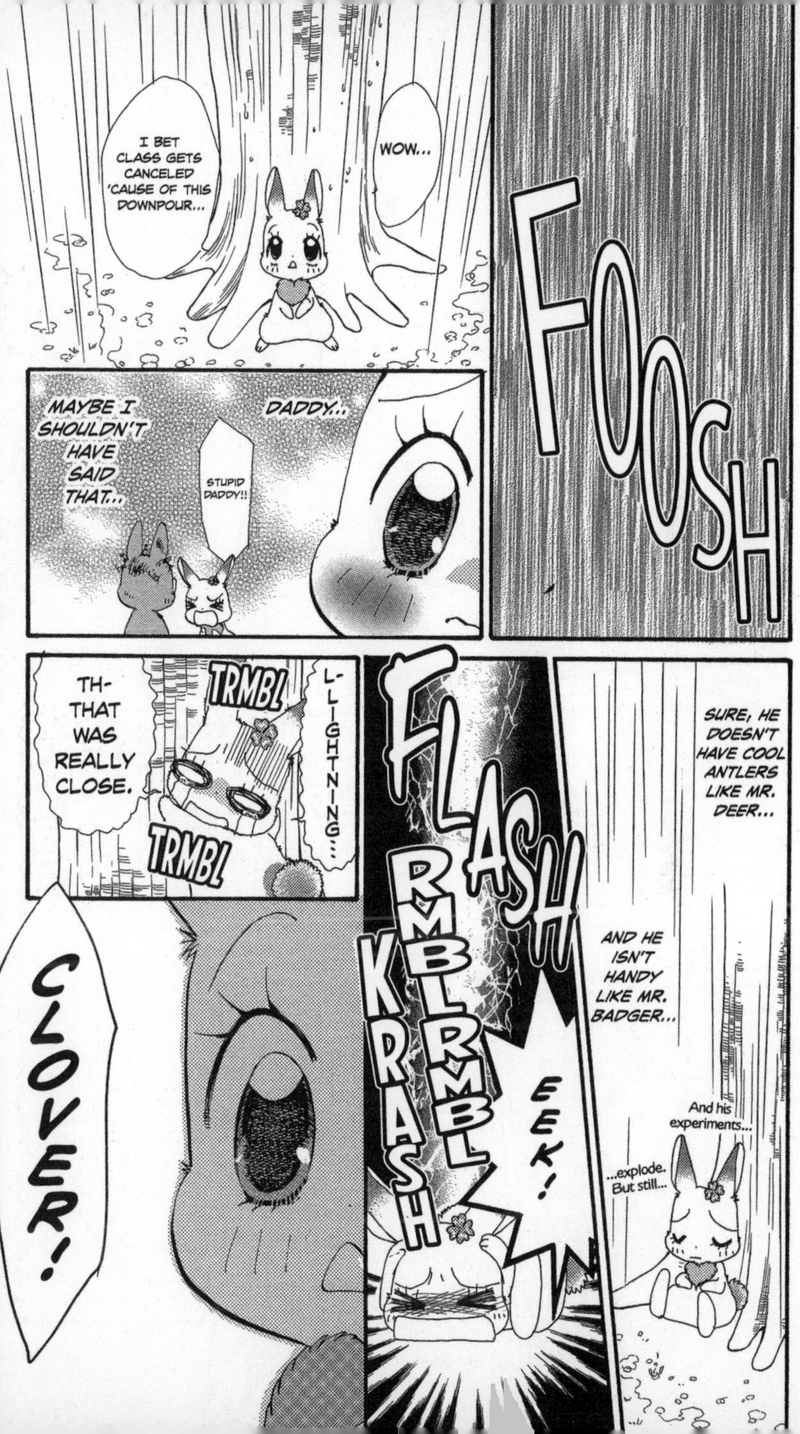
FOOSH
WOW...
I BET CLASS GETS CANCELED 'CAUSE OF THIS DOWNPOUR...
DADDY...
MAYBE I SHOULDN'T HAVE SAID THAT...
STUPID DADDY!!
SURE, HE DOESN'T HAVE COOL ANTLERS LIKE MR. DEER...
AND HE ISN'T HANDY LIKE MR. BADGER...
And his experiments...
...explode. But still...
FLASH
RMBL RMBL
KRASH
EEK!
L-LIGHTNING...
TRMBL
TH-THAT WAS REALLY CLOSE.
TRMBL
CLOVER!

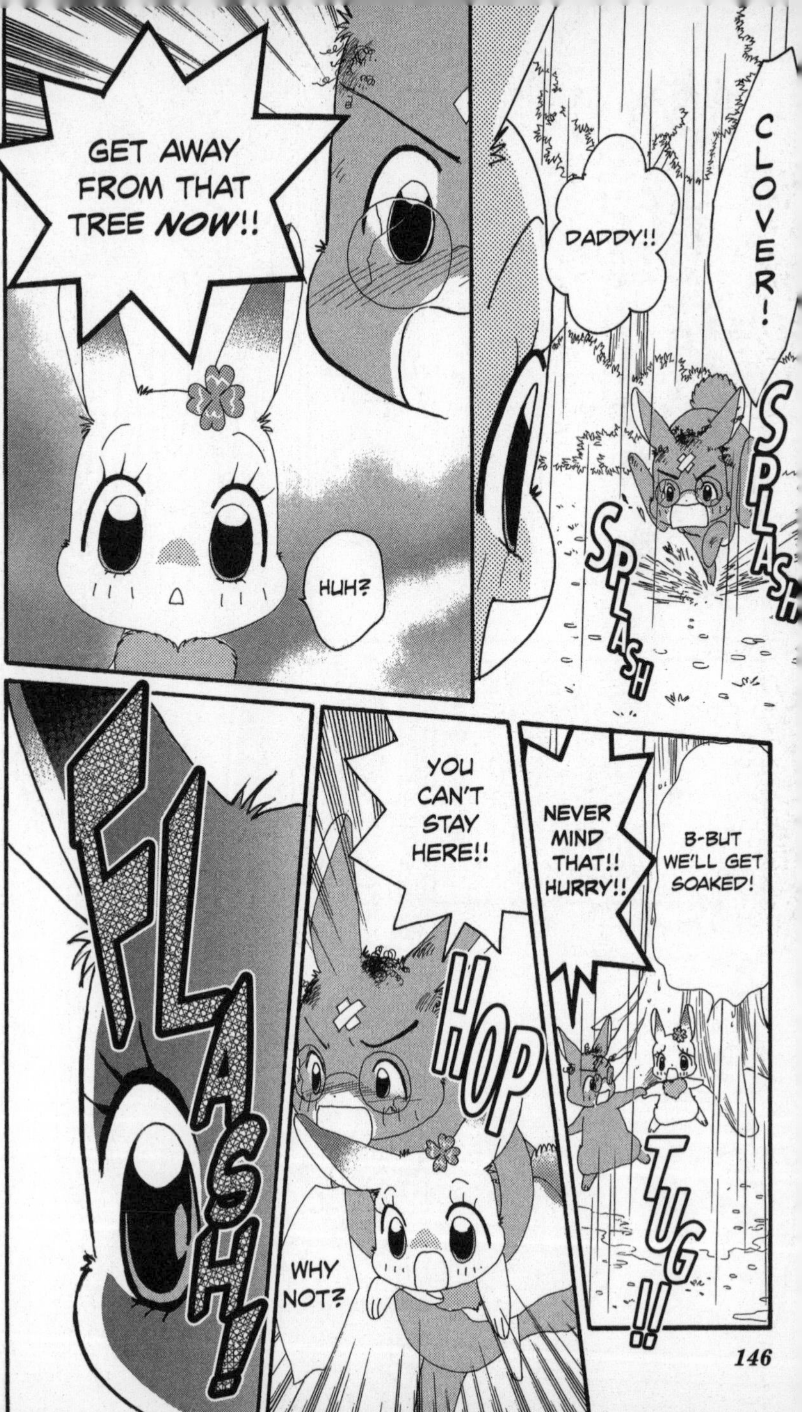
CLOVER!
DADDY!!
SPLASH
SPLASH
GET AWAY FROM THAT TREE NOW!!
HUH?
B-BUT WE'LL GET SOAKED!
NEVER MIND THAT!! HURRY!!
TUG!!
YOU CAN'T STAY HERE!!
HOP
WHY NOT?
FLASH!

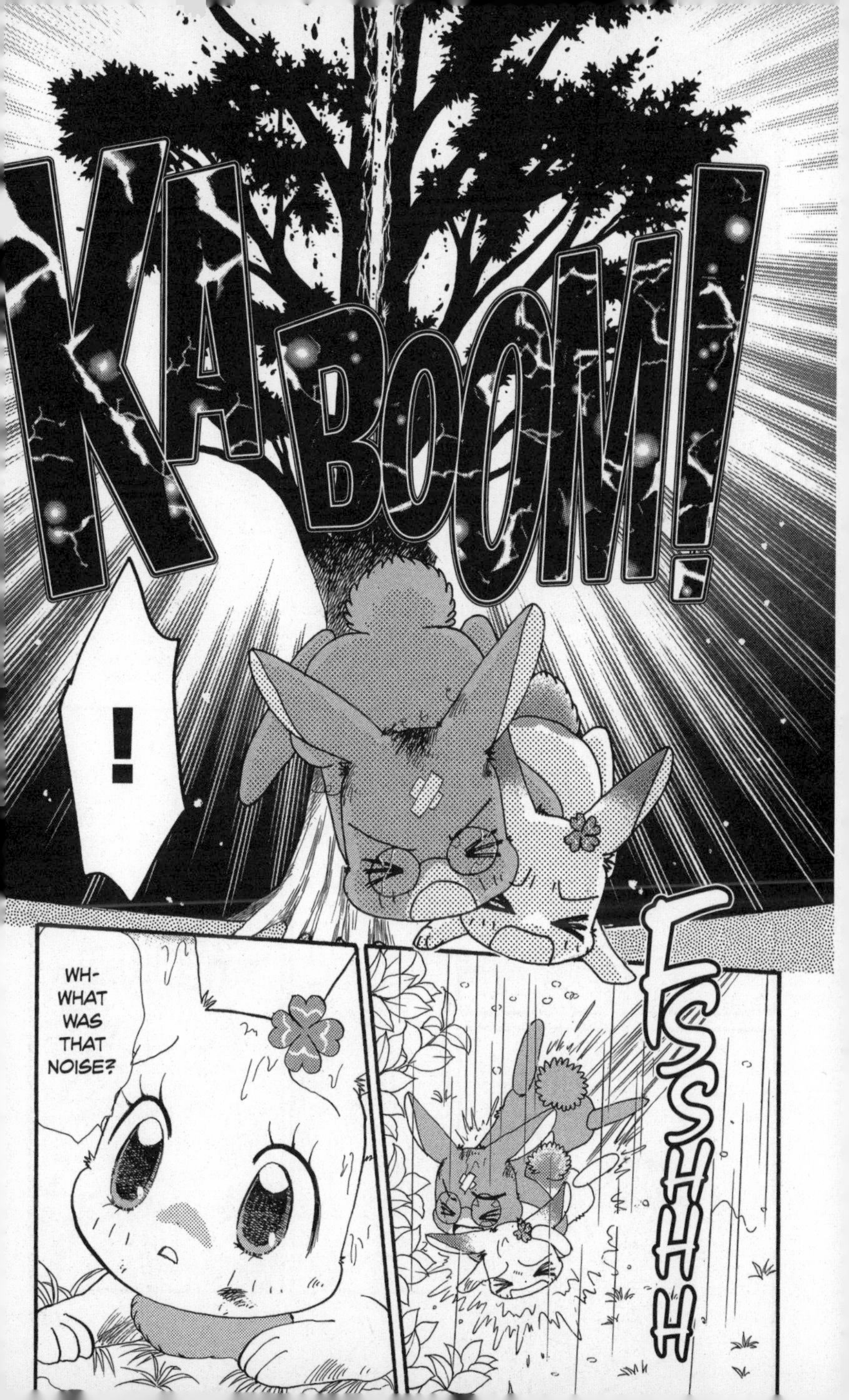
KA-BOOM!
!
FSSHHH
WH-WHAT WAS THAT NOISE?

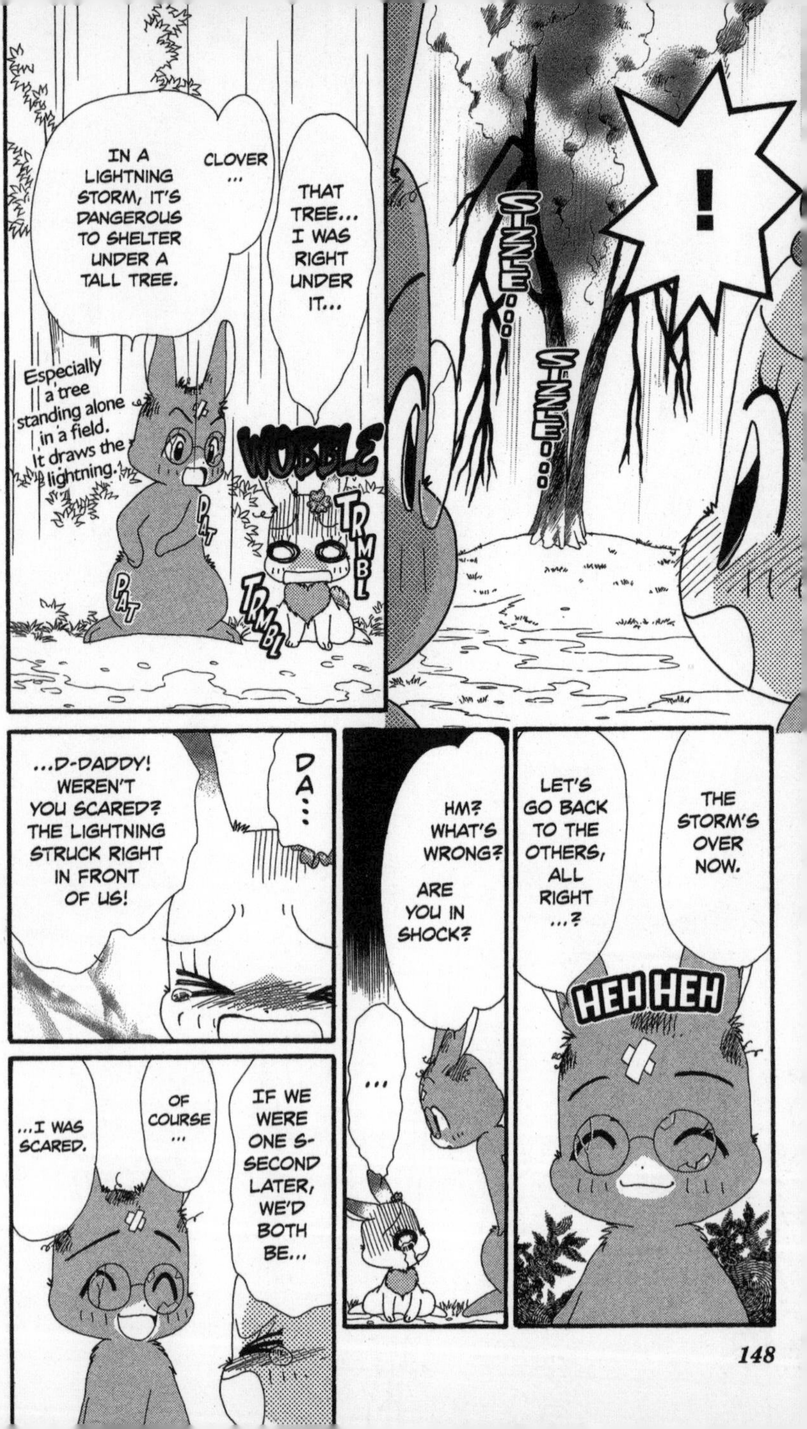
!
SIZZLE...
SIZZLE...
THAT TREE... I WAS RIGHT UNDER IT...
CLOVER...
IN A LIGHTNING STORM, IT'S DANGEROUS TO SHELTER UNDER A TALL TREE.
Especially a tree standing alone in a field. It draws the lightning.
WOBBLE
TRMBL
TRMBL
PAT
PAT
THE STORM'S OVER NOW.
LET'S GO BACK TO THE OTHERS, ALL RIGHT...?
HEH HEH
HM? WHAT'S WRONG?
ARE YOU IN SHOCK?
...
DA...
...D-DADDY! WEREN'T YOU SCARED? THE LIGHTNING STRUCK RIGHT IN FRONT OF US!
IF WE WERE ONE S-SECOND LATER, WE'D BOTH BE...
OF COURSE...
...I WAS SCARED.

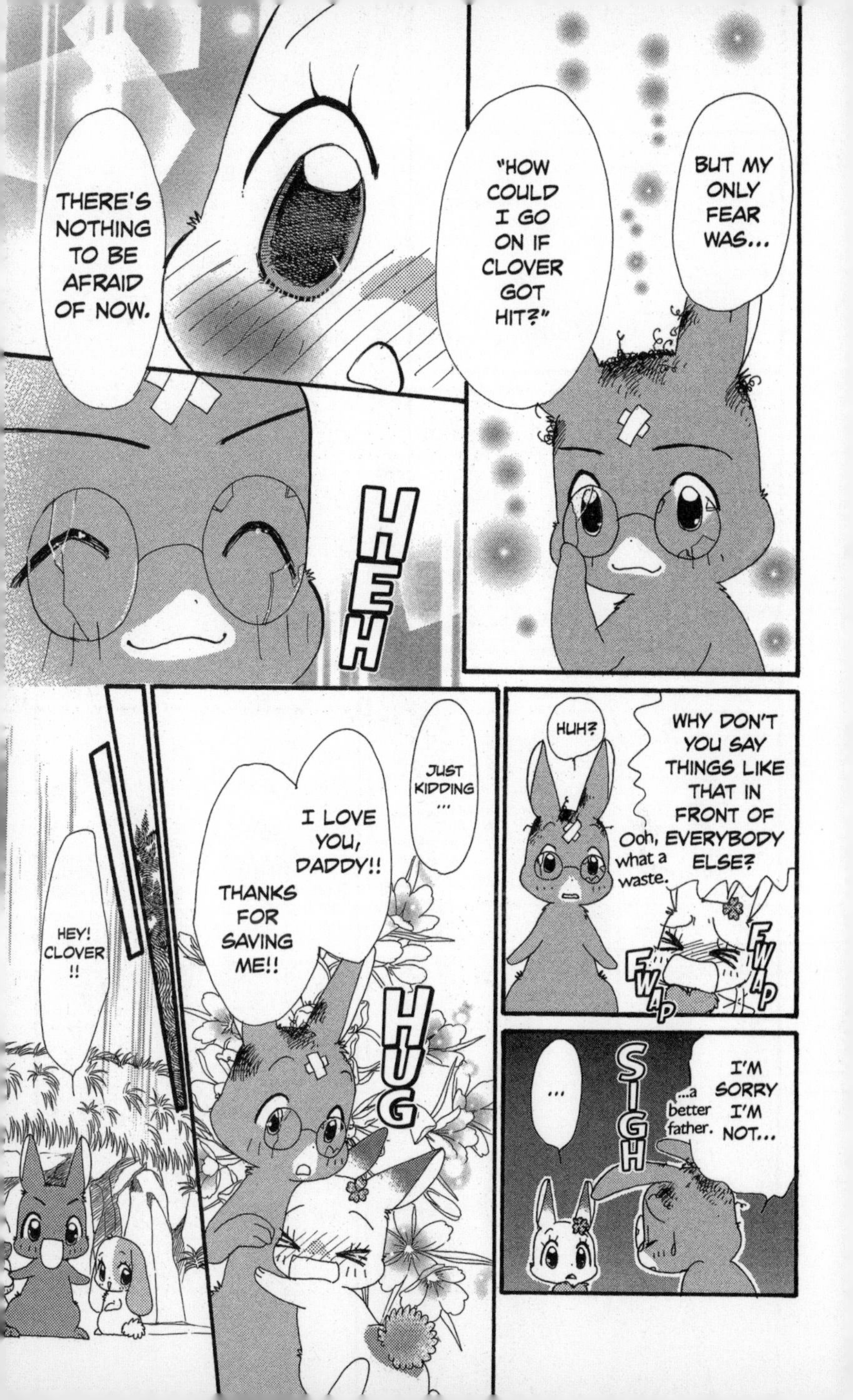
BUT MY ONLY FEAR WAS...
"HOW COULD I GO ON IF CLOVER GOT HIT?"
THERE'S NOTHING TO BE AFRAID OF NOW.
HEH
WHY DON'T YOU SAY THINGS LIKE THAT IN FRONT OF EVERYBODY ELSE?
HUH?
Ooh, what a waste.
FWAP
FWAP
I'M SORRY I'M NOT...
...a better father.
SIGH
...
JUST KIDDING...
I LOVE YOU, DADDY!!
THANKS FOR SAVING ME!!
HUG
HEY! CLOVER!!

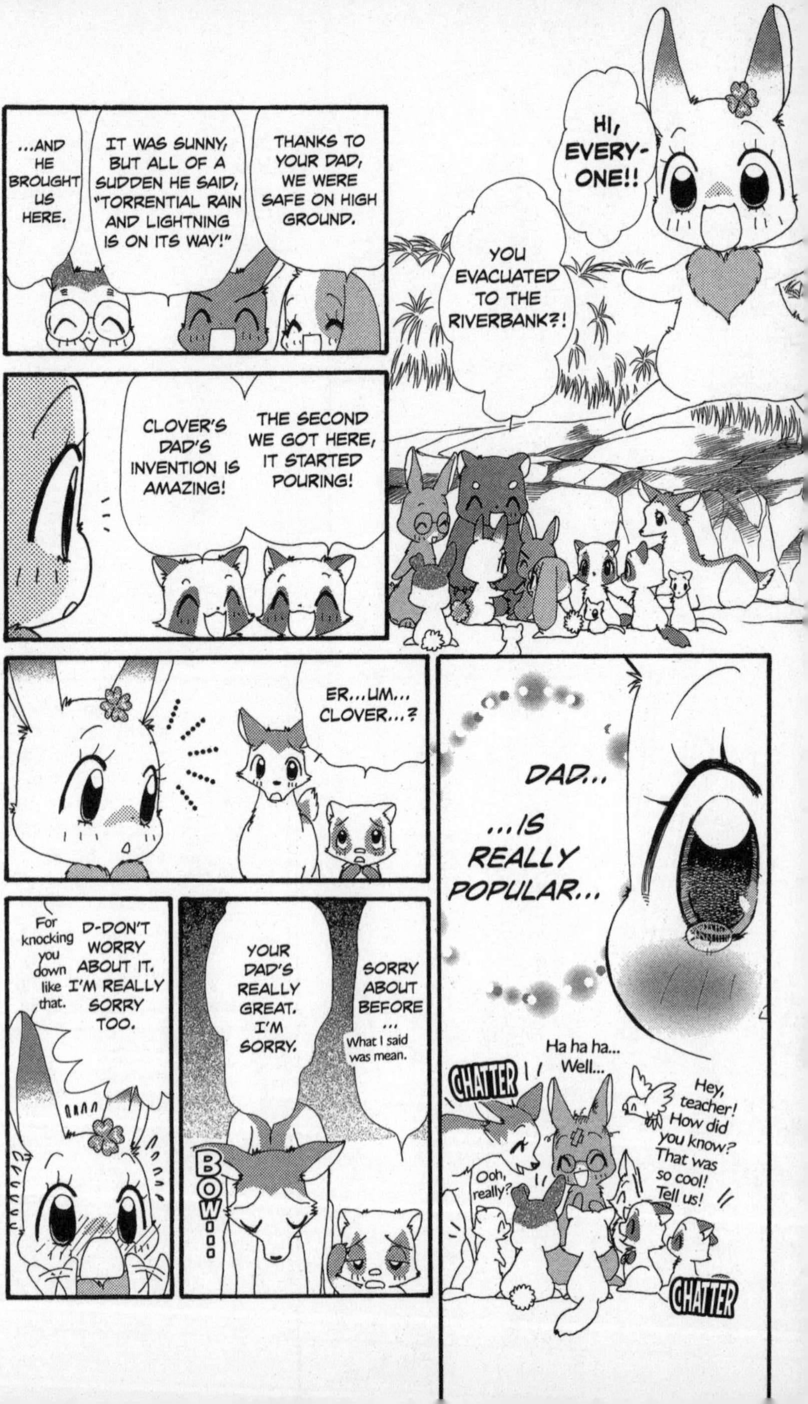
HI, EVERY-ONE!!
YOU EVACUATED TO THE RIVERBANK?!
THANKS TO YOUR DAD, WE WERE SAFE ON HIGH GROUND.
IT WAS SUNNY, BUT ALL OF A SUDDEN HE SAID, "TORRENTIAL RAIN AND LIGHTNING IS ON ITS WAY!"
...AND HE BROUGHT US HERE.
THE SECOND WE GOT HERE, IT STARTED POURING!
CLOVER'S DAD'S INVENTION IS AMAZING!
DAD...
...IS REALLY POPULAR...
CHATTER
Hey, teacher! How did you know? That was so cool! Tell us!
Ha ha ha... Well...
Ooh, really?
CHATTER
ER...UM... CLOVER...?
SORRY ABOUT BEFORE...
What I said was mean.
YOUR DAD'S REALLY GREAT. I'M SORRY.
BOW
D-DON'T WORRY ABOUT IT. I'M REALLY SORRY TOO.
For knocking you down like that.

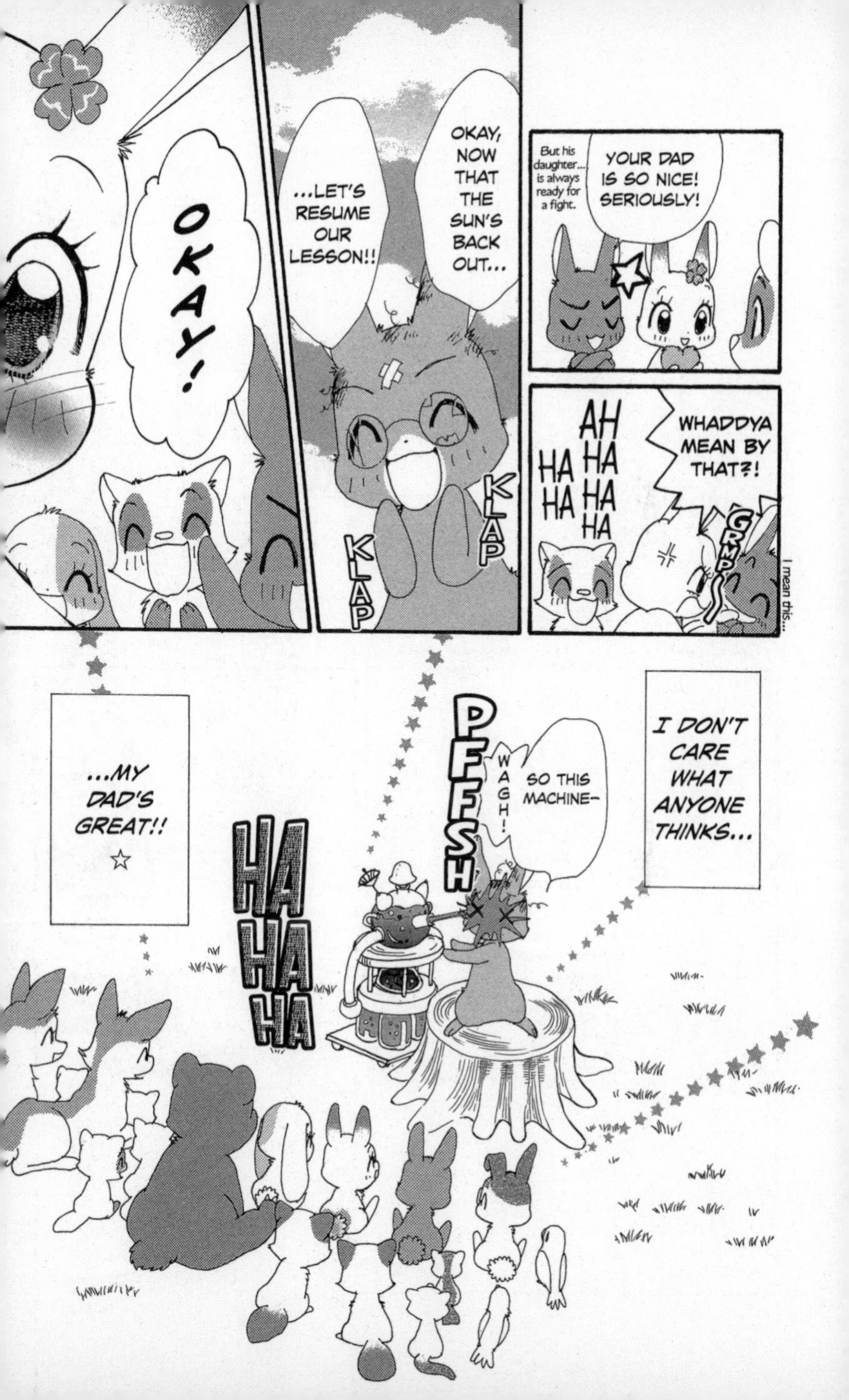
YOUR DAD IS SO NICE! SERIOUSLY!
But his daughter... is always ready for a fight.
WHADDYA MEAN BY THAT?!
AH HA HA HA HA
HA HA
GRMP
I mean this...
OKAY, NOW THAT THE SUN'S BACK OUT...
...LET'S RESUME OUR LESSON!!
KLAP
KLAP
OKAY!
I DON'T CARE WHAT ANYONE THINKS...
SO THIS MACHINE-
WAGH!
PFFSH
HA HA HA HA
...MY DAD'S GREAT!! ☆

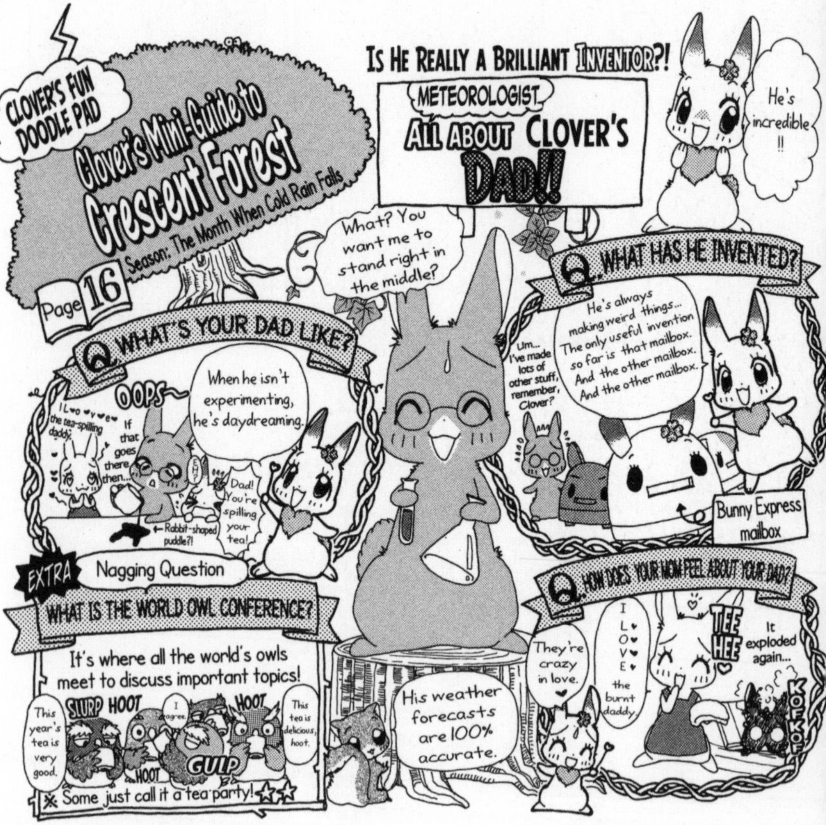
He's incredible!!
IS HE REALLY A BRILLIANT INVENTOR?!
METEOROLOGIST
ALL ABOUT CLOVER'S DAD!!
CLOVER'S FUN DOODLE PAD
Clover's Mini-Guide to Crescent Forest
Season: The Month When Cold Rain Falls
Page 16
What? You want me to stand right in the middle?
Q. WHAT HAS HE INVENTED?
He's always making weird things... The only useful invention so far is that mailbox. And the other mailbox. And the other mailbox.
Um... I've made lots of other stuff, remember, Clover?
Bunny Express mailbox
Q. WHAT'S YOUR DAD LIKE?
When he isn't experimenting, he's daydreaming.
Dad! You're spilling your tea!
OOPS~
If that goes there then...
I L♥O♥V♥E the tea-spilling daddy.
← Rabbit-shaped puddle?!
Q. HOW DOES YOUR MOM FEEL ABOUT YOUR DAD?
It exploded again...
KOF KOF
TEE HEE
I L♥O♥V♥E♥ the burnt daddy.
They're crazy in love.
His weather forecasts are 100% accurate.
EXTRA Nagging Question
WHAT IS THE WORLD OWL CONFERENCE?
It's where all the world's owls meet to discuss important topics!
This tea is delicious, hoot.
HOOT
I agree.
HOOT
SLURP
This year's tea is very good.
HOOT
GULP
※ Some just call it a tea party!

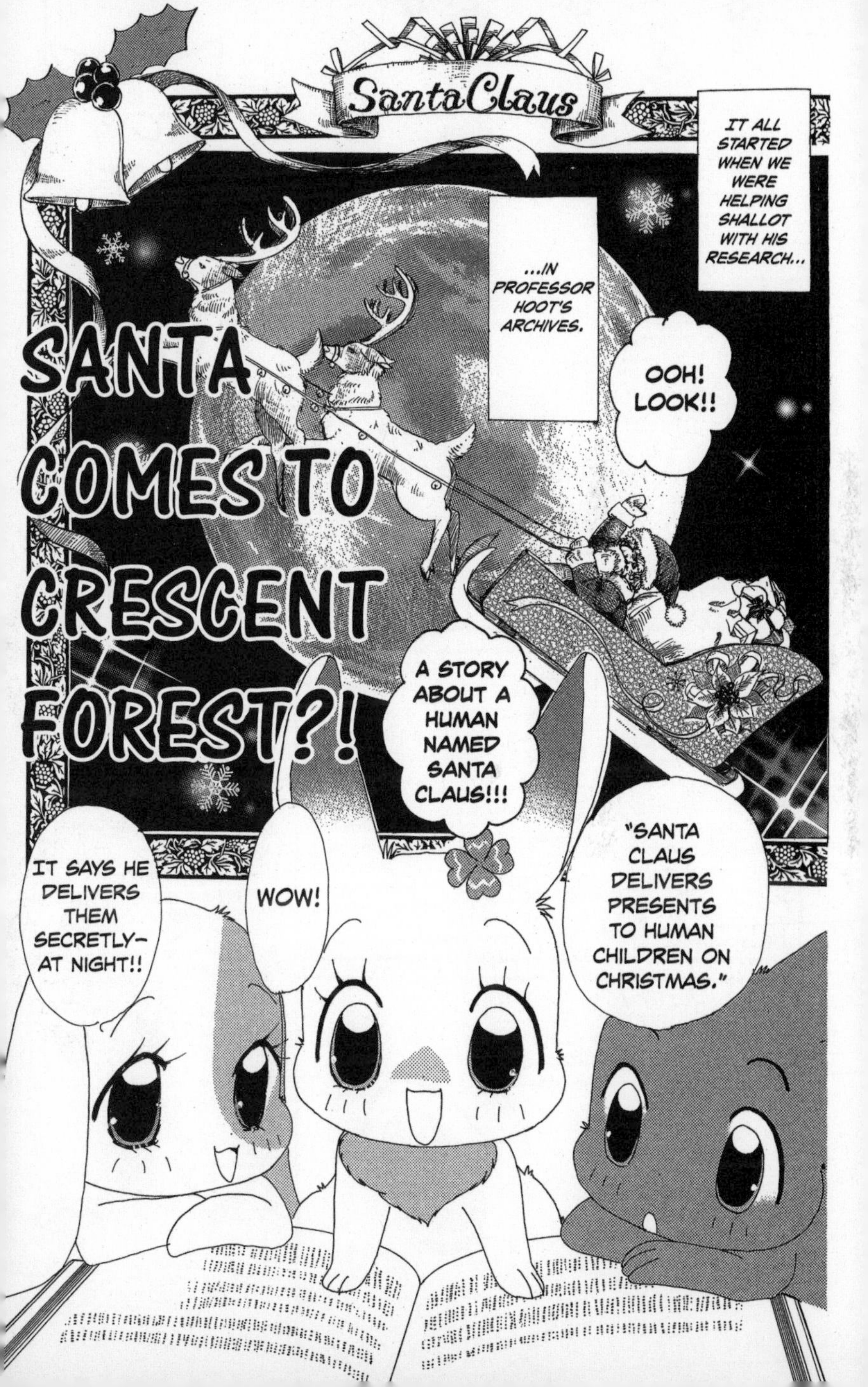
Santa Claus
IT ALL STARTED WHEN WE WERE HELPING SHALLOT WITH HIS RESEARCH...
...IN PROFESSOR HOOT'S ARCHIVES.
OOH! LOOK!!
SANTA COMES TO CRESCENT FOREST?!
A STORY ABOUT A HUMAN NAMED SANTA CLAUS!!!
"SANTA CLAUS DELIVERS PRESENTS TO HUMAN CHILDREN ON CHRISTMAS."
WOW!
IT SAYS HE DELIVERS THEM SECRETLY—AT NIGHT!!

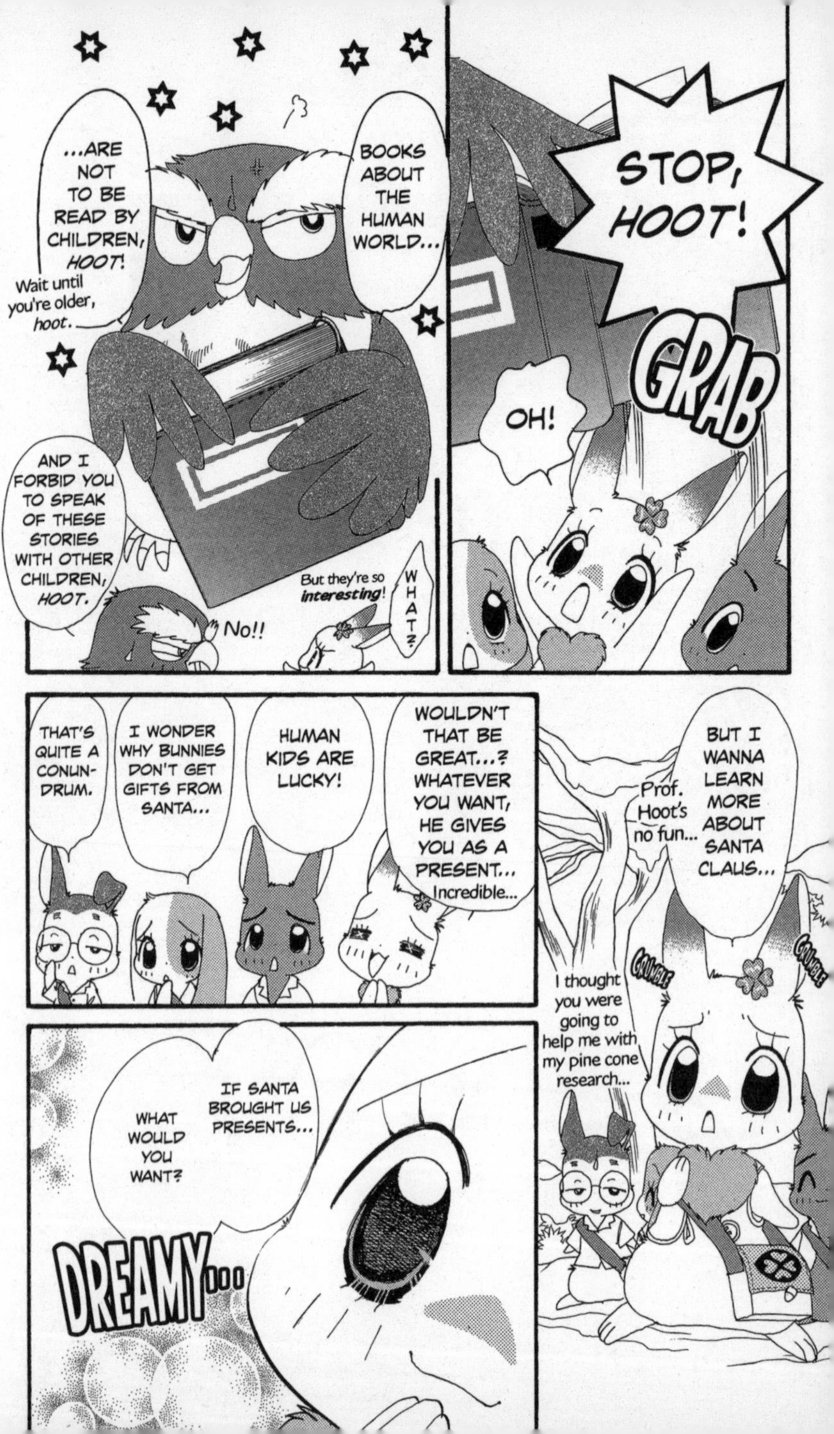
STOP, HOOT!
GRAB
OH!
BOOKS ABOUT THE HUMAN WORLD...
...ARE NOT TO BE READ BY CHILDREN, HOOT!
Wait until you're older, hoot.
WHAT?
But they're so interesting!
No!!
AND I FORBID YOU TO SPEAK OF THESE STORIES WITH OTHER CHILDREN, HOOT.
BUT I WANNA LEARN MORE ABOUT SANTA CLAUS...
Prof. Hoot's no fun...
GRUMBLE
GRUMBLE
I thought you were going to help me with my pine cone research...
WOULDN'T THAT BE GREAT...? WHATEVER YOU WANT, HE GIVES YOU AS A PRESENT...
Incredible...
HUMAN KIDS ARE LUCKY!
I WONDER WHY BUNNIES DON'T GET GIFTS FROM SANTA...
THAT'S QUITE A CONUNDRUM.
IF SANTA BROUGHT US PRESENTS...
WHAT WOULD YOU WANT?
DREAMY...

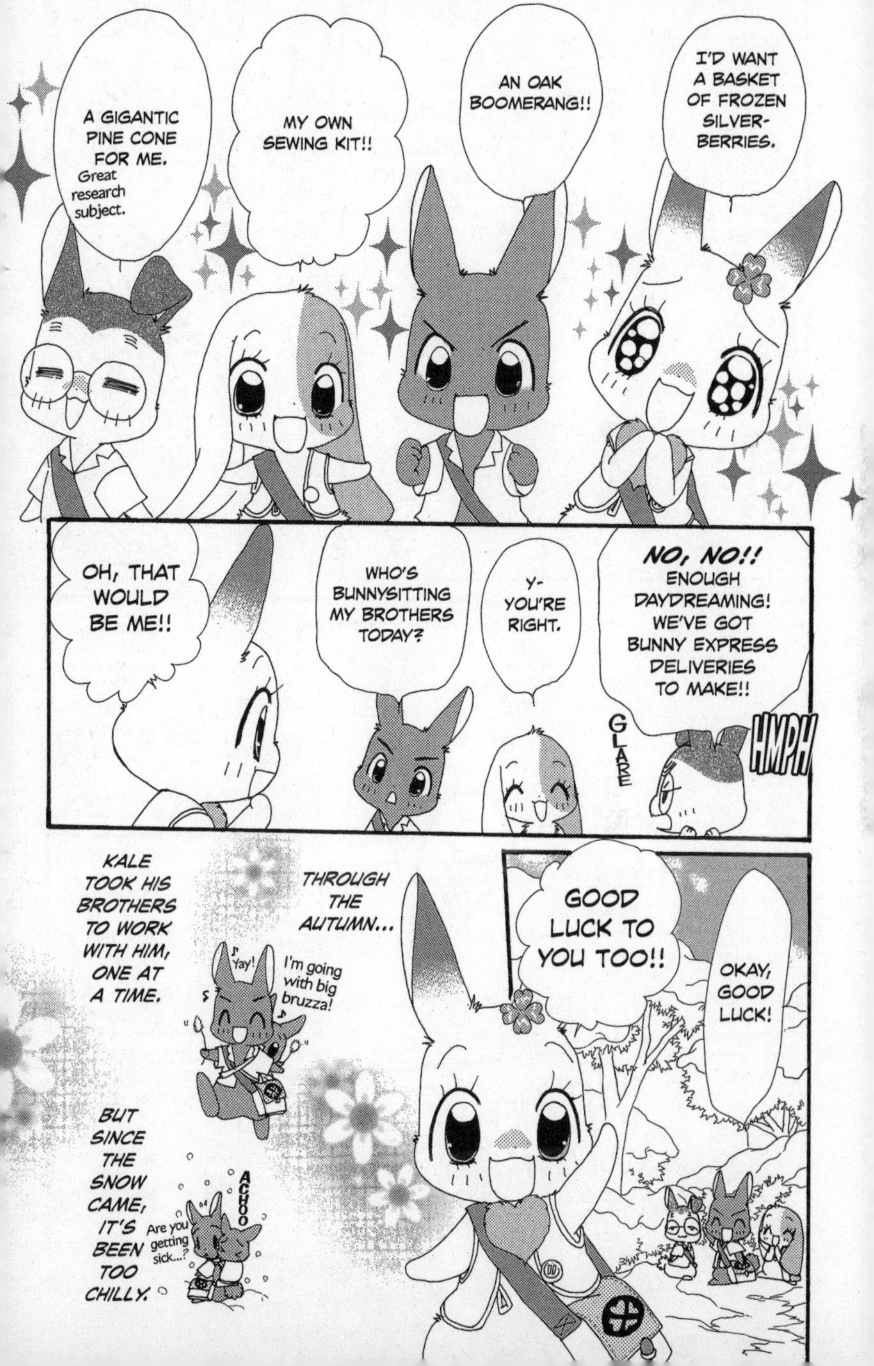
I'D WANT A BASKET OF FROZEN SILVER-BERRIES.
AN OAK BOOMERANG!!
MY OWN SEWING KIT!!
A GIGANTIC PINE CONE FOR ME.
Great research subject.
NO, NO!! ENOUGH DAYDREAMING! WE'VE GOT BUNNY EXPRESS DELIVERIES TO MAKE!!
HMPH
GLARE
Y-YOU'RE RIGHT.
WHO'S BUNNYSITTING MY BROTHERS TODAY?
OH, THAT WOULD BE ME!!
OKAY, GOOD LUCK!
GOOD LUCK TO YOU TOO!!
THROUGH THE AUTUMN...
KALE TOOK HIS BROTHERS TO WORK WITH HIM, ONE AT A TIME.
Yay!
I'm going with big bruzza!
BUT SINCE THE SNOW CAME, IT'S BEEN TOO CHILLY.
ACHOO
Are you getting sick...?

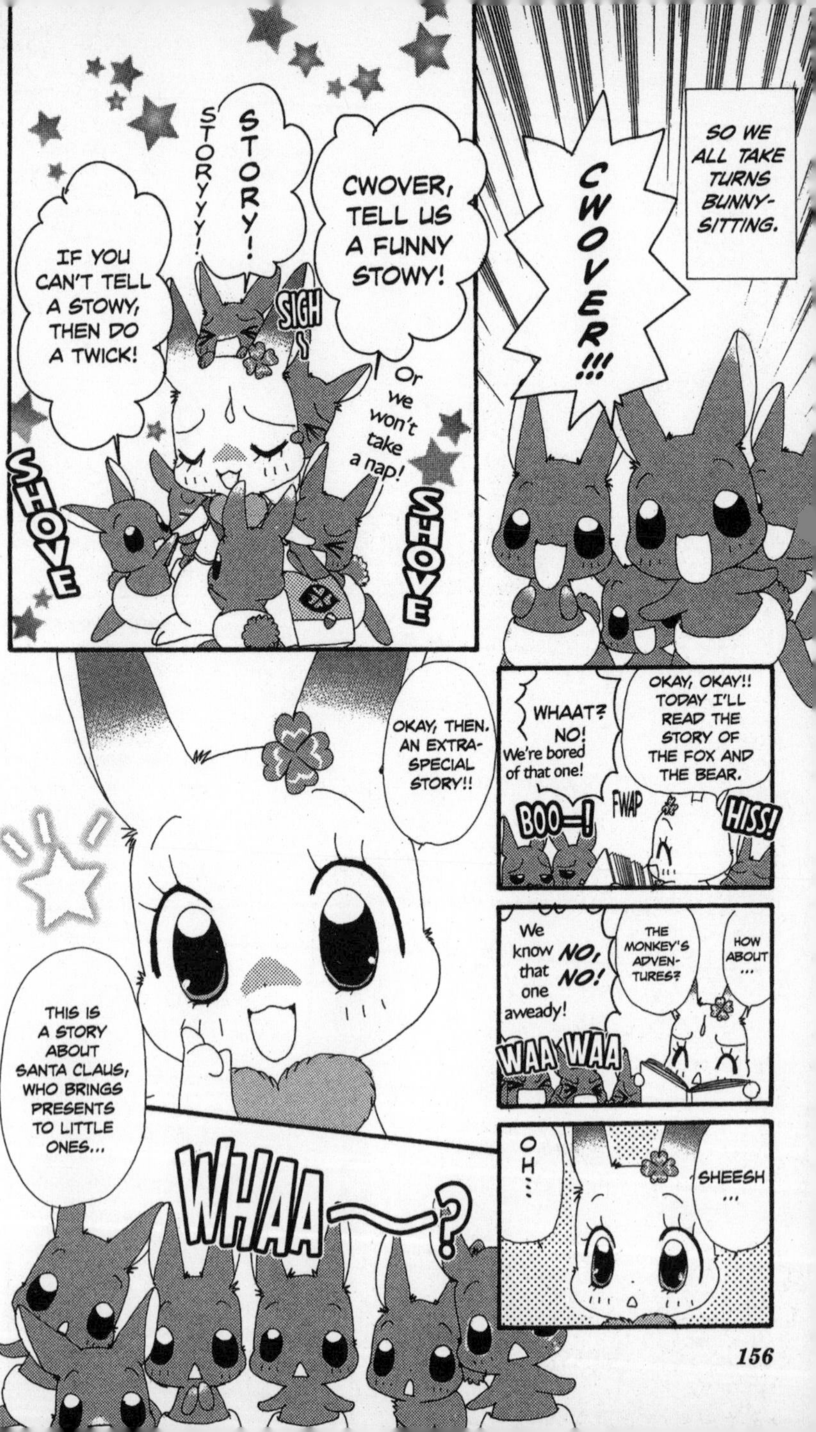

SO WE ALL TAKE TURNS BUNNY-SITTING.
CWOVER!!!
CWOVER, TELL US A FUNNY STOWY!
STORY!
STORYYY!
SIGH
IF YOU CAN'T TELL A STOWY, THEN DO A TWICK!
Or we won't take a nap!
SHOVE
SHOVE
OKAY, OKAY!! TODAY I'LL READ THE STORY OF THE FOX AND THE BEAR.
WHAAT? NO! We're bored of that one!
HISS!
FWAP
BOO—!
HOW ABOUT...
THE MONKEY'S ADVEN-TURES?
NO, NO!
We know that one awweady!
WAA WAA
SHEESH...
OH...
OKAY, THEN. AN EXTRA-SPECIAL STORY!!
THIS IS A STORY ABOUT SANTA CLAUS, WHO BRINGS PRESENTS TO LITTLE ONES...
WHAA—?

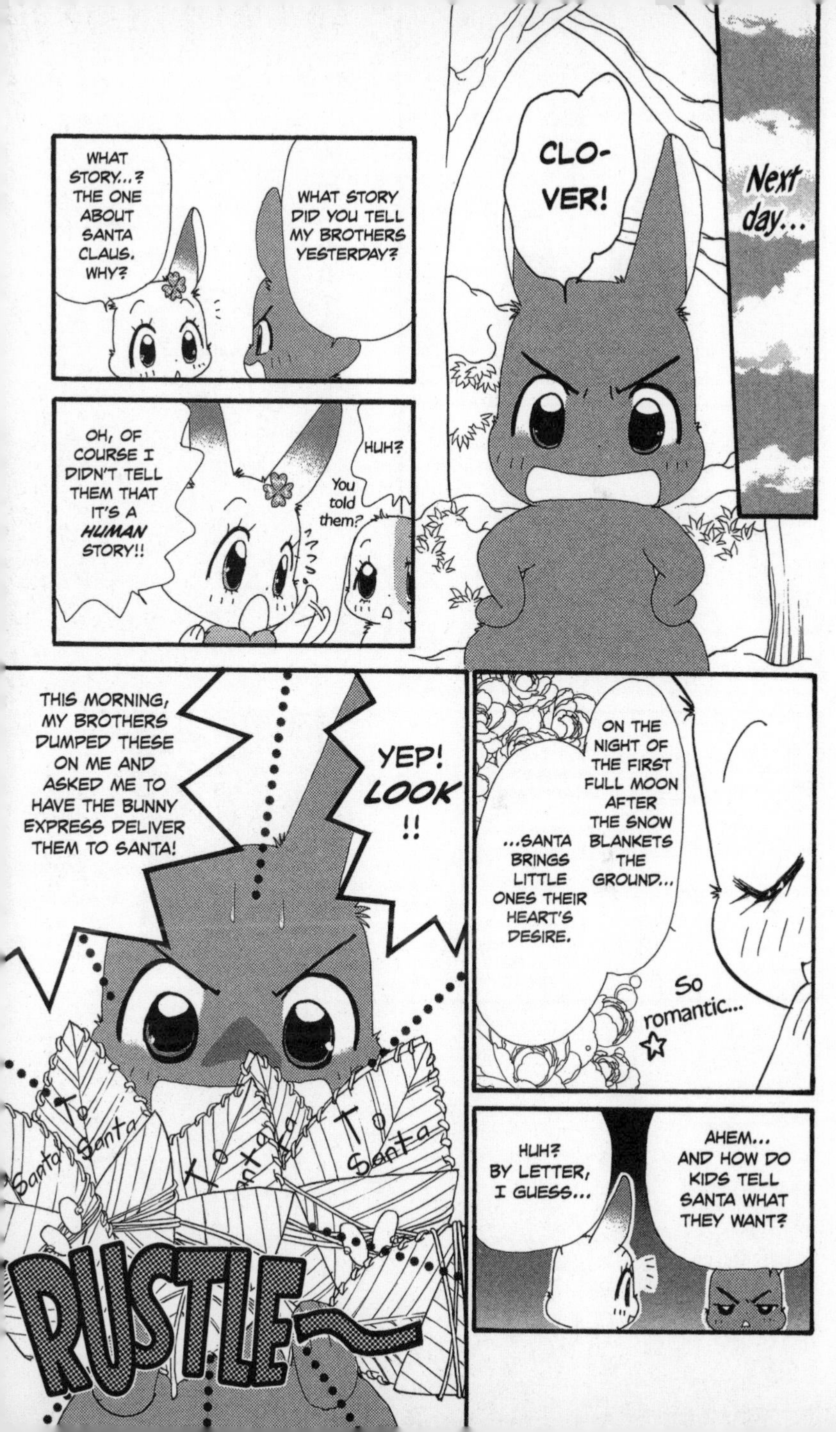
Next day...
CLO-VER!
WHAT STORY DID YOU TELL MY BROTHERS YESTERDAY?
WHAT STORY...? THE ONE ABOUT SANTA CLAUS. WHY?
HUH?
You told them?
OH, OF COURSE I DIDN'T TELL THEM THAT IT'S A *HUMAN* STORY!!
ON THE NIGHT OF THE FIRST FULL MOON AFTER THE SNOW BLANKETS THE GROUND...
...SANTA BRINGS LITTLE ONES THEIR HEART'S DESIRE.
So romantic... ☆
AHEM... AND HOW DO KIDS TELL SANTA WHAT THEY WANT?
HUH? BY LETTER, I GUESS...
YEP! *LOOK* !!
THIS MORNING, MY BROTHERS DUMPED THESE ON ME AND ASKED ME TO HAVE THE BUNNY EXPRESS DELIVER THEM TO SANTA!
To Santa
RUSTLE~

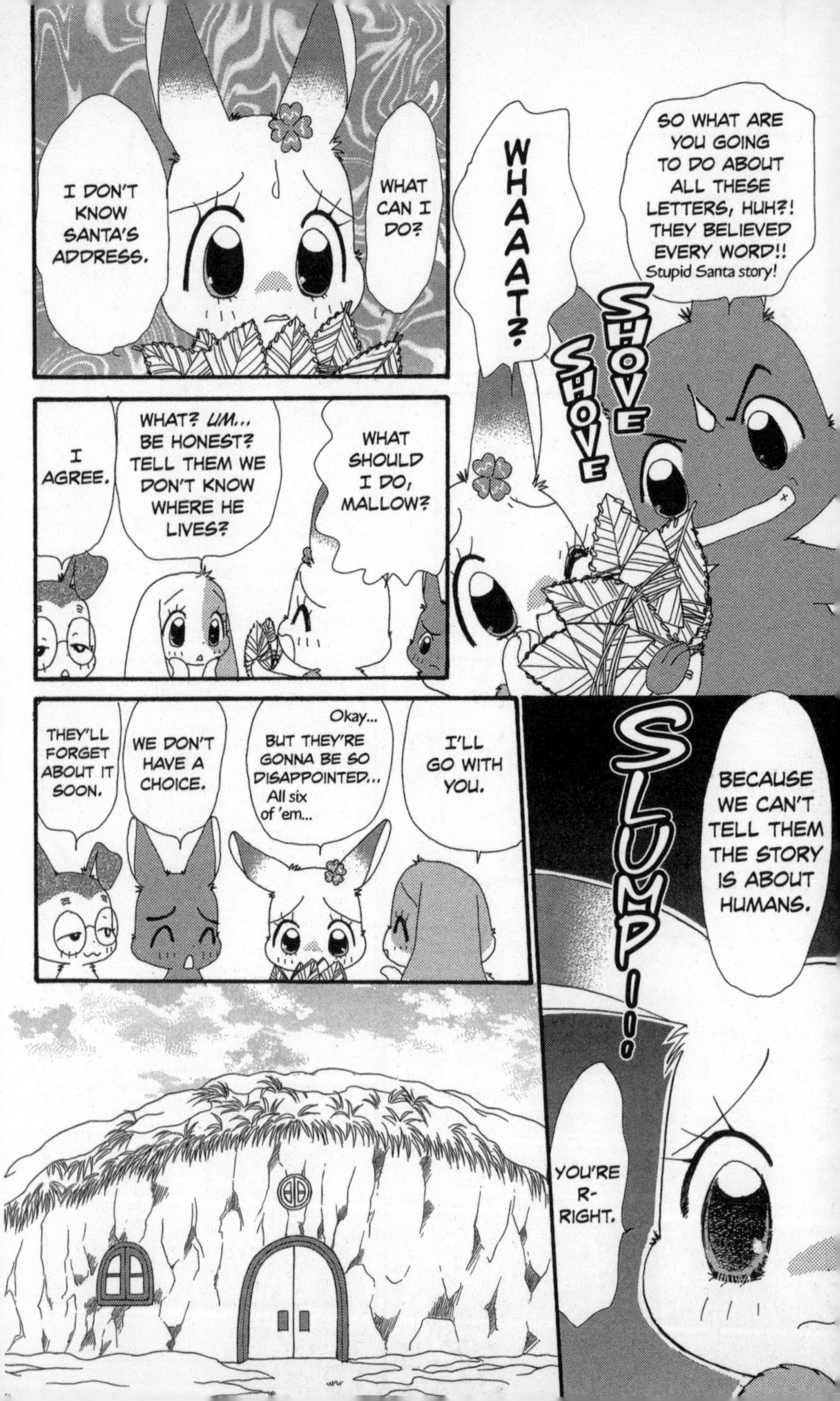
SO WHAT ARE YOU GOING TO DO ABOUT ALL THESE LETTERS, HUH?! THEY BELIEVED EVERY WORD!! Stupid Santa story!
WHAAAT?!
SHOVE
SHOVE
WHAT CAN I DO?
I DON'T KNOW SANTA'S ADDRESS.
WHAT SHOULD I DO, MALLOW?
WHAT? UM... BE HONEST? TELL THEM WE DON'T KNOW WHERE HE LIVES?
I AGREE.
BECAUSE WE CAN'T TELL THEM THE STORY IS ABOUT HUMANS.
SLUMP!!!
YOU'RE R-RIGHT.
I'LL GO WITH YOU.
Okay... BUT THEY'RE GONNA BE SO DISAPPOINTED... All six of 'em...
WE DON'T HAVE A CHOICE.
THEY'LL FORGET ABOUT IT SOON.

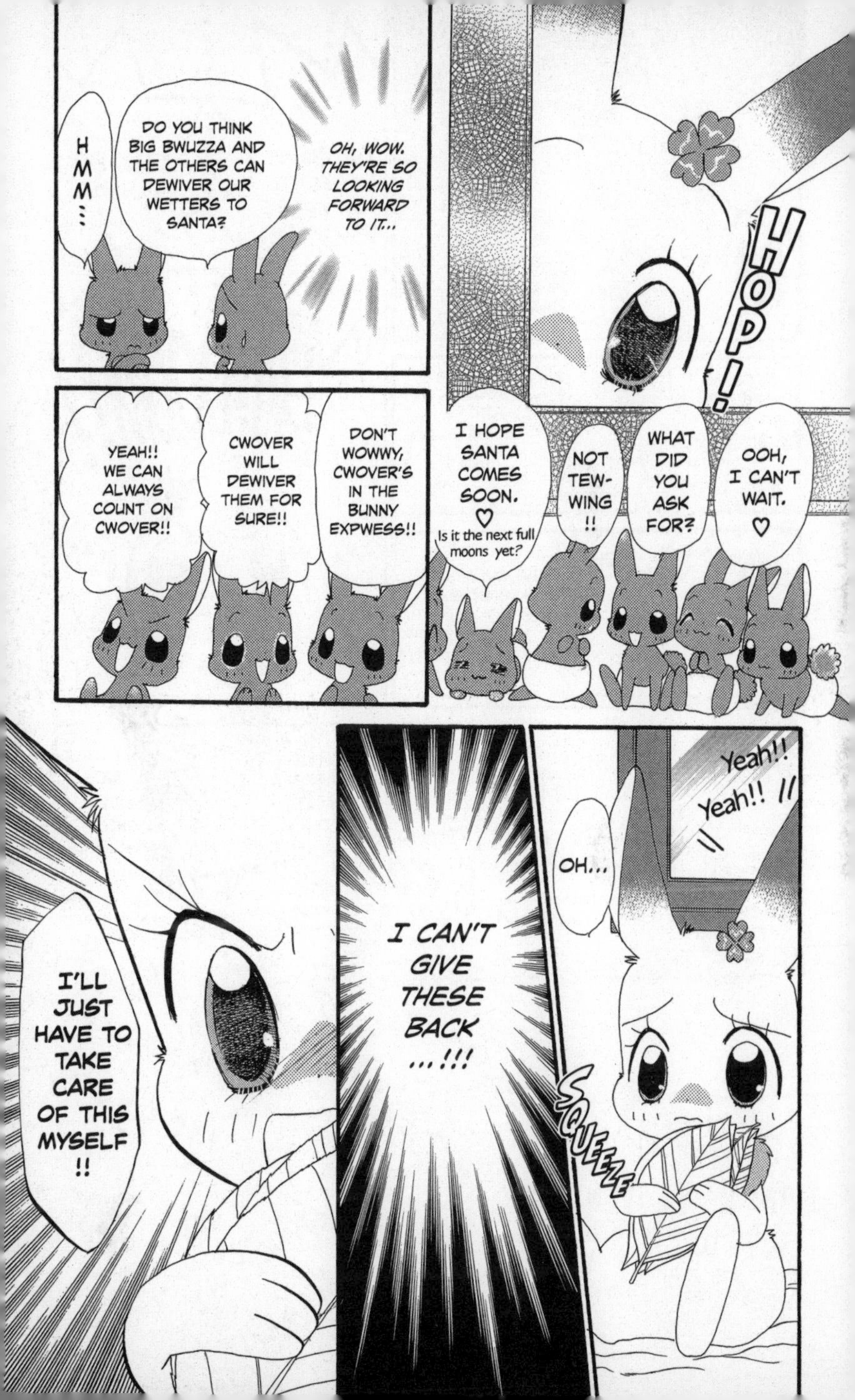
HOP!!
OOH, I CAN'T WAIT. ♡
WHAT DID YOU ASK FOR?
NOT TEW-WING!!
I HOPE SANTA COMES SOON. ♡
Is it the next full moons yet?
OH, WOW. THEY'RE SO LOOKING FORWARD TO IT...
DO YOU THINK BIG BWUZZA AND THE OTHERS CAN DEWIVER OUR WETTERS TO SANTA?
HMM...
DON'T WOWWY, CWOVER'S IN THE BUNNY EXPWESS!!
CWOVER WILL DEWIVER THEM FOR SURE!!
YEAH!! WE CAN ALWAYS COUNT ON CWOVER!!
Yeah!! Yeah!!
OH...
SQUEEZE
I CAN'T GIVE THESE BACK ...!!!
I'LL JUST HAVE TO TAKE CARE OF THIS MYSELF!!

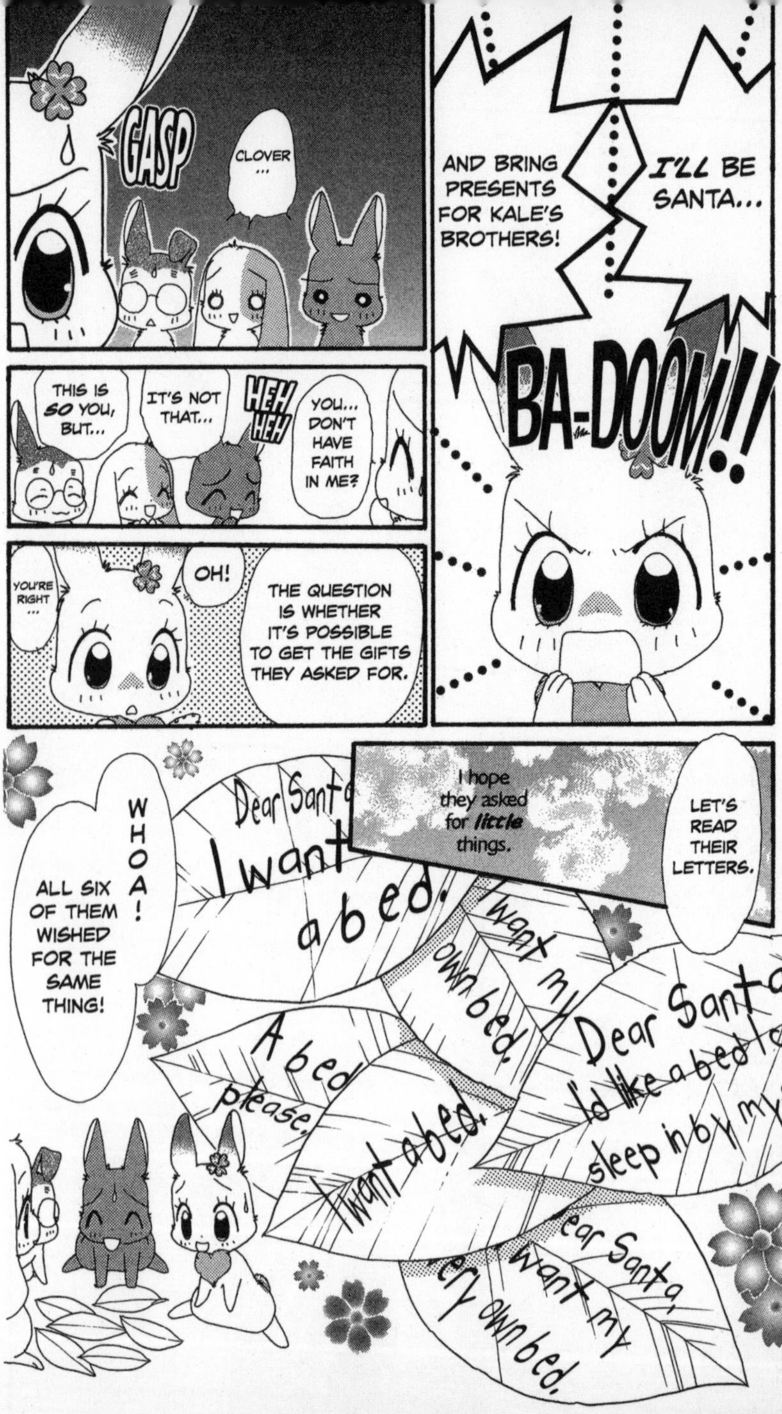
I'LL BE SANTA...
AND BRING PRESENTS FOR KALE'S BROTHERS!
BA-DOOM!!
GASP
CLOVER ...
YOU... DON'T HAVE FAITH IN ME?
HEH HEH
IT'S NOT THAT...
THIS IS SO YOU, BUT...
THE QUESTION IS WHETHER IT'S POSSIBLE TO GET THE GIFTS THEY ASKED FOR.
OH!
YOU'RE RIGHT ...
LET'S READ THEIR LETTERS.
I hope they asked for little things.
Dear Santa, I'd like a bed I can sleep in by myself
I want my own bed.
Dear Sant
I want a bed.
Dear Santa, I want my very own bed.
I want a bed.
A bed please,
WHOA!
ALL SIX OF THEM WISHED FOR THE SAME THING!

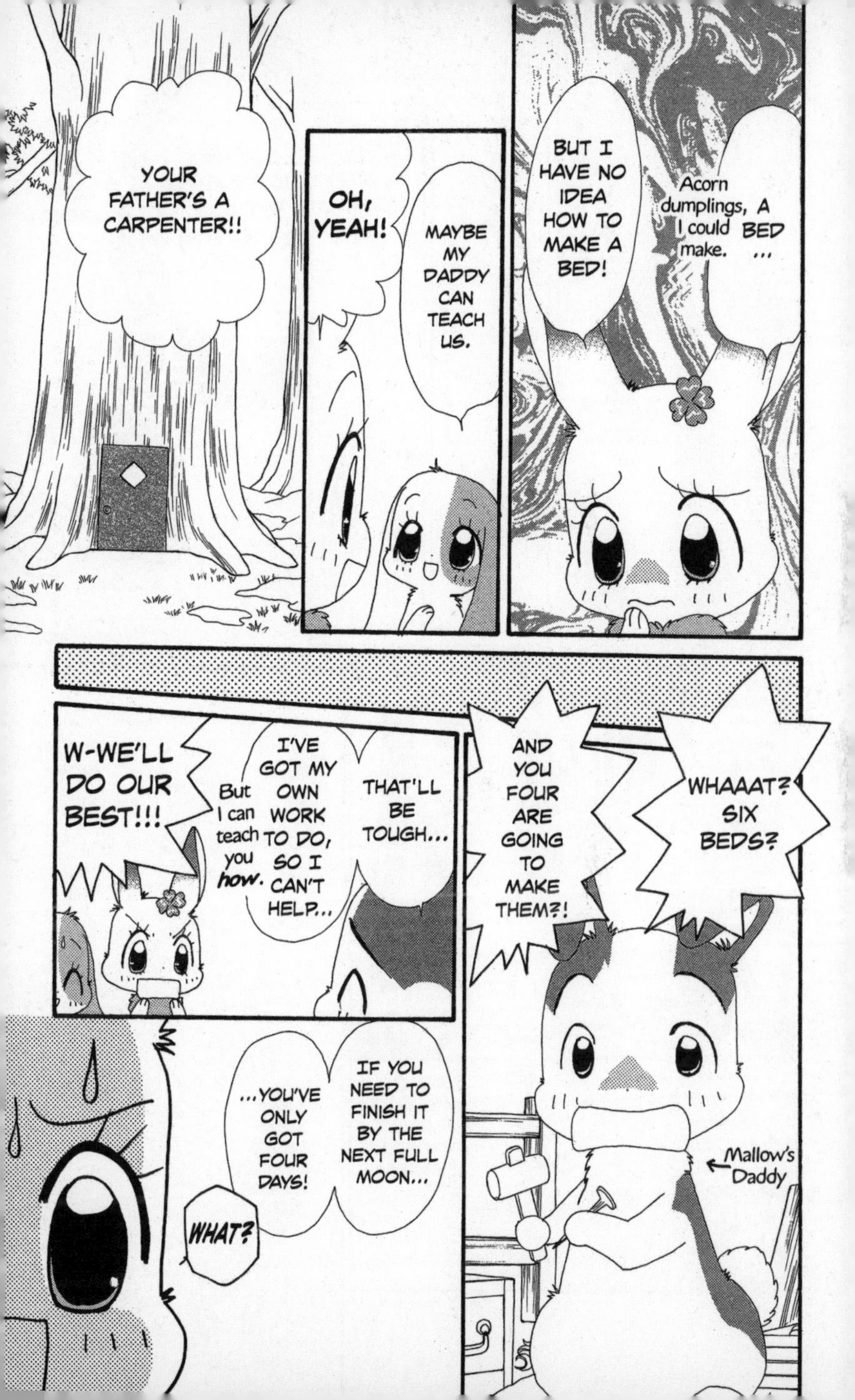
A BED ...
Acorn dumplings, I could make.
BUT I HAVE NO IDEA HOW TO MAKE A BED!
MAYBE MY DADDY CAN TEACH US.
OH, YEAH!
YOUR FATHER'S A CARPENTER!!
WHAAAT? SIX BEDS?
AND YOU FOUR ARE GOING TO MAKE THEM?!
Mallow's Daddy
THAT'LL BE TOUGH...
I'VE GOT MY OWN WORK TO DO, SO I CAN'T HELP...
But I can teach you *how*.
W-WE'LL DO OUR BEST!!!
IF YOU NEED TO FINISH IT BY THE NEXT FULL MOON...
...YOU'VE ONLY GOT FOUR DAYS!
WHAT?

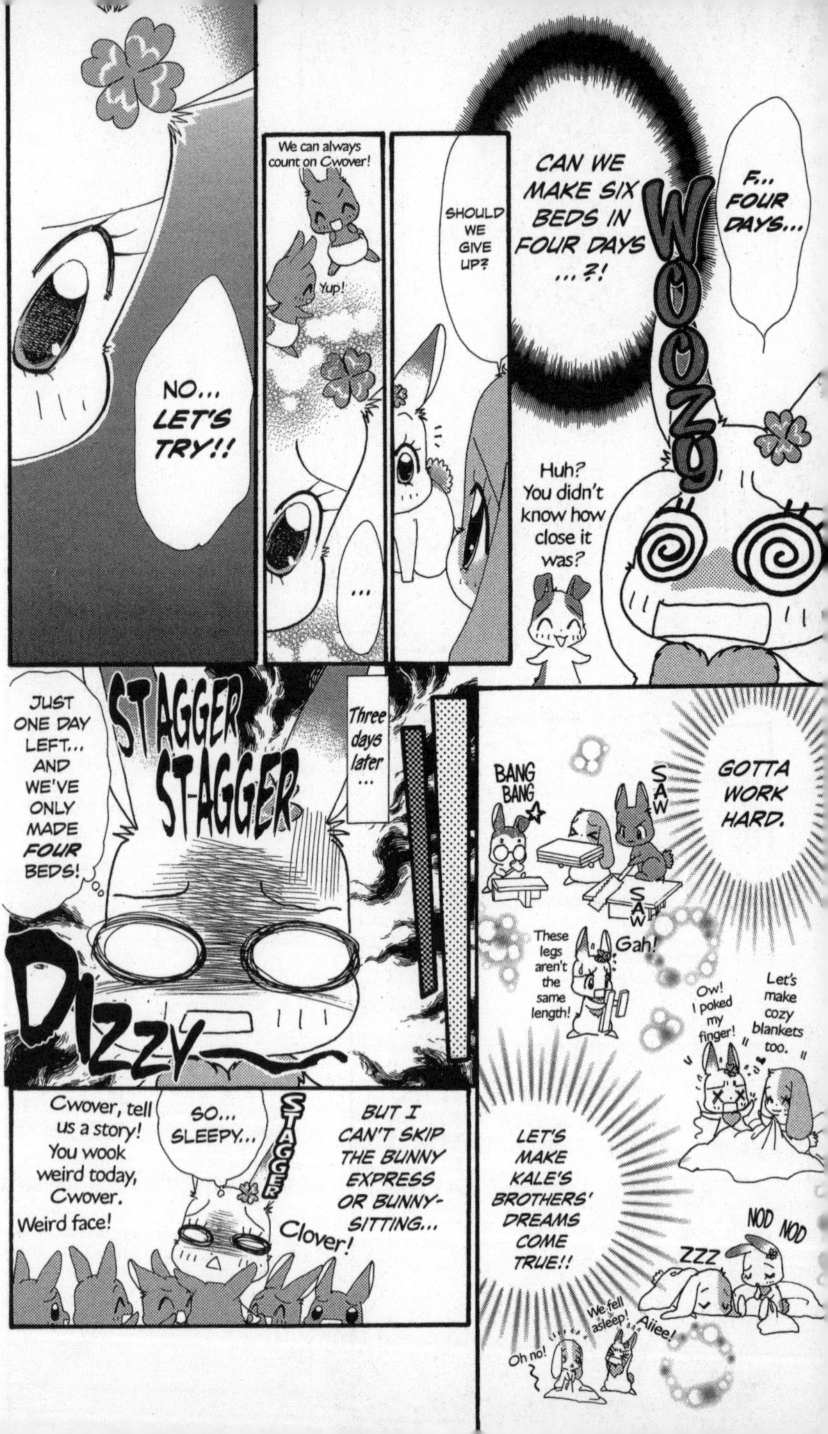
F... FOUR DAYS...
WOOZY
CAN WE MAKE SIX BEDS IN FOUR DAYS ...?!
Huh? You didn't know how close it was?
SHOULD WE GIVE UP?
We can always count on Cwover!
Yup!
...
NO... LET'S TRY!!
GOTTA WORK HARD.
SAW
BANG BANG
SAW
These legs aren't the same length!
Gah!
Let's make cozy blankets too.
Ow! I poked my finger!
LET'S MAKE KALE'S BROTHERS' DREAMS COME TRUE!!
NOD NOD
ZZZ
Aiiee!
We fell asleep!
Oh no!
Three days later...
STAGGER STAGGER
JUST ONE DAY LEFT... AND WE'VE ONLY MADE FOUR BEDS!
DIZZY
BUT I CAN'T SKIP THE BUNNY EXPRESS OR BUNNY-SITTING...
STAGGER
SO... SLEEPY...
Clover!
Cwover, tell us a story!
You wook weird today, Cwover.
Weird face!

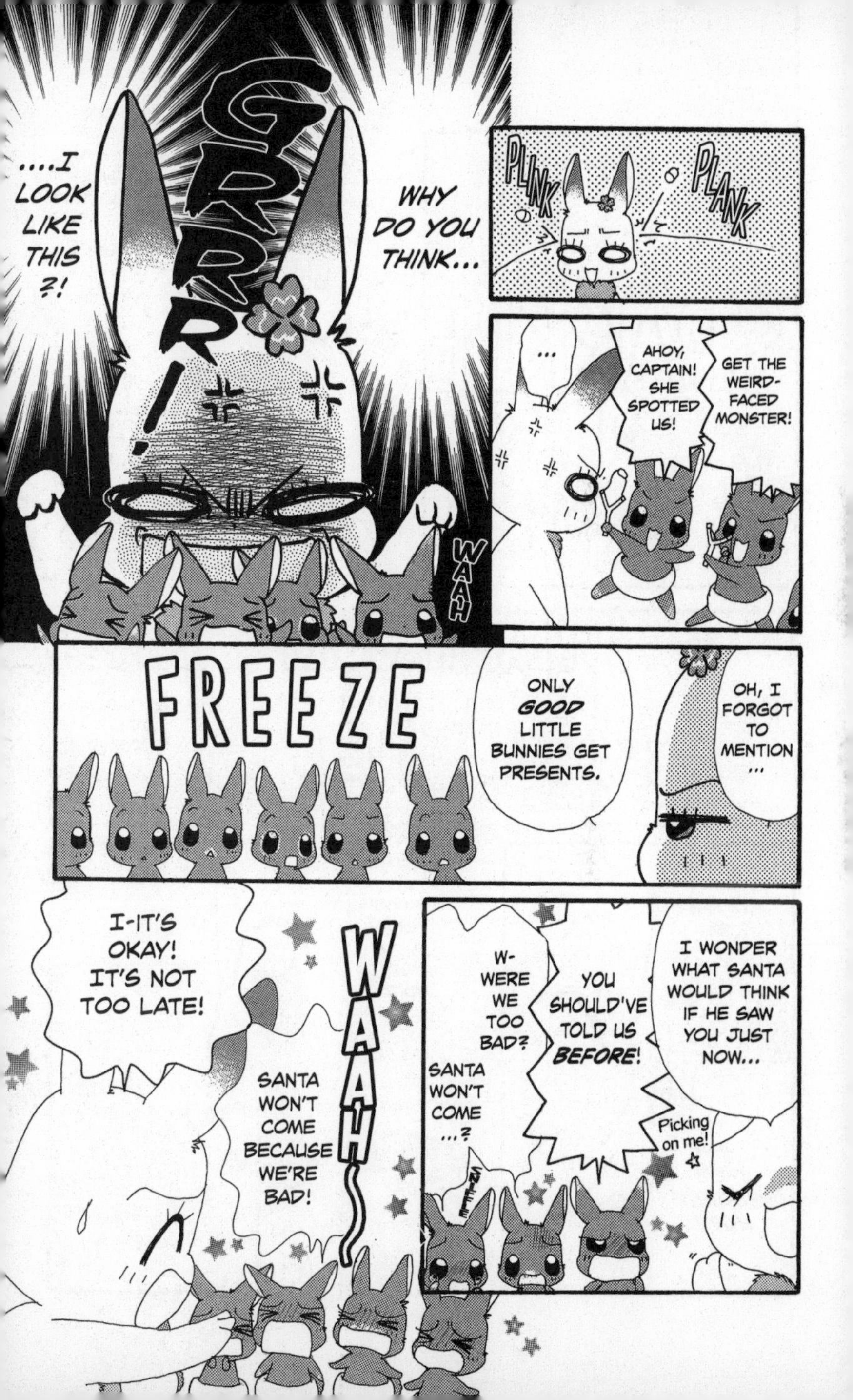
PLANK
PLINK
AHOY, CAPTAIN! SHE SPOTTED US!
GET THE WEIRD-FACED MONSTER!
...
WHY DO YOU THINK...
....I LOOK LIKE THIS?!
GRRR!
WAAH
OH, I FORGOT TO MENTION...
ONLY GOOD LITTLE BUNNIES GET PRESENTS.
FREEZE
I WONDER WHAT SANTA WOULD THINK IF HE SAW YOU JUST NOW...
Picking on me! ☆
YOU SHOULD'VE TOLD US BEFORE!
W-WERE WE TOO BAD?
SANTA WON'T COME...?
SNIFFLE
WAAAH~
SANTA WON'T COME BECAUSE WE'RE BAD!
I-IT'S OKAY! IT'S NOT TOO LATE!

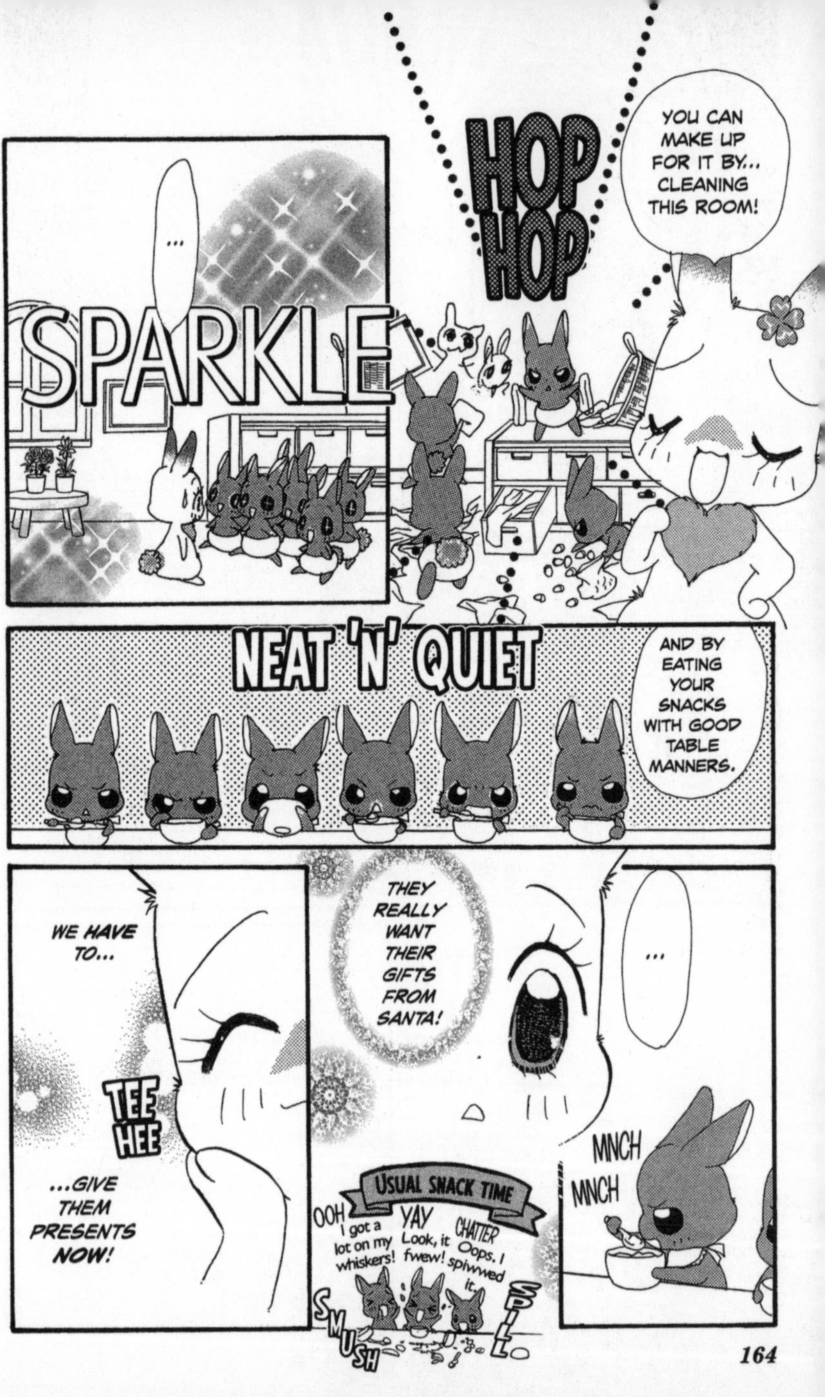
YOU CAN MAKE UP FOR IT BY... CLEANING THIS ROOM!
HOP HOP
...
SPARKLE
AND BY EATING YOUR SNACKS WITH GOOD TABLE MANNERS.
NEAT 'N' QUIET
...
MNCH MNCH
USUAL SNACK TIME
CHATTER
Oops. I spiwwed it.
YAY
Look, it fwew!
OOH
I got a lot on my whiskers!
SPILL
SMUSH
THEY REALLY WANT THEIR GIFTS FROM SANTA!
WE HAVE TO...
TEE HEE
...GIVE THEM PRESENTS NOW!

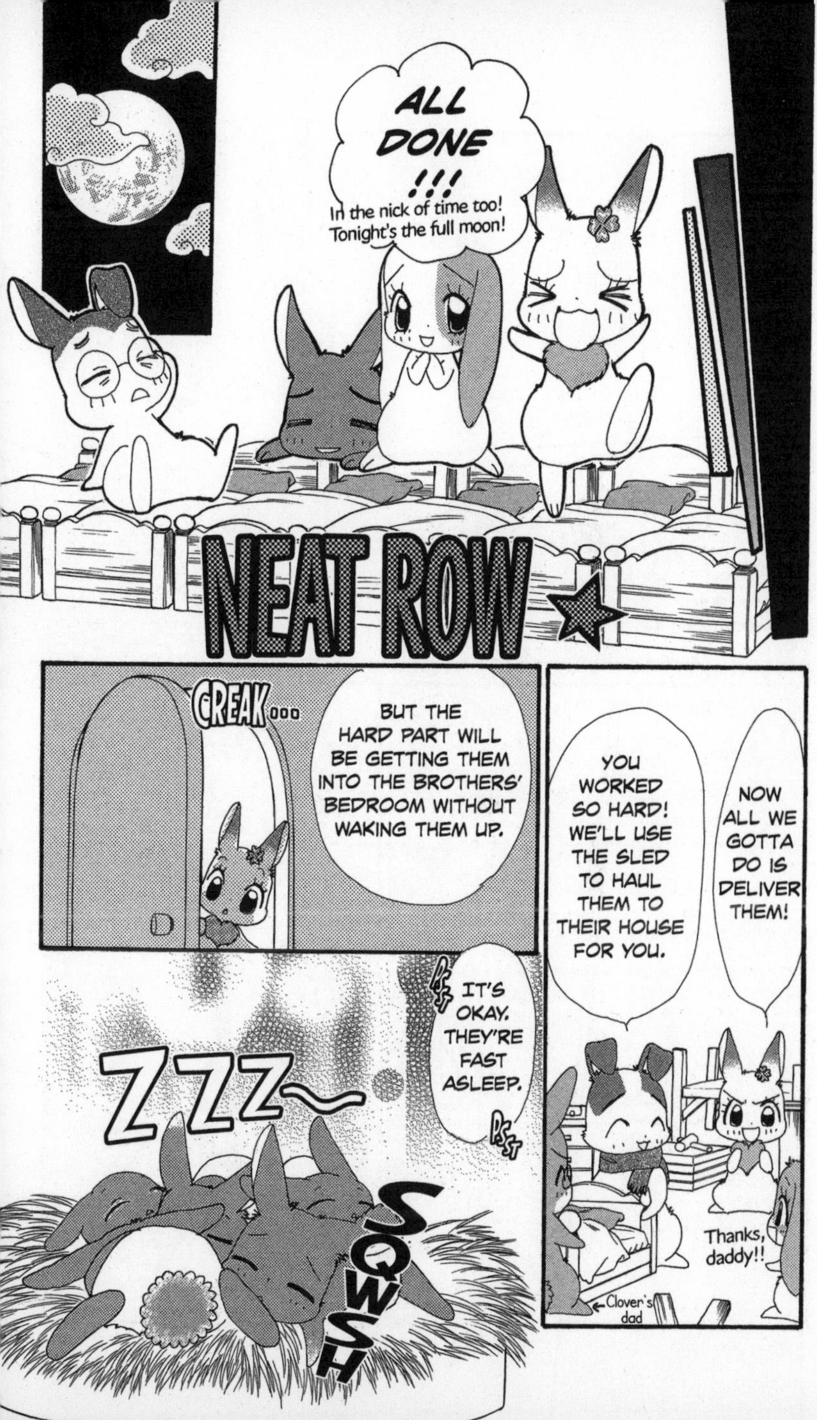
ALL DONE !!!
In the nick of time too! Tonight's the full moon!
NEAT ROW ★
NOW ALL WE GOTTA DO IS DELIVER THEM!
YOU WORKED SO HARD! WE'LL USE THE SLED TO HAUL THEM TO THEIR HOUSE FOR YOU.
Thanks, daddy!!
←Clover's dad
CREAK...
BUT THE HARD PART WILL BE GETTING THEM INTO THE BROTHERS' BEDROOM WITHOUT WAKING THEM UP.
PSST
IT'S OKAY. THEY'RE FAST ASLEEP.
PSST
ZZZ~
SQWSH

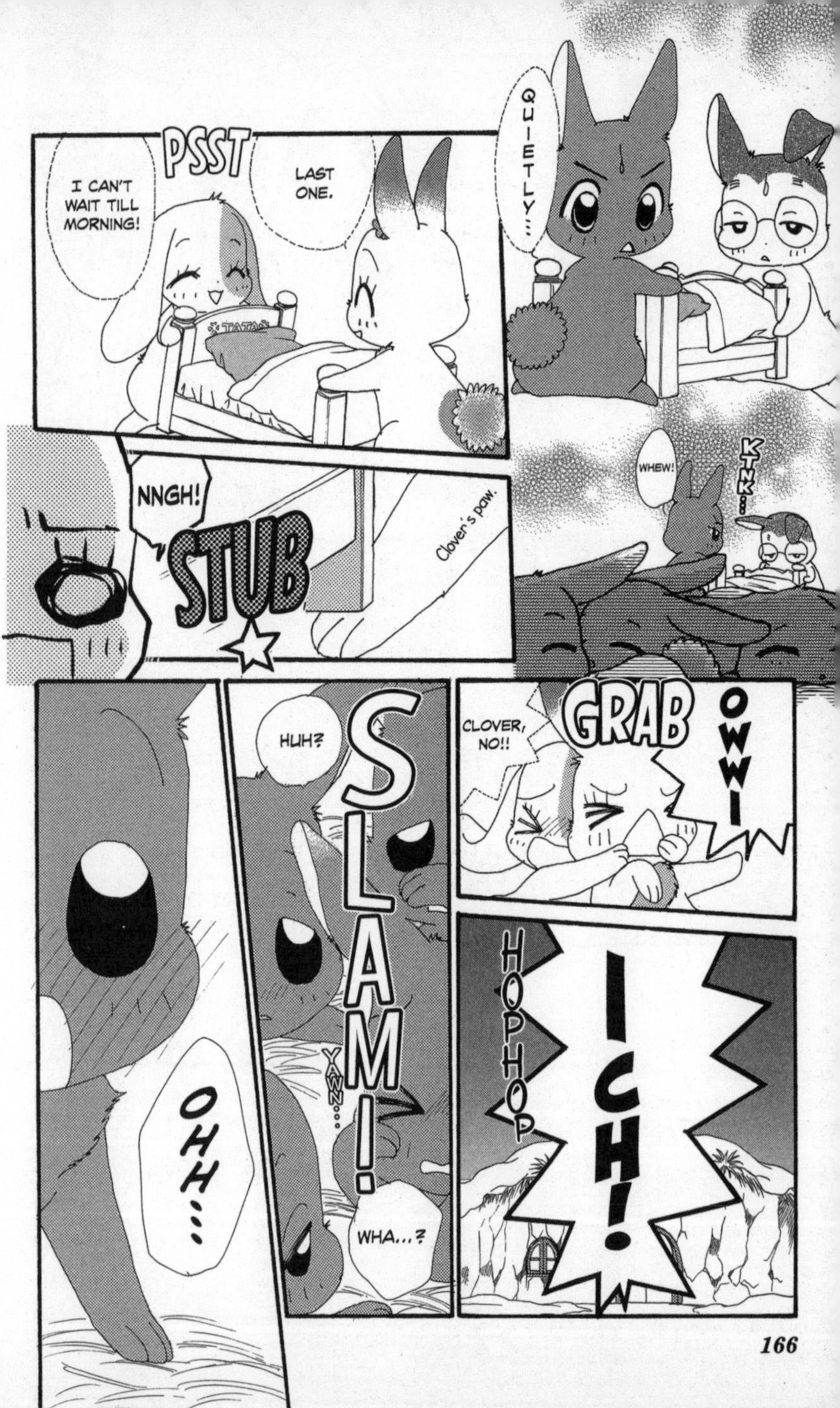
QUIETLY...
LAST ONE.
PSST
I CAN'T WAIT TILL MORNING!
WHEW!
KTNK...
Clover's paw.
NNGH!
STUB
OWW!
GRAB
CLOVER, NO!!
ICH!
HOPHOP
HUH?
SLAM!
YAWN...
WHA...?
OHH...

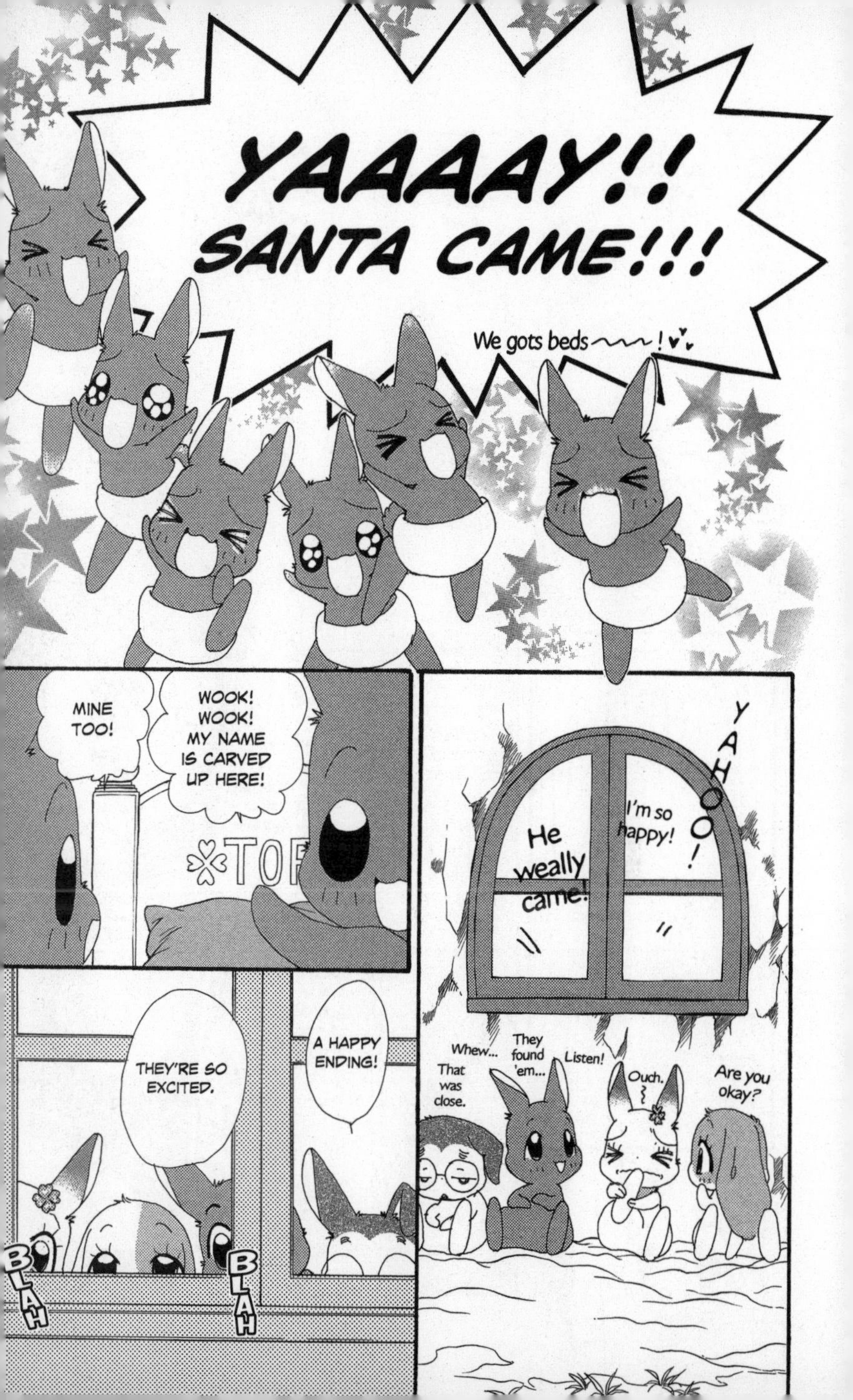
YAAAAY!! SANTA CAME!!!
We gots beds~!
YAHOOO!
I'm so happy!
He weally came!
Are you okay?
Ouch.
Listen!
They found 'em...
Whew...
That was close.
WOOK! WOOK! MY NAME IS CARVED UP HERE!
MINE TOO!
TOF
A HAPPY ENDING!
THEY'RE SO EXCITED.
BLAH
BLAH

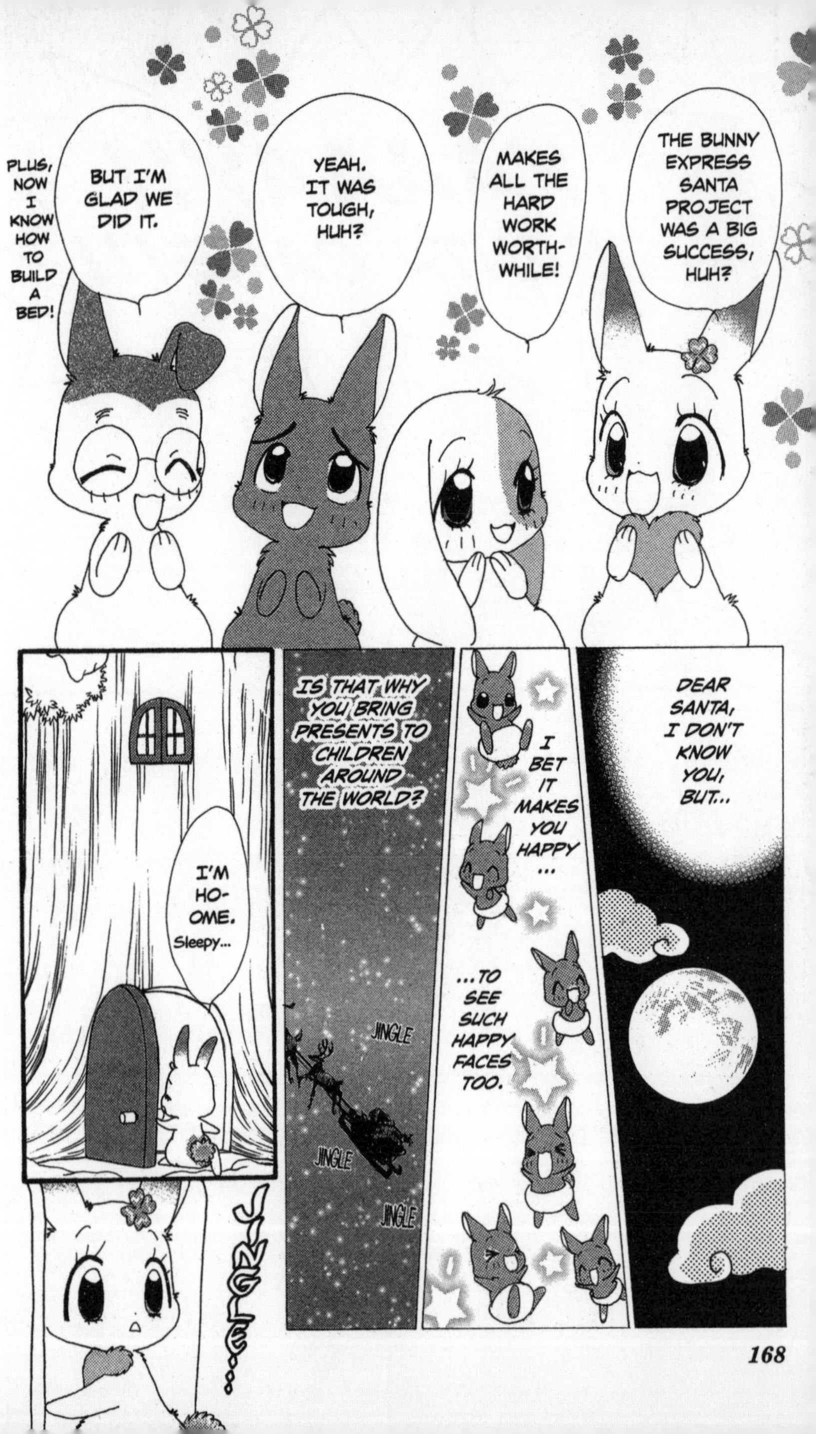
THE BUNNY EXPRESS SANTA PROJECT WAS A BIG SUCCESS, HUH?
MAKES ALL THE HARD WORK WORTH-WHILE!
YEAH. IT WAS TOUGH, HUH?
BUT I'M GLAD WE DID IT.
PLUS, NOW I KNOW HOW TO BUILD A BED!
DEAR SANTA, I DON'T KNOW YOU, BUT...
I BET IT MAKES YOU HAPPY ...
...TO SEE SUCH HAPPY FACES TOO.
IS THAT WHY YOU BRING PRESENTS TO CHILDREN AROUND THE WORLD?
JINGLE
JINGLE
JINGLE
I'M HO-OME.
Sleepy...
JINGLE...

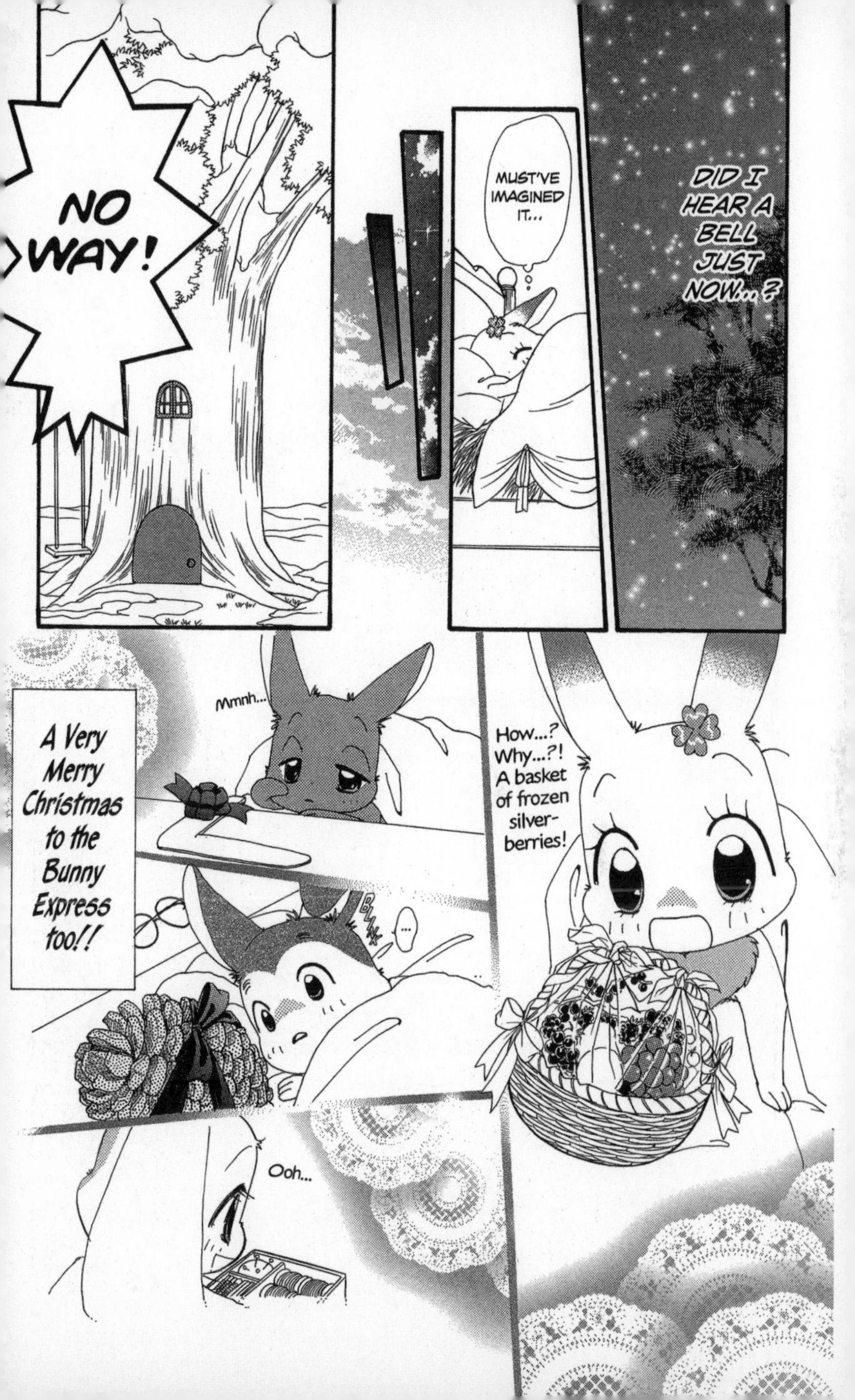
DID I HEAR A BELL JUST NOW...?
MUST'VE IMAGINED IT...
NO WAY!
How...? Why...?! A basket of frozen silver-berries!
Mmnh...
A Very Merry Christmas to the Bunny Express too!!
BLINK
...
Ooh...

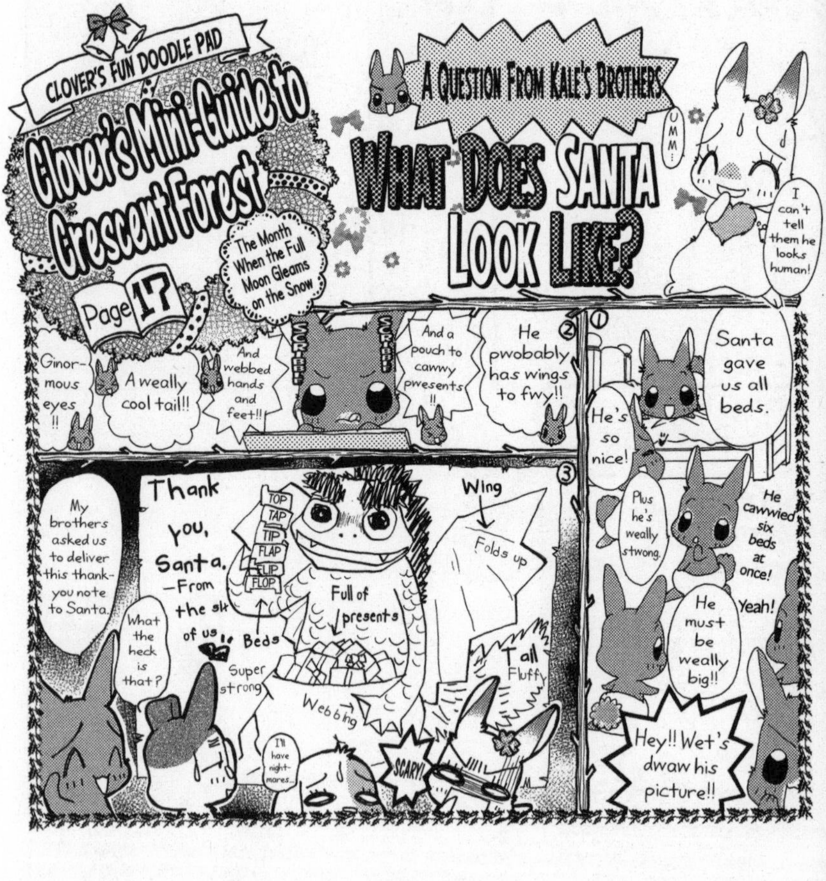
CLOVER'S FUN DOODLE PAD
Clover's Mini-Guide to Crescent Forest
The Month When the Full Moon Gleams on the Snow
Page 17
A QUESTION FROM KALE'S BROTHERS
WHAT DOES SANTA LOOK LIKE?
UMM...
I can't tell them he looks human!
Santa gave us all beds.
He's so nice!
Plus he's weally stwong.
He cawwied six beds at once!
Yeah!
He must be weally big!!
Hey!! Wet's dwaw his picture!!
He pwobably has wings to fwy!!
And a pouch to cawwy pwesents!!
SCRIBBLE
SCRIBBLE
And webbed hands and feet!!
A weally cool tail!!
Ginormous eyes!!
Thank you, Santa. —From the six of us
Wing
Folds up
TOP
TAP
TIP
FLAP
FLIP
FLOP
Beds
Full of presents
Super strong
Webbing
Tall
Fluffy
SCARY!
I'll have nightmares...
What the heck is that?
My brothers asked us to deliver this thank-you note to Santa.

CLOVER'S CHALLENGE

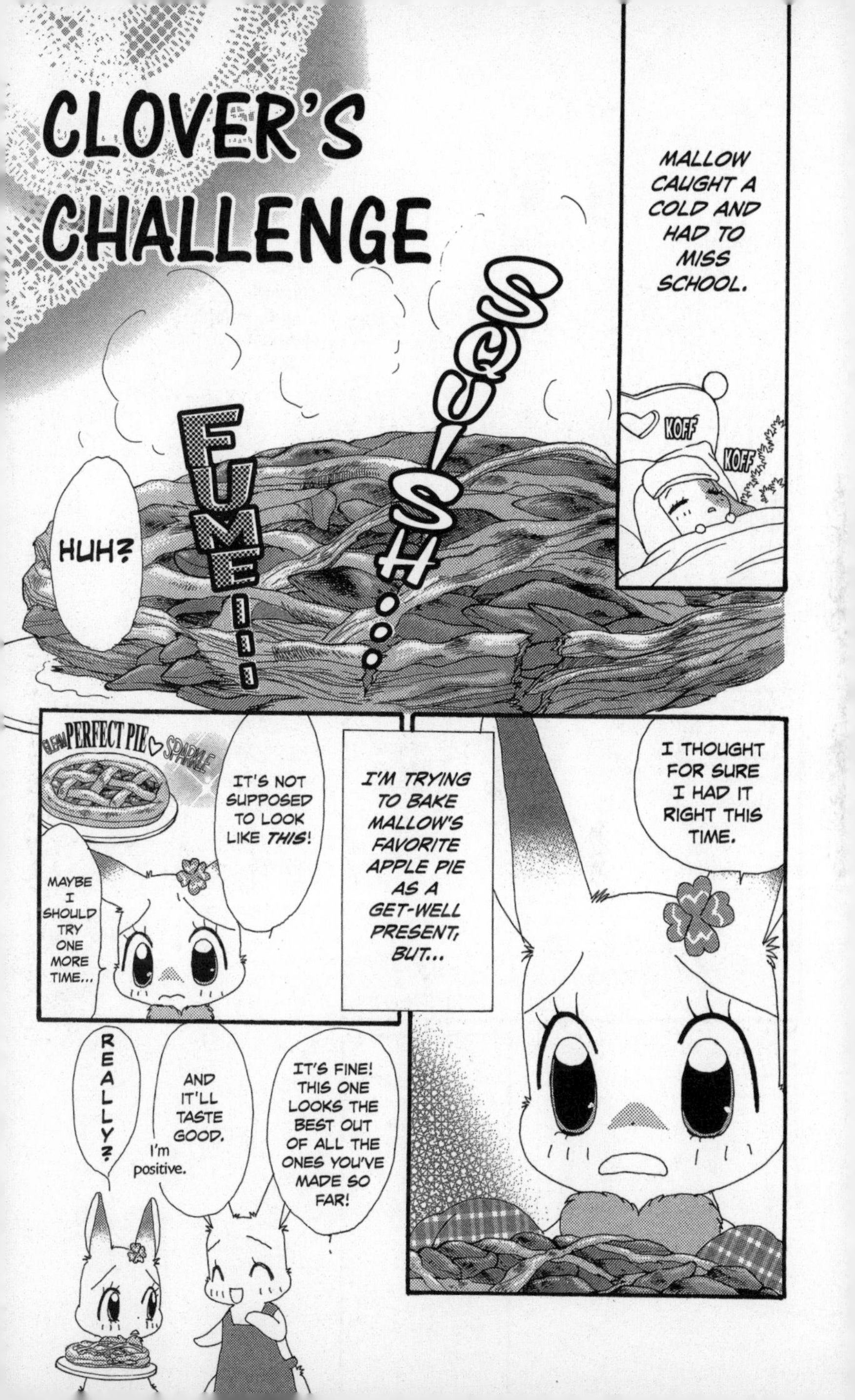
MALLOW CAUGHT A COLD AND HAD TO MISS SCHOOL.
KOFF
KOFF
SQUISH...
FUME!!!
HUH?
I THOUGHT FOR SURE I HAD IT RIGHT THIS TIME.
I'M TRYING TO BAKE MALLOW'S FAVORITE APPLE PIE AS A GET-WELL PRESENT, BUT...
GLEAM PERFECT PIE ♡ SPARKLE
IT'S NOT SUPPOSED TO LOOK LIKE THIS!
MAYBE I SHOULD TRY ONE MORE TIME...
IT'S FINE! THIS ONE LOOKS THE BEST OUT OF ALL THE ONES YOU'VE MADE SO FAR!
AND IT'LL TASTE GOOD.
I'm positive.
REALLY?

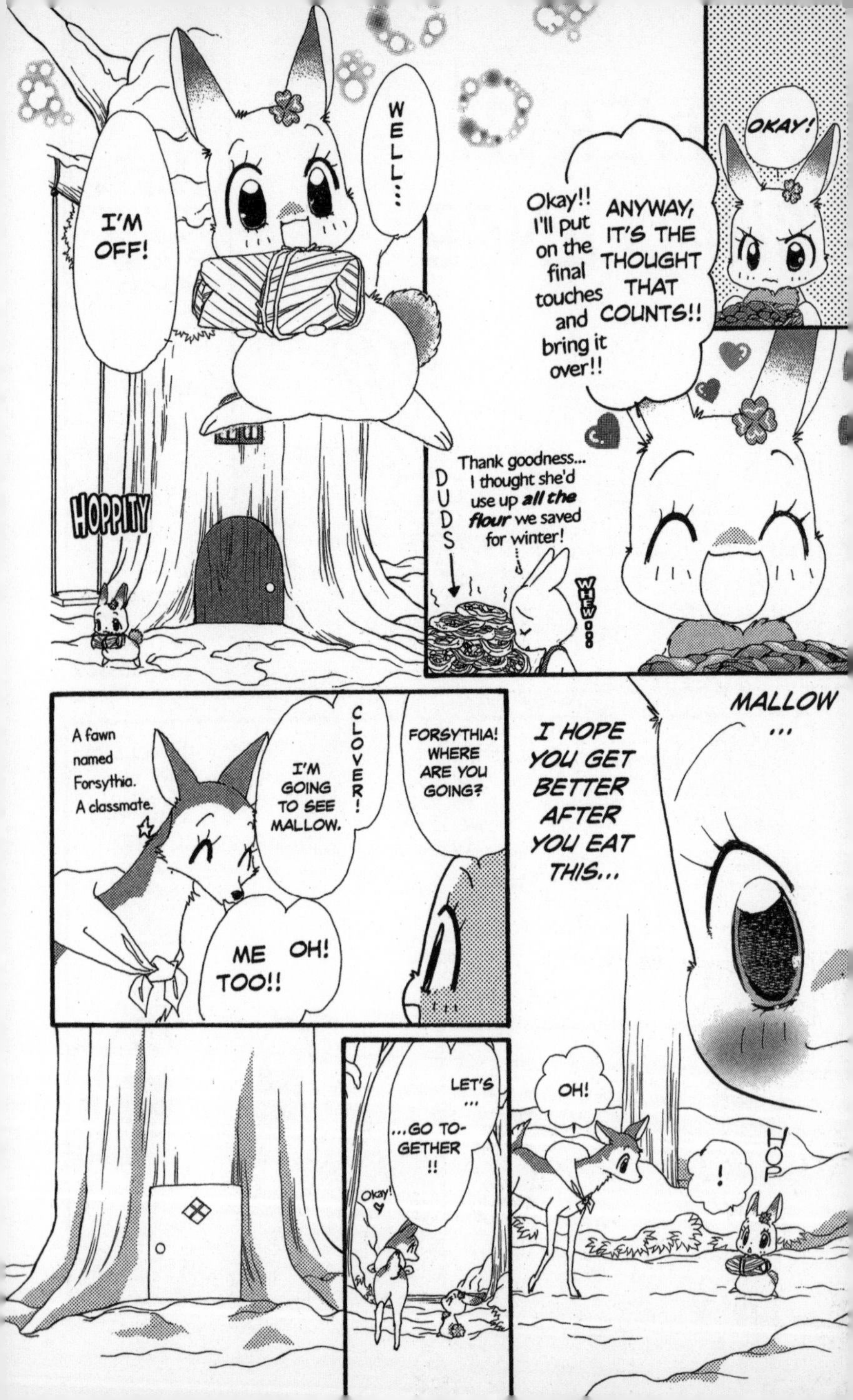

OKAY!
ANYWAY, IT'S THE THOUGHT THAT COUNTS!!
Okay!! I'll put on the final touches and bring it over!!
Thank goodness... I thought she'd use up **all the flour** we saved for winter!
DUDS
WHEW...
WELL...
I'M OFF!
HOPPITY
MALLOW...
I HOPE YOU GET BETTER AFTER YOU EAT THIS...
HOP
!
OH!
FORSYTHIA! WHERE ARE YOU GOING?
CLOVER!
I'M GOING TO SEE MALLOW.
A fawn named Forsythia. A classmate.
OH! ME TOO!!
LET'S...
...GO TO-GETHER!!
Okay! ♥

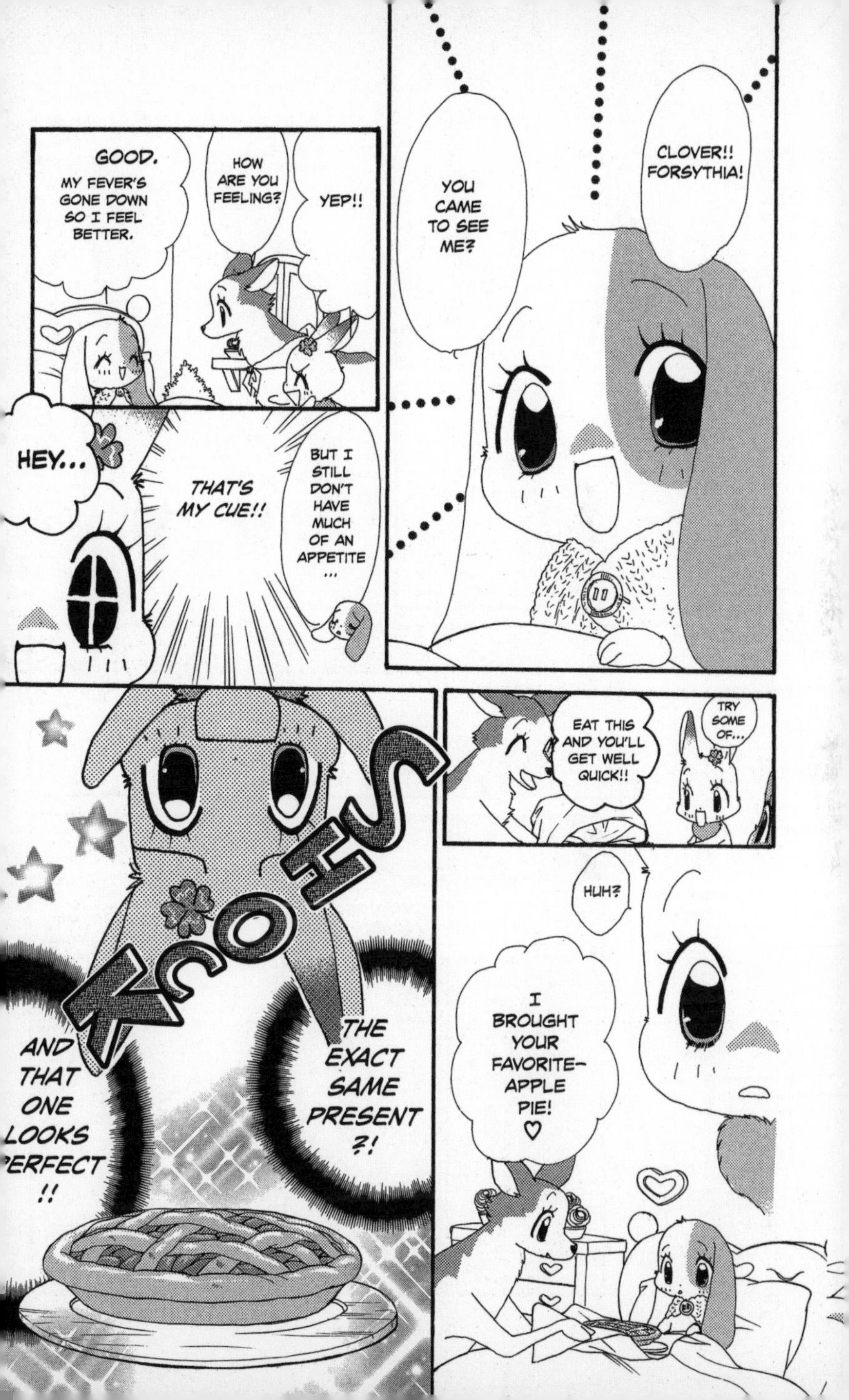
CLOVER!! FORSYTHIA!
YOU CAME TO SEE ME?
YEP!!
HOW ARE YOU FEELING?
GOOD. MY FEVER'S GONE DOWN SO I FEEL BETTER.
BUT I STILL DON'T HAVE MUCH OF AN APPETITE ...
THAT'S MY CUE!!
HEY...
TRY SOME OF...
EAT THIS AND YOU'LL GET WELL QUICK!!
HUH?
I BROUGHT YOUR FAVORITE— APPLE PIE! ♡
SHOCK
THE EXACT SAME PRESENT ?!
AND THAT ONE LOOKS ERFECT !!

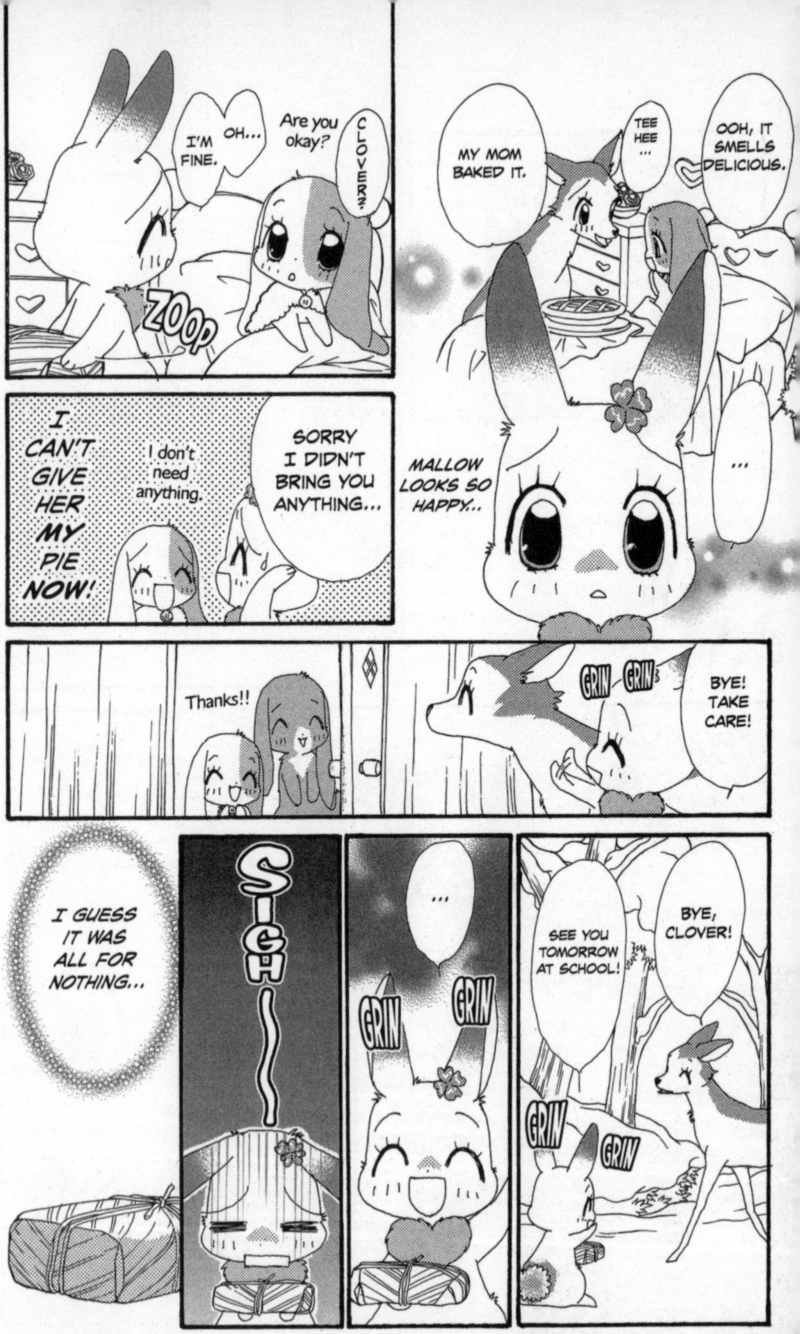
OOH, IT SMELLS DELICIOUS.
TEE HEE ...
MY MOM BAKED IT.
...
MALLOW LOOKS SO HAPPY...
CLOVER?
Are you okay?
OH...
I'M FINE.
ZOOP
SORRY I DIDN'T BRING YOU ANYTHING...
I don't need anything.
I CAN'T GIVE HER MY PIE NOW!
BYE! TAKE CARE!
GRIN GRIN
Thanks!!
BYE, CLOVER!
SEE YOU TOMORROW AT SCHOOL!
GRIN GRIN
...
GRIN GRIN
SIGH
I GUESS IT WAS ALL FOR NOTHING...

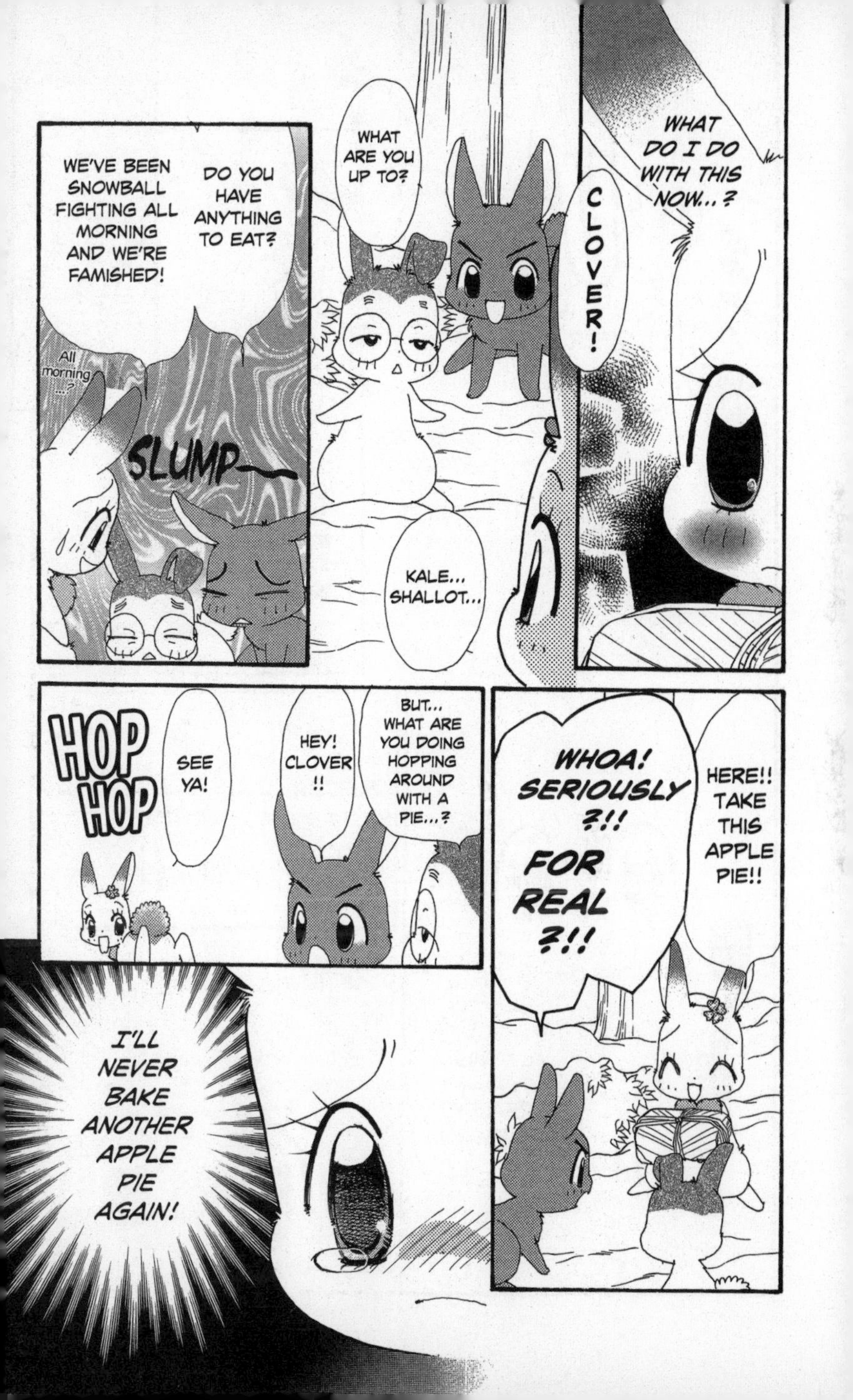
WHAT DO I DO WITH THIS NOW...?
CLOVER!
WHAT ARE YOU UP TO?
KALE... SHALLOT...
DO YOU HAVE ANYTHING TO EAT?
WE'VE BEEN SNOWBALL FIGHTING ALL MORNING AND WE'RE FAMISHED!
All morning...?
SLUMP—
HERE!! TAKE THIS APPLE PIE!!
WHOA! SERIOUSLY?!!
FOR REAL?!!
BUT... WHAT ARE YOU DOING HOPPING AROUND WITH A PIE...?
HEY! CLOVER!!
SEE YA!
HOP HOP
I'LL NEVER BAKE ANOTHER APPLE PIE AGAIN!

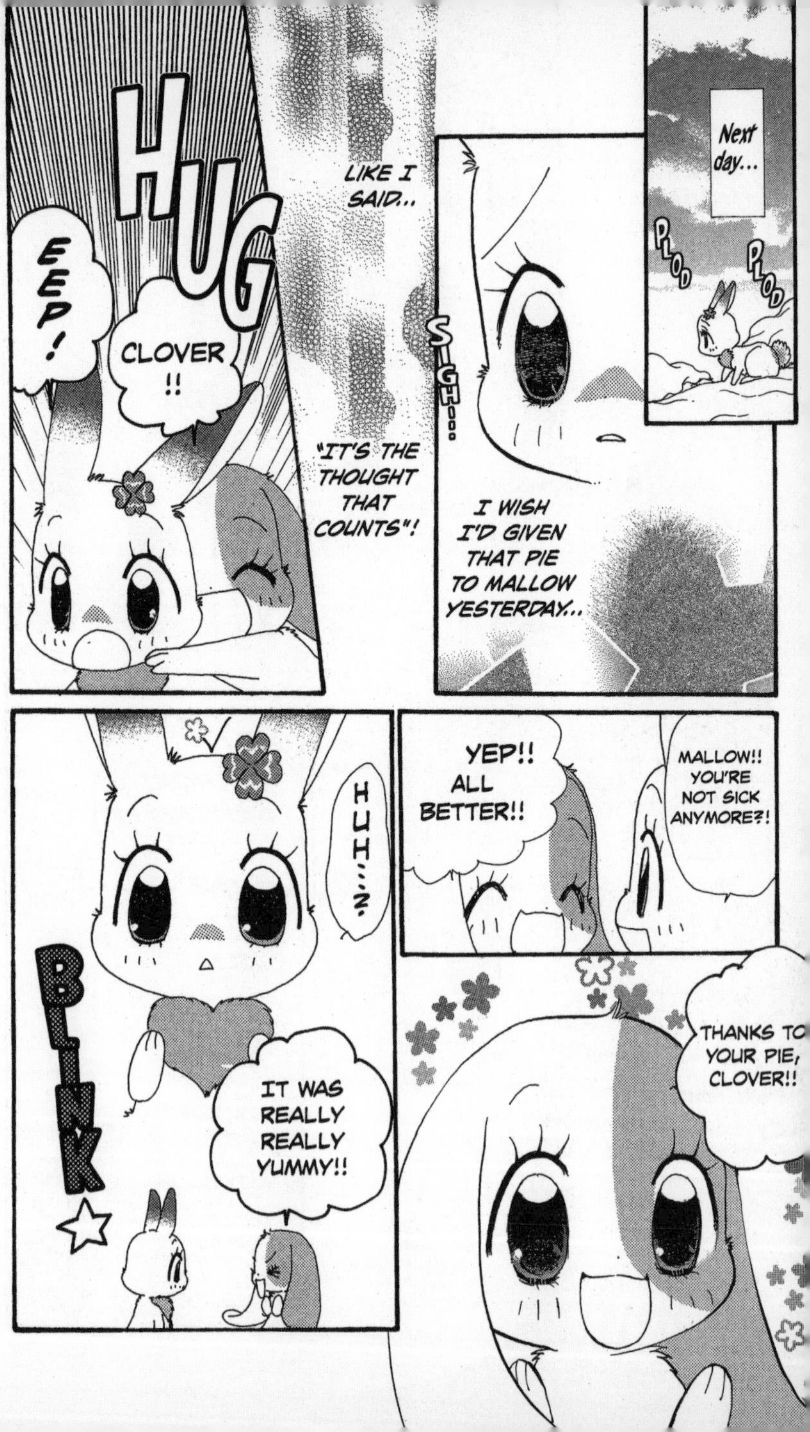
Next day...
PLOD
PLOD
SIGH...
I WISH I'D GIVEN THAT PIE TO MALLOW YESTERDAY...
LIKE I SAID...
"IT'S THE THOUGHT THAT COUNTS"!
HUG
EEP!
CLOVER !!
MALLOW!! YOU'RE NOT SICK ANYMORE?!
YEP!! ALL BETTER!!
THANKS TO YOUR PIE, CLOVER!!
HUH...?
IT WAS REALLY REALLY YUMMY!!
BLINK

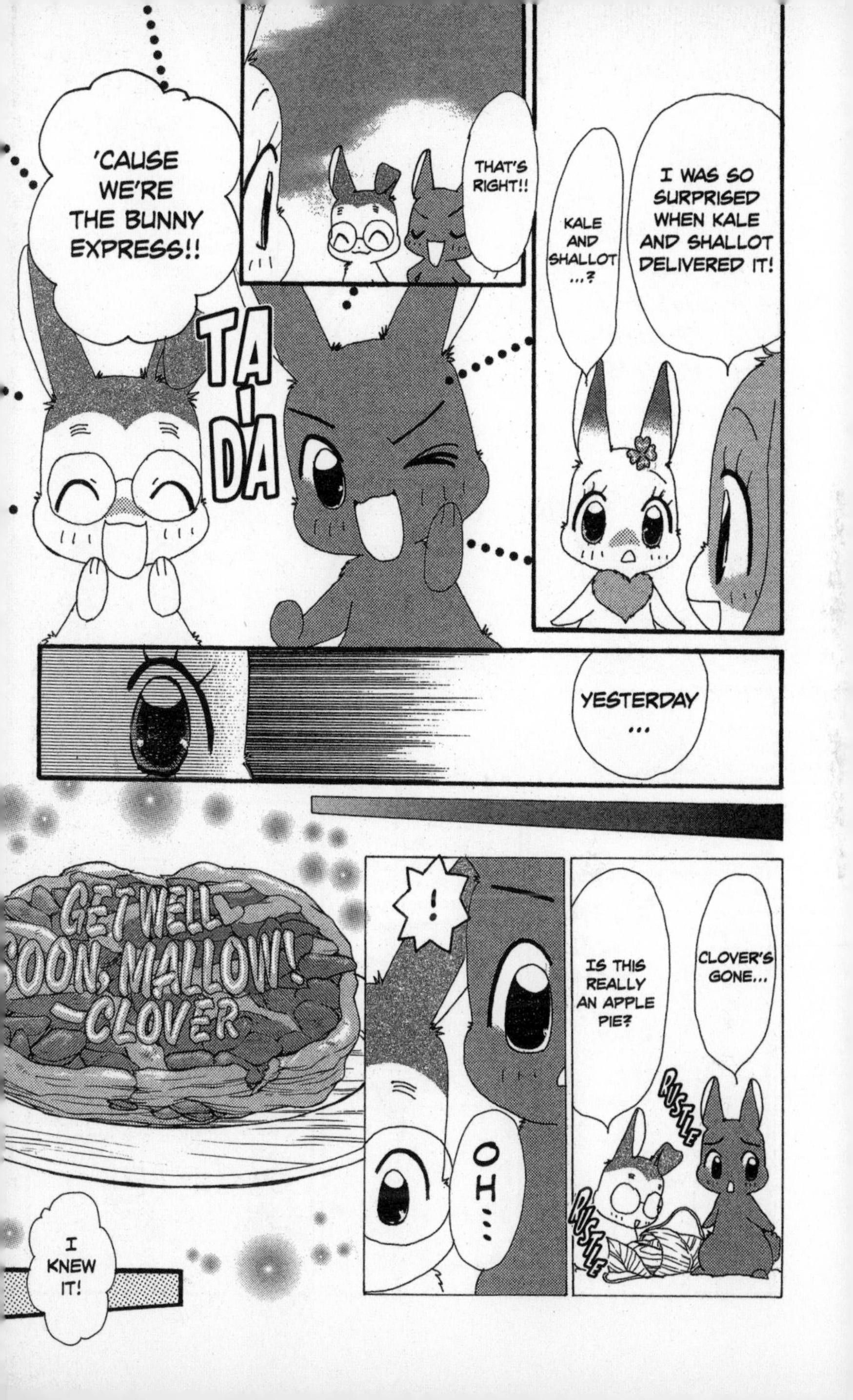
I WAS SO SURPRISED WHEN KALE AND SHALLOT DELIVERED IT!
KALE AND SHALLOT ...?
THAT'S RIGHT!!
'CAUSE WE'RE THE BUNNY EXPRESS!!
TA DA
YESTERDAY ...
CLOVER'S GONE...
IS THIS REALLY AN APPLE PIE?
RUSTLE
RUSTLE
!
OH...
GET WELL SOON, MALLOW! ~CLOVER
I KNEW IT!

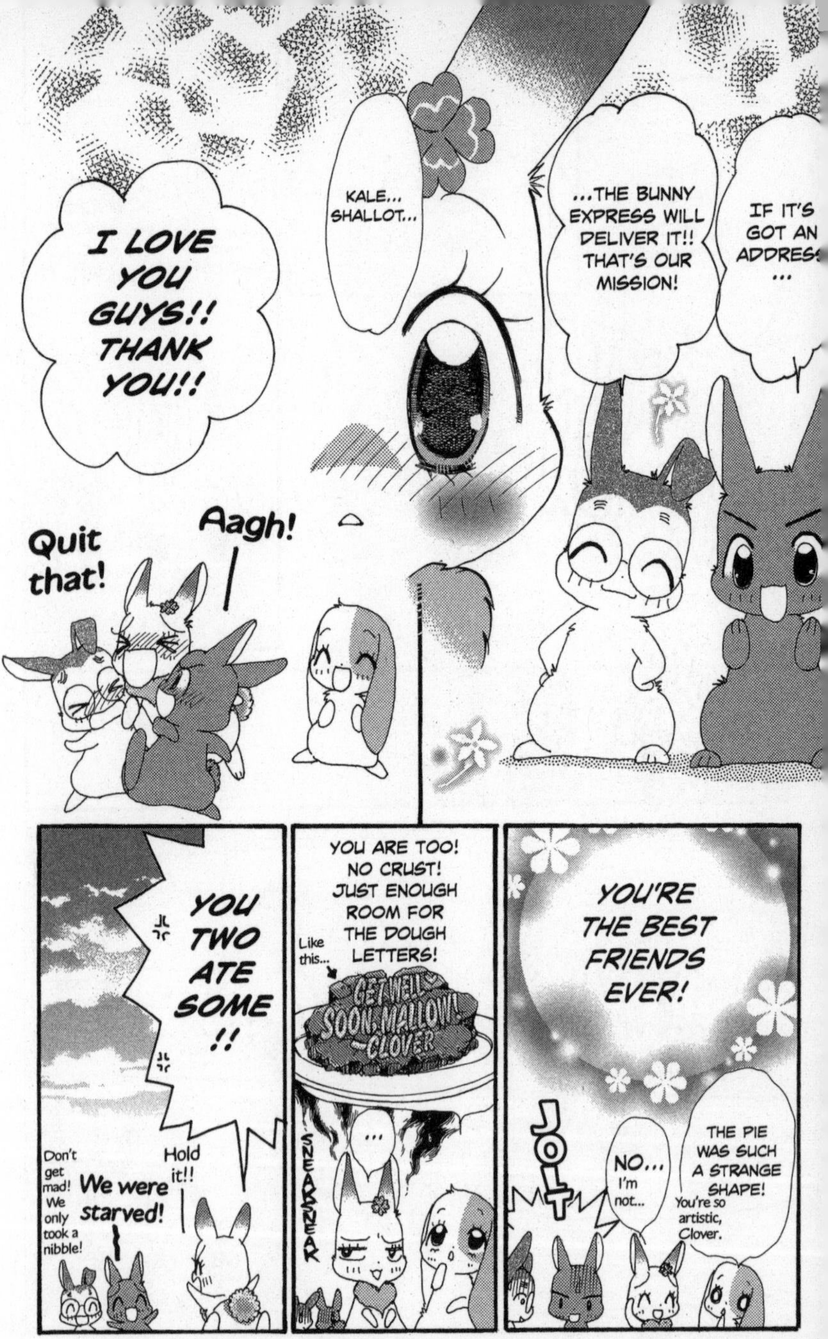

IF IT'S GOT AN ADDRES ...
...THE BUNNY EXPRESS WILL DELIVER IT!! THAT'S OUR MISSION!
KALE... SHALLOT...
I LOVE YOU GUYS!! THANK YOU!!
Aagh!
Quit that!
YOU'RE THE BEST FRIENDS EVER!
JOLT
THE PIE WAS SUCH A STRANGE SHAPE!
You're so artistic, Clover.
NO... I'm not...
YOU ARE TOO! NO CRUST! JUST ENOUGH ROOM FOR THE DOUGH LETTERS!
Like this...
GET WELL SOON MALLOW! -CLOVER
...
SNEAK SNEAK
YOU TWO ATE SOME!!
Hold it!!
We were starved!
Don't get mad! We only took a nibble!

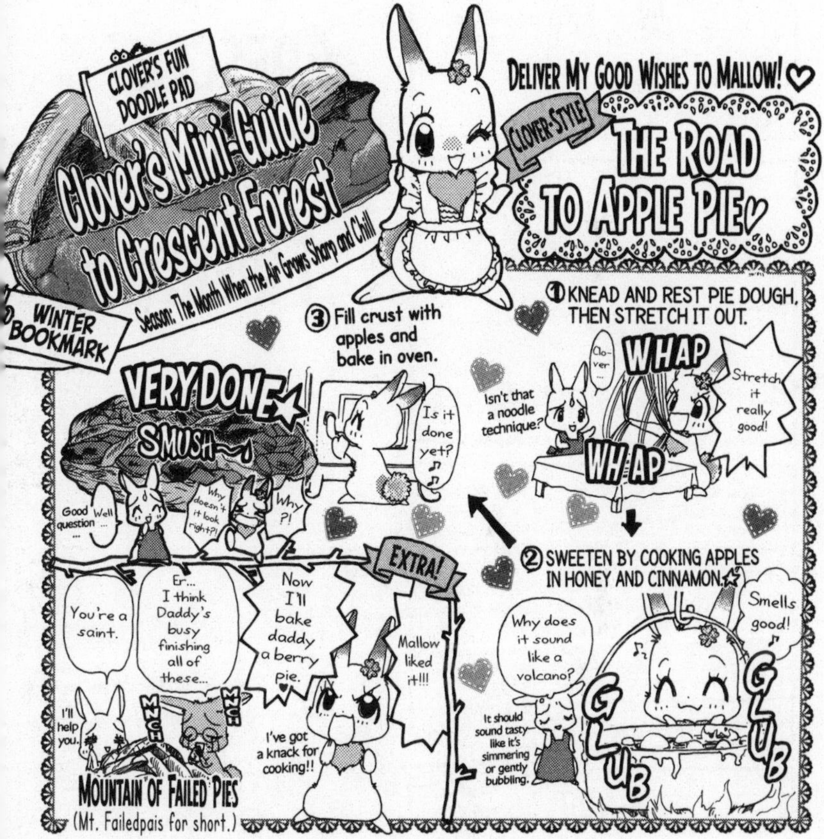

DELIVER MY GOOD WISHES TO MALLOW!
CLOVER-STYLE
THE ROAD TO APPLE PIE
CLOVER'S FUN DOODLE PAD
Clover's Mini-Guide to Crescent Forest
Season: The Month When the Air Grows Sharp and Chill
WINTER BOOKMARK
① KNEAD AND REST PIE DOUGH, THEN STRETCH IT OUT.
WHAP
Stretch it really good!
Clo-ver...
Isn't that a noodle technique?
WHAP
② SWEETEN BY COOKING APPLES IN HONEY AND CINNAMON.
Smells good!
GLUB
GLUB
Why does it sound like a volcano?
It should sound tasty like it's simmering or gently bubbling.
③ Fill crust with apples and bake in oven.
Is it done yet?
VERY DONE
SMUSH~
Why?!
Why doesn't it look right?!
Well...
Good question...
EXTRA!
Mallow liked it!!!
Now I'll bake daddy a berry pie.
I've got a knack for cooking!!
Er... I think Daddy's busy finishing all of these...
You're a saint.
MNCH
MNCH
I'll help you.
MOUNTAIN OF FAILED PIES
(Mt. Failedpais for short.)

CRESCENT FOREST FRIENDS

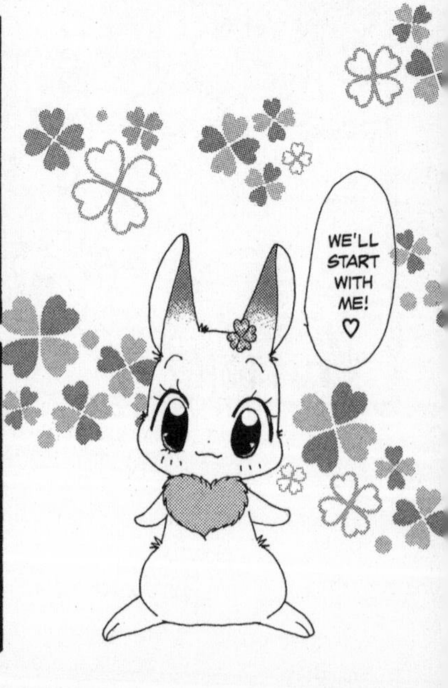
WE'LL START WITH ME! ♡

CLOVER

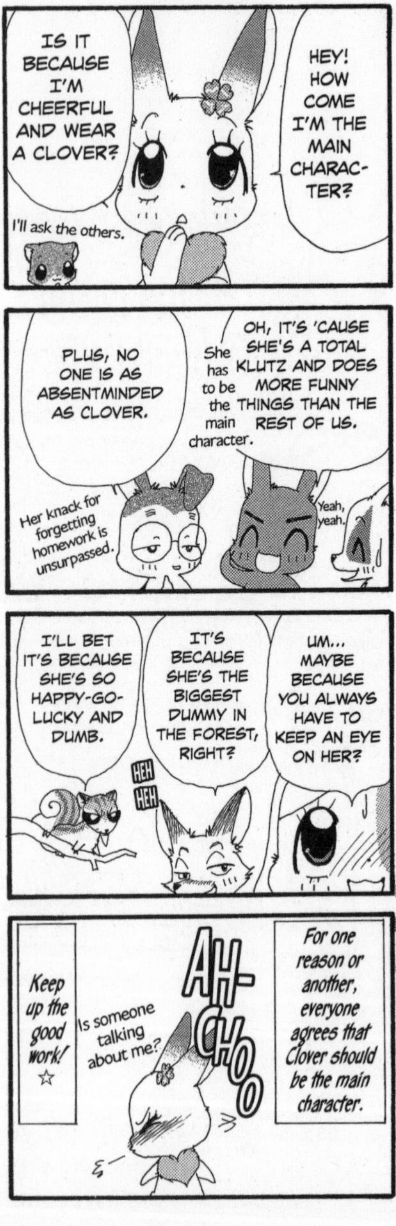
HEY! HOW COME I'M THE MAIN CHARACTER?
IS IT BECAUSE I'M CHEERFUL AND WEAR A CLOVER?
I'll ask the others.
OH, IT'S 'CAUSE SHE'S A TOTAL KLUTZ AND DOES MORE FUNNY THINGS THAN THE REST OF US.
She has to be the main character.
PLUS, NO ONE IS AS ABSENTMINDED AS CLOVER.
Yeah, yeah.
Her knack for forgetting homework is unsurpassed.
UM... MAYBE BECAUSE YOU ALWAYS HAVE TO KEEP AN EYE ON HER?
IT'S BECAUSE SHE'S THE BIGGEST DUMMY IN THE FOREST, RIGHT?
HEH HEH
I'LL BET IT'S BECAUSE SHE'S SO HAPPY-GO-LUCKY AND DUMB.
For one reason or another, everyone agrees that Clover should be the main character.
AH-CHOO
Is someone talking about me?
Keep up the good work! ☆

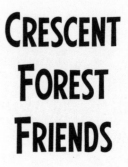

MALLOW

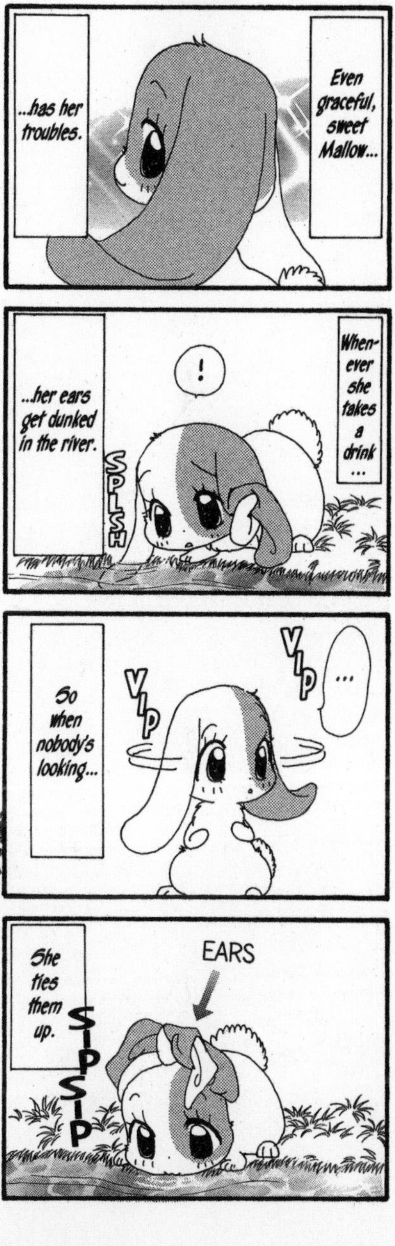
Even graceful, sweet Mallow...
...has her troubles.
When-ever she takes a drink...
!
SPLSH
...her ears get dunked in the river.
...
VIP
VIP
So when nobody's looking...
EARS
She ties them up.
SIP
SIP

Mallow is caring, relaxed, and shy. She's a comfort to everyone.

She says Clover is a comfort to her.

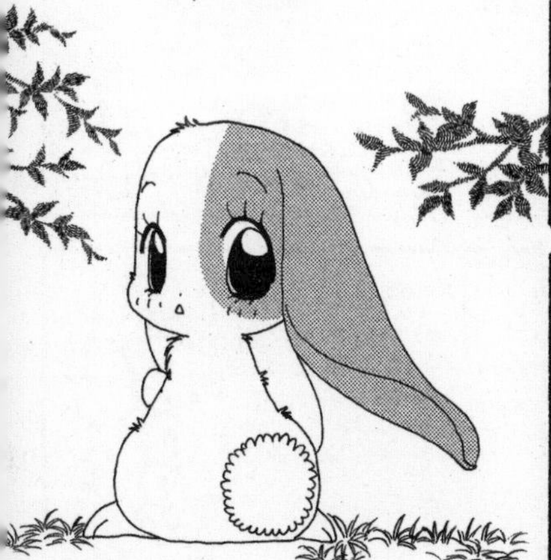

KALE

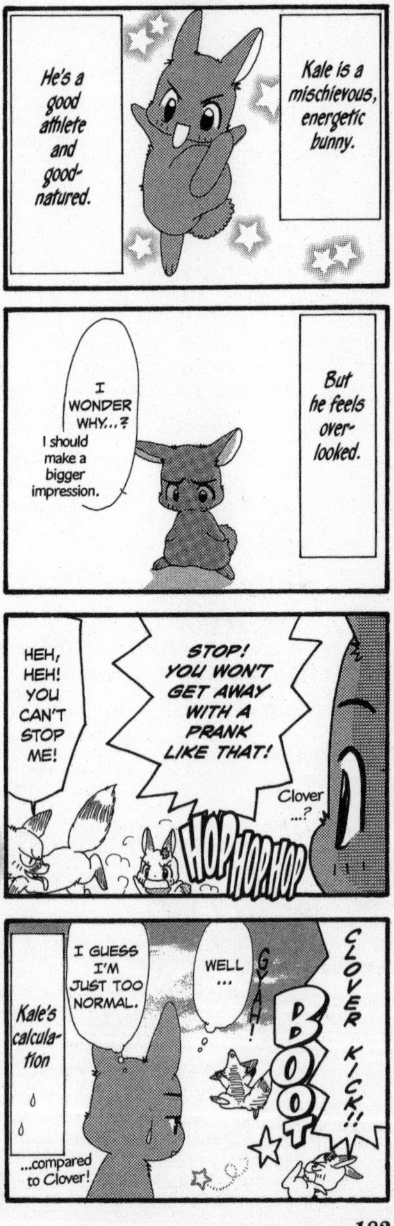
Kale is a mischievous, energetic bunny.
He's a good athlete and good-natured.
But he feels overlooked.
I WONDER WHY...?
I should make a bigger impression.
STOP! YOU WON'T GET AWAY WITH A PRANK LIKE THAT!
HEH, HEH! YOU CAN'T STOP ME!
Clover ...?
HOPHOPHOP
CLOVER KICK!!
BOOT
GYAH!
WELL ...
I GUESS I'M JUST TOO NORMAL.
Kale's calculation
...compared to Clover!

It must be tough having six little brothers...

But Kale loves them all.

And he's good with them.☆

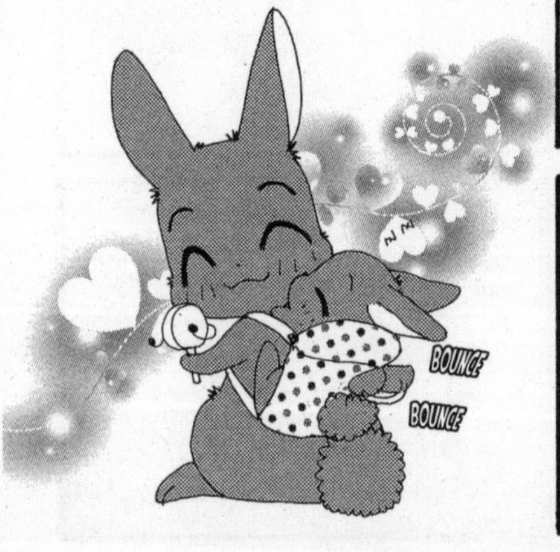
BOUNCE
BOUNCE

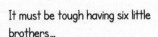

SHALLOT

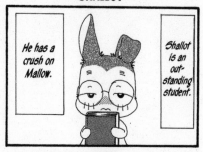

Shallot is an outstanding student.
He has a crush on Mallow.
I LIVE FOR MALLOW'S SMILE!
ZWIP
But ...
HOP
Morning, Mallow!
CLOVER!
...for some reason ...
SWSH
Hey, guess what?!
...even that small wish...
DOES SHE DO IT ON PURPOSE? NO, CLOVER ISN'T THAT TRICKY.
Hey!
You're blocking my view again.
...rarely comes true— thanks to Clover.

He reads thick books cover to cover.

And he is collecting every type of pine cone in the forest.

Pretty impressive, huh?

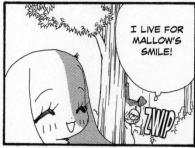

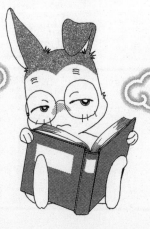

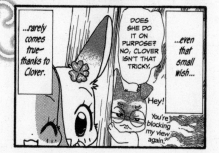

RAMBLER

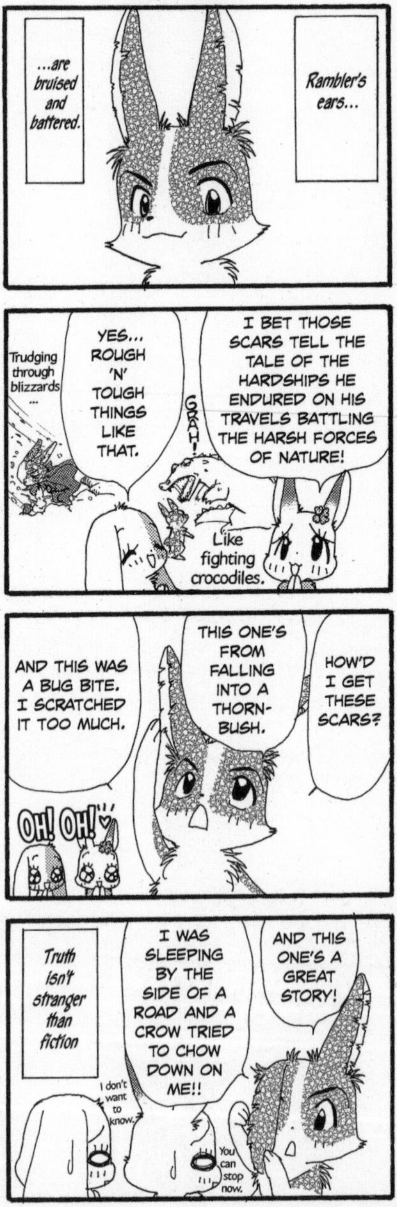
Rambler's ears...
...are bruised and battered.
I BET THOSE SCARS TELL THE TALE OF THE HARDSHIPS HE ENDURED ON HIS TRAVELS BATTLING THE HARSH FORCES OF NATURE!
YES... ROUGH 'N' TOUGH THINGS LIKE THAT.
Trudging through blizzards...
GRAH!
Like fighting crocodiles.
HOW'D I GET THESE SCARS?
THIS ONE'S FROM FALLING INTO A THORN-BUSH.
AND THIS WAS A BUG BITE. I SCRATCHED IT TOO MUCH.
OH! OH!
AND THIS ONE'S A GREAT STORY!
I WAS SLEEPING BY THE SIDE OF A ROAD AND A CROW TRIED TO CHOW DOWN ON ME!!
Truth isn't stranger than fiction
I don't want to know.
You can stop now.

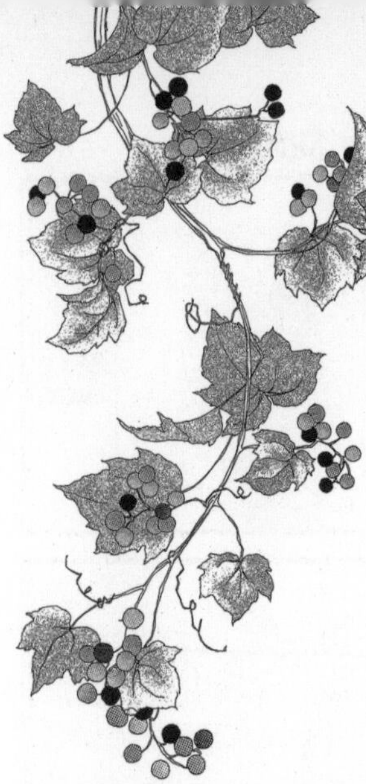

Rambler is a little mysterious, a lot of fun, and popular with everyone.

He lives a life of adventure that's not without its hardships!

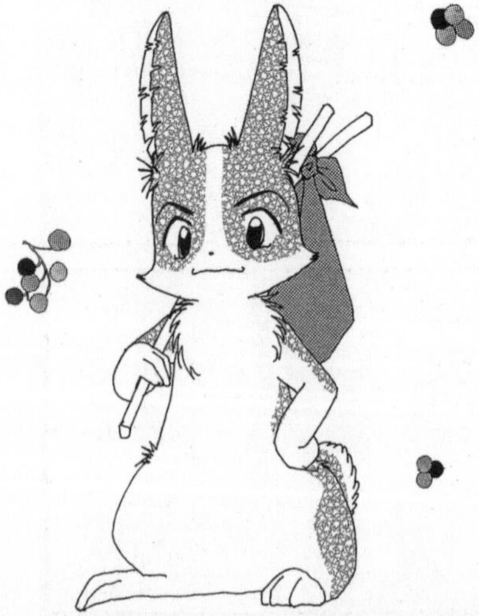

HICKORY

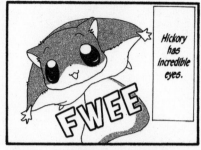

Hickory has incredible eyes.
FWEE
But...
SPLISH
SPLISH
SPLISH
OH! HICKORY! WHAT'S THE MATTER?! ARE YOU SAD?!
DID SOME-BODY PICK ON YOU?!
I'll go beat 'em up for you!
SHAKE
SHAKE
BUGS... BUGS... IN MY EYES...
Lots of them...
Large eyes come with unique challenges.
PLIP
PLIP

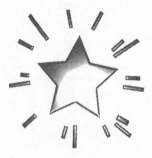

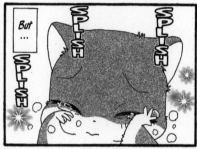

Hickory's voice is melodic and cute.

But he's no chatterbox, so we don't get to hear too much from him. Too bad.

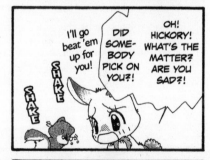

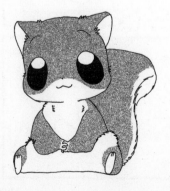

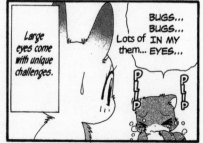

PROFESSOR HOOT

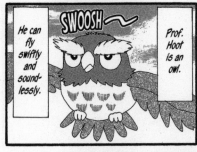

Prof. Hoot is an owl.
SWOOSH~
He can fly swiftly and soundlessly.
He can see in the dark, and his ears are so sharp he can hear a leaf drop.
SNOOZE
Owls are nocturnal, so Prof. Hoot falls asleep a lot during the day.
SNOOZE
BLINK
YOU JUST MADE FUN OF ME, HOOT!
How did you know?
EEK—!
I'm sorry!

Professor Hoot is very strict, but he cares about his students.

Everyone thinks his stories about his younger days are a bit too long...

But no one dares to tell him...

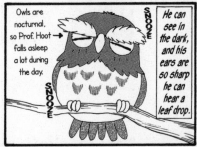

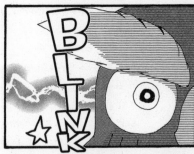

HOOT
Z

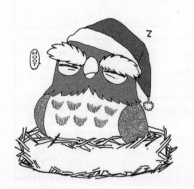

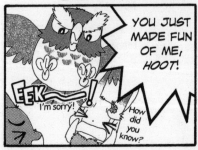

Message From
Sayuri Tatsuyama

A parrot has come to our house. This little cutie is comical, demanding, and doesn't like to be alone.

When I rub its head it talks to me in soft chirps. "Pokkyo? Po po...po?" I sure wish I could understand.

Sayuri Tatsuyama loves furry animals! Before *Happy Happy Clover*, she created a ten-volume manga series called *Pukupuku Tennen Kairanban* starring puppies and other cute pets. In 2001, it was the 47th winner of the annual "Shogakukan Award for Children's Manga." *Happy Happy Clover* is so popular in Japan that it has been made into an anime and a Nintendo DS video game. But they haven't been translated into English yet. Tatsuyama lives in the city of Osaka in Japan. Her dream is to have a huge dog.

Happy Happy Clover

Volume 3 Available Now

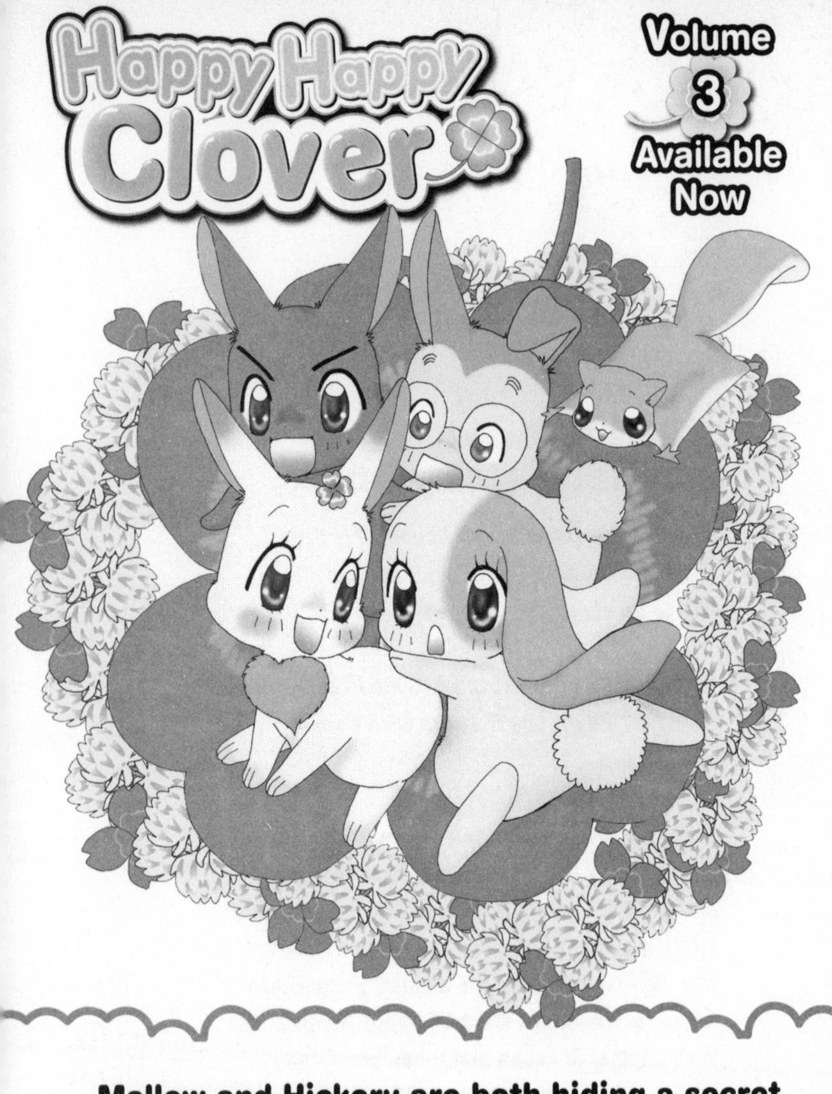

Mallow and Hickory are both hiding a secret, Blackberry gets woken up from hibernation, and Clover casts two magic spells that backfire! Even worse–she has to do chores! *Dust, Clover, dust!*

Take a trip with Pokémon

ALL THAT PIKACHU!
ANI-MANGA™

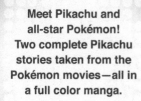

Meet Pikachu and all-star Pokémon! Two complete Pikachu stories taken from the Pokémon movies—all in a full color manga.

Buy yours today!

www.pokemon.com

vizkids

www.viz.com

Hey! You're Reading in the Wrong Direction!

This is the **end** of this graphic novel!

To properly enjoy this VIZ graphic novel, please turn it around and begin reading from **right to left.** Unlike English, Japanese is read right to left, so Japanese comics are read in reverse order from the way English comics are typically read.

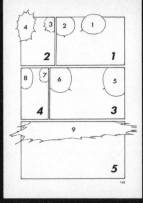

Follow the action this way

This book has been printed in the original Japanese format in order to preserve the orientation of the original artwork. Have fun with it!